'By God, you will come!' Abel said, and though his voice was not particularly raised there was no doubt in any of his listeners' minds but that he was so enraged as to be on the point of losing control. 'You shall see for yourself what you have done by your ways, by your—oh, you *shall* see!'

William's face was white under the smooth fair hair, and his head was thrust forwards in a truculent manner that caused his fleshy chin to double as it rested on the high points of his collar.

'I see no justification for the accusations you are making at me!' he said and his voice was high and thin. 'You complain to me of the whining lies of that toad-eater Conran, you tell me, your own son, that on such a creature's word you are prepared to regard me as a liar at best, a useless fool at worst, and then add to it with *this*? By God, sir, I too have my temper, and I too shall have expression of it, if this nonsense does not come to an end!'

Abel's eyes narrowed and he in his turn pushed his head forwards so that for a moment there was a strong family resemblance between them as they stood glaring at each other.

'Shall you indeed!' Abel said very softly. 'Shall you! Then I take leave to tell you that if you dare to show any tantrums to me, out of this hospital you go, and not to Gower Street, either. My home shall never be open to you again . . .'

D0281746

*Also by Claire Rayner in Sphere:*

# CLAIRE RAYNER

# Paddington Green

## Book III of
## THE PERFORMERS

SPHERE BOOKS LIMITED

A *Sphere* Book

First published in Great Britain by
Cassell & Co Ltd 1975
Corgi edition 1976
Weidenfeld & Nicolson edition 1982
Arrow edition 1985
This edition published by Sphere Books Ltd 1991

Printed and bound in Great Britain by
Cox & Wyman Ltd, Reading

ISBN 0 7474 0742 8

Sphere Books Ltd
A Division of
Macdonald & Co (Publishers) Ltd
Orbit House
1 New Fetter Lane
London EC4A 1AR
A member of Maxwell Macmillan Pergamon Publishing Corporation

# ACKNOWLEDGEMENTS

The author is grateful for the assistance given with research by The Burroughs Wellcome Medical History Library and Museum; Macarthy's Ltd, Surgical Instrument Manufacturers; The Paddington Society; Leichner Stage Make-up Ltd; Professor Philip Rhodes, Dean of St Thomas's Hospital Medical School, London; Raymond Mander and Joe Mitchenson, theatrical historians; the Marylebone Reference Library, London; The Law Society, London; the Wardens and Congregation of the Synagogue of the Sephardi Community, Bevis Marks, in the City of London; and other sources too numerous to mention.

CLAIRE RAYNER

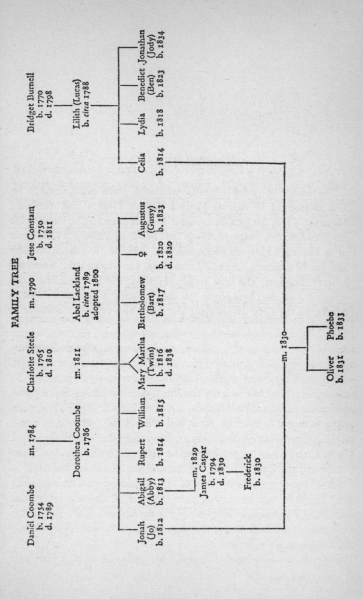

FAMILY TREE

Daniel Coombe
b. 1754
d. 1789

m. 1784

Dorothea Coombe
b. 1786

Charlotte Steele
b. 1765
d. 1810

m. 1790

Jesse Constant
d. 1811

Bridget Burnell
b. 1770
d. 1798

Lilith (Lucas)
b. circa 1788

m. 1811

Abel Lackland
b. circa 1789
adopted 1800

Jonah
(Jo)
b. 1812

Abigail
(Abby)
b. 1813

Rupert
b. 1814

William
b. 1815

Mary   Martha
(Twins)
b. 1816
d. 1838

Bartholomew
(Bart)
b. 1817

♀
b. 1820
d. 1820

Augustus
(Gussy)
b. 1823

Celia
b. 1814

Lydia
b. 1818

Benedict
(Ben)
b. 1823

Jonathan
(Jody)
b. 1834

m. 1829

James Caspar
b. 1794
d. 1830

Frederick
b. 1830

m. 1830

Oliver
b. 1831

Phoebe
b. 1833

## 1

It had been raining since before dawn, a thin icy rain that slicked London with a grey sheen, turning the meaner streets into reeking gutters and the better ones into expanses of freezing mud. It dripped dolefully from the trees on to the greasy pavements beneath and sent the chill striking through to the very bones of the crowds that were already forming along the route between St James's and Buckingham Palace and up Constitution Hill.

It wanted half an hour yet to seven o'clock, but there they were, clustered in little huddles in an attempt to keep warm, chaffering and steaming, throwing ribald jokes at each other about the difference there would be in Her High and Mightiness this time tomorrow morning (if *His* High and Mightiness knew what he was about, that was, which some took leave to doubt), fighting for good vantage points, arguing and screeching and generally behaving as London crowds always did when given any excuse at all to forget the narrow meanness and drabness of their lives. And was not the little Queen's wedding day as good an excuse as they had had since the end of the French Wars? They were going to enjoy themselves, come hell come devil, and in they came pouring, from Hoxton and Stepney, from the villages of Fulham and Chelsea, streaming over the elegant new Waterloo Bridge from Southwark and Lambeth and Camberwell, Londoners on holiday.

Abby, standing at the window of her bedchamber and staring out at the mournful patch of greying grass that was all that was left of the once rural Paddington Green to which she had come as a bride, was well aware of the fact that the day was to be a holiday, and was thoroughly angered by it.

She was as careful and thoughtful an employer as any, she told herself, and saw to it that her people had good conditions and were paid promptly. So their calm assumption that the Queen's wedding gave them leave to depart from the manufactory in the Harrow Road and the work there for the whole of the day, despite the number of important orders waiting to be filled, was plain ingratitude. What was the Queen's wedding to them? Hadn't they their own lives to consider, and the needs of their employer? Who were they to think it reasonable to run wild on the streets today instead of working?

She let the thoughts run round in her head as she stood there sipping her morning chocolate, trying hard not to face the real reason for the deep sense of depression which she knew quite well lay behind her irritation. But she could not keep the thoughts battened down for long, and being Abby, as practical and altogether honest as she had always been, she stopped trying and let her mind do what it wanted to; which was to take itself back to the day eleven years ago when she had looked from her bedroom window on to sheets of rain and thought about weddings.

But that had been her own wedding, not that of a diminutive Queen, and a true love match, not a matter of political importance. But the rain had been the same, albeit it had been April, and not February. She remembered how aware she had been of the warmth of that spring rain when they had arrived here at this house beside the Green starred with daffodils which bent their heads under the great elm trees that had towered over the little house and shop that was to be her new home.

Hers and James's.

It was extraordinary how sharp it could still be, thinking about James. She had long since lost the image of his face, could only conjure into her mind's eye a freckled sandiness, a presence that was pale and thin and ill. Yet thinking of him hurt; or to be more honest, she told herself, it was not the thought of him so much as the thought of herself, her own sense of loss, of outrage, of bitter fury that she should have to suffer so. She had given up so much to marry him; father and mother, brothers and sisters . . . .

Not fair, she told herself now, for the thousandth weary time. I am not fair, for did I not go into it with my eyes so wide open that I saw clearly that my time with him would be short? Did I not deliberately

8

seek him out, deliberately speak to him of my desire for him? I cannot cry hard-done-by now—and yet for ten years that is what I have done. Railed against the fates that selected so good and kind and caring a man for early death; that selected me, who wanted only to be useful and busy and happy, to be so lonely. Not fair, in every sense she could think of, not fair.

She shook herself slightly and turned from the window into the warmth and comfort of her handsome bedchamber, so much more elegant in its furnishings than the house which contained it, to set down her chocolate cup and begin to set about her washing and dressing. Bad enough that the day would be lost to her workers; at least she could be about her own business at her counting house desk. Standing here thinking of past sadnesses would be of little value either to herself or to Frederick; and at the thought of young Frederick some of the desolation that had filled her since she woke dissipated and was replaced by a warmth and pleasure that was very comforting. Frederick with his red hair and narrow green eyes, so much a mixture in his looks of the two men she had always loved most, her husband and her father; Frederick with his sharp wits and wicked little lopsided grin that displayed the big front teeth of vulnerable boyhood; dear Frederick.

And almost as though he was aware of the tender thoughts she had entertained about him, he started his efforts as soon as she entered the little morning parlour to eat breakfast with him. Not precisely wheedling, not precisely nag-nagging, but speaking brightly and yet wistfully of the delights there would be in the streets today, hurdygurdy men and hot-pie sellers and purveyors of sticky sweetmeats; and as he chattered on, with intervals of filling his mouth with hot bread-and-milk, she fought her own deep desire to hide her mood of depression and memories of times lost behind a curtain of ledger work, truly wanting to be the cheerful Mamma he had a right to have. And won the fight and was rewarded by Frederick's shriek of delight and rumbustious hug when she said crisply, 'Well, let be, let be! Eat your breakfast, and we will ride the twelve o'clock Shillibeer's as far as the Diorama in the Park. But you will have to walk from there to the Palace, and it is a long walk! You will not complain about your legs if we go?'

'Oh, no, Mamma! Indeed I shall not! It will be so delightful to see all the people and the bunting and the fine carriages, and they say there are to be fireworks upon the river tonight, and processions, and—oh, so many things! Oh, thank you, Mamma, thank you so much! I had hoped and *hoped*——' and he fell to the remainder of his breakfast with such gusto that he splashed his milk like a silly five-year-old instead of the capable ten-year-old he was and laughed at his own clumsiness with such high delight that Abby found herself laughing too. Dear Frederick, she thought again, and once more shook her mental shoulders against her melancholy; this time with success. Widowhood, for all its pains, could be and often was compensated for by motherhood. She was in many ways a fortunate woman, and well she knew it.

The rain sluicing down his windows in irritable bursts as the wind hurled itself along Gower Street woke Abel some time before Jeffcoate arrived with the brass can of hot shaving water and his freshly ironed shirt. He lay there hunched beneath the blankets staring at the greyness of the window, not moving when the little scullery maid came sidling in to clear and relay and light his fire against the morning chill, cogitating his plans for the day.

It was important that he find time to talk to Conran regarding the tales that had reached his ears about the man's remarks. It was not right that there should be such ill-informed gossip running through the wards and corridors of his hospital, and a stop must be put to it. For all that Queen Eleanor's now boasted twelve wards and a busy dispensary for street patients and for all that there was now a Board of Trustees some five strong, it was still, in Abel's eyes, *his* hospital. Had it not been born of his dreams and his energies, his struggles and not least his and his family's money? Indeed it had, and that sharp-nosed sniffing little creature of a Bursar should know it! How dare he say the things he had said about the way William was handling the consignments of pills and potions from the manufactory at Wapping?

Abel turned restlessly in bed, and bunched the bolster beneath his neck. William. Time would have to be found to speak to him, too, damn it. So much to be done today, as every day, with operations he must perform, his session among the street patients and he had promised to go with young Snow, the surgeon–apothecary sent to him by his old friend Bell from Great Windmill Street, to see some particular patient in whom he had a special interest, down near Broad Street, behind Little Earl Street. At least it was near the hospital, so that shouldn't take more than half an hour out of the day. And perhaps if he postponed one operation on the list, and thus eased the morning's burden, he could take fifteen minutes at the noon hour or thereabouts to seek out the tedious wretch Conran——

A loud and raucous cry from the street below, immediately taken up in reply by jovial shouts from the direction of Bedford Square, pulled him from the depths of thought in some puzzlement; such vulgar dins were by no means a feature of life in elegant Gower Street, and for a moment he frowned, wondering why. And then, remembering, cursed aloud. The Queen's wedding! God damn it all to hell and back, but that would fairly set the seal on the day! With twice the usual number of people in the streets, and the stupid roistering and cele-brating that would be an inevitable accompaniment to the day's activities, the only sure plan he could foresee was that he would be tied fast to the dispensary room mending broken heads and limbs and dealing with the other injuries of the abusive characters who all too often marred a London crowd.

But by the time he was dressed his irritation had subsided somewhat. If there would be tedious and boring aspects to the day's work, there was also the fact that often the sort of injuries sustained in streets as crowded as today's would be could be most interesting. He remem-bered the many such cases he and Charles had pored over on long late nights of work in Charles's anatomy room at Great Windmill Street, or his own at Endell Street, and how he had been able to see actually demonstrated the passage of many of the major nerves that fed the muscles with their motive force. Not as interesting, Bell had often told him a little regretfully, as some of the more spectacular inflictions of damage he had observed upon Wellington's battlefield of Waterloo, close on a quarter century ago, but with their own fascination none-theless.

Charles and his friendship were a great comfort to him, Abel thought now, making his usual morning way to Dorothea's bed-chamber. How he could have borne the past ten years without his unswerving support he could not imagine. Not, of course that it had ever been expected that the situation would last so long. Poor Dorothea, he thought, as he moved across the deep carpeted floor towards the silent bedside to stand in the flickering morning firelight looking down at the thin little face on the pillow. Poor Dorothea. To live in death so long; how could any have foreseen such an outcome to that long ago day?

Charles had said often enough, however, once the first year had passed, that with the devoted nursing Abel insisted she have there was no reason why she should not live her full life span.

'I have seen such cases before, m'dear fellow,' he had once said in his soft Scots burr. 'Dead in the head, ye understand, for the pressure of the injury precludes any passage of sentience from brain to body, or body to brain, but with the vegetative faculties unimpaired. In such cases I have often thought that perhaps the loving devotion of a nurse can be in some sort a handicap to the families of such sufferers——' But Abel had looked at him sharply at that so Bell had nodded soberly and said no more, leaving the unspoken all too clearly understood between them, together with an equally wordless and well understood agreement never to mention the matter again.

He put out one hand now to smooth the pillow beside her head, for the nurse had not yet washed her or arranged her for the day, having gone first to the kitchen to collect the pap on which she was fed, and he noticed almost with a shock that the fair hair was greying quite rapidly. He often noticed such small evidences that she was still physically living—sometimes that her fingernails were long and in need of trimming, sometimes a flaking of the skin upon her birdboned arms—but each time he made such an observation it brought a sharp twitch of surprise, as if each were totally new. For all these years she had lain here unmoving, her face as smooth and young as it had ever been—for why should it ever become lined like others' faces, since no expression or awareness ever crossed its delicate pallor?—and it was hard to remember that this was a breathing living woman.

A breathing living *stubborn* woman, he thought now with a sudden memory of the way Dorothea had been before her injury. Weak, drooping, quite maddening in her meek acceptance of her down-trodden state, and quite immovable on any matter that she cared about. She had made up her mind to wed him, had made up her mind to stay with him, and so it had been. And he knew, now, she had made up her mind that he should one day love her as she loved him, with the same helpless, hopeless, dead sort of love. And hadn't she obtained just that? Standing beside her bed on this cold, wet February morning he knew she had won, and touched her fragile hand in a gesture that said so.

'Good morning, Mr Lackland.'

He turned his head to see Miss Ingoldsby standing quietly just within the bedchamber with her hands crossed before her on her brown merino dress and with her brown hair pulled back into an unfashionable soft knot at the nape of her neck. They looked at each other for a comfortable moment and then he nodded, knowing that now in all truth the day had begun, that he could turn his back on wife and household in the sure knowledge that both would be cared for in perfect detail.

And she returned his nod, as cool as he was, but finding satisfaction in the look of his spare and elegant body, the smoothly thick pepper-and-salt hair that crowned his bony face and the way his sober dark clothes sat so neatly across his wide shoulders, for she was a woman with a passion for order and neatness and methodical living; in her eyes he was a very satisfactory employer, so very reliable and organized a man as he was. He made life in this household much more agreeable than she would ever have thought possible a dozen years ago when she had first entered it as a governess, employed by the rather fluttering and timid Dorothea to look after her younger children. But that had been *before*; so much had happened in this house since then! Now she looked at him approvingly and was content with the way her lines had fallen.

They waited until the nurse returned from the kitchen and then went downstairs to breakfast together, she walking beside him with a bouncy little step that sorted ill with her essential dignity, but which was inevitable in one as small as she was (William often teased her about being 'even smaller than the Queen, and no one is smaller than that!'), and leading the way to the breakfast parlour.

Both Rupert and William were already ensconced at table and Miss Ingoldsby lifted one amused eyebrow at the sight of the latter. It was

13

rare indeed that he was any but last at breakfast, and was all too likely to arrive dishevelled, because he had dressed hurriedly, and foul-tempered for want of sleep, for William was a great reveller and rarely saw his bed until the small hours.

'Oh, don't look so knowing at me, Madam Mouse!' he said now in high good humour. 'I've told you before, I left the schoolroom long since, and I'll have none of your bullying now! You set about someone of your own size if you wish an argument!' and he stretched his long legs under the table and nodded briefly at his father.

Abel paid no attention to either of his sons, only nodding to quiet, drab little Martha at her place at the end of the table behind the coffee equipage; and immediately she bent her head and poured for him his favourite morning brew of bitter black coffee. Miss Ingoldsby seated herself composedly beside Rupert, who sketched a polite if abstracted attempt to rise, and took for herself some bread and butter from the plate set ready before her.

'I have already received some letters this morning,' she said after a short pause which was broken only by the rattle of cups and plates and the slightly noisy gulping of William, who chose to break his fast the very modern way on hot bacon and boiled eggs and cold beef rather than the traditional bread and butter and toast which satisfied the rest of his family. 'And I have messages of affection for you all from Barty.'

There was no response to this from anyone except Martha, who looked up quickly and smiled at Miss Ingoldsby, who smiled swiftly back and went on unperturbed. 'He would appear to be settling happily enough to life in the Shires,' she said, 'for he writes that he is hunting more than three times a week on occasion. I would never have thought such activities would interest him!'

'It's surprising what a man'll do to please a rich wife and her family,' Rupert said shortly, and William laughed and opened his mouth to make some ribald comment and then, catching Miss Ingoldsby's cool glance, laughed again but subsided.

'You may tell him that I look forward to receiving letters of my own from him,' Abel said a little acidly. 'It is gone eight months since his wedding and no more than two letters has he honoured me with! And while I do not in any way grudge you your correspondence,

Miss Ingoldsby, it seems to me a trifle inequitable, shall we say, that you should be the object of so many of his communications.'

'Ah, but you see, Mr Lackland, I *answer* each time he writes,' Miss Ingoldsby said coolly and William laughed even more noisily, throwing back his head.

'She got you there, Father! You are no better with your correspondence than any of us, to be sure, and you cannot blame the wretch if he sickens of writing always into the wind. He need expect no answers from me, that much is sure, for I have far too much to do——'

'I want to talk to you about that,' Abel said, and stood up, wiping his mouth upon his napkin. 'That Conran is getting above himself in many ways, but I must deal with the affair in the proper manner. You must show me the records of the transactions of which he is complaining, and——'

William scowled, and Rupert looked up with a very similar expression on his face, so that for a moment they looked very much alike, with fair rather thin hair surmounting ruddy squarish faces, though Rupert had a more sardonic cast of countenance than the bonhomous William, and a much thinner body compared with William's square solidity. Indeed, William looked far more like the sort of country bumpkin he most despised than the polished man of the town he considered himself to be (and great had been his rage when his sister Martha had once told him that he almost certainly drew his inheritance from his mother's father, Daniel Coombe, who had been a complete countryman, and that he had as much hope of becoming a man of elegance as a cow had of becoming a thoroughbred racehorse).

'I would take it ill, in William's shoes, to see you take the man Conran's part in any disagreement between them!' Rupert said sharply. 'The man is a weasel, with so puffed up an idea of himself that——'

Abel raised his eyebrows. 'I do not consider myself to be taking any sort of stance in the matter! God damn it, I hardly know what the matter *is*! I have heard some stupid gossip, and I have no time for it, so the only thing to do is scotch it! I cannot do that until I have the facts, and so it is of some importance that I discuss it with William first! What affair is it of yours, anyway? You have enough to do dealing with your share of the surgery that bids fair to overwhelm us!

It is William who handles the affairs of the manufactory, not you!'

Rupert was standing up now too. 'That's as may be—but I take leave to be interested when some jumped-up little jack-in-office takes it upon himself to set his face against my brother! The hospital is a Lackland affair, and none have any rights to——'

'Aye,' Abel said softly. 'To an extent you are right, Rupert. A Lackland affair, indeed. *Abel* Lackland. Let's have no nonsense from you about setting yourself in any position of especial eminence! My sons you may be, but Queen Eleanor's is *my* hospital, and you no more important in it than any other of the people I employ there—not in the eyes of those other people. You understand me? In time to come per-haps you will indeed step into my shoes, but a long time to come it will be! Let me remind you, Rupert, that I am barely past my fiftieth birthday and have no notion of letting myself be put out to grass for many years yet! And while I stand there in my place, I can tell you that any matters that need dealing with will be dealt with in the same style, be the persons involved you or Nancy or the dirtiest scullery creature in the basement! No one shall ever say I show favour to any of my family——'

'By God, you're right there!' Rupert said savagely. 'No one ever could. Nor would wish to.'

'If you please, Rupert, Mr Lackland.' Miss Ingoldsby neither moved, nor raised her voice above the usual level, but her words cut easily across theirs. 'I would ask you both to save your breath, for standing here and arguing will start your day off in a very sour fashion! The streets are filling thick already for the processions and you will be hard put to it to make your way through the crowds. Do let me persuade you to keep your discussions for the hospital, for I am sure that after your journey there and time to consider your words you will find a better way to deal than by anger! Forgive my persistence but it really is time that you were about your affairs.'

There was a short silence and then Abel relaxed his shoulders, which had been as stiff and hard as though a board had been set across them, and nodded a little abruptly, but with some return of temper.

'You are right, of course, Miss Ingoldsby. Your pardon, ma'am—and Martha—for our ill manners,' and he turned and looked very directly at Rupert who glared back at him for a moment, and then without turning his head said gruffly, 'Your pardon, Miss Ingoldsby, Martha——' and turned sharply and left the room.

William remained still for a moment longer and then laughed, but there was less of real amusement in it now. He sounded uneasy and yet full of bravado. 'Where would we be without ladies to control our masculine rages! Even you, Father, who are not famous for equanimity, must cool your furies in our Madam Mouse's presence! Well, as she bade us talk at the hospital, we had better go, I imagine. It would take a braver man than I to argue with so formidable an opponent——' and he made a florid bow in her direction, and followed his brother from the room.

Abel too moved towards the door, and then stopped, his hand on the knob. 'I am sorry, Miss Ingoldsby, that you must suffer their impertinence,' he said after a moment. 'I sometimes think it would be better if they too were to set up their own establishments, but——' he shrugged. 'Well, they are men grown, and no longer schoolboys. I cannot always control them as I would wish.' He gave a short laugh then. 'I cannot even control a schoolboy! Oh, I am aware of his absence, Miss Ingoldsby. I may not have spoken of it, but I am aware!'

Miss Ingoldsby, not quite as unperturbed as she had been and indeed with a faint flush across her cheeks, said, 'You need not apologize for Rupert and William, Mr Lackland! You must remember that I had the care of them when they were children, and I am quite able to tolerate their humours. As for Gussy—well, I would ask you not to concern yourself unduly. I will deal with him, with your permission, and he will show regret for whatever escapade it was that kept him from his bed last night.'

'So, he has not returned *yet*?' Abel said sharply, but Miss Ingoldsby at once shook her head.

'Oh, he is back, to be sure, but I cannot deny that it was a shockingly late hour when he did return. However, it is a special time, is it not? It is not every day the Queen is married and——'

'No, thank God, it is not.' Abel said a little savagely, and pulled his watch from his waistcoat pocket. 'And I must indeed be on my way if I am to save anything out of the day. I give you *carte blanche* with the boy, Miss Ingoldsby. I know you will deal with him as is needful.' And he nodded briefly at Martha and went, pulling the door sharply behind him, and gradually the two women relaxed, and looked understandingly at each other as the front door of the house slammed shut, and peace surged comfortingly back into the room.

Miss Ingoldsby poured for herself another cup of tea, and reflected that looking after such a houseful of Lacklands was a far from easy task. But a most rewarding one, her thoughts amended, and her lips curved contentedly as she sat and sipped and stared out at the rain that was still lashing the windows in cold fury, on Queen Victoria's wedding day.

## 2

To the people at the Celia Supper Rooms in King Street, hard by Covent Garden, the notion that any person could possibly forget the fact that today was to see celebrated the nuptials of little Victoria and her German princeling would have been quite absurd. Even before the first drays had come rumbling into the cobbled streets from the storehouses of Kent and the gardens of Surrey and Middlesex, laden with the carefully garnered onions and carrots and sweet wrinkled little last-year apples, they had been busy preparing for the influx of business they expected. Indeed, Letty, the smallest and youngest and cheekiest of the waiting maids, swore that Madam C had not gone to bed at all, for at three in the morning she had found her employer standing beside her pallet, shaking her roughly and bidding her to be about her business.

'There she stood,' she said now, as she sat curled up near the big fire in the main kitchen, before which a half-ox was slowly turning and just beginning to reek and change colour, 'large as life an' twice as natural, not an 'air of 'er 'ead so much as out o' place, 'er gown as smooth as if she'd not so much as sat down, let alone laid down, and tellin' me as I was a lazy cow—me as di'n't get to me bed till gone eleven las' night! I asks yer! 'S far as I'm concerned, mate, the bleedin' Queen can go get 'erself spliced any bleedin' day she likes, 's long as she don't go an'——'

'Are you goin' to whine all day, then?' A tired-looking woman in her late twenties who was leaning against the side of the stone fireplace, her hands curled hungrily round a steaming mug, stared with eyes gleaming with ill temper at the group of girls clustered round the fire. 'Because I tells yer, if you are, I'll set about yer wiv *my* tongue—and me fists—and you'll wish as missus'd take over. It'll be enough to keep ourselves goin' at all today, without you carryin' on——'

'You lay a finger on me, Betsey Brewer, and I'll 'ave Mr Jo on yer, and then where'll you be?' Letty cried shrilly.

'Same place where she was before,' one of the other girls said laconically. 'Oh, can't you just 'ear 'im! "Don't go arguing among yourselves, please not to argue! It do depress me so!"'

There was a snort of laughter from all of them at this and then, as Letty reached for the last hunk of bread soaked in meat juices and dripping, a noisy argument broke out between the six of them; and at the back of the big stone-flagged kitchen, in the darkness by the door, Jonah sighed softly and then slipped back unseen into the passageway outside.

He too had been up since long before dawn, helping by supervising the scrubbing of the big tables to clear them of the evidence of last night's beer swilling, changing the flats behind the diminutive stage, rearranging the music scores, and dealing with the multitude of details that had to be considered when a change of programme was made, as it would be tonight, and had been as aware as any of them of Celia's harrying presence. She had been everywhere this past two hours, ordering, chasing, nagging, occasionally slapping, so that the whole establishment had been in a fever of activity, brooms and brushes and pots whirling.

But now, at five o'clock, with the rain pouring noisily along the gutters outside and the black morning sky just beginning to lift a little over the eastern spires, all was ready. The stage was set, the powdery lime was ready to be flared in the iron holders above the wings, and beside them the new candles were tucked inside their shades above the music stands, while the boards were swept clear and the curtains looped back. The tables shone damply above the newly scrubbed stone flags, and the puddings and pasties, joints and soups, vegetables and syllabubs and jelly creams were all cooking busily in the kitchens. And preparation had at last stopped.

Celia had gone to wash herself and change her gown, ready for the arrival of the market men in search of breakfast victuals, the girls had gone to their own hard-earned breakfasts in the big kitchen, while the two men who worked with them, old Loppy and half-witted Will, together with young Sam the street boy who came and went from time to time to earn himself occasional scraps, had gone to draw the day's beer barrels from the cellar. And Jonah had slipped upstairs to creep into the children's room and look down on their sleeping faces and to touch Phoebe's soft cheek with one loving finger before going to the kitchen himself to see to the making of some breakfast bread-and-milk for them.

Now, standing shivering a little outside the kitchen door in the dark cold passage and smelling the beer lees and faint odour of rotting vegetation coming from the market place so near his back door, he wondered at himself. Was he not the master in this place? Should he not have gone in there raging, as Celia would have done, to lash at them for their insolence in discussing their employers at all, to send them packing, breakfasts finished or not? Why should he stand skulking here, in the cold and dark, wondering whether he should go in to prepare some food for the children, like some frightened alley cat?

Because they are right, his private voice whispered to him. Because it does make me so wretched when people argue, when there are disagreements and shouting and hatefulness. I will do anything for peace, anything at all. Even stand here in the cold, while my own servants roast their toes before my coals——

But even though he tried to persuade himself he was a weak and foolish creature, and tried to whip up his own courage, he knew he could not. He would wait until Celia came sweeping downstairs to scatter her girls about their work before again entering that kitchen, for he could not, would not, face those insolent stares and knowing grins. As ever, he would let Celia handle the matter.

He went wearily upstairs again to the children's room to stand in the doorway staring at their sleeping forms, as he so often did when he was in need of comfort. Life was so often so complex for him, so disagreeable in such silly little ways that he needed the nearness of the children to make himself cope with it all.

Yet it should not be so. He should not be so easily upset by minor irritations, such as ill-mannered servants or drunken customers or bad performers in the company. He should be as Celia was, strong and resilient——

At that thought he smiled a little to himself in the dimness. Like Celia! If only he could be! And how much happier might Celia be if he were? He knew of her unhappinesses, knew of the times she looked at him with her eyes—those deep grey eyes he had first seen staring at him across the Haymarket stage so long ago—dark with the misery of incomprehension. He knew how the passage of the past ten years had hardened and roughened and soured her as they had clawed and fought their way up from the disappointment of failure after failure of his carefully written plays, via the cheapest and dingiest of groups of strolling players, to this modest establishment of their own.

And not so modest any more, after all! They had taken the basement room in King Street as somewhere to live when they had come crawling wearily back to London with two-year-old Oliver, ailing and wheezing and looking fit to die, and Celia hugely pregnant with Phoebe, and somehow by dint of Celia's determination and some good luck (his being engaged for a season as a super at Drury Lane theatre by Edmund Kean, just before he died, had been excellent luck indeed) they had taken the room above and then another, setting themselves up as chophouse keepers. And then, as hungry actors and singers started to entertain other customers for the price of their own supper, had developed the venture into the highly popular theatrical supper rooms it had become.

They owned the whole house now, had converted the entire ground floor into a most snug and elegant place with seating for above seventy-five hungry diners, as well as a neat stage upon which as many as four performers at a time could sing, and a tiny orchestra pit where three musicians could scrape and blow away together. With its red curtains and sparkling Frenchly-fashionable gasoliers and engraved mirrors in gilt frames it was indeed a credit to them both.

To Celia, he now thought bleakly. To Celia, for it had been she who had scraped and saved and planned and schemed and made it all possible, she who had borrowed money and dunned actors and singers and butchers and brewers and coffee merchants, she who had made it all happen. And he knew, now, what had happened to both of them as the years had gone by. As her energy had increased, fed by the success her efforts brought to them, so had her patience with him diminished, and so had he become more and more aware of his own shortcomings. He had looked at her whisking about the rooms and kitchens, and felt his very bones ache with tiredness at the sight of so much sheer animal strength, had doubted his own ability to compete and had shrunk back into himself and to the children, so that she in her lonely frustration had felt it more necessary than ever to work even harder, and thus had made him feel even more useless.

And so it had gone on, until now they lived in so very uneasy a way that they did not even know, most of the time, how uneasy it was. Jonah, always polite and kind and gentle, always eager to do anything she asked him, but knowing himself always a little remote from her, sometimes remembered those early days of their marriage when they had lain next each other in lumpy musty beds in dubious lodging houses, clutching each other in a desperation of loneliness and young doubt and fear, loving each other so much. It was only now that he knew how much he had loved her in those early days, knew how important their closeness had been. Now, when they were so often separated by the exigencies of the business and Celia's abstraction with the details of running it all, he knew that much of their love was in the past. Well, not so much in the past, he amended his thoughts; it was the chance to talk to each other of their needs and feelings that lay behind them both.

Across the room Phoebe stirred and then rolled over to rearrange her sleeping body on knees and elbows, small rump stuck up in the air in endearing absurdity, and he pulled his thoughts away from his wife and the lines in which his life with her had fallen to move across to the child's side and gaze down at her.

He did love her so very dearly, this scrap of a child. Small, bird-boned, and pointed of face, she had her mother's huge grey eyes but surmounted them with winged dark brows and coarse knotted curls that gave her a look of gipsy wickedness that was exceedingly attractive. Fortunately, she did not yet know quite how lovely she was, though she was beginning to discover it from the supper rooms' customers, for they petted her and fussed over her outrageously, and she was learning to be quite an imperious little madam, ordering her brother about with a lordly disdain that made everyone around her laugh and applaud loudly. Even now, asleep in this absurd and favoured position of hers, bottom in the air and head turned sideways against the pillow so that her cheeks crumpled into a grimace, she had an air of self-assurance about her. She had none of the abandoned helplessness that the sleeping Oliver showed.

Jonah turned his head to look at his son, lying sprawled on his back in his truckle bed with his mouth half open and snoring a little, and sighed softly. He was equally beloved but in a more comfortable companionable sort of a way. Together he and his son would watch the women of their family, strong capable Celia and delicious wickedly selfish little Phoebe, moving about them so swift and busy, and would blink and then smile and turn to each other in a sort of silent communion, as if to say, 'They amaze me as much as they amaze you, but that is the way they are, and who are we to do aught about it?' Oliver with his straight black hair that fell always over his forehead and into his eyes, muddily green eyes, round and puzzled and a little short-sighted, Oliver with his fair skin that blushed so easily and burned so painfully in the summer months, quiet, rather slow Oliver with his stocky little body and slightly pigeon-toed walk was a great comfort to his father. And because the child knew it he found his father was a great comfort to him.

Altogether, Jonah thought, looking down on them, they are the most perfect children a man could have. He would never cease to be grateful to Celia and to whatever Providence had so ordained it that he should have the joy of them. If only, he thought as he so often did, if only his own father had been able to find such pleasure in his and his brothers' and sisters' existence, how much pleasanter life would have been for all of them! But that was a thought not to be entertained and certainly not now, for it was close on six o'clock, and already he could hear the crescendo of sound from the streets below that showed the market was shortly to close and the men would come pouring in for their beer and victuals. There was work to be done, and the children must be roused and washed and fed before he could turn his attention to the pulling of pints of ale.

Regretfully he leaned over the table between the children's beds to light the candle lying ready, murmuring their names softly as he did so, for it was bad enough to be roused from a deep sleep without being roused noisily.


The rain made less noise in Grosvenor Square than perhaps anywhere else in London that February morning; it was almost as though the elements, like the rest of the populace of the city, knew that today was

24

to be a most busy one for the fashionable, and showed sympathetic respect by muting their noise. So, no raucous gusts of wind came whistling past the stone-framed windows of the tall and stately grey-fronted houses that marched so arrogantly around the four smart sides. Instead they spent themselves in little whirling eddies of last autumn's dead leaves in the green and railinged central circle, with its fringe of shrubbery and trailing bushes. No rain came hurling itself against those quiet first- and second-floor windows, but instead ran itself politely down the neat pipes and guttering that led it away to the nether regions where it belonged. Only high up in the attics could the rain really be heard, for the angled windows there lay open to the slanting lines, and they pattered irritably and sometimes viciously against them, rattling the panes noisily. But that did not matter at all, for only servants slept in attics, and none cared about the welfare of servants, least of all the elements.

But despite the quietness of the Square outside and the deep comfort of her bed, sitting foursquare and solid in the middle of the expanse of thick-piled Indian carpet which covered her bedroom floor, Lilith was awake. She had been awake for at least two hours, she had estimated, and in that time had swung from rage at her insomnia to whimpering why-should-I-suffer-so? self-pity and back to pillow-thumping anger. But now, as the light began to shred itself against the lightening sky and lifted her room into awareness of morning, she lay with her lace-covered pillows comfortably piled beneath her head, indulging herself with her favourite occupation.

She was counting in her head. Enumerating her assets, totting up parcels of house property and their estimated value; the rents of the tenements she owned throughout the rookeries of St Giles and Clare Market and Seven Dials; the revenues from the couple of market gardens in Hammersmith and Chiswick; the intrinsic value of this house in Grosvenor Square—so physically near to her old home in North Audley Street, but miles away in terms of fashion and the monetary value that fashion lent to an address—the lists of her furniture and plate, her pictures and carvings and glass and silver and all the other kickshaws, her jewellery, her furs, the very clothes that filled her presses—all were itemized, added up and a running balance drawn.

It was a most agreeable occupation, and one which she knew could lull her as no other. Not even in the days when she had been able to call half the London *ton* her lovers, when her bed had known the company of politicians and generals, wits and judges, rich lords and even richer parvenus, had she found such pleasure and ultimate peace in a bed-based occupation.

At seven o'clock, when the rain became careless enough to treat Grosvenor Square to the same drenching downpour that it had hitherto reserved for the less eminent parts of the town, she rang her bell. Never mind the fact that old Hawks would mutter and rage at being called from her own bed at so early an hour; Lilith wanted her chocolate, and wanted it now. And drinking it would help fill in the time between now and nine o'clock when she could hope to see Jody come into her room, bare feet peeping out beneath his befurred dressing-gown, his eyes heavy above his adorably sulky lower lip (for Jody always looked sulky in the mornings) to crawl into bed beside her for their 'morning romp' as she so fondly called it.

Not that he seemed to enjoy the romping as much as he had been used to. At six he was becoming suddenly a boy and much less of a chubby baby. Not that she minded the changes in him; indeed she did not. She revelled in his swift growth, in the rotundity of his belly—for he was fond of food, and it showed in his shape—the heavy sturdiness of his legs, the faint curving of a second chin beneath his dimpled lips almost as much as she loved to look at his silky, curly brown hair and his wide blue eyes, so palely blue that when he looked directly at you, she would tell people, it was as though the clouds had suddenly blown away from the heavens. Altogether, Lilith would say, laughing her tinkling cascade of laughter that had enchanted theatre audiences for more years than she cared to remember, altogether she had become as fond a mamma as any farmer's wife, positively doating over her boy, and finding all good, no ill in any part of him!

Lying now in bed, propped up on cream lace pillows and wearing a silk frilled peignoir in her favourite shade of blue, she felt her lips curve into a smile as she thought of Jody. To think that when she had found herself increasing she had been so furious she had sent his father packing, even before making sure he had made decent provision for his offspring, and had swallowed great quantities of pennyroyal and slippery elm and all manner of noxious draughts in an effort to be rid of the encumbrance. After all, she had been no silly girl when it happened. In the public eye she had been thirty-five or so; in fact she had been a full forty-five, little as she had looked it, and few who would have believed it. To be saddled with a brat at such an age was ludicrous, she had fumed, and had gone on raging and suffering throughout that long and miserable pregnancy, sitting sulking down at Brighton and pretending not to care. She had gone through a long and thoroughly disagreeable labour—much worse than any she had experienced with her other three brats—still hating her ridiculous situation, only to find when the child was put into her arms by old Hawks that some strange alchemy had gone to work, and made her fall head over ears in love with the creature.

Thinking of it now her smile widened until she laughed aloud; it had been so surprising to find herself so *besotted* by a child! She had enjoyed the others well enough, especially the first—for she had been a novelty —but all had become such dead bores by the time Jody had been born that she had quite forgotten how she had felt about them in their infancy. But she knew how she felt about Jody. The sweetest, dearest child, she thought fondly, that any woman was blessed with.

But when Jody appeared at her bedroom door, he was in no mood to be anyone's dearest, sweetest child. He was red with rage, his eyes suffused and his nose running, and he came storming in shrieking at the top of his voice with such a volume of sound that Lilith jumped and spilled the dregs of her chocolate all down her frilled front.

'Dear child!' she cried, as soon as he drew breath and the noise eased. 'What *has* happened? Please, *don't* shriek so, not if you love me! You make my head ache so dreadfully——'

'I shall shriek, I shall, I shall, I *shall*!' roared Jody. 'That hellborn bitch, I'll kill her if you don't turn her off! Do you hear me, Mamma! Make her go away, right now, at once, I shall scream until she does, the cow, the bitch, I'll kill her——' and then he was on his back on the floor, kicking and shouting and throwing himself about in such a lather of temper that his bare legs and behind were a pink blur against the dark brown of his furry robe.

Behind him Hawks came marching in to scoop him up in her deceptively scrawny arms—for she was still as strong as an ox for all

27

she was nearly sixty-five—and hold him at arms' length until he flopped against her with the exhaustion born of his tantrum, while Lilith, now out of her bed with her head between her hands in an agony of concern, stood beside him and tried to make her voice heard above his din.

'What happened?' she managed at last, as Jody subsided to a quieter, if still very audible, snivelling. She held out her arms to him and immediately he was in them, curling his legs around her narrow body so that she reeled a little under his weight. 'Whatever happened to you, my darling? Tell Mamma, and all shall be put right at once——'

'The way to put things right, madam, is for me to set the child across my knee and beat the livin' daylights out of 'im!' Hawks said sharply. ''E's been fit for nothing but a larrapin' since he got out of bed this morning. 'E's thrown his breakfast at Mrs Jennings, 'e's kicked Mrs Castor, and when Mrs Jennings rightly said as if 'e didn't behave, no wedding parade should 'e be took to see, 'e went and bit her. She's bleeding that 'eavy that it'll be a miracle she isn't scarred for life. 'Er arm it was, and 'e ought to be——'

'It's her own fault!' Jody lifted his head from its damp spot on his mother's neck and glared at Hawks. 'So it is! She gave me all the things I hate most for my breakfast and then she took that damned hairbrush to me, and said I could not see the parade, and it's her own fault! Mamma, turn her off! I shan't let her do anything for me, so I tell you, Mamma! I hate her! Turn her *off*!'

'That's the fourth nurse you've let him have turned off since Christmas, Madam Lilith,' Hawks said sourly, 'and I've more sense than to argue with you if 'e demands it, but I tell you it's gettin' 'arder and 'arder to find any as'll take the place. It took me all my time to persuade this one to come, let alone stay, and now—ah, what's the good o' my talkin'! You let that limb o' Satan do all 'e wishes——' She turned away from them and began to clear the chocolate equipage from the bed as Lilith carried her now beaming son to her chaise longue.

'Dear Jody! You must not, you really must *not* treat your nurses so! I must have someone to take good care of you, and how can I if you will be so wilful? I know these women can be so stupid as to make one rage, but all the same——'

He snuggled close to her, tucking his head under her chin. 'Ah,

Mamma, must I have nurses at all? Cannot *you* take care of me? I would like that above all things!'

'No doubt you would, you wretch,' Hawks, scowling, came to stand beside the chaise longue. 'No doubt you would, for you could wind 'er about your small finger any time—I tell you, Madam Lilith, for your own good as well as 'is that 'e needs a firm 'and and none of your mollycoddling ways will be of use to either of yer in the long run! You mark my words——'

'Oh, Hawks, be *quiet*!' Lilith snapped. 'You've been scowling at me long enough! Go away, and tell that woman to pack her box. And seek a better nurse this time, do you hear me? I cannot have these alarums and excursions to drive me wild, not when I have a matinée day to face!'

'Oh, Mamma, you will take me to the parade, will you not? I shan't go if you don't take me, for Hawks is always hateful, and the other servants are so stupid—*please* Mamma, take me to see the Queen in her carriage—Mamma, please?—*please*——'

And it took but little more of his pulling at her lacy wrapper and his impassioned pleading to make her give in, little as she relished the thought of so exhausting a morning as one spent pushing through gawping crowds and on the day of a matinée performance too. But she could refuse this little love of hers nothing, she told him fondly, and together they began to plan the morning's outing.

So when at one o'clock as the bride and groom's procession left the Chapel Royal at St James's to exhibit itself to the waiting crowds of admiring, jeering, gawping, and by now half-drunken Londoners, she and her Jody were there, watching. Not far away in the press of the crowd were Abby and Frederick and even nearer were Miss Ingoldsby with Gussy and Martha; not that any were aware of the others' presence, so heavy was the crush. And Abel, tending the third broken head of the morning in Endell Street cursed Queens and weddings and crowds with a fluent impartiality, for February the tenth, 1840, was proving to be a very busy day and not only for the Queen and her dull Albert.

## 3

Frederick had conversed in whispers all the way home from the Park, sitting there close beside her in the swaying musty dimness of the seven o'clock Shillibeer's omnibus. The three bay horses clattering noisily before them as the vehicle went lurching and rolling up the New Road; the burly self-important conductor in the handsome dark velvet livery who had taken their fares of sixpence a head with such lordly disdain; the other travellers, a dozen or so city men with their well-upholstered wives; all had come in for his wry comments and observations, and Abby had several times to suppress a snort of laughter at the sharpness of his remarks and the edge that he could put into some judgement on a lady traveller's too widely brimmed and excessively feathered and beribboned hat, for he had a dry wit, for one so young, that much delighted her.

It had been a most agreeable day, they both agreed, in spite of the crowds and the rain that had marred the early part of it. The processions had been satisfyingly sumptuous, the sellers of comestibles delightfully ubiquitous, so that even Frederick's ability to eat non-stop had been hard put to it to cope, and the marvellous mock battle fought upon the lake in the Park for the delectation of onlookers had been altogether superb, for at least seven of the frail and overdecorated craft had sunk ignominiously, leaving their crestfallen occupants to struggle muddily to the bank amid the mocking cheers and shouts of the crowd. And then there had been the early fireworks that had starred the grey skies over the roofs of St James's with crimson fire and yellow showers and even, in one particularly breathtaking set piece, a conglomeration of blue and green and orange cascading flame making up a picture of the bride and groom that had left even the indefatigable Frederick speechless. A most *splendid* day, and when at last they climbed down from the omnibus, a little stiff and crumpled, Frederick hurled his arms about his mother with a last burst of energy, and told her she was beyond any shadow of doubt the dearest soul of a Mamma, and he wished for no better life than to spend a million such days in her company. And she had laughed, and hugged him in her turn, and they had made their way companionably across the dark Green, leaving the Shillibeer's men behind them busily unhitching their steaming tired horses, to their snug little house opposite St Mary's Church.

Frederick had produced a couple of jawcracking yawns and gone willingly to eat his supper of hot soup and bread and butter in the kitchen under the watchful eye of Ellie, the little general maid who was the only house-servant Abby felt it necessary to employ, before taking himself off to bed. And so left Abby to take herself to her room to change into a comfortable soft daygown, one of the old grey ones which while being far from fashionable still became her neat well-proportioned figure, and to brush her hair into a tidier mode. She felt at peace and comfortable within herself, for Frederick had indeed been delightful company, and had made her quite forget her morning irritation about the loss of a day's work. And now, it was barely eight o'clock, and there was plenty of the evening left. She would eat her supper and look over the ledgers before bed, and rise early next day to harry them all a little to make up for the loss of production this day.

She went downstairs contentedly to her small sitting room, her favourite room for it looked out over the little garden behind the house, and she could, by straining a little at the window, just glimpse from it the roof of her little manufactory which stood at the corner of Irongate Wharf Road, where it abutted on the Harrow Road. So much of her security and peace of mind was tied up with this house and that manufactory, and so much of her short life with James had been tied in with them both that to sit in one and be able to see the other gave her much comfort.

It was while she was finishing her baked egg custard, having thoroughly enjoyed the dish of crimped cod and potatoes which Ellie had brought to her, that she heard the knocker followed by the soft colloquy of distant voices in the hall. She wiped her mouth upon her

31

napkin and set her tray aside on the little table beside her, but not quite fast enough for the door opened and he stood there, smiling slightly at her. As she made to stand up he said swiftly, 'Please, do not disturb yourself! It is unforgivable of me to visit you on business matters at such an hour, but you were absent from home all day, my messenger said, for I sent him three times. So I took it upon myself to call this evening in the hope you would not object too strenuously to the intrusion.'

'My dear Gideon, as if you could ever disturb me! It is, as always, a great pleasure to see you. Come and sit down, and Ellie shall bring you some refreshment. Have you dined? Well, never mind. I believe you will still be able to enjoy a little of Ellie's baked custard. She makes them very well——'

He settled himself in the chair on the other side of the fireplace with an ease clearly born of long familiarity as she rang the bell. Ellie came and took away her tray and returned almost at once with a dish of custard for the visitor, which he accepted with grave appreciation and immediately set to eating with a neat delicacy in his manners but with obvious relish. And as he ate, Abby sat with her head resting back on her armchair, her hand up to shade her cheek from the warmth of the flames leaping in the little fireplace that separated them and looked at him, liking what she saw.

A tall spare young man, Gideon Henriques, with fine long bones and tapering fingers. He was very pale, but his pallor was a healthy one; no hints of sickness showed in those long white cheeks with their equal clefts where once, clearly, there had been dimples in his childhood; his eyes, which were very dark and fringed with thick lashes that were startling in their effect for the lower lashes were equal in length to the uppers, were clear and shining, quite lustrous in their health, and his hair was thick and dark and curly yet shaped to his long and narrow skull in a most elegant and pleasing manner. Altogether he was good to look upon and she judged herself fortunate to call him her friend.

He looked up as if aware of her scrutiny and smiled slightly, so that the corners of his narrow lips seemed to merge with the clefts in his cheeks, giving his whole countenance a certain mocking quality; but this was in no way a reflection of his mind, for, as Abby well knew from the many years they had worked in harmony as business partners,

32

Gideon never mocked. He might be amused, or ill-pleased, or disapproving, but mocking never, for he was far too sensitive about his own feelings ever to inflict such an unkindness on those of another person.

'And may I ask where you were today that my messenger came back so crestfallen so often?' he said, as he set aside the empty custard bowl, and settled back in his chair. 'I suspect, of course, that I know the answer. I cannot imagine young Frederick allowing you to escape so splendid an opportunity for frivolity!'

'Of course you are right! Where else should we be but admiring the processions?' Abby said, and laughed. 'Oh, Gideon, you should have seen him! He did so relish all of it! The driver of the omnibus allowed him to whip up the horses into Town, and what Shillibeer would have said had he discovered, I cannot imagine, and then of course, there were a thousand things the young wretch wanted to do!'

She launched herself into a spirited account of their day, using her hands occasionally to demonstrate some action undertaken by the lively Frederick, and now it was his turn to sit with his head thrown back against the comfortable armchair and to watch her. And he liked what he saw a great deal more than he found quite comfortable.

He liked the squareness of her face. She was far from being a classic beauty, for her mouth was too wide and generous, her eyes a very ordinary grey, though prettily lashed, and her nose most commonplace. But her brow was deep and wide and her hair, softly and naturally dressed above it, had a delicate brownness that he much preferred to the more startling blacks and blondes that were so admired in fashionable women; and her head was set so elegantly on her firm white throat. He liked, too, the animation of her face, the way her thick dark brows lifted and moved and quirked in response to the things she was saying. He liked the way her neat square hands with their blunt fingers moved so crisply and practically; no fluttering swooning nonsense about Abigail Caspar, thank God. Gideon disliked fluttering swooning women above all things, for they much alarmed him with their swimming looks and speaking glances thrown at him over their expensive fans. He met many such in his parents' drawing room, for he was a more than eligible bachelor of five and twenty and his mother was at some pains to see that he met suitable ladies. But never yet had he seen in that elegant and very costly drawing room any elegant and costly woman who had half as much charm as Abby sitting here in her dull grey stuff gown in her neat and pretty but far from lavishly furnished little sitting room.

'So, you see,' she finished, 'I have just cause to be very fatigued, but you know, now I have eaten my supper I am far from being so! I believe I could work for the rest of the evening to very good effect, and start the day tomorrow as though there had been no enforced holiday at all.'

'Well, if you feel so, I have no conscience about my calling tonight,' he said easily. 'For it is business matters that must be discussed. I am to tell you that I am a little anxious about you, my dear Abby! You have not been showing your usual acumen, I suspect!'

She raised her brows at that. 'Oh? And what error do you *think* you have detected in my ledger keeping now?' and they both laughed at this reference to the time, nine years before, when Gideon, full of the newfound skill of a fresh-from-school accounter, and proud of his status as her prime adviser following his father's sad illness, had thought he detected a great error in the costings of the medicines. He had argued then with Abby at some length, full of cockiness, only to discover that in fact Abby's figures were not merely correct, but a most sophisticated solution to the problem of finding ways to sell her products at advantageously cheap prices. He had been sorely embarrassed by his discovery but she had soon coaxed him out of his young shame in a way that had salvaged his pride; and their friendship had deepened from that day and become far more adult. Before that he had been just Nahum's boy, a gangling, dark-eyed pretty lad in her view. But the dignity with which he had been able to admit his error and the handsomeness of his apology had done much to give him superior status.

Now he smiled again and said, 'Nothing to do with costings, I do assure you. Indeed, Abby, I check the ledgers only because you insist that I should——'

'And I always shall so insist,' she said swiftly. 'I shall never cease to be grateful to your father for had it not been for his good offices when James and I came here to Paddington Green, I believe we should have foundered completely. And had it not been for his unswerving support

34

and concern for me in the years after James's death, I know I should have been submerged totally! Without your money, as well as your friendship and guidance I should be nowhere at all. So check those ledgers you shall, for I am determined you shall know of every transaction and charge upon the books that ever comes!'

'You need not fret about your very small commitment to my father's firm,' Gideon said, and though his tone was mild and his voice light and not particularly emotional, there was a faint flush in those white cheeks, and he looked away from her face to the fire; and Abby too, also a little reddened by the emotion she had undoubtedly been displaying, sat silently for a moment or two. But then she stirred herself and said, 'So! To our affairs. What sin is it that you have discovered me in?'

He smiled at her, glad to recapture the lightness they were usually able to share. 'It is these payments you have been making on Fridays, once a month. You have entered them under "miscellaneous disbursements", but they are so regular in payment—the last Friday of each month—that I am puzzled. What are you hiding behind that bland label of "miscellaneous disbursements"? It is not good business, you know, not to enter in every detail the matters upon which you expend your assets! I have no doubt it is some harmless thing, but if you should choose to sell the business there might be difficulty in explaining it——'

'I shall never sell the business! It is being built up for Frederick, of course!' Abby said, but she was clearly a little put about for her cheeks, which had lost the redness of her earlier emotion, now flamed again, and her eyes were troubled as she looked at him. 'Oh dear, Gideon, I find this a little difficult to explain. It is a matter of some embarrassment for me, for it is a private matter, you see, quite personal, not to do with the business at all——'

Now it was Gideon who became pink with mortification. 'Indeed, then explain you need not! Truly, if it is some matter that does not concern the business, then I wish to know nothing of it! Do remember that I do but examine the books in order to please you, for you will insist upon it, and if I have inadvertently stumbled upon some private matter of your own, I do beg that it remain so! I would not for the world——'

'Oh, Gideon, do stop getting into such an agony!' Abby said, and now she was herself again, her embarrassment quite gone in the face of Gideon's confusion. 'You dear silly boy! As if it were some dreadful matter! You really must not get in such a pother! Of course I shall tell you——'

'Oh, please, do not!' said Gideon earnestly, and leaned forwards to set one hand upon hers as they lay clasped upon her lap. She looked down at the long white fingers, and without moving her own hands looked up into his face, into his eyes very wide and serious as they looked at her, and she smiled almost shyly.

'Dear Gideon, you should not get in such a pother!' she repeated. 'You make a most monstrous mountain out of a minuscule molehill, I do assure you. Now, listen to me! I shall explain about those Friday sums.'

'I wish you would not,' Gideon said again, miserably, but he leaned back in his chair again.

'And I wish that I shall!' Abby said firmly. 'It is my brother, do you see!'

'Your brother?' he sat up a little straighter. 'But I understood that your family had quite—that they did not—that——'

'That they had cast me off when I chose to marry?' Abby said equably. 'You are quite right. My father did, deeply to my regret. I have not seen him nor heard from him this past ten years, I am afraid, though I keep aware of what he is doing. It is easy, you see, in the way of business, to know of his affairs, for when Henry goes about on his selling jaunts, he garners as much gossip as he sells drugs! I know my father to be well, and that the hospital is thriving—he has taken a fourth house there in Endell Street, you know, and has several wards; I have heard of other matters too, agreeable and not so agreeable. My younger sister, Mary, succumbed to the cholera epidemic two years ago——'

'I am sorry to hear it,' Gideon said at once. 'Allow me to wish you a long life.'

She quirked an inquiring eyebrow at him and he looked confused again.

'Forgive me. That is the immediate response all persons of the Jewish faith make to those who have been bereaved,' he said. 'I did it

36

without thinking. I am indeed sad that this should have happened while you were estranged from your relations.'

'I too,' she said soberly. 'I felt it keenly at the time, but more for myself than I had cause to. It is my other sister, Martha, who must have suffered most, for they were twins, you know, and most attached. However!'

There was a little pause and then she went on in a determinedly cheerful voice, 'Pleasant matters have happened too. I saw in the Court pages that my brother Barty has wed himself an heiress! I would never have thought it, knowing what a graceless scamp he was in his childhood!'

Her eyes had darkened a little now, and she was not looking at him so much as through him, and he wanted again to put out his hand to hold hers, but he stifled the wish and sat quietly watching her expressive face.

'Ah well, so be it!' she said after a moment's pause and then went on more animatedly. 'And then, you see, I met my brother Jonah! I was walking in Rotten Row one afternoon, just before Christmas, when the weather cleared at last and gave us a clean frost—you will recall how sadly foggy it had been earlier in the month, and we had all been quite tied to our firesides! Well, there I was with Frederick, and he with his two children! Oh, it was such a delight to see him! His children are quite charming, a most solemn boy of perhaps a year less than my Frederick, and a perfect little bewitcher of a daughter, some two years younger. I was quite taken with them both——'

She sighed sharply then. 'It is such a pity, you know, for neither he nor I have any contact with our father, or our other brothers and sister. It seems so—so *wasteful*, do you not agree, Gideon? I do so dislike the absurdity of family disagreements——'

'Absurd they may be, but powerful they always are,' Gideon said softly, and she looked up at him sharply, for there was an odd note in his voice. But she could not see his face clearly, for the firelight had dwindled as the flames had sunk to embers, and he had one hand shading his cheek. So she went on after a moment, 'Well we decided *we* should at least meet from time to time, for we have no quarrel with each other. And I would have been glad to see his wife—although for my part I must confess it will not be easy for me to be courteous to her, for although she was not herself to be blamed for it, it was her mother who caused my own mother's tragic suffering——' She shook her head a little sharply. 'Well, to draw to an end at last, we met from time to time, he coming here to visit with the children, quietly you know, and I took to giving my niece and nephew an occasional gift, much as you present young Frederick with items from time to time— oh, yes, I know! Never think you are so secret!' She smiled at his obvious discomfiture. 'And I also gave Jonah a little cash to purchase items for them. To be honest, Gideon, I received the impression that it is his wife who rules his roost, and that she controls their purse-strings with such energy that leaves the poor man with little control over his own affairs. It is hard on a man, I think, to have to account for all his moneys to his wife, although of course I know it to be far from rare. Well, there it is, my guilty secret is out! The miscellaneous disbursements are my brother Jonah and his children! I arrange it so that they do not fully realize that this is a regular monthly sum, but I prefer to make sure it is an equal amount, and enter it regularly, for I cannot abide disorder in the ledgers, as well you know.'

He was quiet for a moment, and then said softly, 'You are such a very *good* woman, Abby, are you not?'

'Am I?' she said equably, and stood up to cross the room and raise the flame in the handsome brass oil lamp that stood upon the table in the corner, flooding the room with a new radiance. 'Not at all, dear Gideon! Hardworking you may call me, and practical, and indeed a little dull, for there is nothing of frivolity about me—but good? I repudiate the suggestion. It sounds too spiritual altogether for one of my bread-and-butter nature! Now, we shall ask Ellie to bring us some tea and to mend the fire, and settle to the ledgers, if you can bear to continue work at so late an hour! There are one or two matters I would so much like to discuss with you. Young Henry, for example. He works so well, you know, that I feel there is a real danger that we may lose him. I suspect, from what I have been told by those apothecaries with which he deals on my behalf, that his sterling virtues have been recognized by outsiders and some unscrupulous wretch will not be above coaxing him away from me with offers of better remuneration! I have an idea that we should offer Henry a different form of payment. Not perhaps a greater salary but a bonus calculated upon the volume of sales he makes above a certain level. This will encourage him to work even harder, will help him feel his attachment to me more closely, and will reward me with higher sales, even if Henry must receive more money. What do you think?'

'I think you are indeed a most astute woman of business!' Gideon said, his face alight with good humour as he hurried to help her bring a low table nearer the fire, and set the ledgers upon it. 'That is a most sensible idea for you to devise, in your situation, and shows a foresight that would do credit to a man twice your age, and twice your monetary holdings. We shall look at his efforts, and calculate what it might cost in hard cash. That of course is the key——'

They settled to their bookwork as Ellie came quietly to set her tea tray beside them and to build the fire high with sea coal, but before plunging completely into the affairs of the business, Gideon said a little diffidently, 'I would so much like to know your brother, Abby, if I may. Will you perhaps——'

She smiled up at him. 'Would you, Gideon? Well, why not indeed! You are my friend and business partner, and it is right you should know those of my relations that wish to know me. I shall see what I can contrive.'

He laughed at that. 'You always say that, do you not, Abby?'

'Say what?'

'That you will contrive. I find it most—a charming phrase! I am glad you shall contrive for me to meet this brother of yours. I am most curious to know if he is at all like you!'

She smiled at that, thinking of the way Jonah had stood there in the park the day she had met him, his hat in his hand and his hair blowing in the wind, and his face almost timid as he looked at her, and also remembering the diffident way he had stood here in her sitting room when she had insisted on pressing upon him gifts for his children. 'Like me?' she said softly. 'Indeed, I do not think you will find we are at all alike! But I shall contrive—*arrange* it when I can!'

But when Gideon went home, sitting in the corner of his cold hackney cab as it went rattling back along the New Road to his parents' home above the counting house in Lombard Street, still feeling the warmth of that pretty sitting room and the pleasure he found in the company of its occupant, he remembered that wistful little remark about 'the absurdity of family disagreements' and felt a heavy sadness begin to form deep in his belly, knotting itself into a cold hard lump that made him far less comfortable than he would have wished to be.

## 4

Five students were waiting at the doors that led into the top floor ward of the women's medical house when Abel came clattering up the scrubbed wooden stairs, their heads together and guffawing at some coarse joke or other, but after one look at his set face and the line of his clenched jaw they subsided, seeming to shrink a little from the boisterous creatures they usually were into frightened schoolboys.

They knew their mentor too well to treat him with anything but the most careful of respect when he looked as grim as this; never particularly easy in his dealings with students, in such a mood as he clearly was this morning he could be blistering in his attacks on any lapse of behaviour, intelligence or concern for the patients.

So, they followed him into the big cold room with their heads down and their hands clasped behind their backs, shuffling a little to avoid the most dangerous place immediately behind him, and resigned themselves to a difficult morning.

Each ward-walking day followed the same pattern; they would start at the top of the women's medical house, making their way down through each of the three bleak wards it contained, then go to the men's medical house next door, trailing behind Abel through the dank cellars which had been connected to link the four old houses, finally to walk the six wards of the two surgical houses.

By the end of it, even on a good day, they would be exhausted, heads buzzing with new information, lists of symptoms, medical aphorisms and comments of all sorts thrown at them by Abel, and convinced that never, not if they lived to be ninety, would they learn all that this wretched man expected them to learn before they could call themselves physicians and surgeons.

They knew full well that they were lucky indeed to have places in this medical school; for small an establishment as it was when compared with the great old foundation hospitals of Guy's and St Thomas's over the river, poor in possessions as it was when compared with St George's near the Park or the Middlesex which lay a scant half hour's walk to the North of them, St Eleanor's was one of the best thought-of medical schools in the whole of London and promised fair to produce doctors as great as any that might emerge from other, more august, places. So, would-be Charles Bells and Richard Brights, Thomas Addisons and Astley Coopers and Benjamin Brodies came to Nellie's, as it was vulgarly known, spent their exhausting three years there, and emerged as useful members of their profession, in spite of and because of Abel Lackland.

This morning's quintet, however, seemed likely to flee long before they reached anything like halfway through their course, for today Abel was exceedingly icy in his condemnation of the least error or slowness in response. He nearly reduced Edward Beddoes, the six-foot, butcher-shouldered, square-jawed countryman who had been known to stand up to a charging bull in his father's farmyard without flinching, to tears; he so flicked on the raw the quiet Samuel Carey, who never showed any discomfiture whatever when his fellow students teased him cruelly for his studious ways and careful work, that he actually clenched his fist and raised it halfway to Abel's face. Altogether the morning proved to be even worse than they had feared it would be at first sight of him.

And all because of the half hour Abel had spent, before coming to his ward rounds, in the tiny cluttered office on the ground floor of the men's surgical house where George Conran spent his days scrabbling among his ledgers and accounts, sniffing dolorously into his straggling whiskers and looking suspiciously sideways at any who came at all near him.

Abel had realized full well that he had started the interview on the wrong foot and that much of what later transpired had been his own fault, but that did not ease his anger at all. He had wanted to approach Conran two days earlier, but the Queen's wedding and all the excitement and brouhaha it had caused in the town had kept him so hard at work patching broken heads and reducing fractured legs and arms that not until now, the Wednesday following, had he been able to come to see the Bursar; and he had brought his own irritation at the delay with him.

He had stood there with his back to the small fire that burned dispiritedly in the grate, effectively cutting off any heat to the desiccated Conran, and said loudly, 'So, Conran? What is this nonsense you have been saying about the costs of drugs to Eleanor's being inflated beyond need? If you have any complaints in this area it is right and proper to bring them to me. You do not go bruiting them about the town to your tavern cronies! I will not have the hospital's affairs gossiped over in taprooms, d'ye hear me, Conran? You exceed your office in taking Eleanor's happenings outside the walls of this building!'

'And, if you please, Mr Lackland, you seem to exceed yours in trying to give me instructions about the way in which I perform my functions,' Conran said, in his whiney little voice, so full of subservience, yet triumphant in its self-righteousness. 'For you know yourself, sir, that I was instructed always to take my instructions and to hand my reports to the whole Board of Trustees, and not to yourself alone, sir. After all, it was you that so instructed me, and——'

'Dammit all man, I know that! I made sure the Bursar was answerable not to me personally for the very reason that so much of the money the hospital enjoys comes from my own pocket! I would not have any man say that I have the place run in any but the most pernickety of fashions! But that does not give you the right to bypass me altogether, for I am the one who handles the day to day running of the place, and not the Board! And well you know it! To go and sit in some damned Covent Garden whorehouse and make your whining complaints about the way my son handles the drug accounts is in no way the manner in which such matters should be dealt with. If you have any complaint, make it to me, not to half the neighbourhood!'

'It was no whorehouse,' Conran said, and how his head was poking forwards and his eyes gleaming spitefully. 'But a decent eating place! I know better than to say aught about Master William Lackland in a whorehouse, begging your presence, sir, for it is all Lombard Street to a China orange that he would be there before me to listen! All I did was to take my dinner with Matthew Hodgkin the apothecary and ask him the prices of some of the staples we buy from Mr William, since

43

I was concerned to check the state of the market, and was amazed to discover that we are paying fully twenty per cent more for ipecac and quassia chips, not to mention ginger and rhubarb and squills and other necessaries, and I said to my friend Hodgkin that I was surprised and——'

'Aye—and said it loud enough for half the town to hear, and so talk about ever since,' Abel said savagely. 'William may be no angel in his entertainments, Conran, and I am the first to admit it, but I believe his way of spending his own time is no concern of yours! I know you have not wanted to work with him, from the time he took over the running of the manufactory, but that does not give you leave to spread malicious gossip!'

He stared loweringly at Conran for a moment, who stared back with that sideways glitter of his and said nothing.

'Dammit all, Conran, I hold no brief for the man, my son or not,' Abel burst out, irritated beyond measure by the way Conran was staring at him. 'All I care for is that the hospital shall be run properly! And I cannot have this sort of talk going about outside its walls. I would not have it *inside*, for that matter! You are to stop this complaining and whining of yours, d'you hear me? I've better things to do than deal with the megrims of the Trustees if they hear this Banbury tale of troubles about the manufactory!'

Conran set down his pen and stood up, ostentatiously buttoning his jacket over his scrawny belly, and then starting to remove the calico covers which he had so prudently set over the threadbare cloth of his jacket sleeves. 'That being so, sir, am I to understand I am no longer to take my instructions from the Board, but from you alone? You will forgive me, sir, I am sure, if I think it right to go to the City and discuss the matter with Sir Daniel and Mr Buckle? I would not for the world do aught to cause trouble between you and if I get my instructions from them as well as from you, and hear them with my own ears, why then, sir, I am in no risk of causing any pother! So I will set about——'

'Sit down, you great fool!' Abel roared, and moved forwards from the fire, his head down as rage made his shoulders rigid. 'Do you dare to try your schoolboy tricks with me? We are not engaged in covering up any matter at all. Of that I assure you! If William is not giving

Eleanor's the service it should have, then by Christ, I will see to it that the matter is dealt with at speed! But I will not—I will *not*, do you hear me, have the likes of you rushing about so full of slimy virtue and making a great stick out of nothing! You get on with your task, and I will deal with all matters that are above your reach! I am telling you to mind your business and keep out of affairs that are too complex for you!'

Conran sat down again precipitously, but still had that gleam of spite about him, and even though his voice shook a little and he had to lick his dry lips before he spoke, he remained stubborn.

'I will gladly stay with my business, sir. Indeed, that is all I am trying to do, for it is one of my duties to see the drugs are bought in and to make payments for them, and to do it at the most advantageous rates. It was Mr Hunnisett taught me my business, sir, your own servant as was for many years, God rest his poor soul in peace, and I doubt he taught me wrong. I would be derelict in my duty, sir, if I were to pay these sums out knowing in all truth that I could save four shillings in every pound I disburse. So what am I to do?'

And he sat and stared at Abel and Abel had stared back, knowing the man was right, in part applauding him for his careful watch over the hospital's expenditure and yet hating him—as he had from the time he had first met him—for the unctuousness of his tone and the self-congratulatory way he had of displaying his virtuous care for his occupation.

The fault, of course, was William's, too busy about his whoring and his drinking and his gaming to pay half the attention he should to his work. To keep prices down demanded constant attention to the state of the spice and drug market, frequent visits to the docks to go prowling about the merchantmen, playing one greedy captain off against another as the cargoes were dickered over. It needed concentration and application together with a sharp eye and a healthy appetite for clever practice, all of which this disagreeable, scrawny and altogether hateful little man had, and which William so notably lacked. And that this same hateful little man should be the one to underline William's lacks was galling in the extreme.

So Abel fumed and smarted under his awareness of the whole wretched situation, and George Conran sat and watched him with his face quite still yet carrying in every line of his body a smirk that showed he knew precisely how Abel was feeling and gloried in it.

'So, what am I to do, sir?' Conran said again after a long pause. 'You are so set that I should take day to day instructions from you, and here I find myself sore set about, not knowing what is my duty! I would be glad of a judgement, sir! After all, that was all I was asking of my friend the apothecary, Mr Hodgkin, who knows about such matters—just asking for advice, sir! It goes against my conscience to spend full twenty per cent more for Queen Eleanor's medicaments than I have need to spend, but if you so instruct me, sir, then of course there is nothing more that I can say——'

'Be quiet, damn you!' Abel snapped and then rubbed his face wearily. 'Don't be a fool, man! Of course you must not spend more than is required! God damn it all, the manufactory was set up in the first instance to provide Eleanor's with cheap medicines, and if it fails to do that, then it has no other real function, for the other side of its trade is little enough, in all conscience.'

'—Another way in which William had been derelict in his duty,' a little voice whispered somewhere deep in Abel's mind. The sales of drugs to other hospitals and to those apothecaries' shops which had no Fellow of the Society always on the premises should have brought in a tidy profit, and it always had in Hunnisett's day. Since William had taken over, it had dwindled steadily. It was becoming ever more abundantly clear that it was at William's door that all the real trouble lay, not at this dismal gossiping old woman of a Bursar's.

Again Abel rubbed his face and now he spoke a little less harshly. 'You must, of course, save every penny you can, for the hospital is hard put to it to raise all the money it needs at the best of times. I doubt your friend Hodgkin can provide us with our needs at any saving, so don't go thinking *that*——'

Conran smirked. 'Oh, sir, I was not thinking of any such thing, for he is a man in a very small way of business, I do assure you! But I have heard talk of a man who can provide us for even less than twenty per cent difference, and I am quite set upon seeing him and discussing——'

'Not yet,' Abel said, with a return of the edge to his voice. 'The Wapping manufactory exists solely to provide us, and if I cannot find out why prices have risen so, and see to it they plummet again, why then, I shall close it down! But until I do, then we shall not, I believe, approach any other source. You understand me? We have no special needs at the moment which are unmet?'

'Oh, no, sir, for I have always been most careful to call in all supplies we require well before there can be any diminution of them to the patients. I may not be a surgeon or physician, sir, or one directly concerned with saving lives but I know the importance of making sure the supplies come through, and I spend long hours here, sir, even late into the night, with no thanks or personal recompense, just to make sure that all is as it should be. My function here at Eleanor's may be a very humble one, sir, but I do my best——'

Abel grimaced. 'I am sure you do, Conran,' he said. 'But let us be clear. There is to be no more of this malicious gossip, outside the doors—or within 'em, for that matter—and I will set matters in order at the manufactory! For the rest I bid you a good morning!'

He slammed out of the stuffy little room leaving Conran sitting staring at his books with his mouth curved happily under his straggling whiskers and his eyes very bright when he lifted them to stare out of his window into the street below.

And Abel went storming on his way to his ward rounds to terrify his students, to flurry Nancy and her collection of nurses more than somewhat and even to alarm some of the patients a little (though he was usually well able to treat them with gentleness and concern, however sharp he could be with the healthy). He would have to use some of his precious time to set William right, and it was this that angered him most; bad enough that there had been gossip, that William had been revealed as being incompetent and lazy. Bad enough Queen Eleanor's precious money was being wasted. But that he would have to lose precious operating time in going down to Wapping—*that* was the most galling thing of all. It was little wonder that Edward Beddoes nearly wept, and Samuel Carey nearly struck him. He was within an ace of weeping and striking out himself, he was so put about.

## 5

Jonah had never liked Friday night at the supper rooms, not from the very start. He knew it was, together with Saturday, one of the most important nights of the week from Celia's point of view, for the market men were paid on Fridays and went to work with a will to spend their all as soon as they received it; there was rarely any left for Monday's entertainment once Saturday had collapsed into the small hours of the Sabbath morning, swilled with beer, spent with food, and hoarse with singing and shouting. So Mondays to Thursdays were quiet nights at the Celia Rooms, nights when the better class of company came from beyond the immediate streets of the market to eat and drink and listen to the entertainment. But because they were a better class of citizen they were prudent with their money, and those four evenings garnered only enough to cover brewers' and butchers' bills, to pay the meagre wages Celia gave her people, and to provide their own small family expenses. It was Friday and Saturday that brought in the profits, that made the running of the business worth while at all. And Jonah hated both nights cordially, but Friday most of all.

Tonight he sat in his place beside the small stage wings from which vantage point he controlled the twice nightly show, seeing that each act succeeded the other fast enough and that each musician was ready with the right music in time, watching the crowded floor below him in considerable uneasiness.

Each table was crammed full, extra chairs having been dragged up from the cellars below and in some places two men had to sit crushed uneasily together on one stool, so popular was the Celia Rooms tonight. Beer was slopping over the tables, the floor was awash with it, and the smell was so heavy that it was almost as though a miasma of malt fumes hung over the smoky oil-lit room.

That wasn't the only smell that assaulted the hot air however, for there were game pies on the menu tonight, made of well-hung hares and some venison that Celia had shrewdly haggled from a French packet master, down at Tilbury, and so ripe had it been that a great deal of cloves and mace and cinnamon had been needed in the baking to mask it. And what with the smell of that, the boiled cabbage for which the Celia Rooms' clientèle had a vast appetite, and the reek of heavy shag tobacco added to the all-pervading beer, Jonah felt decidedly qualmish.

Not that anyone else seemed to be aware of the atmosphere, for the men were shouting raucously and with huge good humour at each other, mauling lasciviously at the serving girls' skirts, pinching their behinds and trying to thrust their hands down into the bodices of their dresses as they leaned over the tables to unload their trays; and the girls, accepting it all with a sort of weary familiarity, shrieked and slapped back at them, particularly Letty who was wearing the tightest and lowest-cut bodice of them all.

Down immediately in front of Jonah the three sweating musicians scraped away at the violin, blew anxiously at the flute and thrummed busily at the mandolin, trying to make themselves heard above the hubbub but providing only a whining undertow of thin and tinny music; while from the kitchens came the crash and clatter of dishes, the sound of Celia's voice rising and falling as she harried her sweating scarlet cooks about its stoneflagged greasy expanse, and their hoarse shouts as they rushed between the roaring fire and the table where the orders were spread ready for the girls to scoop them up and go weaving away through the mob to their customers.

Sitting beside Jonah on the floor, with a tallow dip candle carefully shaded with a paper lanthorn, Oliver was sitting hunched up over a book, his fingers thrust in his ears and his face totally absorbed and happy. The weight of his back resting against his leg made Jonah feel a little less anxious, and he glanced fondly down at the boy's bent head and reached down with one hand to brush his dark hair out of his eyes. Oliver looked swiftly up at him and smiled vaguely, shook his hair back into his eyes, and went back to his reading.

The musicians stopped with a final flourish and an attempt at a crashing chord to bow in a perfunctory manner and some of the customers near enough to notice jeered and shouted and applauded ironically, and called, 'Song, song!' And Jonah sighed softly, then jerked his head at the girl standing opposite him in the other wings.

She came bouncing on to the stage, stamped her foot roguishly at the audience which at once set up a roar (for she was an attractive buxom little girl with snapping black eyes and a lively manner which was quite popular with the regulars) and launched herself into a very loud and earthy song about the way London girls got their education. 'I've been tumbled in ev'ry alleyway from 'ere to Temple Bar,' she bawled lustily at the end of each verse, and the men roared their own accompaniment, egging her on, and Jonah sat and watched her and wished, very much indeed, that he liked this sort of entertainment better.

For this was becoming ever more of a thorn in his side. He knew that the show they provided here at the Celia Rooms was good of its kind—indeed, very good. That was why the place was so full and why the profits were rising. As well as Norah Norton, the girl now singing, there were other popular and cheerful cockney performers, all well appreciated by the Rooms' regular customers. Even the quieter week-day ones enjoyed in their more genteel way the choruses and comic jingles with their very direct and vulgarly honest accounts of gutter life in the great city that was London. The regular performers included men who recited; older women who danced; a pair of twin sisters much given to singing shrill soprano songs about Loving Mothers Up In Heaven and Dreams of Happy Days Gone By; Danny Donger, a droll man with a long white face and a shocking cough who would stand up drooping miserably in the centre of the stage and tell one lugubrious—and very lubricious—joke after another, never cracking a smile himself while he reduced the audience to helpless guffaws; and Pretty Polly, Pride of Peckham, as she called herself, a vast young woman of barely thirty who must have turned the butchers' scales at over twenty stone, and whose extraordinary speciality was juggling and acrobatics, in which she would throw her huge and trembling bulk about in cartwheels, somersaults and twists that made the tiny stage shake, and displayed great unappetizing expanses of the flesh which she kept barely contained in spangled tights and a feathered bodice. There were those who played the Jews' harp with enormous verve, others who performed clowns' tricks in classic white face, even a troupe of performing dogs who pranced about on their hind legs, jaws slavering, on wheels and planks their sweating, swearing, wizened little Italian owner spread about the stage. And Jonah hired them all, paid them all, could recognize at a glance any ability to please the customers—and yet despised every single one of the performances he had to watch.

He had tried once, long ago, to explain haltingly to Celia how he felt about the sort of show that was growing up as part of the Rooms' offering. He found it so raucous, so lacking in any of the refinements of music or poetry or artistry which so much mattered to him, that it had a positively physical effect on him. He would listen to Norah shouting the crudities of one of her songs and the flesh at the back of his neck would crawl. He would listen to Danny Donger producing his earthy jokes and his belly would knot itself with sick distaste. And the sight of Pretty Polly, Pride of Peckham, and her quivering pinkness amid the glitter of her tinselly costume was more than he could bear, and he would turn his head fastidiously aside.

Celia had listened to his attempt to explain how he felt about it, his suggestion that they offer something a little less gutter-inspired, and her jaw had hardened.

'It is of little use thinking we can make a living here with the sort of missish entertainment you would offer, Jonah, and so I tell you!' she had said sharply. 'The people in these parts want red meat that is to their taste, and they'll tell us in no uncertain way what they think of bread-and-milk singers just as they would if we tried to sell 'em bread-and-milk slops for their bellies! If we would eat at all we must give the customers what it is they have a taste for, not what you think is more elegant. Much good elegance ever did, come to that! For my part, I am a woman of this world, and a London-born one at that, and I *like* the shows we are getting here! They stink of honest sweat, perhaps, but I like that better than swooning drawing room whines of the sort you would favour——'

And, typically, Jonah had said no more. He was all too keenly aware of his own failure as an entertainer; his plays over which he had been used to work so diligently and with such delight had been poetic in the extreme, full of elegance and artistry, and he shrank inside himself when he remembered how so many audiences had at the very best ignored them, at worst—and more frequently—had jeered and cat-called and shouted obscene advice to the actors. No, he was not a person who had any right to make a judgement on the quality of the entertainment offered in King Street. His job was just to select the best performers of the much hated material, see to it that the show ran smoothly and suffer his distaste in silence. And extraordinary though it was that it should be so, he knew he performed his task very well indeed.

But of one thing he was sure. His children were not to be tainted by these shows. He had long ago given up as a bad job the attempt to get them to their beds and asleep before the entertainment started, for the noise was so great and the music went vibrating through the old house so strongly that it was sheer absurdity to expect any sleep while the programme was going forward, and certainly not a child like Phoebe, who adored the lights and smells and the sound of her parents' eating rooms.

Oliver had been no problem. Given a book, he would sit happily in a corner of the wings totally oblivious of what was going on about him. At eleven o'clock when the entertainment ended he would blink vaguely up at his father when he touched his shoulder, grin sleepily and go obediently off to bed. But Phoebe was a problem.

There was no doubt in Jonah's mind that she must not, on any account, spend the time of the show in the supper rooms and this most particularly because she wanted to so much. He saw her as so vulner-able, so likely to be smirched, to have her taste for true artistry per-manently ruined by these cheap performers, that she needed extra protection. Before it began, he would permit her to flit about among the customers, giggling and sparkling and being petted, but after that, Jonah had told her firmly, she must stay above stairs with Mary, the youngest of the maids and one that was used more to look after the family's rooms above stairs than to serve the customers, although when business was brisk she was sometimes pressed into service in the kitchens.

Phoebe had stamped and pouted and pleaded and wept, but for once Jonah had been adamant, not a little to small Phoebe's surprise, for she was accustomed to having her own way always with her father. She had, usually, but to pout at him and let her lower lip tremble a little and he would melt with love and sweep her up and hug her close and tell her the story she was begging for or take her for the walk she craved, or buy her whatever little gewgaw it was her eye had lighted upon. But her pleas to stay and see the singing ladies and the funny men—they never got her anywhere, and each night she would go sulkily upstairs, her small hand firmly held in Mary's big red fist, to sulk and mutter her way through her supper and generally to torment Mary until she could be persuaded into her bed.

Thinking now about her, as Norah Norton launched herself into her encore, a mock melancholy song about a lost child—'I only wish I'd got him safe in these arms, oh, wouldn't I 'ug and a-kiss him, I never thought 'ow per-recious 'e was, but a child don't feel like a child till you miss 'im——' he let his eyes wander round the room, picking out faces as they gleamed in the red glow reflected from the walls by the candle ends that smoked and guttered in the row of footlights at the front of the stage. And then realized just why he felt so uneasy.

At the back of the room he could see Mary, her big ungainly body lumping itself between the tables as she carried pints of porter and plates of cheese and pickled onions to latecomers who had to settle for these furthermost corners, and at once his throat tightened with anxiety. She must have been working there for some time, he realized; it was only now that he had actually registered her presence. And if Mary were down here working, where was Phoebe?

He began to rake the room systematically with his eyes, trying to penetrate the smokier corners to see beyond the upraised arms of the drunken men waving accompaniment to Norah Norton's song (and she had reached the chorus, a plaintive wail of 'Will no one tell me where 'e's gorn——' which sharply underlined the anxiety that was now thickening in Jonah), almost moving on to the very stage itself in his efforts to make his gaze reach as far as possible.

And then Norah was bowing and cheekily flicking her soiled befrilled skirts up as the audience shouted its approval, and the next act, a girl in short spangled skirts who affected to do classical dancing but who in actuality offered a most outrageous performance that was exceedingly knowing in its inviting gestures, was waiting to come on from the opposite side, and still he couldn't see Phoebe, and wanted quite urgently to climb down from this wretched little stage to go and find her. But he had his job to do, and he did it, nodding to the streaming-faced musicians below, who struck into the dancer's music as Norah came flopping off stage beside him, swearing when she almost tripped over.

'Have you seen Phoebe?' he hissed at her urgently, as the dancer went into a series of pirouettes and leaps that were meant to show as much of her legs as possible to the leering gaze beneath her. Norah stared at him, then shrugged and said, 'Oo? Your kid? I got better things to do than go 'unting a bleedin' kid, mate——' and went thumping off to get the pint of porter she demanded between every stage appearance, and to glower at the audience as they cheered the dancer on stage. She was now getting more and more lascivious in her movements, stroking her own body with her hands, rolling her pelvis and jerking her knees at the front row of men while staring with bright-eyed knowingness at them, her tongue held between her teeth and her lips moistly apart.

This was one act that Jonah disliked above almost all others, for he found it disturbed him in a most disagreeable way; it was not the dancer herself that he found so disagreeable but the looks on the faces of the men who watched her. There had been times when he had found his own face redden with shame at the sight of their half open mouths and glazed eyes as they stared at the girl's gyrations and moved their own bodies in clumsy time with her.

He decided swiftly, and with one downwards glance at Oliver, still oblivious in his book, he stepped back and down the three little steps at the side and pushed through the looped side curtain into the crowded room. He could see less now than he could from the raised vantage point of the stage, and he paused for a moment, wondering whether to go back and look again, then stood on his toes and craned his neck; but still he couldn't see and stood uncertainly trying to decide what to do.

And then he heard it, above the wailing of the music—the flutes and violin making a curiously sensuous sound for the dancer, who was now writhing backwards across the stage, her legs completely exposed—and he pushed forwards through the mob more urgently, towards the direction the sound had come from; for he had heard Phoebe's shrill voice cry out something unintelligible and then abruptly stop.

There was a shout from the audience as the girl on the stage produced another of her erotic movements, one more obviously inviting than any she had hitherto shown, and then there was a sort of hush as the men stared, and Jonah heard it again: Phoebe's voice raised in protest. This time a few other heads turned and the movement was enough to help Jonah push through more swiftly until he reached the furthest darkest corner.

It took another moment for his eyes to become accustomed to the dimness, and then he saw her. Phoebe, her white frilled dress tumbled over her stockinged knees, a black shoe dangling from one foot and the other unshod, and her face flushed. She was sitting uncomfortably on the lap of a vast man who was holding her close in a bear hug, and as Jonah reached her she cried out again, and wriggled on the man's lap, trying to pull away, for he was nuzzling her neck and tightening his arms about her.

For so peaceable a man, Jonah acted with a speed that amazed him, even as he moved. He thrust his hands forward and seized the wrists of the seated man with a grip so hard that it drew a sudden whimper of surprised pain, and then, exerting all the muscle power he had, prised the man's hands apart—and he was a huge creature, with arms as knotted and thick as great wooden clubs, obviously a market porter—at the same time shoving him backwards. And the man's arms parted, and immediately Phoebe scrambled down and ran to clutch Jonah's knees, as the man with ludicrous slowness and a startled expression on his face tumbled backwards off his stool.

Jonah realized that the dancer behind him on the stage had finished her performance, that the bulk of the audience were cheering her and clapping madly, but that some of the people nearby were talking to him above the hubbub.

'Don' you worry none, mister!' One of the men was saying, thrusting his face close to Jonah and leering at Phoebe, who clung closer to her father who had scooped her up into his arms, putting her arms about his neck but smiling bright-eyed and cheerful at the stranger. 'Don' you worry—that's only old Davie! 'E won' do no 'arm to the little miss, no more'n I would, eh, little pretty? Got a kiss for me, then? Eh? Pretty little dilly like you, give you a penny for a kiss, I would——'

Jonah jerked his shoulder at the man, making him fall back, and with one hand pushed Phoebe's face down into his neck, feeling obscurely that that would prevent her hearing or seeing anything else. And then went shoving his way through the crowd, caring not one whit for the customers he sent reeling or the porter mugs he caused them to spill.

Behind him the dancer started another of her gyrations, delighted that Jonah was not in his usual place in the wings to make sure she made way for the next performer, and the audience returned its attention to her, away from the little flurry that marked Jonah's passage through the crowd. At last he reached the door and went pushing through, to find himself in the comparative calm of the passageway, at the foot of the stairs.

He stood for a moment, holding Phoebe close, and feeling the trembling of his barely controlled anger rising in him, and then along the stone-flagged passage the door to the kitchens swung and banged, and Celia came through, her head inquiringly on one side, and her face set as she dried her hands on the white towel she was holding and which made a bright splash against the dull purple of her gown.

'Jonah?' she said sharply. 'What are you doing here? That girl's gone into another encore and the Perry Twins are waiting to go and furious at being held back! Why aren't you in the wings?'

'Why was Mary not above stairs watching Phoebe?' Jonah's voice sounded hard in his own ears, and Celia was clearly startled by the quality that was in its tone, for she sounded much less sharp herself when she answered him.

'I needed her for the back tables. Letty, the wretched creature, has been drinking like the slut she is, and is casting up her accounts into the yard—I shall have to turn her off. She's a useless object—I had to set *someone* to the work, and there was none but Mary. What has happened?'

'He was kissing me, Mamma!' Phoebe raised her head from Jonah's neck. 'He was a nasty man and he made my neck all wet. Faugh!' And she scrubbed suddenly at the collar of her gown. 'And he smelled horrid and kept whispering in my ear and I only wanted to watch the dancing!'

'I have told you time and again you are not to come down here during the performance,' Jonah said harshly, holding her away from him a little so that he could look into her face. 'What were you doing down here at all? The man could not have kissed you at all if you had stayed above stairs where you belong!'

'Mary went down and I heard the music and I wanted to watch!' Phoebe pouted, and wriggled in his firm hold. 'Oh, Papa, do not prose on so! I like the music and the people, and I wanted only to watch and the man said to sit on his lap so that I could see the stage, but he wriggled so, and kept on whispering and kissing but I did no harm, Papa! Do not be vexed, please, Papa?' and she smiled up at him and set her head beguilingly to one side.

But Jonah was not to be mollified, and he moved towards the stairs, holding her firmly.

'I shall take her up and you are to send Mary up to set her to bed,' he said shortly to Celia. 'And then I must talk with you about this matter. No, do not look at me so! I am most disturbed about it, and talk about it we shall. It must not happen again! Now call Mary at once!'

And Celia, after one narrow frowning stare at him nodded her head and went sweeping into the kitchens to seek Mary, leaving Jonah to carry the still protesting Phoebe upstairs to her bedroom.

It was not often he set his face against Celia, he was thinking, but the time had now come. Whatever she said, he told himself, some plan must be made to remove his precious burden from this place. Even if it meant removing her also from his side; a thought which made him move more slowly and heavily as he reached the top of the stairs.

## 6

'Really, father, you are making a great pother over a small matter,' Gideon said again, but he could not look the old man in the face, and leaned forwards to tuck the fur rug more firmly about the lax and bony knees. But the old man twitched irritably at his touch, and pulled the rug up to his waist, and said, 'So? A great pother, is it? Then why should *you* make so much of a pother yourself when I tell you I am not happy in the situation? If it was as unimportant as you say it is, then you would not argue with me.'

Gideon looked up at his father's face then, and could not help but let his lips twitch. 'You are too sharp for your own good, Papa,' he said. 'You always were.'

'Which is why there is so successful a business for you to enjoy, which is why your mother and you can live a decent life in spite of the fact that I am a useless hulk and which is why I am worried about you now. My legs may have turned to a jelly, my brains have not. Move me. I am getting cold. Move me, you hear?'

Obediently Gideon stood up and turned the wicker chair on its spindly single wheel, and pushed it from the long window at which the old man spent most of the day staring down at the hurrying crowds below to the hearthrug where the fire glowed hotly between its highly-polished brass dogs.

There was a little flurry as Gideon settled the chair, making sure its two front legs were firmly set on the carpet, turning the wheel sideways so that it could not inadvertently roll, carefully moving the useless old legs so that they did not press painfully against the wicker sides and rearranging the fine soft shawl over the old bowed shoulders.

All the time his father sat quite still, staring into the fire, his mouth turned down so that the lips seemed to disappear into the carving of the narrow jaws. His usually pallid face, now lit by the clear glow of the fire, shone ruddily under the crest of white hair and his eyes were a startling black in contrast. Usually those eyes were sharp and bright, moving restlessly from side to side as though they would with their eager activity replace the muscle power that had once filled the whole of the long spare body, but now they were still and shadowed, staring out at the world in a sullen anger.

He moved suddenly, grasping one wasted thigh in his long tapering hands and lifting his leg bodily from the extended wicker platform on which it rested, thumped it down again, so hard that the chair rocked and Gideon had to put out a restraining hand, and he lifted his chin at the ceiling and shouted, 'God Almighty, why? *Why?* What did I ever do to *You?*'

Gideon sat very still and silent, watching him, and felt the almost forgotten but now all too vividly remembered sick sensation rise in him. The tragedy of the illness that had done this to his father had been masked at first by the shadow of the greater tragedy that had threatened; nine years ago they had feared he would die, Gideon and his mother. They had sat beside his bed watching that strong figure shrivelled by fever, those intelligent dark eyes dulled with stupor, that elegant face blurred with the threat of death, and they had prayed with all the fervour they had that he should live.

And live he had. But only in half his body.

His legs had quite lost all their power—though sensation had remained, and much was the pain those useless limbs often gave him—his shoulders had narrowed, his chest had collapsed; only his brain remained undamaged, and in the darkest days, just after they had realized that indeed the old man had been spared death, but had been given instead a dead life, Gideon had found it in him to rail against God for treating his father so cruelly, his father who had always been good and virtuous and followed the laws of the synagogue and never done an ill thing to any man.

It was not until a week or so after the commencement of his illness when his father himself had lifted his head and shrieked his enraged frustration at his Maker that Gideon had realized how much worse it would have been to have lost his father altogether. And he had sat, hour after hour, day after day, a frightened but determined fifteen-year-old, talking to the figure in the bed, coaxing, wheedling, admonishing, and eventually even weeping until at last old Nahum had been convinced that his life was worth living, that whatever had happened to him had to be borne as other losses had been borne in the past. He who had watched three of his infant children die had been grateful to have been left with one son to grow to manhood; now he had to accept the fact that half his body had died, but be glad to have his mind unclouded.

This he had told Gideon at last and together they had worked to restore some happiness to their household. Gideon had turned with a will to running the affairs of the business, his mother had worked at coaxing the most that could be coaxed out of the flaccid muscles of her husband's legs and trunk, and the three of them had built up, over the last nine years, a tolerable pattern to their lives.

There were parties, often, at which the old man would sit in the centre of his drawing room ensconced in the wicker chair that Gideon had designed and had built for him, his legs wrapped in a sable rug, his hair gleaming like creamy satin above a cobweb of a shawl spread across the shoulders of a red velvet jacket, beaming at guests, teasing the handsome girls his wife invited to the house, and showing no sign of the exhaustion that always followed such evenings. But that was his contribution to the efforts his wife and son made to their shared life, and neither of them would have made any attempt to protect him from it. That he should entertain, and be interested and busy—that was important to them all; and Nahum would often work over the books with Gideon, often spend long hours talking business and making plans and drawing up ledgers. And Gideon would not only allow him to go on until he fell asleep with the abrupt fatigue of a baby, but drove him on to greater efforts, knowing that this was vital if the man was to find any satisfaction in his life.

And not once, in all the years that had passed since that dreadful winter of his illness had Nahum raised his voice in anger against his God, the God for whom he had a real and very personal love. Until now. And he had done so now because of Gideon, and Gideon felt sick.

He sat on in silence for a long time, willing his belly to settle and relax while Nahum too sat hunched and glowering, and then it was

Nahum who stirred at last and said gruffly, 'I am sorry. You must forgive me for such an outburst. It is a sin, and I am wrong.'

'Oh, sin——' said Gideon almost absently, and moved awkwardly in his chair. 'I am as guilty, if it is a sin, for I was not—I did not *lie* to you precisely, which I would find hard enough to do——'

The old man glinted at him suddenly. 'You would find it hard indeed to have any success if you did for I know the difference between true truth and almost truth, strange as it may seem.'

Gideon smiled back at him, and felt the weight of the afternoon lift a little. 'Well, I know that. Perhaps I *was* making small of the matter when it is not in reality small to me.'

Nahum nodded heavily. 'You think I did not know that? Why else should I be so angered? You must understand, Gideon, that I have little to do, sitting here, but to sharpen my wits. My perceptions are not clouded by outside excitements, for I spend so much of my time within these walls. So, I study that which changes, since the walls remain always the same. I study *you*, your mother and the people who come here to the house. But I study you most of all. For many reasons——'

He paused a moment, and then leaned back in his chair, and raising his hands to his neck began to rub it, and Gideon moved across to him and gently pushed the delicate hands down so that they rested on the fur rug, and began to massage the stringy old neck with strong and even movements which rocked the white head a little from side to side, and gradually Nahum let his face relax so that his mouth lost its harsh lines, and some of the softness of his age came back into the papery cheeks.

'And what have your studies told you, Papa?'

'That you are a good kind boy, that you have a heart that is as big as the Bank of England, that it is time you were settled with a good wife.'

Gideon's fingers stopped their gentle kneading for a long moment, and then, slowly, he started again but said nothing.

'You are five and twenty, Gideon!' Nahum burst out, trying to turn his head to look up into his son's face, but Gideon continued with his massaging and Nahum gave up, letting his head roll again with the movements of the long and powerful fingers. 'Well, you may not wish to talk of it, but it concerns me. You are a man, not a child. You have been a man for some time, and you cannot expect to be a whole and happy man if you do not give your nature its true needs. It is not right that a healthy boy like you should be celibate——'

'Which am I, Papa?' Gideon said softly, still not altering the rhythm of his fingers. 'Man or boy? You used both words. There is a difference——'

There was another short silence, and then the old man burst out, 'Man, man, of course. I know what you are saying to me! That it is none of my concern. Is that it? You are telling me that as a man you are beyond the guidance and interest of a father. That you may think, but if you do, then you are no man, but a foolish boy——'

'I am a man, Papa, in every way. I understand what it is you are telling me, I understand that you are concerned for me——' At last Gideon stopped his massaging and came round the chair to stand in front of his father, his back to the fire so that the light created a nimbus around his tall shape, and his face was shadowed in the dwindling light of the winter afternoon. 'But you must understand what it is I am telling you. There are occasions when I must make a choice between that which will please you, and that which is right for me. They come rarely, these times, and so far they have been almost entirely matters of business. Though there was the matter of my uncle in Madrid——'

The old man's shoulders moved pettishly, dismissing that, but he said nothing and Gideon went on, his voice becoming a little louder as he developed assurance in what he was saying.

'But this time, Papa, the choice is one you do not like, yet make it I have, and remain with it I will. Mrs Caspar had asked me to come to her because she has need of my help and advice. It is a summons that I must obey.'

'But on a Friday night, Gideon, a Friday night!'

'I know, Papa. That is—unfortunate. But it cannot be helped. It is no whim that makes her ask me to come at this time, but a real need.' He reddened quite suddenly, and even in the shadows his father could see it. 'And I am glad she has this need of me.'

'She has always had need of us, my boy,' Nahum said after a moment, and his voice was quiet and matter of fact, and very reasonable. 'In her situation, how could it be otherwise? A young widow, with an infant and no father or brothers who care for her——' He tutted then, in a curiously womanish way, showing on his face and in his voice his total inability to comprehend any family that could leave a young woman alone in such a plight. '—and with a business to run! If it had not been for us what could have happened to her? I look back and remember her husband and her husband's father, good kind men and good friends to me, when there were some that turned their back on me for my religion—how else should it be but that in her widowhood the house of Henriques should be her strength? But Gigi—my dear boy——' and he leaned forwards and set his hand entreatingly against his son's thigh, peering up at him. 'Dear Gigi, see the truth of the situation, I do beg of you! Her need is of a business head, a brother's care, if you like. Do not allow yourself to think it is any greater need than that! Do not commit the great error of—of offering more than you are asked to give.'

More moved than he would have thought possible by his father's use of his childhood nickname Gideon moved forward a little awkwardly and patted his father's shoulder.

'You worry too much, Papa, indeed you do. I am in control of my life and—and my sensibilities, I do assure you! But I feel a close friendship for Abby—Mrs Caspar, and if she has need of me then go I must, be it Friday or not. It is, after all, a blessing to do good works on the Sabbath! Consider it a good work, and do not concern yourself further, please.'

For the rest of the afternoon there was constraint between them, as they worked over the books pertaining to the affairs of their business and of their related business house in Madrid, and in many ways it grieved Gideon deeply that this should be so. But that regret could not be allowed to make any difference; he had decided to go to Abby's the next evening, since she wanted him, and even though he knew that to his pious father—and of course his mother who shared his view of religious matters—such desecration of the Sabbath evening was a matter of vast concern, there was nothing he could do about it. Abby had called, and to Abby he would go.

And so they sat, father and son, in their warm red-panelled drawing room above the hubbub and clatter of the traffic thudding over the cobbles of Lombard Street below them, talking of money, but thinking severally of many very different matters.

*

In the two days that had passed since his disagreeable conversation with Conran, Abel had been debating in his mind how best to deal with the matter of William and his ill-management of the Wapping manufactory. Obviously he must talk to William about it, but William had selected these two days to be absent from the hospital on a buying expedition.

He had taken himself to Bristol, leaving a suave message for his father to the effect that 'the West Indiamen that come into that port carry better quality molasses than any other, and we have need of a good bargain in this commodity' and thus left Abel to simmer away in his anger; not a very politic action on his part, for Abel knew that his anger would be even greater by the time William returned, and that the whole matter would have been much better—and more coolly—thrashed out immediately it had come to his attention. Obviously William knew it too, for he had not been his father's son and business associate as long as he had without learning something of his temper. And that knowledge enraged Abel even more; that William should be so additionally stupid as to compound his stupidity by running for cover in this matter was the outside of enough.

Abel had been reduced at one point during those two frustrating days to considering bringing in another member of the family to deal with the care of Wapping in order to send William packing on to another task (not that finding one suitable for him would be easy). But there was only Gussy now that Bart was married and away and he was much too young and frivolous, and it was not possible seriously to consider Martha, mere female as she was. That there had been a time when he had had a daughter fit to deal with the matter was not to be thought of, he had told himself when there came into his mind's eye a sudden vision of Abby, his wholly admirable Abby as she had been in her girlhood; but telling himself that had been of little help. The memory of Abby had stayed with him a long time that evening as he had gone walking up and down Dorothea's silent bedchamber, from the candelabra on the table by the door to the oil lamp on the table by the bed, over and over again.

And sometimes, mixed with that memory had been a vision of her older brother, the tall and poetic Jonah, and the way he had once sat beside his father's operating table in Tavistock Street, in the old dispensary, watching him work on the sores and wounds and abscesses of the poor of Seven Dials with horror and sickness and misery written all over his young face. That was another memory not to be entertained on any account, and Abel set his jaw and did all he could to banish it.

Not until Miss Ingoldsby came to the room, wrapped in her peignoir, a very austere garment of dark blue wool cut high at the neck and very voluminous about the skirts, her hair tied up prosaically in a white and severely simple nightcap, to tell him that his pacing was keeping the whole house awake, did he realize just how buried he had been in his own concerns.

He stood there in the dimly-lit room looking at her with a faint frown between his eyes, and she stood calmly at the door, her candle-stick in her hand, and looked back at him.

'I am sorry to have disturbed you,' he said abruptly after a moment. 'What o'clock is it?'

'One,' she said, 'or perhaps a quarter hour after. You would be better occupied sleeping, Mr Lackland, than marching about thus, whatever it is that concerns you. You can do little good, I imagine, at the hospital if you are starved of rest and sleep.'

'I do not need much sleep,' he said absently, and after a long pause said sharply, 'Your opinion, Miss Ingoldsby! Is Gussy likely to be of any use to the hospital if I give him work to do? He is, I believe, doing little enough work with Mr Loudoun at school. Is he fit to take up a man's occupation in any way?'

She stood silent for a moment, giving the question the same quiet consideration she would have done had it been mid-morning and she full of energy, instead of as tired as she undoubtedly was after her normal busy day. And then shook her head decisively.

'I think not, Mr Lackland. He is a boy of much charm and indeed can display quite remarkable energy in matters that interest him, but they are generally to do with amusement, I must confess. He is not at all like Martha or Rupert, who are the ones with most ability, I believe. He is, in many ways, closest to Bart and I think will make as advantageous a marriage as did Bart.' She looked up calmly at him and smiled a little. 'Indeed, it is imperative that he do so, for I must tell you frankly, sir, that from his earliest childhood it has been clear to me that without such an arrangement Gussy's life is like to be most dis-appointing to him.'

Abel nodded heavily. 'I thought that would be the case.' He brooded for a moment, and then shook his head, clearly consigning his youngest son to perdition. 'So I cannot solve my problem that way.'

She looked at him for a while, as though considering, and then sighed very softly and came into the room, setting her candle down upon the small table beside the chaise longue and seating herself with her hands folded on her lap.

'If you wish to discuss the matter that is concerning you, Mr Lack-land, then I am happy to render any assistance I may,' she said, and he nodded briefly and again began to walk up and down the room, his head bent and his hands behind his back. And she watched him walk, as he passed to and fro in front of the silent figure that was Dorothea, and waited patiently, showing by no hint or movement the fatigue that filled her, for she had been busy since six in the morning, and would be up at that time again the next morning, in order to see all the household on its way.

'It is William,' Abel said at last. 'William, who is so crass, so stupid, so useless as to display his ineptitude to all the hospital! I do not think he is in any way venial—he is not lining his pockets at Eleanor's expense, whatever Conran may imply. But he is allowing our hard-made money to trickle through his fingers, and I must seek a way to deal with it that will not cause too great an upset at the hospital. Now what say you to that?'

She nodded in comprehension, and then turned her head to one side thoughtfully, and said after her customary pause—for she was not one given to hasty judgements—'I think your error, sir, is in regarding only the members of your family as suitable for these tasks. There must be others you can employ about the Wapping factory! I know William to dislike the work heartily and it is possible that this is why he does it so ill.' She said nothing at all about the possibility of William being less than honest.

His brows snapped into a frown. 'To use some outside person for such a task is asking for trouble. If this man Conran were not in his place, I doubt we would have the difficulty we are having now. It is because he and William loathe each other so heartily, I believe, that there are so many difficulties. The more he goads William, the more neglectful William becomes of his tasks in order to display to Conran that he is a person of worth and not to be so treated by a servant of the hospital.'

'You are shrewd, indeed, Mr Lackland,' Miss Ingoldsby said after a moment. 'William is one much aware of his status. He can be most sharp with me if I exceed my station.'

Abel looked at her quickly. 'I trust he does not give you the insolence that I know he has shown to Conran?'

She shook her head calmly. 'You need not concern yourself on my behalf, sir,' she said and smiled. Not for the world would she have let him know of the many casual insults William had dropped into her lap, the dismissive way he could call her 'servant' and put her firmly in her subservient position whenever she made any attempt to impose her will on him. Nor would she ever let anyone know of the subterfuges she had often been reduced to using, the cajoling and flattery she had offered William many times in order to win her way. She had cared for William for much of his life, after all; she could contain any pain he meted out to her.

'I think, sir, since you are good enough to seek my advice, that the best plan open to you is to seek some other person to employ as the superintendent of the Wapping factory. One who will be fully answerable to you in a way that even the most dutiful of sons can never be expected to be.'

She rose to her feet and picked up her candle. 'I hope, sir, that you will now go to your bed, for I am persuaded that you will make yourself quite ill if you go on missing such a great deal of your much needed rest. I will bring you a hot drink, if you wish it——'

'No—no drink,' he said, and yawned suddenly, a jawcracking gape. 'You are right, of course. I am indeed more tired than I knew. And perhaps you are right about the factory too. I must give some further thought to your suggestion. Not that I can do much until William returns from his jaunt to Bristol. By God, but I'll have much to say to him when he does! I almost relish the thought of it——'

And with a perfunctory nod at Miss Ingoldsby he went, leaving her to extinguish all but the little night light in Dorothea's room, and to make her own weary way to her bedroom at the top of the house.

## 7

The children had been playing in the garden for most of the after-noon, wrapped up warmly against the cold, for a sharp frost had come suddenly to seize London in its white iron grip. Here in Paddington, so near the countryside, it was colder still and the grass of the little garden behind Abby's house was so slippery that it had been possible for the three of them to make a slide. It lay in a glassy stripe gleaming softly in the dusk and reflecting the lamplight from the sitting room window while the children took it in turns to go slithering along its length, arms flailing, scarves flying wildly behind them and their faces scarlet with exertion.

Phoebe in particular was blissfully happy. She was wearing a crimson tam-o'-shanter, in the new mode, and a dark blue heavy cloth coat trimmed with scarlet fringe. With her little black buttoned boots showing beneath her heavily petticoated skirts and her little fur muff she looked even more deliciously gypsy than ever, and it was clear that her cousin Frederick was quite captivated by her.

He stood at the end of the slide waiting for her every attempt, hold-ing his arms wide to catch her as she arrived in a squealing heap, for she fell every time; but clearly without damaging herself, and sometimes it would appear falling quite deliberately in order to enjoy the pleasure of having the sturdy Frederick hurry to scoop her up and set her on her feet and anxiously inquire as to her wellbeing.

Oliver too was enjoying himself but in his own solemn way, plodding from the end of the run back to the beginning each time, his head down and his hands deep in his trouser pockets, breathing heavily, ready to stand there for a second, then to push his hat back on his head and finally, with a careful run-up, to make his stately progression down again, toes turned in ready to brake safely, arms held stiffly outwards. Frederick obviously thought him a very dull dog indeed, and had hardly spoken a word to him all afternoon, close as they were in age. It was Phoebe to whom he gave all his attention, greatly to her delight and much to his own satisfaction.

Watching them from the window Jonah sighed sharply, and turned back into the cosiness of the sitting room. It looked particularly charming in the evening light, for in addition to the oil lamp in the window the fire was burning bright and cheerful, exploring every corner with its clear glaze, and the well-polished old furniture gleamed softly and comfortingly from the walls. The red turkey carpet made the room feel even warmer, but Jonah shivered suddenly as a sharp draught of air slid through the interstices of the window to bite the back of his neck.

'They had best come in soon, I think,' he said. 'It is really very cold today, and they have been out there some time. I would not have them catch cold.'

'Dear Jonah!' Abby said, her voice amused. 'You are indeed a remarkable papa! You talk more like a nursemaid or a besotted mamma than any man I ever heard!'

Jonah flushed. 'I am sorry,' he said stiffly. 'It is a habit with me to concern myself about the children's welfare. There is always so much going forward at home, what with the supper rooms and the kitchens—Celia has so little time and I have fallen into the habit of——'

'Bless you, my dear old boy, I was not criticizing you! Indeed, I find it charming in you that you should be so concerned. But you did sound so—well, never mind. As for their coming in—why, you know, they are not stupid! They will come in when they are cold or bored with their occupation. And I have no doubt their exertions will protect them from any damage from the chill. Come and sit down and drink some negus, do. You are the one who looks in need of some warming.' She patted the sofa beside her invitingly and Jonah, after one worried backwards glance through the window, came to join her.

'Have you thought further about my request, Abby?' he said. 'I would not wish to make a nuisance of myself, but I can think of no other solution to my dilemma. And I cannot believe you will think me too anxious a father in making it.'

Her hands busy among the lemon and the spices and the silver kettle steaming gently over its little spirit lamp as she made him his glass of negus, Abby was silent, and then as she gave him the glass, delicately turning it so that the handle was within his grasp, she said, 'I would not have you think I am not mindful of the links between us, Jo. It has long been a matter of some sadness to me that we—that our family has been splintered as it has. It would be agreeable, would it not, if we were all to be friends? And never think that I consider you to be making your request out of anything but real need. I feel, with you, that the situation you describe is far from suitable for a child of her years. I would not wish it for Frederick and he is older than she, and a boy, to boot.'

He turned the glass between his fingers, staring down into its depths, and spoke with obvious difficulty.

'It was not easy to come to you as I did, Abby, so cap-in-hand. I would not have done so for the world. But—it is not Celia's fault, you know. I would not have you think that. It is simply that——'

'You need not make any apologies or explanations, you know,' Abby said gently. 'Any—any discussion between you and your wife must be a matter between yourselves. I would not for the world interfere in any way.'

He looked up and managed a smile, but it was strained. 'I know that, Abby. You were ever a practical creature, and not at all given to having the vapours over matters that—well, anyway, I know you do not ask me to speak as I do. But having come to you as I have, then you must permit me to be as honourable as it is possible for a man to be, in such a situation, and to explain all.'

She felt her eyes get hot suddenly, looking at him. He was so well set-up a man, so very admirable to look at; and even though he was her brother she could recognize the masculine attraction of him. It was all wrong, she felt confusedly, that so pleasant and so delightful a man should be set to such shifts as he was. And she felt the rare tears prick at her eyes, responding to the deep sadness she felt in him and to her recognition of his embarrassment, and in one corner of her awareness was amazed. She who never cried, who had not wept since James's death, whatever had happened to her, to wish to weep for Jonah! It was most strange.

And looking at him again, she felt a sudden stab of anger against her unknown sister-in-law. What had she done to make him so bedraggled, so down at heel in himself? For all his dress was neat, if not rich, for all his well-polished shoes and clean linen—for Jonah was every inch a well-dressed gentleman—there was something hungry and pathetic about him that was painful to observe.

He was speaking again, his manner gathering strength as his words formed themselves into sentences.

'It is not only the matter of her exposure to the customers on those two nights of the week that distress me. If all I had to worry about were that, why, I daresay it would be possible to find a solution. But the child must learn. And how can she learn her letters in her present mode of life? But in talking to Celia of the matter—and she does understand my concern, even if she does not fully share it——' he looked up at Abby again then, and again dropped his gaze to the glass in his hand. 'And how could she, for was she not herself a child of the theatre? She grew up in much the same surroundings—indeed she was worse off in her infancy, poor girl, for she had no father. And Phoebe does have me. In feeling as I do about Phoebe I am I suppose in some way striking at Celia. Or so she says. And although I can understand that she might feel so, and have tried so hard to convince her that it is not so—I mean, that I do not despise her for her—her family life when she was a child, I do not succeed as well as I should like——'

He sighed sharply, and managed to smile ruefully at Abby. 'My dear, you cannot know how fortunate you are in not having to tolerate the pricks and complications of married life! I envy you your peace and solitude in so many ways.' Again he returned his eyes to his glass, and again Abby experienced some feeling for her sister-in-law. But this time she felt a spurt of sympathy rather than anger. If Jonah were always so ham-handed in his treatment of women, if he could speak so to his widowed sister, what effect might he have on his wife?

And then, remembering the sort of boy he had been, this handsome brother of hers, she sighed softly in her turn. A man of nine and twenty he might be, but in some ways he was clearly still the impetuous self-absorbed youth of sixteen who had caused so much upheaval in his father's house.

'Whatever I say, she flies up into her high trees,' he was saying, 'and although this was always her way, for she is a woman of great spirit, my Celia, on this matter she is particularly—well, difficult. I talked to her of so many possibilities, but none would serve. And I made other attempts to deal with it—like seeking a governess to come to King Street, but that is out of the question. No lady of any reliability would come to such an establishment as ours—I soon discovered that—and those that would, I did not consider suitable.'

He looked up at her with real indignation on his face. 'Why, do you know, Abby, one such person I spoke to told me she would teach my Phoebe for part of the week as long as I would give her the opportunity to sing in the performance, for that was her ultimate ambition! The pert creature! As if I would consider such an arrangement, for was not the whole point of the idea that Phoebe should be kept apart from the theatre and its customers? And besides, she was a shocking singer, with no talent or stage presence whatever. Quite unsuitable!'

Abby began to laugh, throwing her head back and opening her mouth widely in a most inelegant fashion, but her laughter was so real and her enjoyment so great that it was not possible for her even to consider the sort of spectacle she must be making of herself.

Jonah stared at her in amazement, quite unable to see what it was that had so amused her, and neither of them heard the door open behind them or little Ellie's perfunctory, 'Mr Gideon, ma'am,' so loudly was Abby pealing out her mirth. So Gideon stood there for a while watching her, enjoying her delight without knowing the source of it, but responding with a broad smile of his own.

It was not until she had subsided somewhat and was wiping the tears of merriment from her eyes that she became aware of him, and rose at once to her feet to cross the room, her hand held out to draw him towards the cosiness of the fireside.

'Oh, dear, such a cake to make of myself!' she said, her voice still tremulous with laughter. 'But you see, Jonah was so funny!' She looked at Jonah and at the sight of his puzzled face burst into another peal, and now Gideon laughed too, quite unable to resist the infection.

'I wish you would explain,' Jonah said stiffly, as soon as he could be heard, and Abby spluttered a little and blew her nose upon her handkerchief then said, 'It was you, Jo! You complained of the pertness of a would-be governess who had the effrontery to say she wanted to use part of her time to sing upon the stage in your theatre show. And then

—and then you said she was a poor singer anyway! Which I take leave to find so very funny! Do forgive me. I was not mocking you, I promise——' And she caught Gideon's eye and warmed to the way he had lit up in appreciation. In the face of Jonah's incomprehension, it was a great comfort to have with her someone who could share the humour she found in the situation.

There was a little flurry as she settled Gideon in a chair and provided him with negus before refilling Jo's glass as well as her own, and by that time Jonah had recovered his equanimity and Abby her gravity, and quiet came back into the room. There was a pause as they all sipped and the silence between them was friendly though Jonah seemed stiff and less comfortable than he had been when alone with Abby, throwing cold and somewhat suspicious glances in Gideon's direction.

He moved after a while and went over to the window to peer out at the children, now barely visible as the short afternoon merged into the long winter night, and he tapped on the window and beckoned when Phoebe looked up; but she shook her curls with great decisiveness, and went running off again to the slide, and after a moment's hesitation, Jonah dropped the curtain and turned back into the room. Anxious as he was to protect the children from the cold so was he anxious to talk in more depth with his sister; and in the children's presence that would be difficult.

And now there was this caller, whoever he might be, sitting there beside the fire as though he owned it, his long legs stretched to the blaze, and grinning like some damned monkey at Abby. Jonah felt the irritation rise in him, and it made him speak more sharply than he meant to.

'I had hoped to discuss our private matter to the point of completion before leaving you tonight, Abby,' he said. 'But if it is not a matter of convenience for you, then perhaps I should——'

'Oh, Jo, I am sorry!' Abby jumped to her feet, all contrition. 'You will think me quite out of my attic. My dear, permit me to present Mr Gideon Henriques. He is my partner, you know.' She caught Jo's frowning stare and blushed suddenly. 'My *business* partner, you understand.' Then, amazed at the tide of colour that had filled her cheeks, she stepped back so that Gideon could move forwards to shake hands with Jonah and to give herself time to recover her calm. To blush, because of

73

introducing Gideon? The afternoon was proving to be full of strange new experiences for Abby.

'I am happy to know you, sir,' Gideon was saying. 'I have known your sister these many years, to my extreme pleasure, for she is both a diligent business partner—indeed a lady of remarkable acuity—and a good friend. I am happy to have the privilege of extending acquaintanceship to her family.'

'Gideon is to help me decide how to deal with the matter of Phoebe, Jo,' Abby said, and at once Jonah whirled to stare at her with his brows clamped down into a frown.

'Abby, what do you mean, to—Good God! This is a private affair! I would not have it bruited about like some—some ballad singer's wares! Forgive me, but I must indeed protest if you have said aught of my affairs to this—this gentleman. I never met him till now, and you say he knows of such private matters? Indeed, Abby, I am amazed that you should——'

'Jo, for heaven's sake stop getting yourself into such a lather,' Abby said sharply. 'And come and sit down! I have said no word at all about the matter to Mr Henriques although I have asked him here tonight in order that he might help me. And you. If you prefer not to discuss it with him, then that decision must be yours, but I must tell you that in all matters pertaining to my household as well as to my business affairs I involve Mr Henriques because he is my partner—no, Gideon, please do not speak for a moment! I will explain more in a little while, if you will bear with me.'

She turned back to Jonah. 'I cannot help you without Mr Henriques' knowledge of what I am doing, Jo, and so I tell you. I am happy—indeed, eager—to solve this very real problem you have regarding my niece, but you must accept Mr Henriques' concern if you will have mine. And I am sure he *will* be as concerned as I am, for he is a person of excellent feeling.' She smiled swiftly at Gideon. 'I do not know how I should have reared Frederick as I have without his aid, quite apart from any assistance that I have had from him in business affairs.'

There was a silence as Jo stood glowering at her, and then she said more gently, 'Dear Jo! Do not torment yourself. Gideon is my oldest friend, I do assure you! In confiding in him you do no more than confide in me! Please to accept my word on this.'

'Please, Abby—Mrs Caspar—I would not cause your brother any embarrassment for all the world.' Gideon could keep silent no longer and moved forward until he was standing beside her, so that they both looked earnestly at Jonah. 'I can quite understand that your brother has some private matter to deal with, and wishes to keep it private! I would not wish to cause any rift between you——'

'Your presence causes no rift,' Abby said firmly. 'On the contrary. I am at fault here, for I should have told Jo before you came that I had asked you to do so, and told him why.'

Gideon turned to look at her, his face almost childishly creased with lines of anxiety. 'Abby, I must implore you not to force this, whatever it may be, upon either your brother or me! I have told you, you must do as you think fit when——'

'And I have told you, Gideon, that I shall not ever commit myself to any extra expenditure of any kind, however personal it may be, without your full awareness and agreement.' Abby said calmly. 'I was wrong not to have told you of the other expenditure—private expenditure—I made, and to leave it till you saw it in the ledgers was—most improper. It is not a mistake I intend ever to make again.'

'But it was not wrong of you!' Gideon cried, now exquisitely uncomfortable as he felt Jonah's eyes upon him. 'Indeed, you——'

Abby laughed suddenly, lightly, turning away from the two men to return to the fireside. 'There, you see, Jo? How can you not regard us as close friends when we can argue so in your presence! Does that not show you how much of a pair we are? What you say to one concerns the other, so you may as well come to terms with it now! Now, come and sit down and we shall talk of the matter that brought you here!' And she settled her taffeta skirts about her feet with a little flurry, bending her head to smooth the flounces on it.

'You speak as though you were held by the bonds of matrimony, not merely of business!' Jonah said, sulkily, but he moved away from the window and after a moment Gideon did too, making some fuss about smoothing his coat and waistcoat when he sat down, keeping his head bent over the lie of the cloth of his trousers as Abby kept hers bent over the flounces of her skirt. And if both were a little more pink about the cheeks when they did raise their heads, then Jonah did not notice it, for he was thinking about what to do; and reached his decision with uncharacteristic speed.

'If you will explain the situation as I have to you, Abby, then perhaps we can go on from that point,' he said. 'But if you will forgive me, I prefer not to be here while you make your explanations. I recognize you feel the need for it. I do not recognize any need in myself to take part in your decision. So I will go and see that the children come within doors, while you talk, for it is now quite dark and it must be even colder than it was, and the wind I am sure is biting.'

He moved to the door, and looked back over his shoulder at them both, and said harshly, 'I would be pleased, Abby, if you will remember that Celia—that I—oh, devil take it! I have no doubt you will say what you please and when you please, as you always did!' and he pulled the door open with a savage tug.

'Trust me, Jo,' she said, and smiled at him with great sweetness. 'I never treated you ill when we were children, did I? Nor shall I now. If you will take the children to Ellie in the kitchen she will give them some hot broth and dry their boots before the fire.'

And Jonah nodded and with one last sharp glance at the silent Gideon went, closing the door loudly behind him.

## 8

'By God, you will come!' Abel said, and though his voice was not particularly raised there was no doubt in any of his listeners' minds but that he was so enraged as to be on the point of losing control. 'You shall see for yourself what you have done by your ways, by your—oh, you *shall* see!'

William's face was white under the smooth fair hair, and his head was thrust forwards in a truculent manner that caused his fleshy chin to double as it rested on the high points of his collar.

'I see no justification for the accusations you are making at me!' he said and his voice was high and thin. 'You complain to me of the whining lies of that toad-eater Conran, you tell me, your own son, that on such a creature's word you are prepared to regard me as a liar at best, a useless fool at worst, and then add to it with *this*? By God, sir, I too have my temper, and I too shall have·expression of it, if this nonsense does not come to an end!'

Abel's eyes narrowed and he in his turn pushed his head forwards so that for a moment there was a strong family resemblance between them as they stood glaring at each other.

'Shall you indeed!' Abel said very softly. 'Shall you! Then I take leave to tell you that if you dare to show any tantrums to me, out of this hospital you go, and not to Gower Street, either. My home shall never be open to you again. None of the possessions you have collected at my expense shall be available to you, and not a penny piece shall there be from any source over which I have control for you to bless yourself with! You understand me? You deal with this matter in my way, or you go out of here into Endell Street in the clothes you stand up in, and with no more money to your pockets than that which is in them at this moment. Which, I have no doubt, is none at all, for you have had your pockets to let from the day you were admitted to the Society, despite all the moneys you have been paid for the work you have done so ill at Wapping! Oh, don't think I don't know! Don't think I am not full aware of the life you live, you and your whoring and your gaming! How much money do you owe now, boy? And how much time will your *friends* have for you the day they find that I am no longer willing to underwrite you? Think on that! And when you have thought, you will bend your stiff neck and come to see what you have done with your stupidity. I have said you shall see it, and see it you shall!'

'Oh, for God's sake, William, do as you're bid!' Rupert's voice came a little muffled from the window seat, where he had been sitting half hidden by the heavy curtains, and he got up and came across the polished boards to the table on each side of which Abel and William were standing. 'While the two of you stand there hissing at each other like a pair of cocks in the ring, we get nowhere. If m'father's bound and determined that you shall see this operation, then see it you shall! You know that as well as I. Like you, I doubt such observation on your part will do any good. It will no doubt make you feel qualmish to a degree, and if you cast up your accounts at m'father's feet, then he's none but himself to blame for it!' and Rupert looked sideways at his father. 'But if this is his humour, then humour him. You'll do it, willyou nillyou, so you might as well choose to go on your own feet. He's not above having you dragged there by one of his damned students if you persist in your refusal.'

'You can come too,' Abel said shortly, his eyes still on William. 'The case is an interesting one in its own right, apart from what I wish to show this—this *brother* of yours——' and the amount of venom Abel managed to inject into his tone was remarkable '—and perhaps when you have seen the situation you will be less defensive on your brother's behalf and will see what it is that his stupidity is doing! They are taking her to the operating theatre in ten minutes, and you'd best be there. Both of you. I'm tired of being argued with—the time has come for you to do as you're told.'

And he turned and went, slamming the door of the big room hard behind him.

'For God's sake, Rupert!' William burst out. 'I expected better of you! Why did you let me down so? There's no point in this wretched charade! So I see his damnable operation! Much good it'll do!'

'It will make you very sick!' Rupert said and laughed and his narrow face was sardonic. 'You were ever weak in the stomach, as I recall!'

William's face became even whiter, developing a muddy sallowness, and he began to move fretfully about the room. 'Well, you may find it funny, but I do not! And why in hell's name should *I* be the one to suffer all this trouble at his hands? You are as involved as I! And if this doesn't stop, and if you don't pull your weight in the matter then I shall——'

'Oh, be quiet, you fool!' Rupert turned on him sharply. 'I know full well how you feel! But remember, will you, that there is more to concern ourselves with than your discomfiture! You want to be a man in your own right, and not have to go to him cap-in-hand for every penny? So! Put up with the pricks and wait for the fruit! And come and see your operation!' And again he grinned, his face creasing into those faintly devilish lines and he turned on his heel and made for the door.

William hesitated and then seemed to steel himself to action, and moved round the table to follow him. But he stopped as he reached the head of the table, where a carved and polished oak chair stood with its arms spread wide dominating the stretch of polished wood that lay in front of it.

He put his hand on the back of the chair, and looked round the room. 'He shall see,' he said softly. 'Oh, but he shall! When they turn him out of this room, and he can't lord it over the place as though he were God Almighty, then he shall see! I shall turn this room into my private sanctum, for once we are rid of his damned Trustees there'll be no use for such a boardroom as this! And I——'

Rupert, standing in the doorway, raised his eyebrows at that. 'You've a long way to go before you can consider any such new domestic arrangements,' he said sharply. 'And when the time comes, permit me to remind you that you will not be alone in making such decisions. One God Almighty is more than enough for me. You dream too much, William. Too many grandiose plans by far. A little more attention to reality, and a little less to dreaming and you'll fare better. And the reality at this moment is this operation, so face up to it, and come along. Unless you want one of the students to come looking for you?'

They made their way through the hospital in silence, Rupert in the lead and William dragging his feet a little, past the heavy wooden doors that led to each ward, along the narrow passageways reeking of the heavy scent of the sulphur pastilles that burned sluggishly in the corners.

Abel had little use for the purifying and cleansing powers of the pastilles, but Nancy had; and it was she who ran the building with a rod of iron, harassing the scrubbing women who came in each day from the mean surrounding streets and the three scrawny housemaids who lived in the attics with the nurses, until each board was scrubbed almost white, each painted wall washed to within an inch of its life, each window polished till it shone like crystal.

'There's naught like living in a whorehouse to teach you the value of soap and water and elbow grease!' she would say, laughing raucously when the nurses complained about the reek of soap and the throat-catching fumes of the sulphur, or muttered about Nancy's ridiculous demands that the sheets and blankets of each departing patient be changed and aired before another be put in the bed. And she would light more pastilles and harry the maids and nurses with threats and cajoling and shouting and wheedling, so that Queen Eleanor's enjoyed a reputation throughout London of having the least sluttish of nurses, the cleanest of servants, and if not the best of food, precisely, at least the least noisome.

And Nancy would go home to her old friend Lucy, once London's most famous Madam, but now bedridden in her house at Panton Street and complain about how hard she had to work to keep Nellie's running. At which Lucy would snort and say in her wheezy old voice, 'If it's what's needed by young Abel, then do it an' shut yer gob. It's what yer there for——' And Nancy would laugh again, but gently this time, and expertly spoon some gruel into the helpless old woman's mouth before going to her own narrow bed to sleep herself into the energy needed for the next day's battle with the dirt and disease and grime of the hospital in Seven Dials.

There was one room in all the four buildings which Nancy cleaned and scrubbed and took care of with her own hands; the operating theatre at the top of the hospital. It was an awkward room for its purpose in many ways, for it was reached by two flights of narrow twisting stairs, and carrying frightened agonized patients up and down made the students and porters sweat and swear considerably. But it had the virtue of being sufficiently removed from the wards for the shrieks and entreaties and heart-rending wails of patients undergoing surgery to be muffled; and this was important, for even the most desperately ill had been known to hobble away from the care that Nellie's offered when they heard of what happened in that little room at the top of the stairs, in the highest of the attics.

And also, it was well lit. The narrow dormer windows that embellished one side of the room had been supplemented with broad skylights set into the roof, and every week Nancy would tuck up her heavy calico skirts and climb up there laboriously to wash away the soot and grime that London threw from all its adjacent chimney stacks to coat the glass. No matter how bad the weather some light would come struggling in; and even when rain came lashing at the roof in impotent fury or the heavy yellow fog came pressing secretly and lasciviously against the panes so that narrow tendrils of the smoke-heavy choking fumes came twisting lazily through the cracks the room could be used, for Nancy had set to with wood and hammers and nails to make shelves along the walls on which she had set half a dozen of the most expensive of oil lamps, each of which she kept with its wick scrupulously trimmed and for which only the best quality lamp oil was used. No black sooty streaks would spoil Nancy's special room, nothing but the most brilliant of light would ever be allowed to shed itself in this special shrine to the surgeon's art. For Nancy the work she did here, whether it were scrubbing away the heavy clotted blood from the pools in which it had fallen on the planks of the floor, or washing pus from the walls where it had spattered when some great abscess had been lanced, was her eternal thanks to her beloved Abel. If it had not been for him she would have joined her Maker when she was little more than a child, she would tell anyone who would listen to her (and there were not many in the hospital who would any more, for she had told the tale so often that some knew it by heart) and each and every day she thanked that Maker for her deliverance by taking care of her deliverer.

When William and Rupert reached the room on that dull February afternoon, William puffing a little (for his weight was rising steadily, and the narrow stairs were very steep) it was already occupied by Abel and a tall thin young man with a solemn face and a high forehead below prematurely thinning hair. He was standing quietly against one wall, his hands clasped behind his back beneath his coat tails, his head bent as he listened to Abel who was talking vigorously and turning from time to time towards the narrow table in the middle of the room immediately beneath the skylight, on which lay the figure of a woman with Nancy standing quietly just behind her.

The brothers hesitated at the door, and Abel looked up and grunted.

'I am glad to see you,' he said with a sort of mockery in his tone that made William's face flush angrily. 'Mr Snow, you have met my son Rupert, of course. An acquaintanceship with William, however, is a pleasure so far denied you. My younger son, Mr Snow. William, Mr John Snow, of the Westminster Medical Society, and a Fellow of the College. He is here to observe some of the forms of surgery I practise.'

'How do, Mr Snow,' William essayed his usual bonhomie, and advanced across the room with his hand out, and the tall thin man coughed and held out his own to share a perfunctory clasp.

'I'm happy to know ye, Mr Lackland. I believe we are both Fellows of the Society of Apothecaries? I did not realize that you were like your father, however, and interested in surgery as well as the drugs and potions side of our craft.' He had a flat Yorkshire tone to his voice, and a tendency to stare at people he addressed very closely from beneath heavy dark eyebrows, his eyes sharp and extremely knowing.

William reddened again as he glanced at his father and his lips tightened.

'Oh, I am no surgeon, Mr Snow, though I am indeed a fellow apothecary. If my father has been telling you that I am interested in his knives and scissors trade he has been funning you! It is *his* idea that I attend this operation today.' He turned his head to look about the room, but only at the table laden with instruments and the bowls set ready to catch whatever might be needed to be caught, the gleaming

82

lights and the washed walls; never at the woman lying moaning a little on the table in the middle.

'It was no choice of mine,' he finished petulantly and turned away from Snow to go and stand with his back to the wall as far away from the centre of the room as he could be.

'I believe it necessary for all men occupied in the practice of medical care, be they physicians or surgeons or apothecaries, to see as much as they can of all forms of practice, Mr Snow.' Abel was shrugging out of his frockcoat and into the exceedingly old and greenish one that Nancy was holding ready for him. 'For until the apothecary sees the effects of his drugs or the physician the effects of his advising or the surgeon the effects of his cutting, why, they cannot know what it is they are doing! Might as well be a miner digging in the bowels of the earth by the light of a penny dip as to be such!'

'Aye,' said Snow simply. 'Aye. 'Tis a good practice. I was taught so in my student days, in Newcastle.'

'Newcastle?' said William, his eyebrows raised a little. 'Now, where precisely might that be? You must forgive my metropolitan ignorance! For me any place much north of Bedford must be regarded as the back of beyond!'

'Well, at least you know it's in the North,' Snow said after a sharp glance at William's now gleaming face, for the room was getting warmer as the oil lamps threw heat as well as radiance from their tall glass chimneys. 'We bumpkins must be grateful for that, no doubt!'

There was a snort of laughter from Rupert, and William, now quite discomfited, threw him a furious glance, but Rupert merely grinned back at him and turned his attention to the woman on the table.

She was lying on her back, her hands held close to the table by heavy leather straps, and her ankles and knees held equally fast. She was rolling her head from side to side, moaning softly and occasionally opening her eyes to stare blearily about the room, only to close them again with another groan.

Behind her Nancy held a white china cup with a spout and occasionally leaned over and coaxed her to drink some of its contents and the heavy scent of brandy filled the air each time she gulped. She was, quite clearly, completely and helplessly drunk.

Abel moved across to stand at her side and peer down at her and said loudly, 'Mrs Finn! Mrs Finn, do you hear me, Mrs Finn?'

The woman opened her eyes, tried to focus them in the direction from which the sound came, and closed them again, muttering something thickly but inaudibly, and Nancy said cheerfully, 'Oh, she's far gone, sir! I gave her twice the usual amount, poor creature, for I've seen the state of her and 'twill be hell and all its devils as she'll suffer before this day's out. Far gone, she is——'

'By God, but it's no way to treat patients, this,' Snow said abruptly. 'To fill their bellies with brandy before you can touch 'em with a knife! I've no doubt that the brandy makes the blood run more free, and impedes the surgery and the recovery more than is necessary! And brandy or no, they suffer——'

'I'd not be able to touch the woman at all without it,' Abel said shortly, and began to remove the dressing that covered the left side of her chest. 'Oh, I've heard you on the subject before, Snow. Seeking a way to promote insensibility without spirits. But you must admit it's an unlikely idea, to say the least!'

'I'm not so sure,' Snow said, and leaned over to help as the bandages began to unravel. 'I've been hearing of a leech in Shropshire, some twenty years ago. Gave animals carbon dioxide to inhale, as I understand it, and made 'em quite as insensible as any surgeon would require.'

'Aye, but what happened afterwards? Did they wake up again? It might be easier to operate on the insensible, but where's the sense if they don't recover their senses? That becomes the mere *practice* of surgery, not the use of it to ameliorate a man's ills. Or a woman's——'

There was a silence as the last dressing came off, apart from the thick soft moan that the woman produced and they all stood looking at her bare breasts.

On one side the curve of flesh was soft, even seductive, for the woman was quite young, not three and thirty yet, and the nipple stood firm and tiptilted above the gentle swell. But in the other breast the nipple was lopsided, curving over towards the armpit, and though the flesh still looked healthy and agreeable towards the centre of the body, there between the arm and the nipple lay an open weeping sore. Its edges were hard and inturned as though punched out and the veins which ran into it were swollen and tense and dark as they made their tortuous way across the pallid skin. The livid flesh within the ulcerated area looked hot and tight, and Snow put one hand forwards and then withdrew it, and Abel said almost inconsequentially, 'The ancients called this *noli me tangere*, as I recall.'

'Aye,' said Snow. 'Or the Wolf. It is indeed a great eater of flesh. How long since she came to you?'

Abel's voice seemed to harden. 'About five weeks.'

'Five weeks?' Snow looked up swiftly, and frowned. 'Did you try no treatment in that time?'

'Oh, indeed I did!' Abel said, and turned his head so that he was staring very directly at William, who was standing hard against the wall, looking down at his feet. 'Indeed I did. I recommended the application of caustic salve, to burn away the cancerous tissue and promote the granulation of new. Nancy was bid to apply the treatment twice a day, without fail. Did you fail, Nancy?' And still he was staring at William.

'I, sir? Fail your instructions?' Nancy raised her head and stared at Abel with her face filled with amazement. 'Mr Abel! You should know better nor to say such a thing to me! This is Nancy, remember? Not one of yer gutter nurses as you——'

He threw her a swift look and smiled reassuringly. 'I know, I know. You must forgive the stupid question.' He turned his gaze back to William.

'So, the fault, if it is not in the applying of the ointment, must be in the ointment itself. That seems a reasonable supposition?'

Rupert leaned forwards and stared at the ulcer. 'I see no sign of any salve here,' he said and his voice was high and thin. 'You may believe your instructions were fully carried out, sir, but I see no salve here or——'

'Then look at this!' Nancy said loudly, and reached across to scrabble in the bowl where the soiled dressings had been thrown. She pulled out a messy looking piece of greyish charpie, the soft bundle of teased linen threads that Nellie's always used for dressings.

'See this? Look, Master Rupert, and then tell me there was no salve applied! O'course it's not to be seen on the ulcer, on account the stuff was so poorly made that it 'ad no sticking power at all! I put it on the dressing, as you see 'ere if you do but look, *and* set it into its place, and not a bit of goodness come out of it on to the poor woman's body! 'Twas me as told Mr Abel 'is salve wasn't no good! It used to be a good salve, this one did, but look at this and then tell me I ain't done as I was bid!' And she waved the dressing almost under Rupert's nose, so that he reared back, for it smelt foul; but all could see quite clearly the heavy brownish mass that adhered to the cloth and the way it was packed so heavily into the fibres.

'What mixture is it, for heaven's sake?' Snow said, taking it from her hand and peering at it. 'This is a poor quality substance, Lackland, and no mistake. There should be sweet mercury in it, and red lead and balsam of sulphur and——'

'And oil of amber and spirits of wine and opium,' Abel said harshly, 'caustic and soothing in turn, all with a task to do in the concoction——'

'There was no opium in it, I'll tell you that,' Nancy said flatly. She took the dressing from Snow's hand and stared at it for a moment, and then dropped it back into the bowl. 'No opium, on my life as I stand 'ere, for she shrieked pitiful when I applied it, and if there'd bin opium, why, 'er pain would 'ave abated. And it didn't.'

'So, William!' Abel's voice was harsh now. 'Can you perhaps explain the matter? The salve was prepared at Wapping like all the materials we use here. What went wrong with this one? For I have looked in the pots, and I tell you now, they contain a mass of the base, but the minimum—if any!—of the essential ingredients. You must remember that I too am an apothecary, and I know how these plasters and salves and cataplasms you make should be! And I cannot understand why the ones we are here using should be such cheap and rubbishy concoctions when we are paying for the best of quality. Can you help me to understand?'

William at last raised his head to stare at his father and his face was sullen and heavy. He looked at him for a long moment, and then sighed heavily, his nostrils dilating sharply to make his face seem momentarily to spread and soften.

'So, I have been lax in the supervision of the apprentices and they have not been following the receipts as they should,' he said. 'I cannot help that, though, since I must be out and about all the time to the

86

wharves and warehouses buying the materials and the drugs you seek. I cannot do that and be by their side always watching them!'

'Perhaps not,' Abel said softly. 'But if they are not using the materials in the concoctions, William, then those materials should still be about the place. And you tell me they are not! That is what you meant, I believe, when you told me that the stocks of all our expensive medicaments are shocking low? And that the prices have risen so high that you must go and buy at the top of the market's prices, and thus demand more money than we budgeted for Wapping in this quarter?'

William's face changed again, the ready colour rising and then receding like a tide, to leave his face pinched and sallow. 'I cannot discuss that now,' he said shortly. 'You can come and check the stores for yourself if you so wish. Rupert will come with you, no doubt, to see that both our interests are fairly represented——' He looked swiftly at Rupert, but he was looking down at the ulcer on the woman's chest, his lips pursed softly as though he were whistling, and seeming to be quite oblivious of the conversation around him.

'That I shall surely do,' Abel said, and his voice was loud and harsh in the quiet room, obliterating even the sound of Mrs Finn's groaning, which was coming more loudly now, so that Nancy bent over to pour more brandy between her clenched teeth. 'That I shall! But now, William, you shall see the operation that has been made necessary because the salve was not—not as—effective as we hoped, shall I say. That salve, properly constituted and used for a full five weeks, should have halted the spread of the ulcer and hopefully have given us a cure for a while—though she could not hope to live much longer, for the disease is an incurable one. Now, however, surgery is necessary for the ulcer will spread so fast it will eat into her very bones and she will die in greater agony than necessary.'

William moved then, turning blindly towards the door but Abel was faster than he was, and moved across the room with a few easy lopes to grasp his elbow and lead him to the side of the table.

'Stand you there, so you may see each stroke of the knife,' he said. 'It will help, I think, if Mr Snow stands this side of you—aye, thank you, Snow—for then he can hand me the instruments and also see to it that you have a good view of the proceedings. I would not have you miss one atom of it.'

And so William stood, sweating steadily so that rivulets ran down his forehead and the sides of his nose, down his cheeks and on to the starched points of his collar so that they wilted and bent. The light from the oil lamps and the dull grey skylight above him threw every movement of his father's and Snow's hands into sharp relief so that he could not help but watch them, though he tried to keep his eyes closed. But the light seemed to come needle-sharp, pushing in beneath his sandy lashes to force them up and make him stare at what was happening in sick horror.

For all he had trained as an apothecary, had been taught the facts of illness and disease, for all the time he had spent working in Wapping and frequenting the corridors of this hospital, he had never before been brought face to face with the cold reality that was surgery. And facing it now he sweated and squirmed, but watched in mounting revulsion, almost as fascinated as he was repelled.

They moved fast, his father and his brother and Snow. Rupert had moved to stand behind the woman and take her left shoulder in a hard grasp, so that he could fix it to the table with all his weight, while Nancy moved across to hold the other shoulder by leaning on it. Snow took the left arm and bent it at the elbow so that although the wrist was still strapped firmly to the table there was room for Abel to move.

And move he did, taking one of his favourite knives in one hand and a wad of charpie in the other. Stylishly tortoiseshell-handled, with a dull satin grey gleam about its blade, the knife moved with a precision that was sure and swift, cutting in a great curve from the armpit round up to the nipple, and back to the point of the shoulder, leaving the yellow-white flesh to part lazily behind it, and small spurts of scarlet blood to go leaping up into the air with a sort of teasing merriment.

The woman started to shriek, a great breathy high-pitched sound that yet had an undertow, a counterpoint, of thick huskiness, and the sound grew and grew even though Nancy held on to her head and shoulder and tried to contain it, grew until the room rang with sound, and it seemed the air would thicken with it and become foggy, as though the din would become concrete enough to dull the lights and make it impossible not only to see and hear but to breathe and think or even be.

But Abel seemed untouched by it, and went on, applying hot pitch from the bubbling pot on the table beside him so that the dancing little jets of blood were stilled and the smell of singed flesh filled the air to mix itself with the sound of the woman's crying. His knife moved with a great elegance, gouging out the flesh beneath the nipple so that a flap of skin was formed; easing away from the chest wall the ulcerated area, lifting and cutting, manipulating and urging until, quite suddenly there was a flap of dead humanity in his hand, a piece of helpless limp muscle and fat and skin, and he laid it almost tenderly on the table behind him and returned to the body that lay there on the table.

For it was now very like a body, a dead shell, for the shrieking had stopped as the woman fell into a blessed unconsciousness and ceased her heaving and plunging attempts to move and now Abel could work with delicacy, showing his skill in a kind of grace-note way as his hands moved and trilled and spun their web of ties and sutures. The flap came over the armpit, was sewn to the remaining skin on that side so that the remains of the nipple lay. ludicrously and pathetically askew, almost at the side of the body. And then he was done, and he and Snow were throwing used instruments down on the table, and wrapping dressings and bandages into place and the woman was beginning to emerge from the blackness of the little peace she had known to start again her great wailing.

Nancy went to the door, and William for the first time was able to look away from the woman on the table to stare almost blankly at the two hefty men who came in.

'Take her back,' Abel said shortly. 'And we shall hope to see some improvement in her. But I cannot be too sanguine.'

He stood back, and the porters unbuckled the straps and with Nancy's help lifted the blanket-wrapped shape to their shoulders and went stumping down the stairs so that the crying that had become so much a part of the room went fading away in a diminuendo which left them all, and William most particularly, blank and a little dazed.

'The quality of the materials you produce at Wapping does matter, you see, William,' Abel said and his tone was quite conversational. 'If you did not see that before, I think you will now. Good afternoon to you. I must go to the wards for my visits. Rupert? Snow? Will you join me? Excellent. We shall see each other at home, I believe, William. At dinner.'

And it was then, left alone in the too-bright, too-quiet room at the top of the house, that William began to vomit.

## 9

'You make too much of the matter altogether,' Celia said again, and bent her head more closely over her sewing. They were in their little sitting room, the house blessedly silent beneath and around them with only the distant rumbling of the first carts coming into the market over the rattling cobbles to tell them that any but themselves were awake in all London.

Fully two hours had passed since the last customer had gone rolling out into the midnight darkness of King Street, skintight with beer, stuffed with food and dazed with music and brawling, to leave the proprietors to their weary nightly cleaning of their establishment; and now it was done.

Below stairs in the kitchen the last embers of the cooking fires warmed the bony shanks of the girls who had chosen to drag their pallets in front of it to sleep, for it was a bitter cold night, with the frost still biting hard at the roofs and walls of Covent Garden's houses, seeping in through the grimy brick to chill the flesh of all within. Along the passageway Oliver and Phoebe slept heavily, and all over the house the fading smells of game pies and boiled ham, beer lees and tobacco carried ghostly reminders of the evening's business.

Celia had twice told Jonah to go to bed, as she settled herself to the sewing of the spangled costume Norah Norton had torn so badly when one of the customers, in a sudden access of drunken desire, had gone reeling up on to the little stage to grab at her and join in the singing, much to the audience's raucous delight.

'In all truth, the thing is falling apart,' she had said, wearily surveying its bedraggled seams and the trailing sequins on the bodice. 'But it will cost far more to get a new one made than I'm inclined to spend on *that* one. She's not that good a performer, and you must look to replace her, Jonah, as soon as you may. But she'll need it for tomorrow's performance, so mend it I must and now. Do go to bed, and don't stand there gawping at me! I will come as soon as I am done, and I'll be done the sooner without you there——'

But Jonah, tired as he was, had known that he would not find a better chance to talk to her of his plans and arrangements, so had sat down firmly in the chair facing hers and after a moment she had looked at him and shrugged, and bent her head to work.

He had watched her, staring at her smooth dark head in the pool of lamplight, at the way her long fingers flashed and twisted among the crimson and purple and violent green sequins, at the pale line of her cheek and the firm set of her mouth that was beginning to look much more narrow than it once had as lines etched themselves a little more deeply from its corners to her nose. He remembered suddenly and very poignantly the round-faced softness she had had when he had first seen her in the wings of the Haymarket theatre, watching him as he sat in the stage box, and the memory was so oddly painful—and why it should be so he could not imagine—that he blurted it out without stopping to think, without at all choosing his words in a way that would mollify her.

'I am very concerned about Phoebe. It is wrong—very improper—that she should see the things she has to see here.'

Celia bit off a piece of thread, with her teeth snapping whitely in the soft light and began to thread her needle. 'Oh, I know you were put out about it,' she said irritably, and squinted at her needle, 'and talked of nothing else all week. But really Jonah, you make too much of the matter! I told you—it was just one of the customers being friendly. And the child enjoys it, after all! I saw more and heard worse when I was half her age, and went on hearing and seeing it until I was full grown. And I doubt I have come to any harm.'

'I want better for her,' Jonah said stubbornly. She looked up at him sharply under her level brows and then looked down at her work again.

'Oh, I am sorry!' Jonah said, and rubbed his face wearily. 'I mean no criticism of you, and you know I do not. You are every inch a lady, and you have made yourself so, and I know it better than any. But I would wish Phoebe to have to work less hard, to be—to find life *easier*. I would wish Oliver to be a better man than I am—and in saying so I would not wish it thought I am calling myself in any way bad. It's just that—I regard this as part of a father's love. To want his children to have a better life than did their parents——'

There was a silence as her needle flashed swiftly through the torn net, and then she said harshly, 'They have a better life now than they would have had if they had needed to depend on *you*. When you begot them we had nothing to call our own, no roof, no money, no future. Now they are the children of people of property, and if you don't know who they have to thank for that, I do.'

He swallowed before he spoke, and his voice was husky. 'I know perfectly well that I have been a poor provider. That you have worked —that you have indeed slaved to make this place what it is. And never think I do not appreciate the fact. I do all I can to help you, to the limit of my ability. I could not help being without capital. My father— my plays—I wanted to—God dammit, I did all I could!'

He threw himself out of his chair to go moving restlessly about the room, and she followed him with her eyes, and her face creased a little as she looked at the straightness of his back, the broadness of his shoulders and the elegance of his long flanks. He should not still look as beautiful as he had done when she had first seen him, she thought confusedly, when I am so weary; and then as he turned his head to stare at her, his eyes dark and shadowed, she bent her head and began to sew again, but more slowly now.

'I am sorry,' she said after a moment. 'I did not wish to dig at you. Vulgar in the extreme, was it not? But no doubt to be expected of one of my rearing——'

'Oh, for God's sake!' His voice was flat with fatigue. 'Can we talk less of ourselves, for there is no sense in such conversations, nor ever has been it seems to me, and talk only of Phoebe? I told you I was concerned and that——'

And again she repeated it. 'You make too much of the matter altogether.'

'Well, that's as may be,' Jonah yawned suddenly, and blinked. 'We will not talk further of my view of the matter. Whether I have made too much of it or no, I have made a plan. And I wish to tell you that

I have—that it is arranged that Phoebe shall have some education. In a way that will solve many of our—my difficulties, I hope you will be happy about it.'

She lifted her head sharply. 'I have told you, Jonah, there is no money for governesses! Not that you would find one of those milk-and-water misses to come here anyway! You saw what happened when you spoke to Mr Bourne and he sent that girl he knew of—is that what you want? She's better off with Mary and me—when I have the time—and if you are so anxious that she learn her letters then set to yourself and teach her.'

He shook his head. 'I am not fit to teach. I thought of that. And I know that no respectable governess will come here.' He moved across the room suddenly and knelt by her side, putting his hand on hers so that she had to stop her sewing, and peered up into her face. 'And cannot you see that therein lies the root of the problem? If no respectable governess will come here, how can you be so calm about your children growing up here? That we must make our living in this manner is—well, I would be happier with the legitimate theatre, you know that! Where there is some art, some beauty—but we could not earn a living at that and so this is what it must be—but for Phoebe——'

'You make me sick!' she said suddenly, and very loudly, and stared at him with her upper lip slightly twisted so that scorn showed all over her face. 'You, who saw what went on at the Haymarket, who went trailing with me all round those filthy, louse-infested stinking pits of provincial theatres—you tell me that that is in some sort better than the work we do here? So our customers are not smooth and elegant lords and ladies, and don't go about in satin and stinking of their perfumes! I like 'em better with the smell of their work on them, and their leather aprons and their nailed boots! You hear me? We offer honest entertainment here to honest people and I will not have it that it is too low and too inelegant for you or for anyone else! Phoebe will do as I did, and grow up in the world she was born into. And when she is old enough, let me tell you, she can start working, just as do other girls who are not born into the fancy ton! Who do you think you are, Jonah Lackland, to make such a to-do about the rearing of your daughter? Your father was dragged out of the gutter—there was no nobility in him, so there is none in you, any more than there is in me!

I made this house a support for us, as well as our home, and you who go marching about with that sneer on your face, as though some evil smell were below your nose, can think again and stop your moaning over Phoebe! The airs and graces you want to give her will be of no use to her in the world she'll grow up in, I tell you, for it is a hard and ugly world, and the sooner she knows it the better for her——'

He had settled back to sit on his heels and stare at her and the tirade went on, rolling over him in waves of sound as her voice became more and more shrill, and his face became creased and tight, but still she went on, the words pouring out of her.

'—and what of Oliver, hey? What of him? If you care so much for madam Phoebe, what plans have you for your son? I have saved and scrimped and fiddled with money for all these years to give that boy a schooling, planning that when he is of an age he would go away to school, as you did before him, for I too am a parent, and I know, and I care! He shall have at least as good as his father did, even if that father cannot provide it! Even if his father is too set about in his mind over his daughter to look at his son as he ought to, that boy shall not suffer if I have aught to say in the matter! What have you done to prepare for Oliver's education? Nothing! It had been all *my* concern, every bit of it! You moon about, you dream, you go around looking as though you were anywhere but here, and then dare to tell me that you would rather we worked in the legitimate—faugh! You sicken me!'

She stopped at last and stared down at him with her face white and pinched and her eyes very wide open, and he looked back and then nodded heavily and got to his feet.

'Well, I feared you had learned to hate me, and now I know,' he said flatly and turned and went back to his chair. She moved as though she would follow him, putting her hands forward in a sudden entreating movement, but he did not see, and she pulled her hands back then clasped them in her lap so tightly that the knuckles flared whitely among the heavy spangles.

'I do not speak of hate,' she said heavily after a moment. 'I speak of practicalities. You are a dreamer, a great mooncalf of a dreamer and ever were. You have some mad image in your mind of being another Sheridan or Shelley or some such. Well, you are not, nor ever will be.

You tried and you failed. To dream on and to despise what you are and what you do here is plainly stupid. But it does not make me hate you.'

She stopped and then spoke again with an almost visible effort. 'I loved you when I wed you. I loved you when we worked and suffered so in those dirty little towns and when you were so low in your spirits about our situation. I loved when we were so poor that we did not have food to our bellies, beyond what we could pick up in those foul greenrooms. If I loved you then, I see no reason why you should think I could—would feel any different now.'

He sat with his head bowed and she looked at him with a curious sort of anxiety on her face, but he said nothing, just sitting staring down at his clasped hands and she blinked hard, for her eyes had brightened sharply, and she would not have him see it for the world.

The room sank into silence, with a faint hissing coming from the fireplace where a last ember was flaring in the dying fire, and after a while she returned to her sewing, and worked busily at it. And by the time the ember had collapsed into a heap of white ash she had finished, shaking out the tawdry folds and staring at the garment with a critical eye. And then she stood up and folded it and tidily put away her needle and thimble in the pouch of her sewing table, moving softly about the room setting it to rights.

He stirred himself at last and said heavily, 'I have not yet told you what arrangements I have made. I wish you to know of them and would be glad of your approval. I—I was aware of the difficulty of finding money with which to solve the dilemma, and made up my mind to it that you should not have to be fretted over it. There are others who could be expected to have an interest in Phoebe, for she has more in the world than just parents and a brother after all. There are those I thought could be expected to show some concern for her welfare and——'

She was standing very still, her hand on the knob of the door, and her eyes wide and blank in her face, which had suddenly become very white. But he was not looking at her, still sitting with his gaze fastened on his tightly clasped hands in his lap.

'Others?'

Now he raised his head and looked at her, and his face too was bleak and suddenly very tired. He looked much older than he usually did.

'Why not?' he said, and there was a note of defiance in his voice. 'Other people have relations and seek to use their good offices and influence. Why not our daughter? I saw no ill in going to one who is after all a blood relation of the child, and who could be expected to show an interest in her young connection. And if she has the money to spare, with so excellent a head for money as she has—and always had, as I recall—and only the one small boy to occupy her and no husband or such to say her nay, why not? I spoke to her and she has agreed that Phoebe may go to her house each Friday and stay there until Monday and there will be a governess who will——'

'You will do as you please!' Celia said loudly, so loudly that he almost jumped and peered at her, standing there in the shadows by the door. Her eyes were closed and her mouth set in a tight line and he said in a puzzled tone, 'Celia?'

But she shook her head dumbly and turned and pulled the door open and went away, leaving him sitting there alone by the oil lamp, which was beginning to reek and splutter as the reservoir emptied, for it had been burning a very long time; it was close on three in the morning, and noise from the traffic outside was beginning to build up towards morning. The smell of hot lamp oil thickened and automatically he reached out and cupped his hand over the chimney and blew, and the room sank into darkness, leaving him to fumble his way to the door.

Celia was in bed, her head almost covered by the blankets and sheets by the time he managed to find a candle and light it, and he stood beside the bed and stared at her for a while, his face very puzzled, but she lay still as a rock, her body hardly moving in response to her shallow breathing. He sighed and set down the candle and began to undress and slipped into the bed beside her.

For a moment he thought of putting out his hand to touch her, considered moving his body closer to hers, to initiate the little tendernesses that he knew could make her respond and turn suddenly to him in the darkness to wrap her arms about his neck and cling to him with that intense need for his caresses that seemed, he sometimes thought, to have grown over the years rather than diminished. But there was a sort of wall about her, intangible, unseeable, but undoubtedly there and after lying very still beside her for a moment he sighed deeply and turned his back on her and pulled the blankets about his ears to lie and think miserably about the whole conversation, trying to see why she had suddenly become so icy.

The taunts about his uselessness were nothing new; he almost expected those in any disagreement between them and knew in a confused sort of way that she regretted making them almost as soon as she had; but this chill was something quite new. That she should respond to his plan for Phoebe with such cold rage was not at all what he had expected. That she might laugh, might shrug it off as one of his nonsenses had been very possible; he had even for a mad moment hoped she would be glad and would applaud his good sense. But to be so *angry*—why?

'And I did not even manage to tell her where Abby lives,' he thought confusedly, 'or to tell her that she wants her to come to Paddington Green to visit——' and fell asleep in a sudden wave of exhaustion.

But Celia did not sleep for a long time. She lay and stared into the darkness, listening to his breathing thicken behind her, brooding heavily and with a depth of misery that seemed to tie knots in her guts and make her head pound.

After all this time, when they had never mentioned her name once. All these years when she had been as though non-existent between them. They had quarrelled and worried and fretted and she knew she had become harder in many ways, but surely it had not come to this, after all this time——

'She said it would be so,' Celia whispered into the darkness, and behind her Jonah slept on, his breathing bubbling a little, becoming a soft snore, a sound she usually liked to hear. But not now.

*She had said it would be so.* As clearly as though it were being enacted before her eyes, Celia saw herself ten years ago, ten years younger, ten years more hopeful, more foolish, more yearning, standing there in her mother's white and gold drawing room in North Audley Street, staring at her lying there so beautifully on her chaise longue in her blue peignoir, her arms languorously stretched above her curly head and saying '—you may have him, for my part!—for what good he may do you!—I can tell you, you poor thing, he will not forget me—whenever he embraces you, it will be me he thinks of and you will always know it and will always see me there, no matter what happens——'

Ten years. And she had been right. Celia closed her eyes in the darkness of her marriage bed, and tried to shrink into herself, feeling her body crawl at the thought of it. To go to *her*. When they had suffered such hunger and such need and such pain together for so long, to go to Lilith now and to go for *Phoebe*——

The thoughts circled in her head, images of her mother dancing and smiling over her shoulder blurring and shifting to become images of Phoebe skipping and tossing her curls and dimpling her knowing baby smile over her shoulder too, but neither looked or smiled at *her*, neither even cared that it was in Celia's mind they were dancing their mad saraband. It was Jonah they danced for, Jonah, who stood there in the flat landscape behind her closed eyes, smiling and nodding and turning from one to the other, loving and approving, beaming his attention and love at them both. But ignoring totally the person who was most yearning for him.

And then, as she slid deeper into her miserable sleep Celia realized she wasn't even there herself in her own bewildered dream. Just Jonah and Lilith and Phoebe, circling and nodding at each other. Just those three.

## 10

Abby had been working at the manufactory since eight o'clock, arriving only an hour after the workers had come straggling in from their tenement homes in Lisson Green and Tyburn and some from the even further slums that lay hidden behind the elegancies of Baker Street and York Place.

At one time all Abby's workers had lived close to the manufactory at the corner of Irongate Wharf Road, for when James had started there had been little local work, and the poor of the neighbourhood—and there were many—had been eager for the employment he offered. But then had come the steam engine and the railway boom and with it the great plans for the building of the provisional Great Western Railway terminus before which so many of their little homes and alleys had been swept away.

Before that, to start work at seven in the morning had been no hardship, and the work of the factory had been arranged to fit a labouring day that commenced at this time, and ended at eight in the evening. The workers had been content, and with their regular money coming in—some took home as much as twelve shillings on a Saturday night, a full two shillings a day—had thought themselves well placed. And now they still came to work for Abby, even though for some of the displaced people who had formerly lived in Paddington, but who had fled before the all-conquering steam locomotive, it meant a walk of fully three-quarters of an hour there and the same back to reach their homes again. For even though she had found it would be uneconomic to alter the factory hours to suit the workers' new situations, Abby was a good reliable employer, and well they knew it; and she, in her turn had appreciated their loyalty and arranged that each morning there should be brewed for all of them (and there were twenty-five women and children, as well as the sprinkling of men who tended the bigger machines) a great jug of bitter tea, laced with skimmed milk and sweetened with syrup of molasses to be drunk after an hour's work and again at dinner time at noon, and then at four in the afternoon. And they murmured to each other of their good fortune and drank it greedily, slaking their dry throats, for the air of the place was full of floating powder from the medicines, and warming their thin dirty hands against their tin mugs.

Many of them, when they had first come to the factory and had realized that the gaffer was a lady, had been suspicious, even shocked, for what sort of a lady was it that made the affairs of a manufactory her own? Worse still, what sort of lady was it that actually worked there herself, could turn her hand to any of the processes used, could deal with the books, and the packing and the organizing, as she did?

One would-be employee had been fool enough to say so. Standing before her in his heavy frieze coat over a grimy collarless shirt, with his moleskin trousers tied with string below each huge knee and turning his flat cap between hands half as big as hams, he had stared insultingly at the neat young woman who had stood before him, arms akimbo, and told him she was the one to whom he must speak if he wanted employment for she was the guv'nor and there was no man to be sent for, and as he had looked her up and down, coolly insulting, he had growled, 'The only female 'as runs 'er own business is in the tail business. An' I don' want no job in no 'ore'ouse sniffin' round stinkin' skirts——'

And she had raised her hand and struck him sharply across the face, having to stand almost on tiptoe to do it, and for one sick moment they had all stood breathless, watching, tensing their muscles, puny and scrawny muscles though they were, ready to go to this foolish gaffer's defence.

But they had not been needed, for after raising his hand threateningly, the man had looked around him, and, sensing the spirit of the watching women and children had lowered it and spat rudely at Abby's feet, but then gone lumbering peaceably enough away, and they had all breathed again, and laughed and complimented each other on having such a lady as this to work for. The story was told to each new worker, inevitably improving in the telling, and spread about the district so that gradually the force of working men needed had been built up, and none were more ferociously devoted to Abby than they. Strange lady she may be, strange guv'nor she may be, but she was the Missus and that was all about it.

Today, as she stood there among them drinking her tea—and she was not being consciously condescending in doing so, for although Abby could be as delicate as any Belgravia lady in her own little sitting room, here she enjoyed the brew, and lapped it up with real pleasure—while some of the younger of the children who worked for her clustered round her skirts and giggled together as they watched for the chance of second helpings from the big enamelled jug wielded by Mrs Hobson, the most senior of the women, she was very content.

The big dusty room was bright with lamplight, keeping out the dinginess of the March morning, and the wooden floorboards were cosy to bare feet—and few of the children had boots—for Abby kept a great coal slack fire burning at the far end of the draughty old structure that was the manufactory. She had had to tell Gideon when he had mildly demurred at the cost of the fuel, 'Cold people are slow people. The warmer I keep them the better they'll work, and so they'll pay for the coal. And it is the cheapest that I buy, after all——' He had laughed, and agreed that her business acumen, as ever, had proved it ran deeper than mere columns of figures in the ledgers.

She was thinking about Gideon now, standing there before the fire surrounded by the soft chatter of the workers making the most of the five minute rest they were enjoying. He had been surprised at that, too, she remembered, on one of his early visits to the factory, for he knew of no employer who allowed such, but when she had opened her mouth to defend the practice he had laughed and said at once, 'Aye, I know! Tired workers are slow workers, so you give 'em a rest that they may work the better and pay for the lost production—aye, that will be it——' and they had laughed together and she had said perkily, 'Well, I am not wrong, am I? The volume of our production has increased two-fold this year. It cannot be bad to treat my workers so, if they work as well as that!'

But thinking about him now, she was not able to keep her mind entirely to matters of the factory. It had been strange that afternoon, she mused, after Jonah had gone and taken Phoebe and Oliver away with him. They had spent a noisy and contented hour first with the children as they had their supper and although Jonah had been remote and stiff with Gideon, the children with their noisy chatter and laughter and Phoebe's curl-tossing and wholly enchanting insolence had smoothed the time well; and Jonah had managed a reasonably civilized farewell when he had left, although he was put out to discover that Gideon was to remain with Abby for a while longer.

Abby had pressed his hand and said quickly, 'Please, not to worry, Jonah! I have explained all that is needed to Gideon, and when we have deliberated over the details I shall send you a letter. But we will contrive, I am sure. Please do not worry!'

And of course she had been right. She *had* contrived, explaining to Gideon the plan she had concocted to solve Jonah's dilemma.

'The child is my niece after all, Gideon,' she had said earnestly, leaning forward in her chair towards where he sat on the other side of the fireplace. 'And I can understand my brother's anxiety, for I believe that some of these supper rooms are—well, they lack refinement! I do not know the situation at my brother's establishment precisely, but he is anxious, so I must share his anxiety——'

'What does her mother feel?' Gideon asked, almost lazily. To be quite honest, he told himself, he did not really care one way or the other about the matter, but Abby wanted to talk to him about it, so talk she must. And he watched her animated square little face with his mouth slightly upturned into a smile. She was so very agreeable to watch when she talked.

'I don't know! He speaks little of her. I never met her——' Abby leaned back then and stared into the fire. 'I never wanted to, to tell the truth, for I have cruel memories of her mother, and—I have always blamed that woman for much of the tragedy that overcame my family. My own mother's distress, and—oh, that is all ancient history now, and it is stupid and unkind in me to bear any grudge against Jonah's wife on such an account. I have told Jonah so, and bade him bring her to visit me. I would like to know her better, for herself, you know, and not as her mother's daughter.'

'You have not yet told me precisely what is the plan that you have made,' Gideon said. 'You were most anxious that I come here to talk about it, but——'

'Oh, I am sorry! That is so very remiss of me! I prose on and on like some dismal old maid nodding over her crochet! Well, Gideon, the plan I have is this, and you will see why I must have your agreement to it——'

'Abby, I have told you——'

'Aye. Many a time. And I have told you. So hush and listen!' And he smiled at her and subsided.

'Now, my niece needs not only a haven away from the roughness of her home at the end of each week—and you must understand it is not that my brother lacks any awareness of the elegancies of life, but that the nature of the establishment—yes, you do understand! Well, she needs to stay here with me from Thursday until Monday each week, which will be agreeable for me and a pleasure, I suspect for Freddy, and——'

Gideon laughed. 'Indeed, yes! He was quite *bouleversé* by his little cousin, was he not! I did indeed observe it!'

She laughed too. 'Indeed—and it will do him no harm to have one younger than himself about for some of the time. He attends his day school, of course, and has intercourse with other boys there, but here at home he is in danger of becoming somewhat babyfied, for he is the only child after all. To have one younger and frailer than himself to protect and defer to will be excellent for his character, I am sure. But it is the next point upon which I need your guidance.'

'Well?'

'Her father is anxious that she be taught but lacks the funds to employ a suitable governess, even if one of satisfactory character could be found to take the post. I have said I will employ such a one here, but that her duties will not be entirely in the schoolroom——'

He cocked his head at her, for she had hesitated, and seemed embarrassed. 'Are you going to seek other children to come here and take lessons, then? To use the extra time?'

She laughed at that. 'No, such a thought! I cannot imagine myself running a dame school! No, it had occurred to me that a sensible girl, if she had a head for figures, could be taught some of the ledger work, and take it from my back. There is so much to be done in the manufactory itself you see, and I would wish to spend more time there, and with another head to take over from me some of the counting house labour, why I could——'

'Oh, no!' he said swiftly, and she looked at him in surprise, for his voice had been most vehement and he was sitting very upright with an expression of almost ludicrous dismay on his face.

'Why, Gideon! Is it so bad a scheme? I would have thought that—well, that you would see the good business sense of it and——'

He had relaxed a little, and now looked almost sheepish. 'I am sorry, Abby. That was quite an involuntary reaction—of course you are right. You work very hard in the counting house, and any help you can find for your labours there will be good, and meet with all my approval, whatever the cost of such an employee may be. You must forgive my first reaction!'

'I will if I know its source,' Abby said. 'Why were you so adamant so suddenly, and then so immediately reversed your view?'

'It does not matter, really——'

'Indeed it does!' Abby said sturdily. 'Until you tell me why, the plan cannot be put into operation! Jonah—and I imagine Freddy and Phoebe—will be most disappointed of course, but without your full agreement, because she will cost at least forty pounds a year as well as her keep, then naturally——'

'Oh, it was nothing to do with the costs!' Gideon said, and he was most uncharacteristically flustered. 'Indeed, I was not thinking——'

'It is immediate responses that are always the most honest, Gideon! Now tell me what was in your mind, or the whole matter is closed and no arrangements will be made.'

There was a silence and then Gideon said awkwardly, 'I was afraid it would mean I would have to deal with this governess person instead of you, when the books are checked each week. And I could not bear to miss that Wednesday meeting of ours. It is, for me, the high point of my working week. Of all the week, for the matter of that.'

There was a long silence, and then Abby said uncertainly, 'Why, Gideon, that is—well, that is most kind of you. I am glad we are such friends. We always have been, and you——'

He smiled at her, his mouth crooked and his long face with its deep shadowed dark eyes looked suddenly very young. 'I was not thinking of mere friendship, Abby, value it as I do, and always have. I spoke from a more—perhaps more important sensibility.'

He seemed suddenly to have lost his embarrassment and spoke with greater certainty, and now it was her turn to be discomfited.

She got up from her chair in a flurry of soft green taffeta skirts and moved across the room, her hand up to pat her smooth hair into tidiness; a quite unnecessary gesture which spoke clearly of her under-lying confusion.

'There can be no greater sensibility than friendship.'

'Can there not, Abby?' he said gently, and came across the room behind her to put a hand on her arm, and she turned to look up into his face, tipping back her head until she felt the soft knot of her hair on the back of her neck, and knew her face had crimsoned.

'I—really, I do not know, Gideon!' she said after a little pause. He looked closely at her and then nodded, his long face still and quiet and he dropped his hand, and said in a low voice, 'Well, it is a matter to think about, perhaps,' and turned and went back to his chair and sat down composedly.

She stood there uncertainly for a moment, her hand on the little polished table that was at her side, looking at him, and then bent her head in her confusion and saw on the table the little framed miniature of James, the one that had been painted of him just six months before he died, when both had known, though neither had said, that such a picture would be all she would have of him in the years to come.

Across the room, sitting beside the bright fire with his long slender legs outstretched to the blaze, was the boy who had come to her support and guidance in those black and agonizing days when James was dying and then dead; and she looked again at the little painting, at James's quiet pallid face with the reddish hair, so like young Freddy's, glowing above the broad forehead, at the man she had loved so dearly and so passionately that she had abandoned all her family and friends for him. And for a moment she felt so bewildered that she had to close her eyes and breathe deeply to steady herself.

'I can assure you that there would be no change in our present arrangements, Gideon,' she said carefully then, and came back to the chair facing him and settled herself smoothly, and he looked up and smiled.

'I am very glad,' he said simply and it was as though that dangerous moment when so little and so much had been said and almost said had never happened. And she folded her hands on her lap and bent her head and tried to regain her usual composure.

Standing here now in the factory with her heavy alpaca apron over her soft grey gown, drinking strong sweet tea out of a tin mug, she felt again the stir of confusion that evening had created in her, and felt with it a sudden flash of irritation. All had been so smooth and so comfortable for so long; she and Freddy and the manufactory, and Gideon always there in the background, so safe, so secure, so himself; and now for some reason he seemed not to be himself any more. It was very annoying.

She gave herself a little mental shake at that. Of course he had not changed so suddenly. There had been changes in him of course, with the passage of the years, but it was she with her sudden new awareness of him as the person he in truth was, instead of as the picture she seemed always to have held of him, who had been altered. He had been a raw youth in those days when she had first come to know him, when she had been trying to recover from the loss of James, and he from the pain of his father's illness. He had been rather gangling, with his bony wrists and rather thin neck with its prominent Adam's apple, so very young a fifteen-year-old with his tendency to blush and stammer when he spoke to her, that she had felt quite motherly sometimes in her dealings with him. And that had been absurd, she told herself now, for she had been only eighteen herself.

'But I was a widow and the mother of a son,' she whispered into her tin cup. 'I had lived a great deal——'

Perhaps he had lived a great deal, too, in the intervening years? She thought seriously about that, and was puzzled by the stab of feeling that it created in her. Not jealousy, precisely, but a desire to know more of him than she already did. She knew of his parents, of course, of his father's illness and helplessness, his mother's devotion, but beyond that it was all shadowy, remote.

She could imagine him sitting at table with his parents, could actually see how the old man must look, for hadn't he been James's first benefactor, and hadn't he come to see the manufactory once in its early days? But she could not see Gideon at any of the other activities young men might be expected to enjoy. At the theatre, perhaps, or in a drawing room full of people or at a ball——'

'Git goin', yer lazy 'ounds!' Caleb's voice rose shrill and raucous above the soft chatter around her, and she looked up, startled to find that the women were wiping their tin mugs on their aprons and the children were gulping the last dregs of the tea, their usual perquisite, ready to get back to work.

Again she gave herself a mental shake, finished her own tea and gave her mug to Mrs Hobson, who bobbed at the knees as she took it, and old Caleb Garner, the foreman, a tiny man with so many wrinkles in his brown face that he looked like a map, and so toothless that his face seemed to have collapsed like an overripe quince, grinned gummily at her and said, 'We'm startin' on the plaisters, mum, s'mornin', on account young Mr 'Enry says as 'e reckons 'e can get a big run on 'em. Weather's been cruel treacherous, ain't it? Yerss. I reckon as young 'Enry's got the right of it, for onct. They'll be wantin' their plaisters for their congestions an' phlegms an' the like. So we'll be gettin' 'em out today, mum. Unless yer wants summat diff'rent, o'course——' and he twisted his little head and peered up at her, birdlike and sharp as a needle, and she smiled back and said easily, 'Aye, Caleb, that will do capitally! Mr Sydenham knows what he can sell, so we are all in his hands, are we not?'

'You ain't, missus!' Caleb said, and turned to growl at the children who were still lingering beside the tea jug and they went sulkily back to their work benches, ready to pound heavy lumps of kaolin into powder ready to be mixed with wintergreen and oil of cloves to make poultices. 'Us is all at your beck'n'call, and well we all knows it. I tol' Mr 'Enry, I tol' 'im, none of yer orders I foller wivaht missus, and that's the way of it, an' 'e says as 'ow——'

'I know, Caleb,' Abby said, more crisply this time. When Caleb launched himself on one of his regular attempts to remind her how loyal, useful and altogether better and more important than young Henry Sydenham he was, the time had come to put an end to the talk. 'And you are right, of course. Now, as well as the plasters, I'd like some more ipecacuanha mixture put in hand. If the plasters are wanted because of the weather, then the ipecac will be too. Make a couple of gallons, and we'll see how we do. Oh, and the paregoric draught mixture—how's that progressing? Yesterday as I recall, we had no more than three pints in hand——'

She launched gratefully into the day's business, settling Caleb and Joss, the storeman, into a checking of the ingredients needed for the day's output, and then doing her usual round of the benches.

She did not have to for Caleb, who for all his appearance of weakness and frailty was as tough as one of the London sparrows he so closely resembled, having grown up in the gutters supporting himself and a widowed mother as well as a raft of brothers and sisters, was a tough and capable taskmaster. No woman, however tired, however grizzling the baby she might have bound to her back as she worked, would dare to slack when Caleb was about; no child, however small (though no child younger than ten was employed in the factory, for Abby would not take them, not being able to bear seeing such little ones as seven and eight year olds working at her benches) dared fall asleep over his efforts when Caleb's roving eye might fall on them. He could not only be heavy of hand; he could also turn them off, and would without a second thought, for there were plenty more would-be workers teeming outside in the gutters, and he would have no compunction in sending a less than devoted worker back to the hunger and filth outside.

So, he was a good foreman, and Abby was lucky to have him, and knew it; but she liked to walk past each worker's place each day, and had a shrewd notion that her regular appearance had a good effect on them all. She was a lady and they were gutter creatures (though superior gutter creatures, of course, for were they not in regular employment, with homes to go to and clothes to their backs as well as food to their bellies?) and for them to be so close so often to one of the Quality, the people they might see walking remotely about the rich shopping streets like Oxford Street and the Strand, was a rare experience. To be under the same roof as one, even in such conditions as a factory's, was agreeable in the extreme.

They could have such contact with the rich and well fed, of course, if they went to the mission ladies for the gifts of bibles and free soup, but you had to be very humble with them and bow and scrape and be grateful and be told to wash more often (and what an idea, with water having to be carried by the bucketful from the pump, or paid for at tuppence the pail from the water carriers!) and to drink less and to say your prayers regular, grateful to the good Lord for all His gifts. But with Missus, none of this was necessary, for she treated them almost like people of her own sort. At least, she talked civilly to them which was more than Caleb or the other men workers ever did. She was a good lady was Missus, the women and children would tell each other as she walked past their benches every morning, and would grin at her and bend their heads again to their work.

And hard work it was, in all truth. The children were used for the most repetitive labour, pounding whole spices to powder or rubbing down the great iron-hard lumps of clay or zinc, while the women dealt with measuring and mixing, tending the little machines that James had long ago designed and built for his factory. Some were hand operated, with wheels and levers and platforms of heavy metal that moved and turned, creaking laboriously, to cut and roll and coat the pills; some, the more ambitious ones, were equipped with elaborate levers and pulleys and were operated by foot treadles, and they rattled and thumped heavily as they worked.

The machines were getting old now, Abby thought as she moved past them, and saw young Nathaniel Stare oiling and buffing a newly mended arm. He was needed more and more, this self-taught engineer who had come to work for James as a slip of a ten-year-old, and had stayed on to work for his widow. New machinery would cost a lot, but must be thought of. Something else to discuss with Gideon——

She moved across the bare boards, past the great roaring fire, leaving the heavy smell of oil and turpentine and wintergreen behind her to tuck herself into her tiny counting house, with its scrap of red carpet upon the floor, the old mahogany desk and battered armchair and the glassed-in door that kept out the noise and smell but let in light, to settle to preparing the books for the new governess-cum-secretary who was to take up her residence in Paddington Green on Friday coming.

But in reality she was waiting for Gideon, for was not today Wednesday? It was time she came to some sort of understanding of the subtle way the relationship between them had shifted these past few weeks, and she could not do that till she was with him, she told herself.

So, she lifted her head with great eagerness, half an hour later when there was a tap on her glass door, her face alight with pleasure, for it was about the time that Gideon usually arrived. But it was Henry Sydenham who stood there, his hat on the back of his head, his fair hair falling in his eyes, and his round face beaming as he set his fists upon his hips and announced, 'Mrs Caspar! Oh, Mrs Caspar, but you'll never imagine the great piece of business that I have set in hand for us this very morning! You'll never imagine!'

## 11

The room rustled softly with the sound of low-pitched conversation, and William looked about him, well pleased. It had been a gamble, heaven knew, and he was not unused to staking a lot on the single throw of a die; and in this situation, he reminded himself, he had been able to load the die in his favour. He grinned into his collar points. That self-satisfied jumped-up and thoroughly unpleasant sawbones Snow had no doubt found much pleasure in watching his discomfiture at that damned operation, but now he had himself a most enjoyable revenge. To have used Snow as he had to get his father out of the way so that this meeting could be held in the boardroom seemed to William a most deliciously sweet and satisfying retaliation.

Across the room Sir Daniel Cloudesly, the senior Trustee—for he had been one of the two founder Trustees of the hospital with old Kutner, but he was long since dead—stood tall and thin, with his bald head shining egg-like and glossy in the lamplight, listening to the little Pinto who was standing almost on tiptoe to whisper in his ear.

Since he had been knighted by King William, five years ago, a King William suitably grateful for the amount of money Cloudesly's successful engineering projects had poured into the Court, he had become insufferably high in the instep, William knew, and would need careful handling. They would have to appeal to his snobbery, perhaps; there was a man who cared more for privilege and propriety than anything else, a fact that could well be used in dealings with him. Pinto, on the other hand; now there was a different kettle of fish altogether.

William looked thoughtfully at the little Jew, with his narrow dark eyes and sallow skin, his neat and finicky little body, and wondered. He knew, better than most, that Pinto was far from being the traditional Jewish money-grubber of whom people complained even while using them. There were Jews in Lombard Street, heaven knew, who had a vast scorn for any Christian and would cheerfully fleece them of every penny and feel themselves justified. But not Pinto. William could still remember what had happened when he had tried to borrow money from his banking house. The arrogant devil! William thought viciously, with his talk of honour and duty! All because he had attempted to use his father's name to cover a loan, and had not realized that Pinto knew what Abel's signature looked like. But he had been honourable, in his nasty way; he had not told Abel of the encounter he had had with his son, so there had been no repercussions. But there must be care used in the handling of the little Pinto.

William moved his eyes to the next group, where Rupert stood twirling his Madeira between his fingers so that the light caught the swirl of the twisted glass in the stem to send winking patterns across the polished table. He was standing with his head in its usual half-bent posture, looking up from beneath those sardonic brows at Buckle the brewer, whose vast belly with its rope of gold chains stuck out from between the flaps of his frock coat like some great globe. The perfect advertisement for his own brew, thought William, looking with distaste at the man's jowly face, glowing damply as he steamed gently in his own fat; and then almost unconsciously smoothed one hand over his own incipient paunch and looked away to the corner where Ross and Porteous were standing side by side for all the world like a pair of black crows, in identical gleaming white linen, black broadcloth, and with no hint of gold or any adornment at all apart from a sober watch-chain in dull silver to spoil the funereal set of their sacerdotal waistcoats.

But though they looked like clerics, dressed like them, even stood sometimes with their hands in a praying posture like them, there was nothing of the unworldly about these two attorneys at law. The sour visage of the one and the more learned cast of countenance of the other were fronts for sharp legal brains and healthy appetites for money, with no unnecessary scruples about how that money was made. Spirits of the age, both of 'em, William thought fondly, looking at these two most powerful of his allies. And Ross caught his eye and sketched a slightly mocking bow, and pulled from his pocket a heavy turnip watch which he consulted with a portentous air; William nodded briefly and moved into the centre of the room, to stand beside the table with its tray bearing a decanter of glowing amber Madeira.

'More wine, gentlemen? No? Ah—hmm—then, I think—business. Yes? Busy men, all of us, and I have no wish to waste more time than is necessary.'

'And, of course there's no knowing when m'father will return,' Rupert said softly and came to refill his glass, coolly taking the decanter from William's hand. William flushed brick red, and opened his mouth to speak, but Pinto was ahead of him.

'Is there some reason why we should be alarmed at the return of Mr Lackland?' he asked sharply, his head turning from one brother to the other, but looking faintly ridiculous, for each topped him by the best part of a foot, and he had to tip his chin like a child seeking for sweetmeats.

'None at all,' William said shortly, throwing Rupert a furious glance. 'None at all, Mr Pinto. He will have to know soon enough of the matters we discuss today, but I felt it would be—shall we say *kinder*—to discuss the situation with all of you first—as the people most concerned—so that we can, well—settle any necessary matters with the least distress to all concerned. Shall we be seated?'

They sat down, Sir Daniel taking the chair at the top as though by right, and then leaning back and tucking his chin into his collar so that he looked like a bad-tempered penguin.

'For those of you who do not know the reason for this special meeting of the Trustees of Queen Eleanor's this afternoon,' he said heavily, 'I must tell you it was requested by Mr William Lackland here, his brother Mr Rupert Lackland supporting, in order to bring to our notice matters pertaining to finance of which they believe we should have knowledge.' He coughed, and folded his hands on the table before him. 'Has anyone any comments to make before we open the meeting to Mr William Lackland?'

'I am concerned at the absence of Mr Abel Lackland,' Mr Pinto said fretfully. 'This is, after all, his hospital, and I would have thought that——'

'Ahem!' Again Cloudesly produced the affected little cough which he used so often to punctuate his conversation. 'The hospital is by no means the *property* of Mr Abel Lackland! He founded it, most certainly, gave considerable personal moneys to it, was the man who set the establishment in motion. But the property itself—the land, the buildings—are in the hands of the Governors, *ourselves*. I am certainly not prepared to sit here at these Trustee meetings merely to underwrite any decisions already made by one man! If this charitable institution is to be run in a Godfearing and proper manner, then we must set ourselves to the task of doing so with humility and a ready acceptance of our duty. It is our duty to accept the burden of care of Queen Eleanor's hospital. It is not our duty to always make ourselves subservient to the will of one man——'

William smiled again. There had been many occasions when Cloudesly had smarted under the whip of his father's tongue over the years, and well all of them knew it. It was indeed amusing to see how Abel's own actions were contributing to his sons' desires and plans. If only the old man knew, William thought gleefully, and returned his attention to Pinto who was speaking again.

'I would not be happy to be involved in any matters of which Mr Lackland was not cognisant,' he was saying. 'I quite accept what you say, Sir Daniel, but there is a matter of honour here—it is Mr Lackland who has worked so hard, done so much—he is a great surgeon——'

'Oh, come, man!' Porteous said, and his voice was thin and high and sounded a little absurd in a man of his sober mien. 'We all know of the gratitude you feel for him since he cured your—wife, was it?—of a quinsy, but that doesn't make him God Almighty! We can discuss any matters we choose whether he be here to listen or no! He is only admitted to Trustee meetings as a courtesy, by virtue of his position as Chief Surgeon, after all! No doubt your partiality for him is understood and allowed for, for we all know what it is to be concerned about a *wife's* health!' and he looked sideways at Ross who snickered softly, for Pinto's uxoriousness was well known; there was little he would ever do, not even obey the call of nature, it was ill-heartedly rumoured, without discussing it first with his formidable wife, a habit which the other Trustees found most extraordinary; indeed, positively foolish.

'It was my daughter,' Pinto said, and then reddened and subsided. But he sat with his face watchful, and his eyes moved from speaker to speaker as the meeting went on, never missing one word that was spoken.

'Well, *à nos moutons*, gentlemen!' Cloudesly said and ostentatiously took snuff, with a would-be elegant turn of the wrist. 'I have to be at the House of Commons before they rise, Lackland, so I'll thank you to put some speed into the proceedings.'

William stood up. It seemed to him obscurely necessary that he do so, that such respectful behaviour on his part would show them all that he acted only from the most crystal clear of motives, the most caring of reasons. He coughed and took from his breast pocket a small sheaf of papers and spread them on the table in front of him.

'Well, Sir Daniel, gentlemen.' He sketched an ingratiating bow towards the head of the table, and Cloudesly responded with a faint lift of his upper lip, but did not look displeased. 'There are matters of finance that have come to my notice that I believe must be brought to yours. In simple terms, gentlemen, I believe that this hospital is not being run, in financial matters, as it should be, and it concerns me deeply that this should be so.'

He lifted his eyes from his paper for a moment to look at his brother sitting opposite him with his arms folded and his chin tucked in as he watched him, and tried to see some message of approbation in their mocking depths. But Rupert did not move or change his expression at all, and William again coughed, and went on.

'I have been taking care of the Wapping manufactory for some three years now, since old Hunnisett died, and in the last six months I have made an experiment regarding the use of moneys there that will, I suspect, tell you a great deal of my thinking.'

Again he looked up and swept his gaze around the table. Porteous and Ross were looking at him with their eyebrows slightly raised; Rupert had not moved, and Pinto was watching him with eyes as sharp and wary as a fox. Only Buckle, sitting with his belly almost resting on the table, seemed to be uninterested; his pale blue eyes were wide open and staring at William, but had a glassiness about them that betrayed his inattention. William turned his head, and again chose to address Sir Daniel directly.

'You know of course, that we have two sides to our work at Wapping. We manufacture medicines and pills and potions in bulk, for use here for the patients in the wards and for those who come for the outdoors care that is so freely given, and we make similar substances for sale to shops and other establishments. It has long seemed to me that to give away, as we do, the extremely costly medicaments to the scum of these gutters——' and he waved a comprehensive hand at the window which showed a grey and lowering March afternoon sky between its heavy red curtains '—is foolish in the extreme.'

From the corner of his eye he saw Pinto lean forward, his mouth open to speak, and without moving his head he went on very swiftly, 'If the care that is given to these gutter people were of an order to make them fit and well, decent working members of the deserving poor, there would be a Christian virtue in giving them this care, whatever its cost. But in fact, Sir Daniel, gentlemen, I have proof *positive* that the expense being lavished on these people is wasted, quite wasted!'

'What proof?' Sir Daniel said. 'Documentary proof?'

'Better than that,' William said triumphantly. '*Financial* proof!' And again he put his hand in his pocket and this time drew forth a sheet of heavy deckle-edged paper, and put it down with a flourish on the table before him.

'What is that?' Sir Daniel sat quite motionless staring at the piece of paper with the faint sneer still upon his face and making no move to pick it up.

'A Banker's note for the sum of twelve hundred pounds,' William said softly, and at once Porteous leaned forwards and picked it up and began to scan it.

'It is made out to the Trustees of Queen Eleanor's,' he said slowly at length and then looked sharply at William. 'Where did this come from?'

William produced a smile of sheer pleasure. 'Why, Mr Porteous,' he said in the most silky of tones. 'I told you! I have carried out an experiment this last six months. The source of that money is that experiment.'

And more besides, and more besides, a little voice cried gleefully inside his head, and he thought of the fat little sum lying snugly in a private bank, quite unconnected with the hospital, and in the harmless and unknown name of John Grimes. 'I told you,' he said aloud, again, and slowly looked round the table, well pleased, and almost preening.

Even Buckle was alert now, and Rupert said sharply, 'You had best get on with it, William. There's no knowing when he may choose to return. There's a bad injury to a femur above stairs on which he'd like to amputate today if he can, and he'll not spend more time than he must in Westminster with Snow. Get on with it.'

'It is a simple matter, gentlemen,' William said. 'Quite frankly, I have not been carrying out the making of the usual receipts for the hospital medical supplier in the last six months. I have used only ten per cent of the more costly ingredients in each batch. Furthermore I have been making the substances sold to the outside shops and dispensaries in half strength—while not, of course, precisely telling the customer that this was so——'

A faint ripple of amusement spread from Buckle to Porteous and Ross, and William grinned even more widely and went on, 'I have, of course, been buying but not at the usual rates, making sure only that we had enough of the more expensive materials to carry on from day to day. And I know that it matters not one whit if we economize in this matter and that it does no harm to any one, for in that six months not one complaint of poor goods has reached me from the paying customers, and certainly there seems to have been no complaint from those using the drugs and medicines here at Nellie's—Queen Eleanor's.'

Rupert suddenly smiled, a wide and disarming smile, his eyes fixed on William, who reddened slightly, but ignored him. 'And what right would they have to complain anyway? They are set for the grave from the moment they are born, and it is as well that they are, in my estimation. They fill the slums and the stews and the rookeries like the vermin they are, they do no decent work, they spawn thieves and foot-pads and every form of vice and evil, and my father sits here and demands that we lavish all our moneys and our efforts on them, pouring good money down their throats, and to what purpose? When they are given inferior treatment it makes no difference! They die like flies whatever is done for 'em! My father, gentlemen, while I of course owe him the duty of a son, is—how shall I explain it? Rupert—you are a surgeon too! It will come better from you, I know! Will you tell these gentlemen just how exercised in our minds we have been about him and his behaviour here at the hospital?'

Rupert sat still for a moment and then nodded, and William sat down, well content. He had done his part, and done it well; it was now up to Rupert to take over, as they had planned, to speak to these men in a way that would make them see, as clearly as he did, the necessity for changes to be made in the running of the hospital. And the necessity to deal with Abel Lackland.

Rupert remained very still for a moment longer, looking down at the table, and then he lifted his head and spoke in a very soft tone of voice, but one which carried a great deal of conviction.

'Gentlemen, I will not hide from you the fact that this is a painful moment for me. And for my brother. We know our filial duty and would wish to discharge it as would any Christian gentleman. But we find, in all conscience, that we cannot go on as we are without apprising you of the facts.'

He stopped and looked round at them all, and they looked back. Damn him, William thought irritably. He has made them listen much better than I did. He looks so damned knowing—but he's no better than I am! He shall discover that, for I'll not let him ride *me*. Wait until my father's dealt with and then I'll show him——

'—my experience of such matters is quite considerable,' Rupert was saying. 'Afflictions of the mind are many, and I have made it my business to develop an awareness of them. And I must tell you that it is my considered opinion as a medical man that my father is developing *la folie de grandeur*. He believes himself to be above all men's touch. He believes that he knows better than any other how matters should be dealt with. He is convinced that none but he can choose what shall be done in this hospital. Despite, gentlemen, the fact that you are the persons *meant* to make the final decisions! You could put this behaviour down to mere—shall we say—self assurance. But I do not think it is this. I think he is moving into the condition of frank madness, when he will brook no opposition to his decisions. You have all, in your time, had your brushes with him, I believe, gentlemen——'

There was a silence. Cloudesly was sitting staring at the table, and William looked at him and wanted to grin. He remembered all too well the time his father had stood in this room and shouted at this tall thin man in such stentorian tones that he could be heard over half the hospital, about the need for spending more money on the beds and the linen; he remembered how his father had won that argument by the sheer weight of his personality, and he had no doubt that Cloudesly was remembering it too.

And on the other side of the table, Ross, who had been dismissed by Abel at one memorable Trustee's meeting as a 'narrow half-wit, not fit to run a brothel, never mind a hospital'; at Porteous, who Abel so despised that he never bothered to hide the fact and never addressed a word directly to him; at Buckle, who had been referred to by Abel in his hearing as 'a bladder of lard, a glutton, and gormandizer who could not keep his mind, such as it was, above his belly'. Oh, they all had cause to treat Rupert's account of Abel with seriousness. It would soothe many smarting wounds that Abel had inflicted over the years to regard him as not in full control of his wits.

'Well? What would you have us do?'

William leaned forwards. 'I would ask you to accept this money saved for you, and ask you to consider seriously whether we should not make every effort to save more in the self-same way——'

'—and also to consider whether or not the time has come to send my father away from here, and with him his gutter patients,' Rupert cut in, 'and to look at Queen Eleanor's in a new way, and plan to make it the sort of establishment I believe it could be. A more agreeable, successful and certainly financially rewarding one.'

It was Buckle who responded to that, staring at Rupert with his pale blue eyes narrowed. 'How do you propose to do *that*?' he wheezed huskily. 'Make a hospital financially rewarding? Can't be done!'

Rupert smiled that very sweet wide smile of his again and said softly, 'Oh, Mr Buckle, I assure you it can! It should be a hospital for the better sort of person, you see. Not these poor useless hulks that fill the beds now, but decent citizens and householders.'

His smile widened even more. 'People who will pay for their care and treatment, do you see. Who will be glad to have decent medical attention in a pleasant place, and will pay heavily for the privilege. It is an interesting idea, is it not? And only my father, I imagine, with his— peculiar passion for the most undeserving of the poor, will be stubborn enough and arrogant enough, in his incipient madness, to deny that fact.'

## 12

'I cannot pretend I am entirely happy about it,' Abby said. 'No, do not look so put about, Henry. There are matters here of which you have no knowledge and you cannot understand my thinking. I am not complaining of your efforts to obtain this customer for us. Indeed, no, for I can quite see you would regard it as a most excellent piece of business——'

She looked across the room at Gideon, who was standing with his back to the glazed door, his coat held over his arm, and his glossy top hat in one hand, for he had arrived only moments after Henry had come bursting in with his news. 'I am sure you understand, Gideon?'

'I am not sure that I do,' he said carefully, coming further into the room and setting his coat across the back of the armchair and his hat beside it before settling himself into his usual posture of legs-out-stretched comfort. 'No—that is not fair. I understand, I believe. But do I sympathize? That is where I suspect we may disagree.'

'I wish you'd tell me, Mrs Caspar, what this is all about,' Henry said fretfully, and pushed his hair out of his eyes, and for the first time realized that he still had his hat on the back of his head, and snatched it off with his face reddening. It was difficult sometimes to remember that his employer was entitled to the courtesies that a gentleman usually paid to ladies, because he never really thought of her as a lady. But now, with this sudden exhibition of capriciousness, her sex was brought home to him with some force and for the first time in all the years he had worked for Caspar's he found himself looking at her with a some-what jaundiced gaze.

'You must take pity on my foolishness, Mrs Caspar,' he said now, and allowed an aggrieved note to creep into his voice. 'For I must be foolish not to comprehend what the rub in our way might well be. I come in to tell you that I am well in the way of getting one of the biggest—indeed, positively the *very* biggest—order we have ever had, an order that could keep the whole manufactory going with no other customers at all unless I miss my bet, and instead of being hat over the moon, as I thought you would be, you tell me you are not happy! I must be foolish, indeed——'

'Oh, Henry, of course you are not!' she said, with a return of some of her usual crispness. 'I told you, there are matters here you do not know of which colour my view of this order. And let us not get too excited, after all. You have not precisely brought in a definite order, have you? The man has only asked you for samples and a tariff.'

'Only!' Henry stared at her, and again pushed his hair out of his eyes. 'Only, Mrs Caspar? How can you talk so? Don't you know as we offer the most competitive prices of anyone? That there ain't another apothecary anywhere that can compete with us? Indeed, you do me an injustice, ma'am, to imply I can't get this order written firmly in my book before the week is out! Gettin' Conran to ask me for the samples and prices was where the skill lay, if you'll forgive my bumptiousness in saying as much! I've been angling for this contact this last three months! My old friend Matthew Hodgkin let drop to me that the hospital's own manufactory was getting very expensive, and that Conran was getting notions about it all—reckoned the man that was running it was lining his pockets more than somewhat—and I've been nibbling away ever since. And now I come home with the bacon, and you say——'

'Henry, do be quiet!' Abby said wearily. 'I have my own reasons for saying what I do and I do not think they concern you——'

'I think you may be wrong there, Abby, if you will permit me to say so,' Gideon said quietly. 'You have made an arrangement to include Henry within the business on a commission basis. When you did but pay him a salary it was perhaps different. Now, when he enjoys a percentage of the goods he sells, he is entitled, I am sure you will agree, to know why you receive his best success with such scant pleasure.'

'Thank you, Mr Henriques,' Henry said, and turned to look for a chair, at last mollified enough to relax a little, and Abby too sat down behind her tall desk, and set her elbows on it and rested her chin on her hands and tried to think. There was a silence in the little room, broken only by the muffled rattle and thump from the machines outside and a faint hiss from the coals that burned in the little corner fireplace.

'I will tell you the problem, Henry,' she said abruptly, at last. 'And I must ask you to keep your tongue between your teeth, because it is largely personal.' She glanced up at Henry who was sitting very upright on the little wooden chair and looking at her with an expression of high expectancy on his round young face.

'Do you know the name of the man who is in prime control of Queen Eleanor's hospital?'

He looked mystified. 'The man who runs it? Conran is the Bursar and controls the spending of money, and as I understand it he is answerable to Trustees—or—oh, do you mean the surgeon? Mr Lackland? Everyone knows Mr Lackland! Why, he founded the place— came over from Tavistock Street, so I've been told, when they rebuilt all round the Strand there—but know him—oh, no, Mrs Caspar, and glad I am to say that I don't! No one in their right mind wants to know such a surgeon as him, except he can't help himself. I deal with apothecaries—and the physicians sometimes—but not the surgeons. And that is how I like it. They're a hard lot, surgeons. Let the instrument makers and the resurrectionists and their like deal with them and have joy of them, not honest apothecaries' merchants, like us——'

'He is also an apothecary,' Abby said, almost absently, and then went on in an almost casual tone, 'My name before I was wed was Abigail Lackland.'

Henry stared at her, frowning, and there was a short silence. Then he said uncertainly, 'You, Mrs Caspar? A relation, then? Well, you don't say so!' He shook his head, grinned widely, and began to laugh. 'D'you mean to tell me as I've been beating my head against that wall trying to get satisfaction out of that dried up Conran, when you could have gone and extracted the juice from the very top? Well, I'll be——'

'You find it amusing, Henry? Then you lack imagination,' Abigail said crisply. 'If I do not go to Mr Lackland, do you not think it is possibly because it would be—an—an embarrassment to do so?'

Henry sobered at once and stared at her, trying to rearrange his thoughts. As a much loved younger son in a large and very affectionate family of market gardeners (who took a great pride in Henry's learning, for an apothecary's assistant was a good cut above a mere radish grower) he had some difficulty in rearranging his view of family attachments and what was proper behaviour between relations; and his uncertainty returned. 'He is a very *distant* connection, perhaps?' he said carefully.

'He is my father,' Abby said quietly. Henry blinked and again shook his head in bewilderment, and then blurted out, 'Your—*father*? Then why must you deal with business matters as you do? I understood you to be a helpless widow, with none to aid you, and this was why—I explained to my mother that was the reason when she was so——' He suddenly flushed a deep crimson, the tide of colour rising in his face under his heavy yellow hair in a most ludicrous fashion, and Abby could not help but laugh.

'Oh dear, Henry, did she worry and fret when you came to work for me? Fear you were in the hands of some wicked adventuress? Well, she was right to be so careful, for you are a charming young man of great gifts, and would indeed be interesting to such a one! I hope she is now more easy in her mind about you, after these past three years!'

'Oh, indeed, yes, ma'am! I am sorry, ma'am—I meant no impertinence, none at all——' Henry muttered, becoming more and more confused, and again Abby laughed softly and said, 'I must explain a little more, I think. I hope you will understand. I was the oldest daughter of my parents, and grew up in—well, I was much in my father's confidence. It was from him I learned what I know of the affairs of the apothecary's trade, and it was in his shop in Piccadilly that I first learned the rudiments of working as I do on the book-keeping I now deal with here. He taught me much, in many ways, and gave me opportunities to use my own abilities for business that are usually denied to mere females. But my father and I parted bad friends when I was wed. It does happen, you must know, Henry, in many families. That it has not in yours, and that you have no experience of the bitterness and sadness that can ensue when parents and children lose affection for each other, is your good fortune——'

She stopped again and then went on painfully, 'And I must say that we did not precisely lose affection for each other, my father and I.

We—we were so very close through all my life for we have much in common in our characters, and understood each other well, and then James—and the pill-making machines, and——'

She was never to know quite what happened then. It was as though in some way her guard had been let down without her knowledge, that in talking to Henry and being so genuinely amused by his gauche yet charming confusion she had allowed her usually constant control over her deepest feelings to slip. For as she talked, she found the memories came seeping into her mind, first slowly, and then in a sudden great flood. She could see James in her mind's eye, her James as he had been in those days of their strange and strained and yet so passionately happy courtship, could see his figure in all its dear detail in a way she had not been able to for many years. The reddish hair, the worried look that had always been on that pale face, the furrowed forehead bespeaking such concern and tenderness for her; all rose before her vision in knife-edged clarity, while behind him in that theatre of her mind stood Abel, his head bent and looking up at her from beneath his heavy dark brows with those narrow green eyes that she had known and loved so well, an expression of anger and pain and a curious yearning filling his face. And she closed her own eyes sharply, trying to banish those unasked-for visions, and shook her head and tried to speak again, but her voice was choked in her chest; to her own amazement and a curious helpless rage she felt the tears climb needle-sharp into her throat, come pushing against her clenched teeth, up and on, thrusting cruelly against her nose and tightly closed eyelids, until, for the first time, she was weeping, great sobs trying to escape her as she sat with her fists clenched on the desk before her, and tears forcing themselves through her lids to go coursing hot and salty down her cheeks.

It was as though a very small and coolly-collected Abby was sitting perched up in a corner of the room, looking down in unemotional curiosity at the figure sitting at the desk with sensible sleeves set over the cuffs of her grey gown, wrapped in her alpaca apron, her hair pulled into a neat soft knot at the nape of her neck and her face twisted into an ugly grimace as tears ran down the furrows in her soft flesh and her nose ran a little, like that of a child too miserable to know or care.

The little observing Abby high in the corner watched as Gideon stood up swiftly, opened the door and hustled out the bewildered

Henry, thrusting his hat into his hand, then pulling across the door the little curtain of shabby sprigged cotton to close out the factory beyond the glazing.

He came back across the room then to where the real Abby sat still and tense, her fists clenched white-knuckled on the desk before her and making no attempt to dry her tears, for her arms were trembling so much it would not have been possible anyway.

He stood beside her for one brief moment, and then set his hand to the back of her chair and pulled it round, so that the desk no longer blockaded her away from him, and at this point the watching little Abby merged again with herself and she felt his hands, warm and very tender yet firm in their touch on both of her tightly-clenched fists and she heard his voice murmuring softly and very soothingly, although she could not recognize the words he used.

And then he was on his knees in front of her, had moved his hands so that he held each of her arms at the elbow, and gently he urged her forwards, until slowly and gently her rigidly-held back bent and then swayed and she let her neck relax too, until she was sitting there curled up in her chair but with his arms about her and her head resting on the rough fabric of his frock coat, weeping noisily and with the helpless misery of a heartbroken child.

How long they remained so she could not tell, for she abandoned herself to the luxury of her distress, letting the sounds of her crying pour from her to be muffled in his coat, but gradually the paroxysm passed its peak and then began to subside until she was sobbing gently against him, luxuriating, almost, in the feel of the cloth against her wet cheek, the smell of the damp serge and the sense of agreeable exhaustion that filled her chest and limbs.

He moved softly then, fumbling in his pocket with his right hand while still holding her close with his other arm, and then she felt his handkerchief, soft cambric smelling faintly of bay rum, against her face, and she sniffed, and obligingly he applied the handkerchief to her nose and said softly, 'Blow!' and she did and then, at last aware of herself, pulled away from him and sat up and scrubbed at her cheeks with the handkerchief and smoothed her hair with one still shaking hand.

'I—please to forgive so shocking an exhibition, Gideon,' she said huskily. 'I cannot imagine—I do not know—perhaps I have been overtaken by some irritation of the nerves due to an impending disorder of some sort. A fever perhaps—I felt quite well this morning but—indeed, I cannot imagine——' and she shook her head, and again blew her nose and looked very directly at him, difficult as it was to meet his eyes, for she was most ashamed of her outburst.

He was still kneeling there in front of her, sitting back on his heels with his hands resting on each knee and looking up at her with an expression of such warmth and kindness on his face that she felt her already hot cheeks respond, and she wanted to look away, but felt somehow it was necessary that she hold her gaze, that not to do so would be in some way even more shameful than the tears she had shed; so she sat there looking steadfastly at him.

And he looked back at her, at the reddened nose and the slightly swollen eyes and the blotchiness that still filled her cheeks, and thought he had never seen her look more desirable and charming and altogether everything he most admired in a woman. That woebegone face between the neat, even severe, style of her hair above a gown so unadorned and practical, made an almost ridiculous contrast. She looked both mature and interesting, yet so vulnerable and so very young, that he wanted, yet again, to hold her close and croon soothing sounds into her ear, to make her safe and happy and free her of the need ever to weep again. So, kneeling there looking up at her, Gideon had to face the truth that he had been trying to deny for so many months, the reality of a situation that he had tried so hard to convince himself was within his own control, yet he now had to admit had him totally in its grip.

'Dear Abby,' he said very simply. 'Dear, dear Abby, I do love you so very much. More than you can possibly imagine.'

## 13

Abel had chosen to walk from Gower Street to the hospital, refusing the blandishments of the cab drivers, even though it would be the third time that day he had covered the mile or so that lay between them, swiftly traversing the windy grey streets in that long loping stride of his.

He had first walked through the dawn-dark streets to the hospital from his home just after six in the morning, following a hasty breakfast of bread and butter and bitter coffee provided by a neat and alert Miss Ingoldsby (and it never entered his head to wonder why it was that she was always up and waiting for him in the breakfast room, whatever time he chose to leave his bed, merely accepting her presence as being as natural and as unneedful of explanation as the rising of the sun each morning) and had worked there operating and dealing with street patients until eleven o'clock.

Then, more black coffee, this time provided by Nancy, yet another woman whose eternal presence and automatic care of him he took for granted, and the return walk to Gower Street, He had dealt with private patients there until three in the afternoon, and had hated it as much as he ever did.

Oh, to be sure, sometimes the private patients would come to him with real ills that warranted his time and effort, and for them he could show gentleness, concern, all the attributes that his hospital patients took for granted. But too many of them were frippery women, attracted by his dark good looks and heavy brooding air which they were stupid enough to consider romantic; and they he despised so heartily that he could hardly bear to speak to them civilly, for few of them had really interesting symptoms, and those complaints they did have could usually be traced to over-indulgence in food and wine and laziness.

He would tell them so, most brusquely, and charge them twice his usual fees, and they would meekly tolerate his animadversions on their behaviour and personal habits and pay all he asked to quiet Miss Ingoldsby, who kept his accounts with the same meticulous care she gave his household, and go away swooning with the experience to tell their friends he was as coarse and cruel as any footpad, but made them feel *so* much better; and then would come back again and again, and bring their friends.

So Abel would grit his teeth, and go on treating them with scant patience and downright rudeness, just as his old friend John Abernethy, who had taught medicine at St Bartholomew's twenty years ago, had advised him.

'They pay the rent and the butcher and the other damned duns, these wretched people,' Abernethy had growled at the young Abel setting himself up in his first private practice. 'And the worse you speak to 'em, the better off they are.'

And he had been right. It was close on ten years since Abernethy had died, Abel thought now, making his way back again towards Endell Street, but nothing changes. Private patients are as stupid as ever, and still must be tolerated because of the need to make a living, God damn it! If only it were possible to work only in the hospital, where there was real illness, real need of him. If only he did not have to pay the way of so many who depended on him, both at home and at Endell Street. If only!

He tucked his chin deeper into the beaver collar of his coat as he went hurrying along Gower Street with the wind whipping mischievously at his ankles and making his coat flap heavily about his knees, past the heavy new buildings of University College and on through the budding greenness of Bedford Square.

Ahead of him Oxford Street teemed and roared with traffic, its cursing drivers and plunging sweating horses and the great crush of clattering swaying carriages and cabs and carts pushing against each other through the mud of the crossings. That hasn't changed, he thought sourly, as he plunged into it to make his way across the greasy cobbles through the hooves and sparking iron-ringed wheels with all the eel-like swiftness of a street arab, for the skills he had learned long ago in his gutter childhood were something else that remained unaltered.

Moving onwards through the stinking narrow alleys and past the filthy hovels that flanked each side—and which were held together by little more than the accreted dirt of decades of human misery and degradation, and so thrust together in painful tightness that no inch of habitable space was wasted by the rapacious landlords who owned the properties—he felt the old depression creeping up on him.

He had been born—so far as he knew—in just such a hovel as one of these; had somehow survived the dead weight of the poverty of these slums, had grown strong and clever and impudent enough to actually gain pleasure and knowledge from them. But then he had escaped; and fortunate though that escape had been it was not complete, for his painful childhood had left a canker behind. As long as he could remember he had been eaten with the urgent desire to do something about this hateful network of decayed and miserable dwellings where hundreds of thousands of people eked out their miserable existences. Every day he walked through this way; every day he suffered a little more at the sight of it all. It was foul, it was evil and he hated it with a hate that bit deeply into his mind, making him ever more sour, more morose and more angry. He could see no redeeming aspects anywhere he looked in these tumbling stinking acres in the heart of prosperous London.

Yet they were there. The flaring windows of the gin palaces might offer no real escape from the misery of life in Seven Dials, might in truth add a greater burden of starvation and cruelty and agonizing pain to the people they filled with raw cheap spirit and then threw into the alleys to die in sodden misery; but while they lit the dripping gutters and sour dirt-encrusted walls with their cheerful light, they gave a little warmth to the view, a glimpse of laughter and joy and human pleasure.

And there were some people who looked less grey and dejected and swollen with hunger than others. Girls whose young prettiness could be seen beneath their dirt, who had decked themselves with cheap beads and gewgaws they bought from the street vendors and from the market in Leather Lane, over towards Holborn, whenever they could steal or cadge a penny for them; children who danced, barefoot and ragged but with vast enjoyment and shrill giggles and shouts to the tinny music of the hurdy-gurdy man; whistling boys who bought—or stole—for themselves hot mutton pies from the many reeking steaming cookshops along the alleys, and then went skipping across the mud filled with satisfaction at their feasts; even the thin and hungry women in their threadbare shawls, standing gossiping in the corners as he went by, showed in their loitering their sense of pleasure in the imminence of spring, for windy though the March afternoon was, there was some hint of warmth in the fetid air, a promise of faint blueness in the slivers of sky that showed above the crooked broken chimneys and the sway-backed rooftops above their heads.

He had needed this walk this afternoon, more than a little; not for the value of its physical effects but because he was still most exercised in his mind about the matter of William and the manufactory. He was puzzled too, for Conran had told him that morning, when he had gone to see him about the matter of taking in two more students whose fees would go towards employing the extra nurse of when Nancy stood sorely in need, that 'the Trustees had said he was on no account to make no changes in the establishment without it first came before them.'

Abel's brows had snapped down at that. 'Oh? And when did the Trustees give such instructions?' he had asked. 'For there has been no meeting since——'

And Conran had smiled and said innocently, 'Oh, sir, did you not know? Why, there was a special meeting here yesterday. Just a short one, do you see, but a meeting none the less, and after, Sir Daniel himself did me the honour to come here to my little sanctum and give me my instructions. Mind you, sir, I was not told anything about changing anything I'd already done—only about future changes, do you see. So I said naught about the matter of you agreeing I should see at what sort of prices we could buy medicines elsewhere——'

The Trustees meeting at the hospital without his knowledge? That had been most strange! Abel had mulled that thought over as Conran had gone prosing on.

'A young man of whom I have great hopes,' he was saying. 'Bright, you know, sir, and most respectful—*most* respectful. An unusual quality in young men these days. *Some* young men——' and he had looked sideways at Abel to see if he had recognized the dig at William. 'And more than willing to let us have samples and prices to the best of our needs and his supplying. He says as he can save up to full twenty-five per cent on our present outgoings, and you said yourself, sir, as if Wapping proved too costly for us to use, why you would close it and let us buy elsewhere and Mr Sydenham is a young man as I think will give us excellent service——'

'Yes, no doubt,' Abel had said absently. 'No doubt. I leave the matter with you. As long as you keep your tongue between your teeth, and get on with what's to be done, I'm content enough.' He turned as though to leave the little office and then came back and said abruptly, 'Who called this Trustees' meeting?'

'Why, as to that, sir, I'm sure I couldn't say——' Conran looked sharply at him, his head on one side. 'To be sure, sir, I assumed as you was absent for your own reasons. Knowing as I do the way you feel plagued by the waste of time in the boardroom, I made sure as the reason you was not there was—well, sir, shall we say your own deliberate forgetfulness. But if they go meeting without telling you at all, why, sir, then I would say there was matters afoot that——'

Abel had pulled his thoughts together at that point and looked sharply at the old man who was staring at him with a most knowing and penetrating gaze, and said quickly, 'You presume too much, Conran, as ever! The meeting indeed was one that escaped my memory. I have better things to do than sit prosing like foolish old women nodding over a dish of tea.'

But all the same he had sent a messenger with a note to Sir Daniel, demanding to know why he had not been apprised of yesterday's meeting in time to attend it, and seeking to know what had been decided, for how else could he run the affairs of Nellie's? The answer, he hoped, would be waiting his return to Endell Street. Until he received it there was no point in considering the matter further.

Instead, as he picked his way past a costermonger's stall where onions and carrots and bunches of earth-encrusted turnips were being sold by a shrill child in a torn gown and wearing a man's flat cap on her tumbled hair, over the slippery mess beside a neighbouring itinerant seller who was plucking and gutting scrawny chickens and

132

throwing the offal on the stones at his feet, he thought about William.

Even after seeing that operation the wretched boy had been unable to understand what it was his father was trying to explain to him, but had stood there in the drawing room at Gower Street, his hands in his trouser pockets, his legs straddling the hearth in his favourite pose of easy devil-may-care man-of-the-town and stared sullenly back at Abel as he had talked, and talked and talked. And all he would say in response was that 'there had been no dirty dealings, if that was what his father suspected', which had infuriated Abel even further, for he had made no such accusations; he was concerned only with efficiency, and so he said in very round terms. And William had simply stood and stared at him with eyes as round and hard as pebbles and shrugged his shoulders.

Thinking of that now, as he walked on along St George's Street towards the pump at Broad Street, thence to bear eastwards through the slightly more respectable alleys and narrow lanes to Endell Street and the hospital, the decision moved full fledged into his mind. He had thought about it, been angered by it, and now he knew what was to be done. He would not go to Wapping to check on stocks as William had tried to goad him into doing. The amount of time that would waste was absurd, and he suspected William knew he would feel this, and that this was why he had suggested it. No, he would waste no more time at all. He would close Wapping altogether. If Conran indeed could supply them with such savings through this man he knew why suffer this wretched problem any longer? The time had long since gone when he had felt any real interest in either the manufactory, or the spice warehouse and business of which it was a part. Jesse Constam had cared about it in his time, had left it with its valuable revenues to Dorothea, and thus it had become a part of the founding of the hospital. But its time had passed, and to own it any longer was more than a waste of time—it was foolish. He would sell it, just as he had sold the shop in Piccadilly, after Abby——

Again, he refused to allow himself to think of Abby, and instead set himself to thinking about William again. Something would have to be done to set him to work, in such a way that he could be watched and chivvied and generally taught the importance of his business. He might not be a surgeon, but he had been taught to be an apothecary, after all, and could be trained further under his father's eye to become some sort of a physician, no doubt, if not a particularly gifted one. Abel thought suddenly of John Snow, so very mature and developed a man as he was, yet still young enough to be his son, and wondered bleakly why none of his own sons had turned out as capable as that taciturn Northerner, as willing to listen and learn and yet to think for themselves.

He stopped on the corner of Broad Street and St George's Street, unwilling though he usually was to waste time, to collect his thoughts even further.

Such a sale could bring in considerable moneys; enough to purchase another house in Endell Street to add to the hospital? Now, there was an attractive thought!

Ten years ago Gandy Deering, buying up old property in Tavistock Street to clear the way for his elegant Exeter Hall (and much as Abel had sneered at it at the time, he had to admit now that it was a handsome edifice, and much improved the Strand frontage) had fallen into his hand like a ripe plum. He had gained the three houses that had become the first Queen Eleanor's almost by default, and great his satisfaction had been at the time, except for what had happened in the buying of the third house. But that was something else that must not—could not—be thought about. And then, the sale of the Piccadilly shop had brought enough money to add the fourth house that made up the present structure. Would the sale of Wapping bring enough to buy even more property, to extend the hospital along virtually half of one side of the street, facing the old Wren church?

He pondered hard on that, trying to judge the possibilities, and then sighed softly, for on one side of the hospital lived a corn chandler, and his business, using the big backyard and stables that lay behind it, was far too profitable for the man to sell at any but a high price; and on the other, Abel recalled, lay what purported to be a lodging house, but was known throughout the district as a most successful and popular bagnio. Whoever owned that would not sell in a hurry, either.

Of course, he could go again to talk to his old friend Lucy in her even more successful house of ease at Panton Street, for she was always glad to see him, and would, he knew, do anything to please her Abel with her far from inconsiderable fortune. Gone seventy she might be, vast and wheezing and helpless in her great bed because of her ulcerated legs which were no longer able to hold up her swollen bulk, and blue about the lips and over-red about the face as she had become, yet beneath her unprepossessing exterior lay a mind as sharp as ever it had been, as ready to see a good business deal as anyone with twice her mobility. But because she was so willing, and still loved him so dearly, he could not go to her, unless, of course, he was in desperation.

And he had to smile a little wryly then, for he was not in desperation and well he knew it. There had been a time, of course, when he had been bursting at the seams of his old dispensary, when finding better accommodation had been a matter of urgent need, but that was no longer the case. Now he had twelve wards and a big operating room, space to see a goodly number of street patients each day, and if he grew the place to ten times its size it still could not accommodate the whole of the sick and poor who needed it. Only a hospital that covered the whole of Seven Dials would hope to be big enough for that and to try to make that happen would be lunacy, not honest ambition.

His thoughts would have gone wheeling even more furiously through his head, had he not suddenly become aware of a soft mewing sound behind him, as though a small and frightened animal was shut up somewhere, and he realized it had been going on all through his thinking, a counterpoint to his mental effort. He turned his head with some irritation, for small and pathetic though the sound was it had a penetrating quality that was beginning to grate on the nerves.

He was standing near the open door of one of the little houses, not a hovel this one, where none cared for comfort or warmth or decency or anything but the mere existence of a roof, but a carefully tended home. He could see through the door that there was a scrap of drugget on the floor, so thin and worn that its colour could hardly be seen, but it was there, and well washed besides, and beyond it hung a piece of flapping thin material, vaguely blue and very faded and heavily patched, but a clear attempt at a curtain.

It reminded him powerfully and suddenly of a room he had seen somewhere else, long ago, and he blinked and tried to bring into focus the image that was hovering on the edge of his mind's eye; a shabbily carpeted floor, a blanketed little bed, a scrubbed wooden table with blue cups on it, a little fireplace where a few sticks burned brightly, and before it a figure crouching, holding bacon on a fork and turning it in the flames to toast it. A slight figure, narrow and yet with a curve to the back that could clutch at the throat, and looking over the shoulder at him a face so bright, so vivid, so full of colour and life as it sparkled up at him that his young heart turned over——

He had to do something active to banish that painful and most unwanted memory and almost without thinking he moved forwards and gave the door a sharp push, without knowing what he expected to see. At once he felt the resistance behind it, and pulled back as the faint mewing became a more definite cry.

He put his head round the door, screwing up his eyes against the dimness, and then as his vision adjusted, he could see. There was a child there behind the door, a scrap of a creature some fifteen months old, he estimated, sitting with little sticks of legs stuck out at sharp angles to its body, its hands lying in a helpless sort of way on its minuscule lap, and its face streaked and crumpled with tears. The nose was running profusely, the eyes were red-rimmed and the little object looked altogether as miserable a creature as any he had ever seen.

At the sight of him the baby began its weak howling again, a little shriller this time, and lifted small and very dirty hands to cover the crumpled face. Abel made a soft irritated noise between his teeth, and moving carefully insinuated himself around the door and bent to pick up the child.

It resisted a little, pushing its puny arms against his chest, and turning its head away, crying louder than ever, and he rocked it gently for a moment, holding it close in his experienced arms, for although he had dealt little with his own children in their infancy he had handled many hundreds in his hospital; and gradually the child's cries eased until it was doing little more than whimpering softly and staring at him suspiciously from under half closed lids.

He could see now that the child was wearing quite decent clothes, not the usual rags he was accustomed to seeing on Seven Dials infants, and even had a napkin tied around his buttocks—a wet and reeking one, but still a napkin, a rare object to find in these poverty-stricken slums, where babies were lucky to have a sheet to be wrapped in and had to lie in their own ordure and tolerate it.

As well as being better dressed than most, the child was better fed too. Thin as he was, Abel could feel some weight there, could recognize the firm muscle and flesh on those birdlike bones, and the belly was decently flat, not swollen with hunger as was usually the case.

He looked at the child, and the child looked at him, and then turned his head towards the curtain at the end of the little passageway, and now Abel heard it too; another faint sound of a human voice, and he moved towards the curtain, the baby straining away from him with arms outstretched towards it, now making a definite sound with its whimpers; 'ma-ma-ma-ma'—— the eternal cry of every human baby seeking its mother.

Abel, shouldering aside the curtain and stepping through, found himself in a room in which there were not the usual deal boxes serving as table and chairs and piles of rags to be used as a bed, which was all most homes in these parts boasted, but real furniture. He could see a tall mahogany chest, a piecrust table, a pair of neat chairs, and against one wall a bed, a real bed with a post at each corner and heavy blankets on it.

Again he had to wait to accustom his eyes to the dimness, for the furniture was so dark and heavy it blotted out what little light came from the tiny window in the far wall; and since that gave only on to a stinking little enclosed yard, with an open midden in the centre, it let in little of the March daylight. But after a moment he could see.

There, lying on the bed under the heap of blankets was the wasted figure of a girl. She looked very young in the dimness, very small and fragile, and for a moment he doubted she could be the infant's mother, but at the sight of her the baby had restarted its caterwauling, holding out matchstick arms even more urgently, and she turned her head on the pillow (and that too was a surprising sight, for who in these parts had pillows with white linen covers on them? Abel thought) and moved her shoulders as though she too wanted to extend her arms.

Abel moved across the room to her, stepping carefully in the gloom, and leaned over to set the child beside her. Now she managed to extricate herself, and moving with what seemed an infinite languor reached for the baby, who crept immediately into her arms, tucked his head into her neck, put two fingers in his mouth and started sucking noisily on them; and almost at once turned his head again so that although he lay close beside the girl, and still kept pressed hard against her, he could observe every one of Abel's movements with one watchful eye.

'I found him behind the open door,' Abel said gently. 'And since the door was open, no doubt he would soon have found his way out into the street. And that is no place for so small a creature.'

'No,' she said. Her voice was so faint it was little more than a breath, and she turned her head closer to the child, and seemed to tighten her grasp on his small body, but again with so effortful a movement it seemed to be lazy. But Abel knew disease when he saw it, and after a moment he sat down beside her on the bed, and pulled off his glove and felt for her wrist.

Her pulse was thin and thready, and she was cold to the touch, and after a moment he said quietly, 'How long have you been so?'

She looked up at him and he could see her more clearly now; pale, so pale as to seem almost yellow and her eyes, which in health must have been a most charming blue, were red-rimmed and cloudy. Her hair was thin and a nondescript brown, and he could see her chest beneath her cotton shift, bony and moving with such erratic rhythm that it was clear that each breath was an effort.

'Peter—he had to go to work——' she said, and still her voice was breathy and very low. 'Two weeks ago, I think, and the woman didn't come when she saw I was ill——'

She closed her eyes for a moment, and seemed to fall into a light sleep; after a moment Abel increased the pressure of his finger tips on her wrist and she opened her eyes again and looked at him in blank puzzlement, then her face cleared and she said again, 'The woman didn't come. The baby—he is—no one has fed him. And he fell down from the bed and crawled away. So frightened—so frightened——'

Tears had escaped from beneath her closed lids now, and she was weeping with the sudden helplessness of the very weak. Abel nodded with sudden decision, and stood up, looking about the room.

'You have a key?' he asked, and then repeated the question more loudly. She woke and her eyes moved and looked at the Welsh dresser that stood against one wall, adorned with cups and bowls and platters, and he nodded, and went over to it and rummaged in the various dishes until he found it, hidden behind a jug.

'We shall lock the door, so none of your neighbours can pay you unwelcome visits,' he said crisply. 'And you will find all well when you return. Come along——' He moved back to the bedside, leaned down and with one sharp tug pulled up the bedding and wrapped it round the two of them, and picked them up bodily, slinging her into his arms as easily as if she had been no bigger than the baby; and indeed his burden seemed as light as an infant, for all he was holding them both.

'Where—no—put me back——' Fear gave her the strength to struggle; she was like a small and captive bird that could be held in one cupped hand, and he said brusquely but with an underlying warmth, 'To a room at the hospital where you will be looked after. You have nothing to fear from me. I am Mr Lackland——' She stopped struggling and looked up wonderingly at him and then tightened her grasp of the baby, let her head fall against his shoulder and closed her eyes.

'Even there——' she murmured after a moment. 'Anywhere. Feed him for me——' then she lay very still, and he did not know whether she had fallen asleep or swooned, and either way it did not matter.

He locked the door of the little house and tucked the key carefully into his waistcoat pocket, looking about him sharply before moving away down the street, but none seemed to have noticed or cared what was happening, with the usual Londoner's disregard for anyone's affairs but his own. So, satisfied that no would-be thief had seen him and would know the place was empty and worth the robbing, he set off swiftly for the hospital. Nancy would take this pathetic little woman and her baby to her capacious self and feed them and care for them and he would see what ill it was that afflicted her, apart from hunger and neglect (and he suspected from the look of her that she had chlorosis, that her blood was thin and weak and useless to her, and that she needed much feeding up with stimulants and tonics and good red meat) before sending her home to her little house. And perhaps by then, Peter, whoever he might be, might have returned. That was not Abel's concern, and he gave the matter no further thought.

But he was thinking about the matter of William again, and the money that would be available to him from the projected sale of the Wapping establishment. Not more hospital buildings, but more of the hospital's care—*that* was what was needed, he was thinking, as he carried his pathetically light burden along Endell Street and up the steps of the first of the medical houses.

We shall start a visiting service, sending students and perhaps nurses and whoever we can prepare for the work to go about the streets and houses and look for such cases as these, people too weak to come to us for the care they need, too frightened, perhaps, to seek us out. The hospital was there for those that would come to it; well and good. Now, with William's help, he would send the hospital out to those who had need and could not come of their own volition. Surely, even inefficient and lazy William would see the good sense of such a scheme.

Abel was almost happy as, with his burden held close, he ran up the first staircase in search of Nancy.

## 14

On Sunday morning London woke to one of those absurd blue and white springlike days that sometimes catch the metropolis completely unawares. For the past week there had been grey days of blustery winds which had sent street dust flying painfully into eyes, skirts whirling immodestly above chilled female ankles and top hats tumbling into the gutters, while slates and chimney pots crashed about the roofs and doors and windows rattled furiously in their frames. In the weeks to come there could be more such days, and worse, too, with rain and sleet and even snow, for that could come even in April to cover the cobbles with icy treacherous slush.

But today there was a sky of so tender a blue that even the most curmudgeonly of citizens felt his heart lift a little, and only the softest of little clouds decorated the sky without blocking the warmth of the early sun. The streets looked washed and clean—as well they might be after the assault they had suffered all week—and the gardens and parks glittered with crocuses and snowdrops and early daffodils.

The hot muffin and new bread sellers going early about the streets seeking breakfast-time customers for their wares did a spanking business, and went home long before they usually did, all wares sold and their pockets cheerfully chinking, to take themselves and their families out for the day to sample the rural joys of Hyde Park and Kensington Gardens, or even as far afield as Highgate Hill and Hampstead Heath, lying fresh and lush with the earliest of young greenery on the roof of London far to the North.

Abby woke early, and smelling the newness and brightness of the morning could not wait for Ellie to bring her chocolate but went padding along the passageway and downstairs to collect her own hot water to wash, only to find that Frederick and Phoebe had risen even earlier, for they were in the kitchen stuffing themselves with hot toast which he was making before the banked-up kitchen fire and then besmearing plentifully with butter and honeycomb for her.

Abby stood for a moment at the top of the steps that led into the basement kitchen, looking down on them and smiling a little. The red tiled floor was chequered with the light which came pouring in through the railed area window, and the scrubbed deal table in the middle sat in a little pool of spilled sunshine of its own with Phoebe perched on it, her white muslin skirts spread about her, and her black stockinged ankles and black buttoned boots swinging cheerfully. She had managed to dress herself well enough, though her scarlet sash was untied and the buttons at the back of her dress were unevenly matched with their holes, but her hair had quite defeated her, and lay on her shoulders in a tumble of unbrushed black curls. Her face was streaked with honey and she was holding in both hands her enormously thick piece of toast (for Frederick had cut the bread most inexpertly, as the remains of the loaf on the table beside Phoebe showed) and eating very seriously indeed.

Frederick, crouched red-faced and sweating in front of the fire, with one piece of bread on a long fork held to the glow in one hand and another dripping buttery honey in the other, looked totally absorbed in his efforts. His neat brown broadcloth trousers and white cambric shirt were covered with a towel he had tied across his chest under his arms, and his thatch of thick springing hair had been vigorously brushed up over his broad forehead to make a halo which shone redly in the sunlight. He looked most careful and responsible and very aware of the seniority of his ten years over Phoebe's seven, and together they made up a picture of contented youngness that was very appealing.

'Good morning!' Abby said briskly, after a moment and came down the steps and Freddy looked up and grinned cheerfully at her.

'Oh, Mamma, could you not sleep either? It it not the most *perfect* morning? The birds woke me so early, and I looked out and the Green looked so splendid! So I crept in and woke Phoebe and she said she was hungry, and—oh, dear——' for his toast was beginning to smoke threateningly. 'Oh, well, never mind! I can scrape off the burnt bits, I daresay! Mamma, shall I make you some toast?'

She laughed. 'I think I will wash and dress first, thank you Freddy, and then wait for Ellie. Did you wash, or is that a question which will embarrass you?'

'*I* did not!' Phoebe announced in a muffled voice, for her mouth was full. 'Because I will be just as dirty again very soon, for Freddy said we shall go to the park immediately after breakfast and play and run and that will make me very dirty!'

'Indeed?' Abby said. 'And what about Church, young sir? And Miss Phoebe's lessons? You know she must read with Miss Miller today, at least for a little while, for Phoebe cannot have lessons every weekday, as you do, but must do all that she can on the days she is with us.'

'Oh, Mamma, cannot we go to the park after Church, then? And could not Miss Miller talk with Phoebe a little about natural philosophy and so forth, as we walk? That is what Mr Corrigan does with us when the weather is too agreeable to be wasted indoors in the schoolroom. We walk about the wilder parts of Hyde Park and he discourses on the beetles and botany and so forth and we learn a *great* deal, and it is most healthy for our lungs. Mr Corrigan says so, and I am sure Miss Miller will say the same, for she looks a most sensible person!' He scrambled to his feet. 'Are you sure you would not like this piece of toast, Mamma? It is only a *little* burned, and the honey is very good and will quite disguise the black bits——'

She laughed and began to fill a brass can from the big kettle that was steaming gently at the back of the big range. 'No, you have it, Freddy, for I am sure your need is greater than mine. As for the park and Mr Corrigan's natural philosophy—well I have no doubt your young Mr Corrigan means well, but you will agree that you learn more at a desk with your books than you ever do skipping about the grass!'

'Oh, please, Aunt!' Phoebe cried, and scrambled down from her perch on the table to pull at Abby's peignoir and look up at her with grey eyes wide and appealing. 'I should like Miss Miller to teach me botany and beetles in the park above all things!'

Abby looked down at the small face with its pointed chin and soft dimples and dark lashes and could not help but smile, for the child was a most beguiling little creature, and she wondered for one brief moment who it was she looked like, for she had none of her father in her physiognomy. Was she then more her mother's daughter? It would be interesting to know, but Celia, Jonah had told her in some embarrassment, had refused the invitation to visit her sister-in-law's house, in spite of the fact that her child was to stay in it for four days of each week, and the two women had never met in the past so it was not possible for Abby to make any such judgements. Although, she thought fleetingly, there is perhaps a little of her grandmother about her, with those curls of hers and that charm.

She shook her head with a sudden involuntary movement and looked at Freddy, who was staring at her with his red head cocked on one side and his green eyes full of hope, and dismissed as ignoble the moment of doubt that had crept into her. Of course she was doing the right thing in having Phoebe here, both for her niece's sake and for her son's. The boy had blossomed in the little time he had known her, becoming quite gentle in his attentions, controlling his natural boisterousness for her in a way that any mother must approve of; to regard small Phoebe with any sort of suspicion simply because she had once met the child's grandmother and had good cause to dislike and fear her, would be most unjust.

So Abby smiled, and picked up her can of hot water and turned back to the steps to return to her room to wash and dress. 'Well, we shall speak to Miss Miller and see what we can contrive!' she said. 'And when Ellie comes down, young man, see to it that you tell her you have eaten breakfast already. There is no need for her to waste time or food preparing more for you, if you are going to be too full to eat it!'

'Oh, we will not be too full!' Freddy said airily, and bit hugely into his toast. 'For this is only a *little* breakfast, you see! We shall be quite ready for the usual one, shall we not, Phoebe?' And Phoebe nodded vigorously, unable to speak for her full mouth.

It was while she was eating her own more frugal breakfast that the letter arrived from Gideon.

'My dear Mrs Caspar,' she read, and raised her eyebrows momentarily at the formality of it. 'Will you be free to take the air with me this afternoon, in Kensington Gardens? On such a balmy day, I have no doubt, Master Frederick and Miss Phoebe will find some occupation to employ them there, and there are matters I would wish to discuss with you which may well be brought into review on the pleasantness of the Broad Walk. Please to tell my messenger that I may attend you at Paddington Green shortly after one o'clock? I hope indeed you will feel able to do so, and oblige Yr most Sincere Friend, Gideon Henriques.'

She sat for a long moment staring out at her little garden where the daffodils were starring the grass under the faintly green branches of the little tree that grew there, finding it difficult to order her thoughts. She had been feeling like that for the past three days, ever since her own absurd loss of control—as she now saw it—and Gideon's startling reaction to it.

She had managed to dismiss his declaration of affection at the time with a light remark and had got to her feet with what dignity she could muster and asked his pardon for her foolishness, then begging him to excuse her; and he had stood and looked at her in silence for a moment and then nodded, and turned and picked up his heavy coat and tall glossy hat, and bowing with that faintly formal air that he sometimes adopted brushed her hand with his lips and made his adieux She herself had taken half an hour to collect herself, and then returned with apparent serenity to her day's work, soothing Henry, who was still bewildered and indeed doubly confused by his employer's extraordinary behaviour, and giving him leave to take samples and the tariff to his hoped-for new customer. There would be time to be worried about what to do if an order were offered; until then, when it would be necessary, she had vowed, she would not concern herself with the problem of how she should behave in the matter.

And she had told herself, too, that she would not concern herself further with the matter of Gideon's extraordinary declaration. He is very young, she had adjured her own mind. Too young to realize that his emotion is not love, as he believes it to be, but mere pity excited in his sensitive heart by the sight of a weeping widow. It is no more than that. It cannot be more than that.

But even as the sensible part of herself said this, several times (and she recognized the significance of the fact that she had to keep repeating it) her emotions were not so sensible, but played quite outrageous tricks on her; as for example making her chest suddenly constrict at the sight of a tall and slight man striding along the Harrow Road and bearing a fleeting resemblance to Gideon's back view, or making her go off into a brown study, staring out with unseeing glazed eyes at the factory through her office door instead of concentrating on her work.

It has indeed been a comfort to her that Miss Miller, the new governess and secretary, had taken up her residence at Paddington Green. When Abby returned there in the evening she had to make an effort to converse with the girl, for she was shy and quiet, and to teach her the new tasks to do with the manufactory for which she would be responsible; and that effectively controlled thoughts of more personal matters. And when she went to bed she was much too weary to lie and ponder for long, and slept as quickly as was her wont; but she did dream a little, and somewhat disturbed dreams some of them had been.

Now this letter; for a moment she wanted very much to send the messenger away with some Banbury tale of having the headache or being otherwise indisposed; and then she shook herself in some irritation. It was quite absurd to react so to Gideon, her good friend and business associate, the man she had known since his gawky boyhood, who was so much her junior! And anyway, her practical mind whispered, you must see him on Wednesday at the manufactory, so what difference to ride in the park with him today, in such lovely weather?

So she sent the messenger back to Lombard Street with her acceptance of the invitation and told Miss Miller and the children of the projected jaunt, much to the latter's delight, and then went to Church as usual, neat and quiet and proper as befitted the widowed mother of a hopeful young son, and worked very hard at keeping her mind on Collects and Lessons and Sermon instead of the pleasure that she would undoubtedly find in the afternoon sunshine of Kensington Gardens. And if she were to find embarrassment as well as pleasure, well, that too was something she would worry about when it happened.


'I know no other way to convince you!' Jonah said, and cut savagely into the beef on his plate. Sunday should be an agreeable day, free as it was from the pressures of work in the supper rooms, the day when they could be as other families and share a noonday luncheon at a reasonable time, instead of snatching a hasty meal in the middle of the day's bustle. But today, despite the sudden improvement in the weather, was proving far from enjoyable for Jonah. Not only was he missing

146

Phoebe's company with much more keenness than even he had expected—almost to the point of regretting his careful plan, a selfish thought he did all he could to banish—but also because of Celia.

For a full week she had hardly spoken to him at all, addressing him only in monosyllables when she had to, and quite clearly deliberately avoiding any possibility of prolonged conversation between them. She had gone about the work of the establishment with a relentless energy that had left the servants even more than usually exhausted, and had dealt with a savage intensity with all that needed doing. The kitchens had been scrubbed and burnished to a pitch of cleanliness that was remarkable, and the supper room and his little stage gleamed with beeswax polish and newly buffed brass and well brushed velvet.

At the end of each day she had somehow contrived to be in bed and asleep before he came to their room, or busied herself about the house for so long after he had gone to bed that despite his best efforts to remain alert he was fast asleep when she came to slip into bed beside him.

He had felt her brooding presence, though, all the time, and sometimes seemed to feel her eyes upon him, dark with suspicion and deeply troubled. But when he turned his head to look at her across the supper rooms or over the dining table she would be sitting with her eyes hooded, ostensibly quite unaware of him.

Until this morning, when she had burst out with her extraordinary attack, and he had been quite stunned with it; and then, when he had realized just what it was she was saying, he had been fool enough to laugh.

'To *Lilith*? You thought I had taken her there? Oh, really, Celia, that is the outside of enough! As if——'

'As if what?' she had flared at him, sitting up against her pillows with her bedgown clutched about her shoulders—for she had greeted him with her fury as soon as he had opened his eyes to the glitter of the morning sun on the blinds. 'As if you would think of such a thing? Don't tell me you have not wanted to go to her, these many, many times! Don't tell me you have not yearned for her and lusted for her these many many years! Do you think I am a fool? She told me—oh, she told me, and that hellborn bitch knew what she was saying—she told me you would always want her, and she was right, for have you

147

not taken Phoebe to her, have you not chosen to let her suffer as I did at her wicked cruel——'

It had gone on and on, as he had sat at the edge of their bed staring at her in sleep-dazed amazement as the words came tumbling out of that pale face above the unmoving and rigid body sitting there absurdly framed by the brass rails at the head of the bed, her arms folded with fierce self-protectiveness across her breasts, and her eyes almost black with the fires of her rage and resentment and fear.

He had spent a good hour, when at last she had ceased her railing, in trying to convince her that it was to his *sister* he had taken Phoebe, and that it was Abby and not Lilith who was providing this help to their daughter, although prudently he did not mention money or that Abby had been in the habit of presenting him with extra funds for some time. Quite apart from his own shame at the situation, he had no wish to add fuel to the flames of her unreasonable rages.

At last he had managed to soothe her and when, later in the morning while she was supervising the preparation of the luncheon in the kitchen, he had time to himself, he took Oliver for a walk, grateful for the opportunity to restore his own peace of mind.

These moods and rages of hers were becoming more alarming, he told himself, as they walked along King Street towards Bedford Street in the warm sunshine, passing the little flatfronted houses of their neighbours as they made for the peace of the railed churchyard of St Paul's, which lay in the corner between Bedford Street and Henrietta Street, boxed in with tall houses which frowned down on the little green patch of headstones and grass that lay at their feet. She had ever had a hot temper—and he remembered with a twist of his mouth the way she had once turned on him in her mother's drawing room one snowy afternoon, long ago, believing him then to be her mother's paramour and attacking him with a huge venom—but it was, surely, getting worse?

There were times when she shrieked at the servants in such an access of fury that it seemed her eyes would burst out of her head; it was small wonder that they were all so frightened of her—and worked so well. Anybody would do all they could to escape the risk of a lashing from her tongue; and sometimes she would hit out physically too, laying about the girls' scrawny backs with whatever came to hand, be it broomstick or pot lid. It was only because work in the neighbouring rookeries of Seven Dials, Clare Market and the Bermudas was so hard to come by that the poor wretches tolerated her at all as an employer. And she fed them reasonably well of course, and that was what mattered most.

For himself, it was becoming more and more wearing to be always worried about the state of her mind, and he closed his own mind against the way she could make him feel when she was in one of her blacker moods. He loved her in so many ways still and although he often felt helpless to express the feelings and needs he did have for her he wanted to make her happy, if that were possible.

Sitting now in the churchyard, as Oliver went bumbling happily about among the gravestones, reading such Latin inscriptions as he could find—for he was proud of the newly acquired scraps of the classic tongue his father had taught him in recent months—Jonah turned his face up to the warmth of the young sun, his eyes closed, and wondered bleakly whether there was a more than reasonable cause for her rages. She had once told him that her father had been in some sort disturbed in his mind, had died in a lake in his own grounds. Perhaps the man, whoever he had been—and Celia, poor girl, had never known his name, let alone the man himself—had suffered some maggot in his brain that led him to the crime of suicide.

Jonah shivered a little at that thought and opened his eyes to stare sombrely at the trees above his head. He had heard often enough that people who did that were more than wicked, were mad as well, and that was a thought to make any married man and hopeful father shiver. And he lowered his head to look at his Oliver, now crouched before a moss-encrusted stone, carefully spelling out the words at which he was staring with his shortsighted gaze, and shivered in actual fact. No, he must not think of Celia in these terms. Not when there were Oliver and Phoebe to consider too. Her angers and her sulks were just that; merely expressions of a volatile temper. And somehow he must help her see that this time she was wrong in her judgements, that her rage was quite ill founded.

He tried again during luncheon to persuade her to come to visit Abby and discover for herself the truth of all she had been told, and all the time she resisted until he had said again with a sudden sense of rage on his own behalf that she was cruelly unjust not to come to see Abby and ask her for the truth of the situation, for he knew no other way to convince her; and she had looked at him for another long moment and then quite suddenly nodded.

'Very well. We shall go to your sister's house. If you are so determined,' she said and her voice though still cold and clipped at least had lost some of its anger; and he smiled at her in deep relief and Oliver looked up from his plate and blinked at them both, and then returned stolidly to eating. Jonah said almost jovially, 'That is splendid! This afternoon, then? I had arranged to go to collect Phoebe to bring her home at six o'clock, in time to send her a little earlier to bed, for she will be fatigued with the newness of her situation, no doubt. You will accompany me then?'

Oliver lifted his chin at that. 'You said you would take me to the Gardens this afternoon, Papa, to sail my boat on the Long Water,' he said and Jonah bit his lip. He had indeed made some such vague promise during their return walk along Bedford Street.

'There will be time enough for that, I think, as well,' he said after a moment. 'Celia? Shall we walk in the park with Oliver and then make our way to Paddington Green from there? It is a lovely afternoon, after all——'

And to his surprise she had agreed, and returned to picking at her own hardly eaten meal, her head bent. He had looked at her, saddened at the sight of her pale cheeks and the violet smudges beneath her eyes, and had put his hand out impulsively towards her across the table. But she had not seen it so he had returned in silence to his own meal. Perhaps, when this afternoon was over, she would be happy again, he told himself optimistically. Perhaps.

All over London that morning and early afternoon, people looked up at the sky and smiled and told each other what a capital plan it would be to walk in Hyde Park and Kensington Gardens to admire the spring flowers and enjoy the fresh air and sunshine and see the new French fashions that would be sure to be paraded all along the Broad Walk and Constitution Hill on such a day. And little boys whooped with joy at such parental good sense and went to rummage in toy boxes for last year's sailing boats to launch upon the Long Water by the Serpentine in competition with other small boys' much inferior vessels.

Jody Lucas, for example, was quite sure *his* boat would outshine any that they saw there and he informed his fond Mamma as soon as she awoke that, weary as she was after last night's late performance at the Haymarket and the crush of a party that had followed it at the Earl of Arundel's house, that that was where she was to take him that afternoon.

## 15

The children were so cock-a-hoop at the sight of the handsome
yellow landau, drawn by a pair of perfectly matched bays, in which
Gideon arrived at Paddington Green that any embarrassment Abby
might have felt at their meeting was quite lost in loud juvenile excla-
mations about the elegance of the yellow velvet fittings inside, the
splendour of the folded leather hood outside, and the spiritedness of the
horses.

Phoebe had stepped fearlessly to the head of one of the animals, her
hand outstretched to pat its nose, but it had tossed its head in great disdain and bared its teeth momentarily so that she had squealed and
jumped back to be caught by the ever watchful Frederick, and this
little episode had made them all laugh; so that they were all well
ensconced behind the liveried coachman before either of the adults
had the opportunity to exchange more than the most commonplace of
words.

But once the vehicle moved off, the horses lifting their heads in great
style, for they too seemed to be infected by the gaiety of the sunshine,
and the children kneeling up on the seat immediately behind the
coachman so that they could watch his expert handling of the ribbons,
they could speak without fear of being overheard.

But for a little while they did not, sitting side by side in some stiff-
ness. Abby hiding a little behind her open parasol, a very pretty
confection of cream silk and ribbon which most charmingly set off her
straw bonnet with its fashionably short brim lined with blue satin and
tied with rose spotted veiling. She had dressed with especial care for
her drive, choosing her dark blue velvet cloak with the half cape
sleeves and grey fur trim to set over her blue satin gown; and even had

Ellie help her redress her hair so that although she still wore much of it in the usual soft knot at the nape of her neck, there were some soft curls escaping on each side of her bonnet to frame her face.

She had not thought particularly of what she was doing in making so much effort with her toilette, until now; and she felt quite extraordinarily embarrassed, more so than she would have thought possible, when Gideon at last broke the silence between them by saying gravely, 'You look most delightful today, Abby. You quite outshine the sun.'

She felt her face stiffen with shyness, and was annoyed with herself; she, a woman of almost eight and twenty to be as put about by a prettily turned male compliment as any sixteen-year-old! And she turned her head to look at him and make some casual remark, but could not, for he too had clearly made great efforts with his appearance, wearing a most beautifully cut frock coat with very French-looking braid frogging fastening it over a shirt of blinding whiteness beneath a black silk cravat set in position between high collar points with a very handsome gold pin. His top hat with its rakishly elegant curling brim was set at an angle on his dark head, and he smelled faintly of eau de cologne. And quite involuntarily she smiled hugely and said, 'My dear Gideon! You outshine us both! Such perfection of linen and such an effulgence of silk hat! Really, my dear, there can be no man to hold a candle to you for dress this side of Kensington Palace!'

And now it was his turn to be confused and he bit his lip and shook his head, and blinked, and then they both laughed, and at last they were comfortable again, and could sit and talk companionably as the landau went bowling along Wharf Road, crossing the smartness of Praed Street on its way to Polygon Street, which would lead them over the Oxford Road to enter the Park near the Serpentine.

'I am glad the children approve of my equipage,' Gideon said. 'Do you think they will be disgusted if they discover that it is not precisely my own, but that I took it from the livery stable for the afternoon?'

She laughed. 'Oh, I doubt that Frederick will care one way or the other! He enjoys that lack of awareness of material wealth which can be so charming in a child. It is yours for the afternoon—that will be enough to please him. As for Phoebe—well, I cannot say! She is my niece, I know, but I have little real knowledge of her in terms of character, for this is the first of her visits since the plan was made. Ask me in a few months' time about her views on property, and perhaps I will be able to advise you!'

'Unawareness of property may be charming in a child,' Gideon said, 'But when Frederick is older he will care more, I think. He will have to, will he not? As the only son of a widow it will be incumbent upon him to concern himself with your affairs as well as his own in due course.'

She looked sideways at him, frowning slightly. 'Are you telling me you will not be available to watch over my affairs in time to come, Gideon? That I must already start training Frederick to the tasks of——'

'Oh, no, indeed no!' Gideon said hastily. 'It is my full intention to continue in my present capacity with the Caspar business interests a long as those interests wish me to do so! No, I meant something quite other, I do assure you.'

He stopped then, and looked at her very directly, and she looked back at him, a little surprised by the intensity of his gaze. 'I meant only that the time will come, I think, when Frederick will need to know that I could well maintain this equipage for myself, if I chose to do so, and that I prefer to use the stables because there are fewer problems for me in so doing.'

She laughed. 'My dear Gideon! Why should Frederick care a whit, one way or the other? You speak in riddles, really you do!'

'He is your son, Abby. That is why.' He turned his head to look out at the houses they were passing, new houses with yellow stucco fronts and very modern iron balconies decorating their upper stories. 'A good and caring young man in the position in which he will find himself will be most concerned to know the monetary affairs and intentions of those gentlemen who display an interest in his Mamma.' Now he turned to look at her again. 'After all, my dear Abby, you are a woman of some substance, are you not? The manufactory brings you a comfortable income, and you own the premises, as well as your house at Paddington Green and——'

Quite suddenly she blushed hotly, and turned away from him to stare in front of her at the coachman's back and the lavish display of frilled drawers and petticoats offered by Phoebe's excited back view as she hung happily over the driver's seat to call encouraging 'Giddaps!'

at the horses. She realized now—and she knew how belated that realization was—just what it was that Gideon meant in talking so of the hiring of his landau, and did not know how to handle the conversation at all. Not with the children there, at any rate; and she bit her lip and tried to calm her mind, for she was thrown into a state of confusion that was very alien to her usual good sense.

'Forgive me,' he said after a moment, and his voice was flat. 'I did not mean to discommode you in any way.'

'Oh, I am not—I mean——' she began, and then to her intense relief Frederick suddenly whooped and turned in his seat to cry, 'Mamma! Oh, Mamma, can you not see which way he has brought us? Look! There are the Tea Gardens! Oh, please, Mamma, Mr Henriques, may we not stop? I am sure Phoebe would like to see the archers and the bowling, above all things! And perhaps we——'

'Oh, yes, please, Aunt!' Phoebe too scrambled round and turned her pleading eyes upon Abby. 'I should very much like to see—what was it Freddy?' She pulled on Frederick's coat and he grinned and said, 'Why, the people with their bows and arrows, shooting at targets! And there are some that bowl, you know, and all about are tables where you can sit and drink lemon sherbet and have little almond cakes and——'

Gideon gave a crack of laughter. 'I had forgotten the great hunger of boyhood, Frederick! How long is it since you ate your luncheon? Fully an hour, I'll be bound! Oh, indeed, lemon sherbet and almond cakes it must be if you are to escape imminent starvation! We shall indeed stop—Chaplin! Please to pull up at the tea gardens, on the corner of Oxford Road!'

'Bott's tea gardens, not the Crown!' Frederick said urgently, 'For the cakes have no flavour to them at all—and there is no archery!'

'Yes, sir!' cried the coachman, his back straightening, for he knew as well as any of them that the gardens offered good ale to servants as well as more delicate sustenance for their betters, and the landau came clattering to a stop by the gateway that led to the neat and pretty tea gardens that dominated the corner of Polygon Street, overlooking on their western side the black waters of the Grand Junction Canal.

The children went skipping away with great glee, and Gideon laughed indulgently and told Chaplin to return in half an hour and offered his arm to Abby, and after a moment of hesitation she accepted it and let him lead her to a table that was set beneath a vividly flowering forsythia bush, to settle her on a little iron chair before ordering a plate of the much admired cakes and glasses of lemon sherbet for the children.

She consented to take a glass of ratafia for herself, and when the comestibles were brought by a perspiring serving woman—for the gardens were very busy on so pleasant a day and she had to bustle considerably to serve all the imperious customers who demanded immediate attention—and the children had gone off clutching their sherbet glasses and with their cakes tied in Frederick's handkerchief to watch the archers, she sat and sipped and did all she could to collect herself, for she was now determined that matters between Gideon and herself must be sorted out, and that quickly. It was quite absurd to go as they were in such a pother.

She lifted her chin and opened her mouth to speak, and at the same moment he too started to speak, and they stopped and then both tried again, and laughed, and Abby said practically, 'Really, this is quite absurd! We must stop behaving like a pair of children no older than those two——' and she turned her head to look across the gardens to the butts, where the diminutive figures of Frederick and Phoebe could be seen watching the busy sportsmen, Phoebe jumping in delight as each arrow went singing through the air on its way to the straw targets.

'The feelings I entertain for you are far from those of a child, Abby,' Gideon said in a low voice, and put out his hand to set it warmly over hers where it lay on the green painted iron table, and at once she pulled her hand away and said severely, 'Gideon, this really will not do! I am deeply ashamed that I should have lost control as I did last week. I can only put it down to some temporary aberration or—or—irritation of the nerves. But you must not, indeed you must not, persist in this foolish——'

'What is foolish about loving, Abby? I do not think it is foolish. You may call it painful, or delightful, or misery or joy or anything of that sort, but foolish—no, never that. How can it be foolish to love you as I do?'

She looked up to see him gazing at her with his eyes so dark and wide open that his face seemed almost gaunt, and she shook her head and tried to speak but he put out his hand and touched her lips and said, 'No, please, will you let me speak first? I have suffered so much this past few days, for want of the chance to speak to you. I have ached with words that I must pour out to you—you must let me have relief of them. I love you so much, Abby, that it bids fair to turn my life quite into a turmoil. Indeed, it already has, for I cannot work or think or even live properly, I am so set about. I would not wish you to think that this is some sudden whim, or that I have spoken as I have out of—out of some youthful notion. I have loved you, I think, for many, many years. And now I can contain it no longer. There are so many difficulties, so many rubs in my way that I hesitated for a long time to tell you of my feelings, of my wishes and most urgent desires for you—for us. But last week your—your sensibility, your concern for your father, your understanding of the love that must lie between you and him, whatever has happened to keep you apart these many years—all that made me see that—well, I was perhaps unjust in feeling it wrong to burden you with my difficulty in loving you, but that you would understand, and——'

He shook his head and swallowed and she had to look closer at him then, for she had thought that for one moment she had seen his eyes glitter as though with tears; but he had closed them, and when he opened them again he was once more in command at himself and managed to smile at her.

'There will be so many difficulties, dearest Abby,' he said and his voice seemed stronger now, had lost the undertow of tremor she had heard in it. 'So many that I feel I am no gentleman to speak to you now in these terms. But speak I must. Dear, dearest Abby, if you will consent to be my wife, I will be the happiest man in all the world, and will promise to take care of you, and watch over you and love you as no husband ever has. Please do not reject me, Abby. I don't think I could bear it——'

There was a long silence as she tried very hard to understand not so much what he had said but the sense of enormous warmth that filled her. Did she reciprocate his feelings as he would want her to, or was she simply as flattered as a schoolroom miss at being regarded with such affection? Or was she responding to him out of gratitude for his friendship, or was it simply that she had been so lonely for so long?

Thoughts and unformed emotion jostled in her and all she could do was shake her head and look at him, at the hopeful way he sat with his head cocked on one side, at the expression of boyish eagerness on his long face, and the words came out of her without any conscious thought on her part.

'Oh, dear Gideon! You are so *very* young!'

He pulled his hand back as though he had been stung and she saw the bones of his jaw become a hard line.

'I wish you will not laugh at me, Abby! I do not find my feelings a matter for levity. I had thought you more——'

'I am not laughing! I would not dream of being so—so *inelegant*,' she cried, and then struck by the ineptitude of the word she suddenly laughed and he looked at her and blinked and then laughed too.

'Inelegant! Well, I had not thought of *that*! Forgive me, Abby, I should know better than to think you would behave like a silly girl. I know, of course you would not laugh at me—but for God's sake, don't be kind, either! I could not bear the insult of your kindness. I want your love, and no less than that. You may be concerned that I am younger than you, but you have barely three years more than I after all. And I have lived a long time in these past seven years. I have served my time for you, in many ways——'

'I did not mean to be unkind, Gideon,' she said gently. 'Indeed I did not. And never think that I look at you with some sort of auntish indulgence. It is not so much that I see you as so young, perhaps, as that I see myself as so much too old. I——' she stopped and shook her head. 'It will be difficult for you to understand, perhaps, the way in which I think of you. You are my friend, my very dear friend, and I cannot imagine coping with the business, or indeed my private life, without you. You have been there beside me for so long! At the beginning, when you were so very new—and—well, you were but fifteen, you know!'

'I know,' he said. 'But a man grown, for all that. Man enough to see you for the woman *you* were—and you were but eighteen yourself, remember!—and to value you and admire you for your courage and your good sense and your wit and——'

'Please, no catalogue,' she said, and heard the catch in her own voice, for she was curiously affected in her breathing now, finding it difficult to be unaware of the rhythm of her own pulses and the need to breathe evenly. 'I do not deny you were very—very mature in many ways, Gideon. But even so, you *were* very young, and I knew it and in some sense have never been able to forget the differences between us. I the widow with a child, at the end of a way of life, and you so very fresh and——'

'At the *end* of a way of life?' He spoke very strongly now, and pulled his chair closer to her side, and put both hands over hers on the table. 'If you talk so then you are not the intelligent woman I took you for! You had been wed barely more than a year, you were hardly out of the schoolroom when your husband died, and you say that was the *end*? I could say that I too was at the end of a part of my life! My father, who had protected me and loved me and cared for me was ill, and I had to protect and love and care for *him*. You had Frederick and Caspar's business to worry about, I my parents and my parents' business. Where were we so different?'

She sat very still, looking down at his hands, pale hands with tapering fingers and almond-shaped nails, holding her own clenched fists in a warm strong grasp, and her breath was coming still more unevenly now, for the sensations that were arising in her were so unfamiliar as to be almost unknown to her. But they were not quite unknown, and as though she were looking through a gauze curtain she saw herself and James, clutching at each other in a sort of wild desperation on an old sofa in the little office behind the Witney shop in Piccadilly, felt the same cold and yet burning shiver against her skin. And she looked up at him and moistened her lips with her tongue and said uncertainly, 'James——'

He nodded, in complete comprehension. 'There would be no disloyalty to James in loving me,' he said very gently. 'It has been almost ten years, Abby. Ten years is long enough to mourn. He would not have wished you to be alone so long. I remember him only faintly, I must confess, but in my memory he was a kind and caring and gentle man. One who loved as a man should love, not wishing to own the object of his love, but wishing only your happiness. He did not do as so many husbands do, and leave his property to his son, so that no other man could ever benefit from marriage to his widow. That is what most prudent and selfish men do, when they fear that they have a mortal illness. But your James was most determined that it should be arranged that you should have sole control of all your property. My father, I know, did all he could to persuade him otherwise, for my father was—indeed, still is, an experienced man of business with solid views and careful notions. But your James wished only for your happiness and security. And I believe that he would be glad for you if you could love again.'

He smiled crookedly then. 'I cannot say he would be glad if you chose to love *me*. But I would, Abby. Oh, I would——' and he bent his head and lifted her hands to his lips and turned them palms upwards and kissed them, and she felt his mouth warm and damp through the network of her gloves and again that shiver moved across her back and she tried to tug her hands away, but he would not release them, and pulled her even closer; and she could look down on to the top of his head, at the way his hair curled softly over his ears, and she closed her eyes and yet again tried to think clearly. But it was very difficult while he held her hands so very tightly and kissed them so very urgently. It was almost improper, indeed, that a man should be able to put so much passion into kissing a woman's hands, she thought confusedly, and again pulled back, and this time he let her go and thrust his own visibly trembling hands into his trouser pockets and leaned back in the absurd little green iron chair, and took a deep breath.

'You see what you do to me,' he said huskily. 'There are times when —when I feel I will burst for want of your touch. When I sit beside you at that desk of yours in your counting house and feel my very bones ache with want of you. Oh, Abby, I am no boy, believe me! I am a man with a passion for you that——' and he shook his head and tucked his chin into his collar and stared down at the grass at his feet.

She too was more shaken than she wanted to admit, still feeling that turmoil of sensation in her skin and in her belly, and ashamed and bewildered by it. Whatever he said about James—and she knew he spoke no more than the truth about him—there was in some sort a sinfulness in feeling like this in the presence of any man but James. She closed her eyes against the bright sunshine of the day and tried very urgently to conjure up a picture of her dead husband. And could not, and wanted to cry.

But that would never do, and she snapped her eyes open and cast about wildly for something to say, and remembering, said, 'You—you spoke of difficulties. What difficulties?'

He shook his head. 'I—I think I prefer not to speak of them just yet, after all.' He managed another of those twisted little smiles but his eyes were not happy. 'It is important to me that first you—that we—I need to know that you share my—recognize my love for you. And in some sort accept it. I do not ask for the passion I feel for you to be returned now, but I need to know that it could be—in time.' He leaned forward again, and looked at her very closely, 'And perhaps I may be arrogant, but I rather think that I am not, for I believe it could be that you will, one day—that although you are a little confused and unsure of yourself now, when you think about it you will find in yourself the concern for me that I have for you. I think so. Which is more than to hope, is it not?'

She shook her head, and wanted to look away, but could not. Those eyes with their heavy lashes were so very close to her, and bore in their depths a tiny reflection of herself, a small figure in blue sitting under a yellow flowering bush and she looked at herself in that tiny picture and knew, somewhere deep inside herself, that he was right. But knew too that she needed time, to think, to be alone, to feel, and to judge her feelings.

He leaned back after a moment, and a curiously pleased little smile curled his narrow lips, and he said softly, 'Well, we shall speak of this again, Abby. Chaplin is waiting there by the gate to take us on to the park, and the children, no doubt, will be upon us in a moment. We cannot talk so easily now as I would wish——' He turned his head to look about the crowded gardens, at the fashionable ladies in their handsome toilettes sipping their tea and ratafia in the sunshine, at the men in severe black paying polite attention to them and he threw her a slightly wicked glance. 'Indeed, to talk to you as I *really* would wish we must be quite alone and within doors. Which, to use your own words, dear Abby, I shall contrive.'

He stood up suddenly and held out one hand to her, and she reached up to her bonnet and set it aright and smoothed her velvet cape and stood up, and he bowed over her hand before tucking it into the crook of his elbow, and they walked in silence across the grass to the gate. Gideon lifted his chin at the coachman, standing obediently beside the landau, and indicated the children away across the gardens at the butts, and the man touched his hat and went to fetch them, leaving the two of them standing each side of the horses' heads, and Abby, still confused, made some play of stroking the velvet nose of one of them.

'I had almost forgot, Abby. My mother asks me to bid you to dine with us. She does not entertain very much, you understand, because of my father, but we do have small parties from time to time. I think it is perhaps time you met her, would you not agree?'

He tried to say it casually but she felt the sense of importance in his tone, and looked at him, over the bay's twitching ears, and still stroking its nose stared at him, and for the first time that afternoon he reddened, and she smiled.

'I see,' she said softly. 'I see. Well, I think I shall be happy to accept your invitation. But please, dear Gideon, do not read into that acceptance more than I mean in making it. I simply say I will be happy to dine with you and your parents. No more.'

And he nodded, and said, 'Of course I understand!' but his face was alight with pleasure as Chaplin came back with the chattering children, and settled them again into the landau before handing Abby ceremoniously after them. And when he took his seat beside her, and again tucked her hand into the crook of his elbow and she felt the warmth of his body so near to hers, she felt a little shiver once more move through her, and could not decide whether it was pleasure or satisfaction, or a curious running anxiety.

And as the little carriage went curving away towards the greenery of the park and the sparkle of the Long Water by the Serpentine, with the horses' hooves seeming to rattle in time to the dull beating of her own pulses in her ears, she still could not decide.

## 16

Abel sat in the corner of the cab, leaning forwards with his elbows on his knees as though by sitting so impatiently he could hurry the vehicle on its way. Already the man was whipping up his horse as hard as he could and the dusty old hack swayed and rattled furiously over the cobbles as it went hurtling across Bedford Square, so that William in his corner was tumbled about like an egg in a basket, greatly to his discomfiture.

'Really, father, I see no reason why you should respond with such ridiculous haste to the woman!' he said pettishly as the cab bounced over a rough patch in the road and made him strike his elbow painfully against the side of his seat. 'And I certainly do not see why I should have to accompany you. If you choose to be at the beck and call of the hospital on Sunday as well as every other day, that is your affair. Bad enough you insisted on talking of hospital matters today. I for one have better things to do with a pleasant afternoon than concern myself with workaday affairs. And I cannot see why——'

'Stop your whining,' Abel said harshly. 'And use your head. Nancy is no fool—she has more sense in her little finger than you and half the hospital have in all your bodies put together, and if she says the matter is of some urgency then it is. And since it concerns the woman I brought in from the streets and these are the ones you will be having care of, then you might as well start as I mean you to go on, and see her now, and——'

'I told you——' William gasped, as the cab hurled itself round a corner, 'I told you I see no reason why I should do any such thing. The matters at Wapping are well enough—the Trustees——'

'To hell and damnation with the Trustees!' Abel said, and leaned out of the window to see where they were, and then seized the door handle, for the cab was now rattling along Broad Street, and would be at the steps of the hospital in another minute or two. 'They'll do as they're bid, and that's all about it. I've decided that the place shall be sold, and sold it shall be. It remains in my possession, and I decide its disposing. As for you——' The cab stopped and he leapt out almost before the wheels had stopped turning. 'You may do as you choose as far as living in my house is concerned. Stay or depart, as you please. But if you depart you take nothing with you, and if you stay you work among the outdoor patients as I have told you. Pay the man——' and he went running up the steps of the hospital leaving William red-faced and furious to settle the cabman's demands.

Nancy was waiting at the top of the first flight of stairs in the women's medical house, peering over the balusters with her face twisted and anxious and her look of relief when she saw Abel was almost ludicrous.

'Gawd, but I'm that glad to see yer!' she said, and hurried to help him pull off his coat. 'Wouldn't 'ave called yer today for anythin', thought it'd do you a bit o' good to be abroad in the sunshine and all—but this——' she shook her head, and set his coat over the baluster rail. 'If I'm wrong an' you tell me to go and boil me 'ead, I'll be that pleased. But I don't think you will——'

'So? What is it that made you send in such a rush?'

'That girl—Ellen Merrick—the one you brought in off the street with 'er baby—he died.'

'Died? The child? But *he* was well enough! It was the mother that was ill! Chlorosis, I believe, and much in need of——'

She nodded. 'Aye, so you said. And I thought the same, and fed 'er as best I could and gave her ipecac and squills in black cherry water for her fever, and thought at first that was the cause of the looseness she started. So then I gave her rhubarb and nutmeg in aqua mirabilis but it made no odds for she got the gripes and started such a flux as could not be kept up with, and when it changed and showed the rice-water look, why I——'

He stood very still. 'Rice-water?'

She nodded, and her face was very grim. 'Aye. That was this morning. I feared at once what had happened and set to wrapping her limbs

164

in hot cloths, for she got the cramps and started to vomit, and that turned to rice-water too, and she was yellow as a guinea and had such spasms with her cramps that I was hard put to it to hold the poor creature down, she was raging so. And thirsty—and the babe was there and quiet enough, and lying still, and she fretted about it, and I said it would be seen to—and when I picked it up the poor little thing began to go into such convulsions, and I saw it had been purging as bad as its Ma. And then it started the vomiting too, and the fits got worse and then it died.'

She shook her head. 'The mother breathes yet, though not for that much longer, I'm thinking, but what am I to do? The place is as full as ever it was, and there's nowhere I can move her to be apart and the miasma will spread, and there we are—I 'opes as I'm wrong, but I don't reckon I am——'

He stood very still, his eyes half closed as he thought, staring unseeingly out of the window at the end of the passage at the sunlit rooftops of the Dials. Then he said harshly, 'Is it known?'

She gave a crack of laughter at that, but there was no humour in it. 'Could I be standin' 'ere like this if it was? I've worked it out—if there's three of those nurses as'll stay when they find out, I'll be doin' well. Chances are there'll not be that many. And you can't keep it quiet that long, for there's some as are bright enough to know what's what. I told Jane when she took the babe to be readied for its burial as the child 'ad the convulsions with its teething and she looked at me very sharp and then looked at the poor Ma, and I thought she'd say something then, but she went off, and did as she was bid. Still an' all, I'm worried——'

'Aye,' he said. 'Well, I'll see the girl,' and he turned on his heel and went into the long room that stretched from front to back of the house, Nancy at his heels.

The women in the beds that were ranged against the walls on each side, some propped up on pillows, some lying flat with blankets pulled over their heads, were quiet. There was none of the usual desultory hum of talk that even a room full of sick women can produce; instead there was an air of watchfulness, a sense of waiting and fearing that was as real as the patches of sunlight on the scrubbed wooden boards of the floor and the grey blankets and striped ticking pillows on each of the beds.

He stood still for a moment, not wishing to show any unusual signs of hurry to alarm the patients, and the smell of the place entered him, that mixture of tired wasting human bodies and human living mixed with the distant scent of long since eaten and forgotten food, all over-lain with the sickly fumes of sulphur from Nancy's eternally burning pastilles. But there was a new scent in the air today; the effluvium of the disease he always feared would find its way into his beloved Nellie's, the disease that had always stalked the streets of the Dials to send ripples of fear washing through the greasy alleys and gutters filled with rotting rubbish and sour mud.

Over the years at both Tavistock Street and Endell Street there had been alarming cases, but they had turned out to be other diseases; bad enough in themselves, but none so bad as this. Typhus and diphtheria, scarlet fever and even the smallpox—these had come to the beds of Nellie's and some had lived and some had died, but none had set in train the disaster they might have done had they chosen to spread. But on those occasions, he thought bleakly, he had known what the distemper was as soon as he had set eyes on it, and had set the patients away on their own, and none had handled them but Nancy and him-self, for they both enjoyed to a marked degree the surgeon's special health which protected them from contagion.

But this time he had brought a case right into one of the wards, to share the same air and the same light as forty other women; this time he had said it was chlorosis and he had been wrong. It was almost amusing in a way; he had seen the symptoms and said it was chlorosis. And it was cholera. Spell it but a little differently, and what a difference it made!

He moved then, almost savagely, tightening his muscles like springs and going down the ward in a controlled rush that made the women about him seem to shrink even more, and then he was beside the bed in the corner where lay the figure of the girl he had scooped up from her home in Broad Street to bring here.

He stood and stared down at her, and almost marvelled. She had been slight enough when he had first seen her, pallid enough, ill enough, but now it was as though she had been shrunken to half the creature she had been then. Her face was gaunt, her eyes seeming to blaze out from under the ridges of her brow like great carriage lamps.

They were red-rimmed and staring, the lids pulled painfully back as she looked up at him, and he could see that ill as she was, wasted as she was, yet consciousness remained with her, for she was looking at him with an appeal in her expression that was almost desperate.

He bent then, tucking his heels under his haunches, so that he crouched beside her, and she managed to turn her head on her pillow and look at him even more entreatingly and tried to speak; but her tongue was swollen and would hardly move, and her lips were cracked and crusted, and all that came out was a husky croak.

But he knew and said softly, 'He is well enough. He is fed and is clean and comfortable and is sleeping in a little basket in my own room. We set him there that he should be well. Your baby is well enough——'

And she sighed softly and closed those staring eyes, although the lids would not completely cover them, but left a rim of yellowish white showing beneath the sparse fair lashes.

He knelt there a while longer, and then very gently set his fingers on the fragile wrist that lay so laxly on the grey blanket, and felt the sluggish heavy pounding of her pulse and murmured, 'Her blood has thickened——' and Nancy nodded and said in a harsh whisper, 'I tried to get 'er to drink, but it was of no use. She cannot swallow—oh, Gawd, she's off again——'

For the little body had started to writhe as cramp moved into the wasted water-starved muscles and the eyes opened again and the cracked lips stretched over the swollen tongue as she stared in helpless terrified fury at the world she was leaving behind; and Abel knelt there beside her and watched her dying and could do nothing.

They settled her after a while, soothing the dry mouth with scraps of charpie soaked in oil of roses, trying to force some liquid past the clenched teeth, but knew it was waste of time and effort, for the girl could hardly live another half a day, if that; and when she had at last stopped convulsing Abel stood up and looked down at her lying there with her breath moving that tiny cage of protruding ribs that was her chest so shallowly that it hardly seemed to move at all, and felt the old familiar anger rise in him. It should not be so, it was evil that it should be so, the most grievous of insults that it should be so when all around him in the broad rich London streets men of fashion paraded in suits of clothes the price of which would feed one of these starving creatures for a month; where women wore clasped around overfed necks jewels which would raise enough money to build half another hospital such as Nellie's. Yet this girl lay here dying and breathing out her contagion to kill hundreds more like her, and he still had not enough money or people to do what needed to be done. His rage rose and filled his mouth with its sour taste, and he clenched his jaws and it settled again; but it was still there, as real and solid in his belly as though he had swallowed a plateful of meat.

William was standing at the foot of the stairs when they came down, his hands clasped behind him under his coat tails and staring sourly at the wooden bench against the wall. He was kicking moodily at the wooden box with the slit in the top which stood beside it begging mutely for donations to Nellie's funds, but he stopped and looked up quickly when his father and Nancy reached him, and he scowled and said, 'For the love of God, Nancy, get me a drink, will you? I came here so fast after eating I bid fair to be sick with the pain of my digestion. And if you can see to it that it's brandy, so much the better.'

She sniffed and said shortly, 'Brandy's a rare luxury at Nellie's, as well you know. You can have half a daffy o' gin, and that with water to it, for I've little enough to spare for those as is 'avin' surgery and 'as a real need of it.' But she went away to the kitchen quarters in the basement obediently enough, and William turned to look at his father and said harshly, 'Well? Is the pother done with? I have matters to attend to and would wish to be away from here.'

'No doubt,' Abel said shortly. 'But you cannot. You will be needed. So will Rupert—and all others I can obtain.'

'Oh? And for what?'

'Cholera,' Abel said abruptly.

William went a sick white.

'Cholera? You need *me* to—what good am I to deal with cholera? I have not been near a patient these three years or more—I have been a man of affairs, as well you know! Set me to cholera patients, and you set me to become one on my own account—no thank you, sir! You must make do with the people you have. If you have that many cases here then——'

'We have not—yet.' Abel said shortly. 'But I am not too sanguine.

The woman has been in the ward with forty others. It will be a miracle if the contagion does not spread and miracles do not usually happen in Seven Dials. The nurses and the women who come in will not stay once they know the disease is here so we will need all the help we can find. You and everyone else. As for risk—don't be a fool, man. You are fit and healthy and well fed and take the same risk every time you walk through the alleys between here and Gower Street.'

'And well I know the danger in those streets!' They both turned as Nancy came rustling up the basement stairs, a glass in her hand, and William grabbed it from her without a word of acknowledgement and drank its faintly clouded contents almost at a gulp, staring at his father over the rim of the glass, then wiping his mouth with the back of his hand with a savage gesture that seemed very incongruous in one so elegantly dressed. 'Aye,' he said then, thrusting the glass back towards Nancy without looking at her, his eyes never leaving his father's face. 'Well indeed do I know the danger in these streets! You may walk in 'em if it suits you, but I will not! I take a hackney to come here, the safe way, when I must, like a gentleman——'

'A little less of your so-called gentlemanly ways and you'd be more good to yourself and to those about you!' Abel said contemptuously and William flushed brick red and snapped, 'Well, I was born in a decent house with an honourable lady to call my mother so I cannot help but show some awareness of gentlemanly ways! It is no fault in *me* that you are less nice in your tastes!'

He stopped and bit down hard on his tongue, for his father had whirled at his words and was staring down at him from his greater height with such venom in his expression that William felt as though he were a child of seven again, a child who had transgressed against his father in some unknown way and had to cower against the wall to escape his wrath.

'Are you sneering at me? You with your niggling nasty little mind and your lazy swaggering ways? Sneering at me because I lacked the benefits I have struggled and suffered to give you? By God, I'll give you something to turn your nose up at, you——'

But William was no coward. For all his deviousness and his greed and his desperate self-aggrandisement he did not lack for courage, and he stood foursquare in front of his father, his chin thrust forwards and his eyes wide and glittering, speaking in as level a tone as he could muster.

'You may rant and bully as much as you wish. You may treat me with the same contempt you used against me in my boyhood to shrivel my very soul. You may try to drive me away as you did my sister and brother before me. You may try every muscle you wish, but I tell you this, I will not come here to deal with these patients, should every nurse and surgeon in the place desert it. I will not work among patients *ever*, so your scheme for sending me scouring the gutters for more half-dead rats and useless thieves and pimps and tails for you to practise your great surgery on won't wash! And nor shall you act the Caesar and sell Wapping from under my feet, for that is *my* establishment—aye, it is! My mother's father owned that business before you, and I shall use the Trustees to see to it that it remains not only for me to run as *I* think fit, but that it will go on supplying your precious Nellie's as it always has! I am sick to death of you and your overbearing bullying ways, and you may as well know it!'

And he seized his overcoat from the bench, took his hat in his hand and slammed out of the door with a violence that Abel did not know he had in him. Standing there in the dim passageway staring after him Abel felt the only stirring of respect for his third son that he could ever remember experiencing. But behind him Nancy stood slowly rubbing the glass she held against her apron and biting her tongue to keep back the words of scorn she ached to pile on the departed William. She had no respect for him at all, nor ever would have. Much as they would need help at Nellie's in the difficult time she knew was to come, she for one felt they were well shot of William Lackland.

## 17

As William's cab went rattling noisily through the sunny streets of Covent Garden on its way to St James's—for he felt the need of the company of good friends at his club in a way that was almost like a hunger for food—he wanted to kick himself. To have let his anger get the better of him in such a way as to virtually tell the old man of his plan to override his authority had been a piece of self-indulgence which, he did not doubt, would cost him dear. But the sight of him standing there with that look of sureness on his cold closed face, with that cool handsomeness that his son had always admired and wanted for himself and been so hopelessly aware that he lacked, had been more than he could tolerate.

Now, remembering the conversation in detail, he moved pettishly in his seat and wondered what the deuce Rupert would have to say; enough, no doubt, to leave scars, for Rupert had a wicked tongue when he wanted to employ it to hurt, as William well knew. The telling of Rupert would be almost as disagreeable as remembering the telling of Abel.

He watched the streets go by the dusty little window; Long Acre and Leicester Fields, Lisle Street and Coventry Street and on through Regent's Circus into Piccadilly; but he saw little. His mind was a turmoil, with thoughts of what he must do to further his designs about the future of the hospital, fears about his inevitable brush with Rupert, and his concern about how much longer he could continue, as they had agreed he should, to make medicines in the way he had been doing at Wapping. They had been lucky to avoid confrontation with his father before this, he told himself gloomily, for we have been at it for months now, and he's no fool, bully and devil incarnate though he may be——

His father. Travelling through London's streets on that unseasonably warm Sunday afternoon in March he found himself trying to cast his memory back to other years, other conversations with his father; why had the two of them become so set against each other? Were other men on such uneasy terms with their Governors? Surely not! Surely this man was unique in being so harsh, so unapproachable, so altogether lacking in any of the usual fatherly virtues?

He had heard schoolfellows talk of their fathers in easy comfortable terms, making it clear that they spent time in their company that gave both parties pleasure; remembered old Sellars, his closest friend in his apprenticeship days, whose father had gone gaming with him, had taken him on his first visit to a brothel, and generally busied himself about his son's worldly education; and tried to imagine Abel behaving so with himself or Rupert or the others. Had he ever done so with Jonah, the older brother William could only just remember, upon whom he had not set eyes for ten years or more?

But he could not put his mind to so impossible a task as to picture such scenes as his imaginings were trying to conjure up, and he abandoned the attempt. He must accept that, for whatever reason, his father was not his friend, nor ever had been. His harshness was a part of him like the colour of his eyes or the shape of his head and anything that happened now as the result of his sons' unwillingness to tolerate any longer his heavy-handed rule was his own fault.

'I wonder if he was so with Mamma.' The thought came into William's mind as his cab arrived at the portico of his club in St James's but he pushed it aside immediately. Thinking of his Mamma was something he had long since trained himself not to do, just as he had long since given up visiting her in her silent room. There were some things no man should have to do, and thinking about and visiting a relation in her state was one of them.

By the time William was ensconced in the gaming room in his club, a glass of brandy at his side as he watched a needlesharp game of faro, the sun was beginning to lose some of its brilliance, for it was now past four in the afternoon, and evening was not far over the horizon. But the crowds in the park were as thick as they had been all day and the hurdygurdy men and the sellers of sweetmeats were plying a most satisfactory trade among the people of the poorer sort who had come to stroll along the shores of the Serpentine in the midst of their fashionable betters and to make audible remarks about the quality of their dresses.

Jonah, with Celia on one arm and Oliver hanging on to his other hand, was uneasy, feeling obscurely as though he belonged neither to the quality nor the others. At one time there would have been no question in his mind; he would have known himself undoubtedly to be one of the *ton*, a man of fashion fully entitled to take the centre of the pathway, probably driving his own elegant equipage along the wide paths to bow to and be bowed to by acquaintances that he might meet.

But that belonged to the old days, before his marriage, and he tried to see himself as he had been then in his extreme youth, and could not. How could he, when for so long he had worked in that tawdry, noisy, smoky establishment that he and Celia had created? It was because of the time he spent there that he no longer felt able to include himself among the people with whom he most wanted to belong; the comfortable men of stature and elegance and ability.

He was not one of the other sort either, he told himself, looking sideways at the parading women in their gaudy feathered hats and blowsy pinned-up gowns, the men in their flat billycock hats and shiny serge coats. Work cheek by jowl with them I may, but I am not such a one, I am *not*, nor ever will be. Nor shall the children. And his hand tightened on Oliver's so that the child looked up at him, a little surprised, and then pulled his hand away and said, 'Papa, may I not sail the boat here? I am sure it is a very good place.'

'The Long Water will be better,' Jonah said. 'We will be there soon——' And more pleasant, his mind added. About the shores of the Long Water the gawpers and shrill cockneys tended not to go, leaving the way clear for the quieter and more worthy people and their children. Oliver would be better there.

Celia, walking beside him with one hand holding her green plaid skirt above her neat black boots, and the other tucked into the curve of his elbow, was happier than she would have thought she could be. For days it had hung over her like a great thick fog; the sick dull anger, the blackness of her mood, the ever-simmering rage barely below the surface of her mind. All the time the vision of *her* had been lurking at the edge of her consciousness so that she had been sure that if she could but turn her head swiftly enough she would see her, standing there laughing and jeering and then ogling Jonah, and Jonah staring back and smiling and becking and nodding at her——

But then, in that white hot flash of rage that had woken her that morning from an uneasy dream, that had made her turn viciously on the bewildered half-asleep Jonah at her side, she had found salvation; in shrieking of her rage and hurt and fury, she had found the way to lose it, and she smiled a little at the shimmering black water beside which they were walking, and then lifted her chin and looked up at the sky with its now thinning but still spring-like blue tenderness.

She felt her spirits lift until it was as though she was in the clouds herself and floating up there full of joy and peace and comfort. She had been wrong, she had been wrong, and Jonah loved her and only her. She had been full of fears of nothing. Lilith was far away and could not harm her. No longer just at the edge of her vision, but far behind her, that was where Lilith was. And she tried to ignore the fact that the vision had not completely gone away and was as happy as she knew how to be.

The crowds were less now, as they approached the Long Water, and they could see the trees on the other side in Kensington Gardens lifting their naked branches, and just beginning to blush greenly with new buds, and elegantly dressed couples strolling among them, and Oliver pulled away from his father's hand and ran for the bridge to gallop to the very middle and stand above the centre arch and stare down at the sluggishly moving water.

'Papa!' he cried, as Jonah and Celia came up to him. 'Papa, it looks very deep! Is it so? Could my boat be lost here? Could my sailors drown here?'

Jonah stood beside him, resting his elbows on the parapet and staring down at the opaque water and his own and Oliver's reflection in it. Beside him Celia too bent her head to look down, and for a moment the three of them surveyed their wrinkled moving faces as little breaths of wind sent eddies moving across the mirror surface.

'Indeed, your sailors could drown here,' Jonah said then, and smiled faintly at Oliver's serious expression. 'Real people have done so, you know! But I don't think you need fear for your sailors or your boat today. It is not precisely rough, after all.'

Oliver stood on tiptoes again to look dubiously over the parapet at the water. 'Well, not at present. But it might become so. Real people, Papa? Who?'

'Oh, a lady drowned here that I know of. A poet's wife, she was——' He stopped and shook his head. 'To be sure, this is a melancholy matter to discuss on so sunny an afternoon! We shall go and sail your boat and make sure your sailors come to no harm! Come along, and we will launch you and you shall be the admiral.'

'What poet, Papa?' Oliver, as dogged as always when in search of a new piece of information, tugged again on Jonah's coat-tails and, with the unending patience he always displayed when dealing with his children, Jonah launched into an account of the poet Shelley, and how his wife Harriet had ended her own life by throwing herself into the Long Water, and Oliver listened and nodded and began to ask questions about what happened to people when they drowned.

Beside them Celia suddenly shivered, and pulled her green woollen mantle more snugly about her shoulders and said sharply, 'I think you had best get on with your sailing, Oliver. It is not so warm as it was, and we must soon, I think, go in search of a hack on the Oxford Road and fetch your sister——' Oliver nodded and ran to crouch at the edge of the water and, with great caution, pushed his small craft out on to the smooth surface.

'I shall stay here, I think,' Celia said and stopped at the foot of the bridge, 'for the ground looks a little marshy there, and I abominate muddy boots. You go and play with him, if you wish——'

Jonah nodded and gave her hand a squeeze and turned to go. And then stopped and turned back to her and said impulsively, 'I am so glad we took this walk, Celia. It is not often enough that we can enjoy these family pleasures. If Phoebe were with us, it would be quite complete, would it not? Perhaps, as the summer comes on and the weather improves we can make more time for ourselves and come here more often? You work so very hard, my dear, and I am sure it is this that so— that upsets your nerves, you know, and makes you anxious. You were not always so—so——'

'So captious?' she said harshly, and looked up at him, her mouth hardening, but at the sight of his squarely handsome face and the grey eyes so filled with affection for her she softened again and spoke more gently.

'You may be right. I am sorry if I am sometimes—difficult. I do not wish to be so, indeed I do not. But the blackness comes upon me, you know, and I cannot always see beyond it, and I think and think, and the ideas go about my head in such a turmoil. It could be that I become fatigued, perhaps, but I know of no other way to do what must be done except completely. The work is there, and if I do not keep after people, naught is done as it should be and, well——' she shrugged, 'then I become more angered than ever. But I will try. If you wish me to——'

'I do indeed wish you would,' he said earnestly. 'I will do all I can to ease the burden—if you will permit me. But you are a very determined person, Celia, are you not? You always were. You determined to wed me, and so you did and here I am——' and he laughed.

She felt the chill move into her again. She had said she would wed him and so she had. Not for her the usual maidenly waiting to be wooed. She had set her cap at him, and he had succumbed. That was the way of it, and she could not deny it. But if only it had not been so! If only she could remember Jonah seeking her, wanting her, yearning for her as she had yearned for him! But it had not been that way! It had been Lilith for whom he had yearned and wanted and sought——

'He is waiting for you,' she said, her voice flat, and he peered at her for a moment and then nodded and went down the slope of the bridge to crouch beside his son and send the boat moving further out, with the aid of a stick Oliver had found at the water's edge. And she turned and rested her arms upon the bridge and watched them; and tried not to brood further, feeling the thin afternoon sun slanting across her back, watching the water's faint movement and the dancing reflections of the light in her search for peace and quietness in her mind.

And it did help her, that quiet time. The sounds of the Gardens receded into the back of her mind, and the glittering water she was staring at grew and grew until it seemed that all she could see was radiance and movement, with a faint green line that was the trees and grass at the edges of her vision. And she felt warm and comfortable, as though her body had melted away, leaving only her awareness there leaning on the stone bridge in the sunshine.

So, when the sound pulled her out of her reveries, it was almost shocking in its effect. The sound of a child shrieking, with shouted unintelligible words momentarily rising above the hubbub and then being overcome by an even more violent shriek, and she lifted her head and tried to clear her vision of the greenish blur that the light had left there, and stared in the direction of the sound.

Further along the bank, separated from the bridge by knots of people and children and boats and foreshortened by the distance were two women and a child. One, obviously a lady in a plum-coloured walking gown and most sumptuous furs, was standing with her hands held to her head in some distress, while the other, equally clearly a servant in her sombre black mantle and severely untrimmed bonnet, was holding a child who was kicking and thrashing about in a perfect paroxysm of temper. Beyond them, on the water, could be seen the probable cause of his rage—a large and very costly toy boat lying on its side shipping water and gradually disappearing from view; the kicking child raised its head and saw it sink deeper and wailed even more loudly, if that were possible.

Just below her Oliver stood up and tried to see what was happening, but could not and pulled on Jonah and cried, 'Papa! What is the noise, Papa?' And Jonah too stood up and lifted his chin to stare along the water's bank to see if he could identify the source of the fuss.

Up on the bridge Celia blinked again, and her sight began to clear as she cupped her hands over her eyes to shade them, and now she could see beyond the little group that was attracting everyone's attention another small party, this time made up of a man, a woman in blue, and two children, and one of the children, a boy with red hair, came running along the shore towards the shrieking child, and with the long stick he was holding in his hand leaned over and reached for the sinking boat. The stick, by some small miracle, managed to tuck its tip under one of the sails just before the vessel finally disappeared, the boy began to draw it back, with great care, and there was a splatter of applause and laughter from the watchers.

Almost at once the shrieking child stopped his hullabaloo and scrambled out of the restraining black arms that had been so grimly holding him, and in the sudden quietness Celia heard Oliver's voice below her cry, 'Why, Papa! Look, Papa, there is Phoebe! Is that not Phoebe? Is that my aunt? And Frederick? It must be——' and he started to run along the edge of the water, slithering and sliding dangerously in the mud as he went twisting and turning among the people who stood between him and those he wanted to reach.

And at once, Jonah ran after him, calling back to Celia over his shoulder, 'The foolish child—he'll fall in the water——' leaving her still standing there with her hand cupped over her eyes, staring along the shore and feeling a shock of coldness filling her as though the Long Water itself had started to rise with stunning speed to encircle first her legs and then her belly and her chest until the chill reached her throat and bade fair to choke her.

For not only had she recognized her daughter; she had also recognized the woman in black, now standing and pulling her skirts to rights, for the child had made unmerciful attacks upon her.

Hawks.

Hawks of the sour visage and even more sour temper. Hawks who had reared her and her sister and brother and treated them all so casually with what little energy she had left after tending the only person for whom she had any real feeling. And Celia felt her eyes move sideways as her gaze was drawn to that person, the woman in plum-coloured velvet by her side, who was now bending over the child and his recovered boat and saying something to the boy with red hair who was standing awkwardly next to her.

Lilith. Her mother. Lilith.

Even before Oliver and Jonah had reached the point halfway between herself and the two women, even before the woman in blue and her tall elegant companion had also converged on the group, Celia had turned and started to run across the bridge, back towards the Oxford Road, stumbling over the grass with her skirts held in both hands and totally unaware of the curious stares and occasional jeers that followed her. All she knew was that he had lied to her. Jonah had lied to her. He had told her that he had not taken Phoebe to Lilith, and he had lied to her. He had brought her here to mock her with his lies, to make her suffer and sink even more deeply under the cloud of the knowledge that he had lied to her for all these years. Lilith, Lilith, Lilith, was the only person he had ever cared for.

It was beginning to grow dark when William left his club to stand on the steps looking down into a St James's vivid in the glow of its elegant new gaslight, pulling on his gloves while his handsome malacca cane was tucked under his arm and his glossy hat was set at an angle on his head. He felt jaunty, pleased with himself and with the brandy warm within his belly. It had helped to clear his thinking, that brandy, and he was grateful to it. He may have blown the gaff to his father, but it need not make any difference, his brandied thinking had told him. The old man could be stopped from selling the Wapping manufactory, one way or another. The first step was simply to make Wapping indispensable and that meant preventing Nellie's buying its medicines from any other source. He must discover just where Conran planned to do his buying and move in ahead of him. However much some other establishment might be interested in doing business with Nellie's, there were ways of persuading them not to. Or at least to hold off for a while. He was enough of a businessman, William told himself in satisfaction, to handle other businessmen. So, to Conran in the morning and then his father would see a thing or two!

He ran down the steps and hailed a hack, bidding it to take him to Panton Street. Tonight he was definitely in the mood for agreeable female company, and he was whistling between his teeth as the cab made its way across the town, through Piccadilly on its way to the lights and glories of the Haymarket and its environs. It had been an unusual Sunday, not only in the way of weather, but in what had happened in it; he might as well have a little fun with which to finish it off.

Long after the last of the sunlight had unwillingly left the sky over the rooftops of St James's Abel was still at the hospital. He had gone prowling from ward to ward, trying not to let the patients who lay there watching him dumbly with their dull eyes know how worried he was, but unable to keep all his anxiety under hatches. It showed in his tight shoulders, in the controlled movements of his head as he turned to look at the people under his care, in the smoothness of his expression and the low even notes of his voice. When all was well in his domain he did not mind scowling his disapproval or shouting his annoyance. His sudden flares of temper were well known by all, from the most senior of the students to the most insignificant of the kitchen maids, and were in a strange manner a source of admiration. Abel in a rage was so strong, so much the master that even as his people cowered under his blistering tongue they felt security in him. But this quietness, this stillness, was something quite other, and in an ill-understood manner very alarming; and as he went by them the patients turned restlessly on their harsh ticking mattresses and pulled the rough grey blankets over their shoulders, trying to seek the peace of mind that would let them sleep.

Until at last Nancy was able to get him to leave the wards with their flickering smoking penny dips set on shelves in the corners to give a little light by which the night watcher could see when she made her occasional rounds of the long rooms, and make him go to his office to drink the brandy she had set ready for him.

'You have need of it,' she said shortly when he tried to push it away. 'You've 'ad a bad day an' you won't be no good to none of us if you don't get the knots out o' yer muscles, an' I knows no better way. So get that dahn yer and shut yer talking.' And he had drunk the brandy and gradually relaxed his shoulders a little; but his face remained brooding and dark as he sat and stared into the few coals that burned dispiritedly in the little grate.

'We have perhaps two days before we can know,' he said abruptly after a long pause. 'I have never yet been able to decide precisely how long it takes a miasma to work in a man, once he has taken it in, but I have never known it less than two days whatever the disease. There is naught we can know till then. And nothing we can do.'

'Oh, there is much we can do!' Nancy said sturdily, and nodded her head encouragingly at him. 'I shall set them all to scrubbing and cleaning tomorrow so that——'

'Oh, Nancy, what good is your housewifery?' Abel said wearily. 'I know you mean well, and it is always agreeable to be in rooms you have a care of, for I like the sight of well washed boards as much as any.

But it cannot do anything against the miasma of disease! If that were enough, why, we should not have the contagion here at all. Your soap and sulphur would have sent it packing when I brought the Merrick girl in. But it did not. We have cholera within our doors and God damn it all, I *brought* it in! Had I stood at the door hat in hand and invited in Death himself with his scythe at the ready I could not be more culpable.'

'Such talk is stupid, and I for one won't listen to it,' Nancy said calmly, and refilled his glass. 'As for my scrubbin' being of no use— well, that's as may be. Mr Snow always reckons as we does better with those of our patients as 'as operations 'ere than they do anywhere else, and 'e says its on account of the operating room's so well took care of an'——'

'Snow,' Abel said, and looked up and pushing away his glass with a suddenly vigorous movement got to his feet and looked about for his coat. 'Snow will help, *and* will have ideas of ways to contain the infection! We were talking of just such a matter only a week or two gone. Where's my coat, dammit? I—oh, thank you——' as Nancy fetched his coat from the back of the door and held it out for him. He shrugged it on and she brushed him down, standing back to stare at him with a judicious eye, and then nodded. 'Aye, you go and talk to Mr Snow. And then away home to your bed, for you'll be no use to none of us if you don't get yer sleep. An' not a soul shall I let in nor aht o' the place till you comes in the mornin'. The cholera may a' got in to Nellie's, but it'll 'ave the devil's own job getting aht of 'ere if I 'ave anythin' to say about it. Come on, now, Mr Abel. All's not lost yet! We've only 'ad two deaths from it, and one o' them a babe no stronger than a breath o' wind in August, so there's nothin' to get yerself into such a to-do over. You go 'ome an' you'll see different in the mornin', I've no doubt.'

He looked back at her from the door and after a moment nodded, still unsmiling but not as tense as he had been ever since he had arrived in the sunlit afternoon that seemed so long ago now. 'Aye,' he said. 'Aye, you may be right. I doubt it, but you may be right. Anyway, there's nothing I can do here now. Goodnight to you, Nancy.'

But long after he had gone she stood there staring at the door he had closed behind him, her lower lip caught between her teeth. She knew as well as he did how empty of true reassurance her words had been. Tonight was but the lull before the storm, of that she was sure. Two dead of cholera already—and God alone knew how many more were to follow.

## 18

'I have not been completely honest with you, Abby,' Gideon's voice came strained and thin from the darkness, and she leaned forwards in an attempt to see him, but the light from the streets outside was not sufficient to bring more than the faintest of glows to the interior of the carriage.

'Oh?' she said easily. 'I cannot imagine you ever being mendacious, Gideon! Are you about to tell me that we are not on our way to dine with your parents after all but that you are going to abduct me to Gretna Green or some such place?'

It was extraordinary how merry she felt; how pleasant all about her seemed, how altogether contented her mood was and had been for the past two days. She had told herself repeatedly that Gideon's declaration of love and his proposal of marriage were delightful compliments but no more than that, that she had no notion of accepting a young man's attachment as anything but transient; that she was a sober staid widow who had neither the desire nor in all likelihood the opportunity ever to wed again. But it made no difference to the way she felt, to the lightness of heart that simplified even the dullest of her chores—like teaching the mouselike Miss Miller her bookkeeping methods—that made her suddenly discover herself humming a vague melody as she went about the day's work. Even now, sitting opposite him on the way to dine in Lombard Street at the house of his parents, she could not be completely serious. There were bubbles in her mind, and she could not but enjoy them.

'Oh, we are indeed going to my parents' home,' Gideon said. 'But I told you it was—was just a simple party, did I not? That my mother had a notion to entertain? It is that that is untrue.'

'Well, you had best confess all, Gideon, before we arrive, for I would not for the world be embarrassed by any ignorance,' Abby said gaily. 'Is it to be a great ball instead of a simple party? Or a masquerade? Or perhaps we are to dine al fresco in the middle of Finsbury Square!'

'I wish you will not make fun of me, Abby,' he said a little plaintively. 'This is a matter of some importance to me.'

She was contrite at once. 'Oh, dear Gideon! I am sorry! Please to forgive me, but I have been so—oh, I don't know! So full of levity this past few days! I must behave myself—I am at risk of being as giddy as young Miss Phoebe!'

He leaned forwards in the stuffy darkness and reached for her hand and even through the kid of her own glove and the heavier leather of his he felt the warmth of him and there was a little answering throb of heat within her.

'I am very happy to hear you say so. It fills me with the hope that I am not altogether unconnected with your mood. Please go on feeling so, Abby. Please—even when I tell you of my deception.'

She began to feel a little apprehensive. 'Dear boy! You must tell me at once!'

'I am not a boy, Abby, but a man, and you must remember that!' There was a note of acerbity in him. 'Although I must confess that I have perhaps been a little juvenile in misleading you about this evening. Well, to be short—you are the only guest we have tonight!'

'Well, that is no matter! I did not dress as for a great fashionable crush, but for a pleasant quiet evening, so——'

'And it is not an ordinary dinner we shall be having. You see, Abby, tonight—oh, there is so much to explain! I should have done so on Sunday when I first broached the matter!'

He leaned back into the darkness of his corner again. 'Abby, do you know anything about my faith?'

She became cautious. 'Not a great deal, Gideon. I know you are a Jew, that you go not to church but to your own place of worship, that there are those who——' she stopped.

'Aye. Those who despise us.' His voice was harsh. 'Well, that is a matter to which all Jews are accustomed. We have been hated and driven out wherever in the world we have been. It appears to be our destiny. Your own people drove us out of this country many years ago.'

'I did not know that.'

'Few do. But we were allowed to return, during the Commonwealth, you know. About two hundred years ago. That was when my forebears came to live and work in London, but we still have relations and many friends in the old country. In Spain. Jewish family ties are always close, and my own has never lost contact with its roots in Madrid.'

'I do not see why you are telling me this,' Abby ventured. 'It is very interesting, of course, but you said you had misled me and must explain and——'

'I am explaining. About my faith. It is one, Abby, that is more than just a matter of attending church and making worship. We, the Jews, we follow our faith in every matter. In the way we live and work and eat—and—everything. There are many religious duties that are carried out in our own homes, as well as in the place in which we worship. The synagogue, you know.'

'Indeed? That is most interesting,' and she could think of nothing more to say, and was deeply puzzled, for he was clearly most disturbed about what he was trying to tell her.

'Tonight is the first night of Passover. Tonight we commemorate the story of Moses and the way the Jews were driven from Egypt——'

'I know of that, of course,' she said, seizing gratefully on her long-ago biblical education. 'The giving of the commandments and so forth.'

'Aye. The giving of the commandments. And it is a commandment to us that we must always remember what happened in those distant times. Tonight we remember. There will be a service at the synagogue, and afterwards a festival meal. It is this to which my father bade me bring you. I—I am afraid you will find it very strange tonight. It will not be the sort of evening you expected at all. And I tell you now that I am sorry I did not tell you sooner of my father's wishes and give you the opportunity to decline.'

His voice sounded heavy and now it was her turn to reach for his hand in the darkness.

'I would not have declined, Gideon. If this is a matter of religious importance to you, then I am gratified and most touched in my heart that your father should think well enough of me to bid me share it with you. I remember him as a gentle and kind man and most honourable, and this is very much the action of a gentle and kind man.'

There was a short silence, and then Gideon said quietly, 'I hope you will always see him so, Abby. As a gentle and kind man. I love him very dearly.'

'I know you do,' she said and tightened her grasp on his hand before letting go and leaning back. 'I know you do.'

'And I love you, Abby, in a different way, of course. A most urgent, needing and——'

'You promised you would not speak of this, Gideon,' she said swiftly. 'You too must be honourable.'

'I am trying to be.'

She smiled in the darkness. 'I know. And in general you succeed. Now, stop fretting yourself about this evening. I have no doubt it will be a little strange to me, and somewhat confusing, for I must confess I was never particularly interested in matters to do with the church—indeed, I regularly commit the sin of falling into a doze during Mr Barker's no doubt estimable sermons at St Mary's—but I trust I have been well enough bred to be able to comport myself with dignity. I will give you and your father no cause for offence, Gideon, I do promise you.'

'It was the risk of offending you that concerned me. We have arrived,' and he leaned forwards to open the door as the hack came to a stop. 'I have already committed some sort of sin, in my father's eyes, you know, Abby, in driving to bring you here. It is forbidden to pious Jews to travel on festivals such as this one tonight. But I prevailed on him to forgive me.'

He led her through the darkness of the street to a heavy doorway. 'Well, we are here. You will see we make our home above our banking house, Abby. We could not move further away, to more fashionable parts, since my father must live within walking distance of the synagogue. Although it is many years since he could walk——'

The stairs that faced her on the other side of the door were broad and covered in a heavily-patterned Persian carpet held in place with brass clips set into each tread. The walls were panelled and bore paintings in ornate gilt frames and brass sconces bearing fat wax candles, all burning very brightly, and there was a small brazier of fretted brass filled with glowing charcoal standing in a recess halfway up the flight. The place was warm and bright and very inviting, and she let her cloak slip back from her shoulders as Gideon stood back and let her precede him up the staircase.

At the top of the flight a soberly blacksuited footman took her wrap and Gideon's coat and hat and stick and went soft-footedly away, and she looked about her at a hallway as warm, as well lit and as elegant in its furnishings as the staircase had been. She would have stopped to admire the pictures here but Gideon was looking at her with his face very still and grave, so she smiled up at him and said lightly, 'Come, Gideon, you fill me with apprehension! I have not seen your father these many years, but I remember him as a man of great charm and urbanity. You need not look so alarmed—I doubt he has any more anxiety about meeting me again, than I have about meeting him! Or is it your Mamma that concerns you? I am sure we shall rub along famously——'

He smiled, and his shoulders relaxed a little. 'Forgive me, Abby, I am, no doubt, being over-anxious. But I do so wish you and they could be—as I would wish you to be. But perhaps I wish for the impossible——' and he turned and opened one of the heavy mahogany doors and stood invitingly aside so that she had to enter and could not answer him.

The room was big—bigger than she had expected, knowing it to be in a far from ordinary house, set as it was above a bank, and even brighter and warmer than the parts of the establishment through which she had already passed. The colour that dominated it was red, a rich hot red so unlike the cool white panelling and delicate mahogany furniture that was so fashionable a feature of most houses she visited that she blinked. There was a hint of strangeness about the room that she could not at first identify, a sense of the faintly exotic, and then she realized that this came from the hanging oil lamps, in the same delicately fretted brass as the brazier on the stairs, and the very splendid oriental carpet which hung on the wall that faced the pair of tall windows, now shrouded in crushed velvet curtains of the deepest crimson.

Before the fire, which was piled high with sea coal and comfortably blazing, was a wicker chair, and in it a man she recognized as Nahum Henriques; but not because of his appearance.

The Nahum Henriques she had known had been a square man, broad of shoulder and vigorous in his movements, as black haired as Gideon and with a pair of fine dark eyes that had looked very directly at her.

The man sitting there with a cobweb of woollen shawl about his shoulders and a rug across his knees was shrunken and clearly carried no atom of excess flesh on any part of his body. He had white hair and a face so spare of flesh that it looked like polished bone; but the eyes were the same, very dark and very direct and impulsively she held out both hands and moved across the room towards him in a soft flurry of cream-coloured taffeta skirts.

'Mr Henriques! How happy I am that we meet again! I am sorry to see you looking to be in poorer health than I remember you, but happy indeed to see you as well as you are! It has not been kind in you to refuse to be visited all these years.'

He looked up at her, and lifted his thin pale hands to accept both of hers. 'I did not precisely refuse, Mrs Caspar. I simply had no wish to impose myself, in my limited state, upon the sensibilities of others. An invalid is a very tedious person to have about one, after all.' He dropped his eyes then and said with a curious punctiliousness, 'I have not seen you since the death of your husband, my good friend James Caspar. You will permit me to offer my condolences, and to wish you a long life, despite the time that has elapsed.'

She inclined her head in quiet acceptance, and after another of those penetrating looks he smiled suddenly so that his whole face lifted and became more like the broad and vigorous one she remembered.

'You have changed for the better in these past nine years, Mrs Caspar! I remember you as a pleasant enough young woman, but little more than a schoolroom miss after all. Now, you are a most handsome lady——' he dropped her hands and she reddened a little.

There was a soft sound behind her, and Nahum said, 'You have not, I believe, met my wife, Mrs Caspar. Leah, may I present Mrs Caspar. You will perhaps recall Henry Caspar—Mrs Caspar is his daughter-in-law.'

Abby turned and sketched the courtesy demanded of a younger

woman presented to an older, and looked with real interest at Mrs Henriques, trying to ensure that her intense curiosity did not show in her face. She had been told by James, she remembered, that Mrs Henriques was a retiring woman of piety and duty who rarely went abroad but spent her time about the matters of her household, which was why they did not meet. 'Nahum Henriques may be a business partner, Abby,' James had said, 'but his wife is a most aloof lady, so you cannot ever look to her for friendship——'

Looking at her now, she saw a woman of surprising tallness, thin and with a back as straight and narrow as a board. She was wearing a dress of very plain cut, quite unadorned with feathers or fringe or any of the braided trimmings that were so fashionable now, but of a most rich deep-green silk that shimmered and whispered with every move-ment she made. Her face was pale and framed by thick glossy hair of a blackness untainted by any hint of grey and pulled back severely from her brow into a tight knot at the nape of her neck. Her eyes were very dark, like those of her son and husband, but of a deep brown richness that was very startling in its effect. She had the same lashes that Gideon had, long and thick and of equal length at both top and bottom and her brow was smooth and quite unfurrowed above them. Abby thought her one of the most striking women she had ever seen and felt suddenly exceedingly dowdy, in her fashionable cream gown with the brown braid trim on the skirt and the amber ribbons that dressed its yoke.

'I am happy to make your acquaintance, ma'am,' she murmured, and Leah Henriques smiled, a cool and seemingly friendly smile, but it did not involve those heavily lashed eyes at all, and she said in a voice that was low and very slightly accented. 'I am happy you were able to accept our invitation for this evening, Mrs Caspar. I remember your father-in-law well. He was a man of most high seriousness. It was sad that he should have died so young, as sad that his son also suffered the same fate. Families can be unfortunate, can they not, in their experi-ences? So much is handed from generation to generation, I find——'

'I did not know my husband's father,' Abby said, and felt a curious unsureness within herself. This was indeed a strange woman; it was not easy to feel comfortable with her. 'But my husband told me that he had cause to regard you and your family as his very good friends.'

'Business associates must enjoy the loyalty and goodwill that is implied in friendship, of course,' Mrs Henriques said. 'It is, naturally, a different sort of friendship from that enjoyed on a purely social level. Forgive me, Mrs Caspar, if I do not offer you refreshment now. Perhaps my son will have explained about this evening——'

'I know that it is a——'

'A festival,' Gideon said, and smiled at her, and she smiled back and said, 'Thank you. Yes, a festival. It is kind in you to include me in so—in a matter that is of such importance to you.'

'We felt it would be of abiding interest to you to see a little of the way Gideon must spend his life,' Nahum's voice came heavily from behind her. 'You have become very good friends, have you not, over the years while you have needed help and guidance with your business? You are thrown much into each other's company.'

She felt herself redden a little. 'I am most grateful, indeed, for the guidance you and Gideon have always provided to Caspar's,' she said, knowing her voice to be very formal. 'I have long wished to express to you in person my appreciation of the investment and involvement in my affairs that you have offered, for without it, I am afraid, my life—and that of my son—would have been quite insupportable. But you preferred to retain your privacy at all times, and I respected this——'

'I do not seek thanks, Mrs Caspar,' he said, and his voice was equally formal. 'The house of Henriques is, I trust, one of probity and honour. We involve ourselves only in good business endeavours—good not only in the sense of being successful in fiscal terms, but in the matter of their prosecution. Your business has been from the start one that must excite the admiration of any man of affairs, being based on good sense and a proper concern for the welfare of the customers you supply. We should not have financed you otherwise. So you must not thank us, but your own sound business attitudes. Indeed it is we who must thank you, for we have from the beginning enjoyed a reasonable return from our involvement in your affairs.'

'And shall continue to do so,' Gideon said, and his voice came to Abby as a comforting sound, for she had begun to feel most embarrassed. 'And now, I insist we shall not mention business matters any more at all this evening. Mamma was about to explain, Abby, that we do not generally take any refreshment before dinner, on the

Passover Festival, for it is a meal of some—some solemnity. But I am sure if you have any wish to——'

'I wish only to do as you do,' she said swiftly.

'Then perhaps you would care to accompany me when we go to the synagogue for the service that commences the festival,' Leah Henriques said. 'Gideon and I must go and it is my husband's sadness that he is rarely able to make the journeys. He does so on the High Holydays, of course——' she stopped and smiled at Abby, and again she seemed to display kindness and friendliness, although her eyes remained bleak. 'That is in the autumn months of the year. But tonight he will remain here until we return for the meal. I had thought to ask you to remain with him, but now, I think, perhaps it would be better if you accompanied us. If you wish to do so, of course——'

She looked beyond Abby to Nahum, and Abby turned her head and saw his returning glance and as clearly as if they had spoken she knew some communication had passed between them; a question had been asked and an answer given. And she felt a sudden pang of loneliness, of painful longing for the days when she had had someone to whom she could so talk, when there had been for her that communion with another mind that was so warming and so needful for any sort of real happiness.

She felt Gideon's hand on her arm then, warm and reassuring, and she looked up at his eyes, those dark and so very handsome eyes, and felt the reassurance he was offering her move into her mind, and relaxed and smiled at him, wanting him to know that she understood and felt better; and he nodded softly and moved away to his father, to re-arrange the rug about his knees. And she realized suddenly that just as his parents had shared a moment of silent communion, so had she and Gideon; and the warmth and sense of joy that had been so much a part of her these past two days came surging back into her, almost doubled in its intensity. She looked at Gideon's bent back, at his dark head bent over that white one and recognized in herself a great tenderness and sense of comfort. In this strange room with these somehow alarming people, he was the source of all that was peace and security.

She lifted her head to find Mrs Henriques looking at her very directly, and she felt herself flush a little and said, 'I will, of course, do as you wish. I am your guest, and more than happy to fall in with any plans you have made for me.'

'I believe you will find the synagogue service one of interest,' Leah said. 'You will forgive me if I fail to introduce you to any of my acquaintance we may meet, however. As is the case with so many peoples who have suffered the pain of being spurned and disparaged, even persecuted, there is among our community an—an occasional unwillingness to accept outsiders. I trust you will not condemn us for this.'

'Really, Mamma, you make us sound like very ogres.' Gideon's voice was light, but Abby could see his jaws had tightened and his head was held up at a sharp angle. His mother looked at him, smiling faintly and said, 'Well, perhaps. I am sure, however, that Mrs Caspar will forgive me. I wish only to explain as much as I can of our ways. There is so much to know, is there not? If you will come with me, then, Mrs Caspar? Nahum, I would wish you would use the time to sleep a little, to strengthen yourself for the Seder. You will have much to do when we return! Gideon, I think we must go, for it is getting late——' She bent and kissed her husband's forehead and turned and left the room, and Gideon took Abby's elbow in his and led her out too, to the footman who was waiting ready with cloaks and Gideon's hat.

Together they went down the stairs and out into the chill of the evening, where the last of the day was finally being extinguished over the western roofs, to walk eastwards along Lombard Street, into Gracechurch Street and thence to Bishopsgate, hurrying past shuttered counting houses and the tall silent grey buildings.

'We are on our way to Bevis Marks, Abby,' Gideon said softly, as she hurried along beside him in the darkness. 'As I explained, we cannot ride there, for that is not permitted to us. But it is not far to walk—it is in the shadow of Houndsditch. And we will be there for only a short time. The service lasts perhaps an hour, and then we shall return to my father and the important part of this evening's celebration. I—I hope you will not be too confused by it all.'

'I am sure I shall be most comfortable,' Abby said a little breathlessly, for Mrs Henriques was setting the pace and walked unusually rapidly. 'Quite sure.'

But within herself, she knew that knowledge and understanding were jostling for recognition. She knew she was beginning to understand why she was here on this rather chilly evening in March, hurrying through the sober businesslike City of London streets on her way to a most exotic and alien experience.

## 19

'But you cannot do it so, Mr Snow!' Nancy said urgently. 'Send 'em out to their 'omes and not only do you tell the 'ole world as we've got the fever 'ere at Nellie's, and send 'em all into the terrors, but you sends the disease aht into the streets. And then more an' more of 'em'll get it, and want to come 'ere to be took care of, and we're worse off then ever we were. And so are they——'

Snow shook his head, impatiently. 'Nay, Nancy, you mean well, I have no doubt, but you do not understand the matters of which you speak. The disease *comes* from the streets! It is the dirt and the hunger and the misery in which they live that makes it flourish so! To send the people from here to their homes won't take the disease there. But it will protect 'em from the severe form of it that has come to the hospital——'

She shook her head stubbornly. 'I don't see 'ow you can be right, beggin' your pardon, Mr Snow. If it was like you said, and a matter of dirt and 'unger, why even if we brought in 'undreds of 'em to Nellie's, they wouldn't die of it, would they? Nor would they pass it on to other people already 'ere. This place ain't dirty and stinking, as well you know. It's scrubbed and clean and fresh as you like, an' the patients gets good food and plenty of it so they ain't 'ungry. If it was like you said, why then, all we'd 'ave to do is bring in all the people as get fevers, and they'd get well again. But it don't 'appen that way, do it? They comes 'ere, and the patients as we've already got get the fever from 'em. So as I see it, it must be somethin' to do with the people that 'as the disease for I swear it's naught we give 'em in 'ere. They carries it on 'em—and gives it to others. So sendin' these patients aht'd be a terrible thing, because it'd spread the contagion worse'n ever.'

Snow gave a sharp little snort, and then said patiently, 'I can understand your thinking, Nancy, but you do not have the right of it, all the same. I cannot deny we do not know yet the precise mechanism of the disease—how the patients pass it to each other, as indeed they do, and why some have mild symptoms and live and others severe ones and die, and why the disease can run through a town like a fire.' He shook his head, 'Like it did in—when was it?—nine years ago, in 'thirty-one. All I can say is that I believe it would be better to send out the patients not yet afflicted and deal only with those showing symptoms, and wait till all subsides and then go on from there. But it is your decision, Lackland——'

They both turned and looked at Abel, standing there at the window of his little room and staring out at the milling crowd below in the street. They were the street patients and were showing signs of restlessness, peering up at the windows and calling out raucously, and some of the livelier children were actually clambering up the railings and leaning over in an attempt to look in through the close drawn curtains, for it was past nine o'clock, the time when the doors were usually opened to their daily inrush.

He looked up as they stopped speaking and stood staring at them, and then shook his head. 'I don't know. If we did but know the mechanism of the spread it would be a guide. Is it miasma or is it something in their constitution? If it is the latter it makes no difference what we do. They'll live or die accordingly. But if it is in the hospital and we send 'em out, they will die for they already will have the disease, and if it is in the streets, and we send 'em out, why then, they die just the same, for they are weak enough, in all conscience, and will fall like flies.'

' 'Tis in the air they breathe when they're near one as is ill, and that's the way of it,' Nancy said stubbornly. 'I may be no physician, Mr Abel, Mr Snow, but I knows what my common sense tells me. An' when I sees what 'appens when we got no cholera in Nellie's, and then one patient with it comes in and 'ow it spreads itself to seven patients in a matter of days, then it says to me as it'd be criminal to send the other patients out until the fever's run its course. As it will——'

'Aye, when they are all dead,' Snow said harshly.

'That's as may be,' Nancy retorted. 'I've as good an idea as yourself of what can 'appen, but at least if they all dies in 'ere, that's all as dies in't it? Send 'em out to the streets and it's thousands, not 'undreds that go to fill their graves. If they've got the fever, as well they might 'ave, for we've 'ad cases in every ward bar one, then this is the place they ought to stay. That's all we can do to contain it.'

Abel nodded, suddenly and sharply. 'I believe she is right, Snow. Oh, I know the theory of it all, well enough! I've talked to 'em all—that accoucheur from Aberdeen who told me he was taught by his master—Gordon, I think his name was—that the childbed fever was spread in a hospital by the hands of the midwives and was in the very fabric of the wards, and now Chadwick and his inquirers——'

'Arnott and Southwood Smith?' Snow grunted. 'Aye, I know 'em—and there's another—James Kay. I've talked to them too, and while I can see that there is good to be done in seeking the source of disease in the gutters the patients come from, I cannot see that you do your hospital any good by keeping the as yet untainted here to take their chance. I would never do so at Westminster.'

'You do not at Westminster have slums pressing as close to your walls as we do here,' Abel said dryly, and after a moment Snow nodded.

'Well, that is true enough. As I said, you know your own business best. Shall you keep 'em here then?'

'Yes. We'll keep them here. As Nancy says, bad enough some shall die. But worse if the whole district catches it.' He drew a deep hard breath. 'Oh, God damn it all to hell and back! If we did but know for certain how it was spread! If it were in the air alone, it would stay in but one ward. But it does not! It started in the women's medical ward here, and then showed itself two houses away and three stories up!'

' 'Tis you and your nurses that go from ward to ward,' Snow said. 'You do perhaps take it on your persons——'

Abel shook his head vigorously at that. 'Oh, no! I told you, I know of the way fever can be carried on people's hands! Neither Nancy nor I nor Jane Weekes—and only we three had touched Merrick and her baby—went to the men's surgical ward—we took good care not to go anywhere but where we had already been, and perhaps already done the harm. We left the care of those men to the people who were already in contact with them. And yet it spread——'

'Well, at least we can keep it here within these walls,' Nancy said grimly, and turned to the door. 'Until the nurses find out, of course——'

'Well, that should prove it either way,' Snow said almost jocularly. 'If the nurses leave you, and cholera breaks out around their homes, why then, we know that you were right and I am wrong. But if it doesn't——'

'If it doesn't I'll be glad to 'ear it,' Nancy said sharply. 'This ain't no sort o' wager, Mr Snow! It's a matter of decidin' what's best to do in a bad situation not to make it a sight worse!'

Snow looked at her and then nodded, his solemn face breaking into an unaccustomed smile. 'Aye, Nancy. You are a very good woman, and a splendid nurse indeed. If they were all as caring as you the sick people who come to us physicians and surgeons would be better off. As it is——'

'As it is I've got work to do,' Nancy said, flouncing a little but clearly not unpleased. 'On account I knows as sure as I'm wastin' time standin' 'ere those nurses'll be scarperin' as fast as their lazy good for nothin' feet'll take 'em. Real scum, that's what these nurses are. Real scum. There isn't one as I'd trust as far as I could throw 'er——' She pushed the door open. 'I'll send the street patients away, Mr Abel? Tell 'em as there's no treatment to be 'ad today?'

'Aye, tell 'em not till further notice is given. Quite apart from the contagion, there'll be no chance for me or any of us to look at 'em——'

'Are your supplies secured?' Snow said practically, as Nancy went rustling away to open the great door and shout at the people outside to go away. 'Food and necessaries? For once the word gets out—as it surely will—you'll get little help from any of your usual tradesmen.'

Abel nodded. 'Nancy is a careful woman, and so is the Bursar. A sour-faced complaining whining maggot of a man though he is, he does his work well enough. I checked as soon as I got here this morning. We have food for eight days, except for milk, of course, but they can do without such luxuries as that. Bread and water is no unusual diet for these people. If we are reduced to that here after a week, well, we must think again. But we can manage well enough to start with.'

'You do not get your water from the main pump in Broadwick Street?'

Abel shook his head. 'No. We found we had a well of our own when we opened the cellar of the third house. We draw what we need from that. It is a good well, fed by a spring quite near the surface. It is only in the driest weather we must use the pump.'

'And the nightsoil men? Will they continue to serve you?' Snow asked shrewdly and Abel grimaced.

'I doubt it, man, I doubt it! You know perfectly well they will not handle such situations as this. The more they are needed, the less good they are! No, we shall have to burn what sewage we cannot deal with in the cesspit. And hope the disease runs its course before it loses its usefulness. Oh, God, man!' He rubbed his face wearily. ' 'Twill be the devil and all if it goes on like this! Seven cases, so soon! And two of 'em babies at the breast! You'd think they took the distemper in with their mother's milk, they get it so fast! Well, I'd best be about it. Thank you for your help, and for coming to see us, Snow. We welcome it. And you'd best be on your way now, had you not? You will have your own more fortunate people at Westminster to see——'

Snow shook his head and smiled thinly. 'Well, no, I think I shall stay if you will have me, Lackland! After all, it could be your common-sensical Nancy is in the right of it, and I will take the disease with me, having been here among its miasma! They have doctors in plenty to manage at Westminster, more than you have here, and half the work. So I'll stay about, I believe, and see what I can do with you. And I am interested, besides. Maybe, being here, we can see some evidence of how the damned disease does take itself so fast about among the poor and hungry! As I say, if you will have me——'

'Have you?' Abel grunted. 'Good God, man, I'd be clean out of my wits not to snatch at you! You are more than welcome, more than welcome. And if you find the answer to the contagion here at Nellie's —why, none will be more pleased than I will. But it's the patients I must turn to now. Shall we about it, then?'

And together they made their way up the stairs to the long rooms above where frightened patients lay in rows, covertly watching each other for signs of the disease they most feared, and the disease they knew had come creeping into the place where they themselves had come, so hopefully, to be cured of other ills.

## 20

It was when they reached the synagogue itself that the full strangeness of it all moved into her so that in some peculiar way she no longer felt like herself at all. She was a different person, going through the actions demanded of her, moving, sometimes speaking, always looking and listening but not ever being involved in any real sense. It was like that painful afternoon when in the familiarity of her own little counting house in Irongate Wharf Road there had been a separate little Abby, sitting aloof and cool, watching all that befell the physical Abby far below her. That little Abby was sardonic and amused, even mocking, and for the whole of that March evening a shy and worried and deeply bewildered Abby shared an uneasy communion with her.

Moving through the darkness she had become aware of other figures joining them, of voices speaking in a strange lisping way, but not using words she could comprehend, of hats being doffed and bows being exchanged, until they were passing through a pair of heavy wrought-iron gates of most elegant design into a courtyard which was cobbled underfoot and surrounded by the shadows of low buildings huddled close.

There was a single lantern burning dully above a wide open pair of huge iron-studded wooden doors and they halted there for a moment, part of a small crowd which was pressing forwards, and Gideon murmured in her ear, 'We must separate here. You will go up with my mother to the Ladies' gallery——' And then he was gone, and she was following Leah Henriques up a narrow flight of wooden stairs that were so ill-lit that she stumbled a little.

But at the top she caught her breath, and stood and stared and had to screw up her eyes against the brightness. She was in a narrow gallery which ran round three sides of the building; a gallery with rows of benches upon which well-dressed women were sitting close together, and edged with a low diamond-latticed screen which made a delicate fresco above the body of the building.

Leah Henriques was moving forwards, past women who nodded and whispered to her as she passed, and she nodded back and smiled, and Abby, following her, felt curious eyes upon her but could not actually catch any direct glances for they all wore large-brimmed hats behind which they could hide their faces.

'Space at the front is a privilege reserved for me by virtue of my husband's position in the congregation,' Leah Henriques whispered, as they sat down. 'He has always been much respected. He was once a most hardworking warden of this place——'

But Abby could do no more than nod her head in response as she looked downwards, for the sight that met her eyes was quite stunning in its effect. Seven vast candelabra with swooping curves of brass and elegant curling sconces, each blazing with two tiers of candles, hung at her eye level over the centre, and she could feel the heat of them moving across the air to strike her cheeks with gentle fingers. The light glittered on polished brass, on painted plaster, on ancient wooden benches and twisted polished rails.

Immediately below her was a dais, railed with curling wooden balusters, with two flights of carpeted steps to give entry to it, and with a reading desk covered in heavy green cloth at its front. Behind it clustered more benches, and before it, leading away to the far wall where there was no gallery but which was pierced by a pair of tall windows with myriad leaded panes edged in a most vivid blue, were rows of sombre pews.

It was the far wall which most engaged her interest then, for the space between the handsome windows was dominated by a huge wooden cupboard-like edifice which bore a pair of great wooden doors, flanked by two more doors of the same heavily-polished wood. They were inlaid with gilt, and a fan-shaped architrave surmounted the central doors, while gilded leaves and garlands and shells, richly clustered and entwined, embellished the other two. Before the central door on an intricately curved and decorated bracket hung a pierced brass lamp within which a little light glowed dully, while above it soared a most curious object, to Abby's bemused eyes.

Surrounded by small squared and richly carved pilasters and surmounted by a pointed arch were a pair of round-topped black-painted panels, each bearing gilt characters of so foreign an appearance that they filled her with a very curious foreboding. She looked at them again and faint memories of her schoolroom days with Miss Ingoldsby and seeing Hebrew script in an old book jostled in her, so that when Leah Henriques beside her, following the line of her gaze, murmured, 'Those are the Ten Commandments, given to Moses for us,' she could nod and understand.

Her eyes were becoming more accustomed to the brightness now, and she looked away from the walls and furnishings of the synagogue to the people below, and marvelled again.

Only men. A mass of men in sober black clothes were sitting there below her, but each of them looked exotic in the extreme for over their shoulders and looped across their backs they wore great white silken shawls. Even from up here she could see how very costly and beautiful they were, many embroidered in rich detail in silk of the identical colour of the fabric upon which the stitches were set, so that they looked as though they were embossed, all edged with a heavy silk fringe of great length which lay across those prosaic black coats and trousers in incongruous frivolity.

Some of the men had their shawls pulled up over their heads, and were bent over their books and swaying to and fro with a curious brisk movement as they read, their lips moving, and indeed the whole building was filled with the soft deep buzz of masculine voices as the men muttered and murmured, and almost without thinking Abby said softly, 'They are praying.'

'Yes,' said Leah, and raised her head from her own book to look at Abby. 'They are praying aloud in the house of their God. It is customary with us,' and she bent her head again, and Abby, looking at her, saw her lips move and heard the soft whisper of her voice as she said her strange and lisping syllables. The book she was using was also written in Hebrew, Abby could see, and she looked away again, embarrassed. It was almost as though she had been prying in a secret letter about personal matters that were not meant, nor ever could be meant, for her eyes.

So she looked down again beyond the lattice of the screen and now saw that every head was covered. Some of the men were wearing top hats, and some round black skull caps, but the effect of that sea of covered heads was the same; she could feel a sense of solemnity, of a dignity born of practices hallowed by centuries of unchanging observance coming up at her in great waves with the heat of the candles and the soft rise and fall of the praying voices.

She turned her head then, her eyes pulled almost against her will towards the dais and now she saw Gideon there, standing with a white shawl about his shoulders and a skull cap on his head about which his glossy hair sprang rich and buoyant.

He was looking at her with his eyes wide with some sort of appeal, and she stared back at him for one long unsmiling moment, and then bent her head a little. And he looked back at her, and she felt the way he relaxed and could be comfortable, and knew he had recognized her assurance of her own wellbeing, there far above him, and was comforted in her turn.

She did not know at which point the private praying ceased and the service proper began, but she became aware of a single voice that rose above the others; a voice of great sweetness and richness, making deep throaty sounds and sending notes of pure tone and perfect pitch soaring into the hot air. Entranced, she turned her head to look and saw a big man wearing a shawl of surpassing richness above a black cassock, so heavily bearded that greying curling locks were spread on his broad chest. Behind him boys' voices took up the music, and it filled the building with such sweetness that suddenly her eyes stung and her throat contracted at the loveliness of it.

And so the time went on and she sat there in a sort of enchantment, listening and being soothed and then uplifted and then soothed again by the changing pattern of the singing, feeling the blaze of the candles on her face, and the scent of wax heavy in her nose.

And when with much pomp several of the men moved slowly to the vast doors at the end of the synagogue and opened them to bring out great scrolls clothed in silver armour, tinkling with silver bells and wrapped in velvet cloths, to parade them all about the building while men bent their heads before the words of God being carried before them, and touched the passing scrolls with the fringes of their shawls and kissed the fringe in an aching need to have contact with the wisdom of their chosen God, she was not surprised.

Indeed, she could no longer be surprised by anything, and she watched the procession, and listened to the sonorous and incomprehensible reading from the scroll and watched the silver objects lovingly borne back to their secret place to be locked up again under the eye of the watching single light that hung above it, and was very aware of the two separate selves that were Abby. Marvelling puzzled Abby, sitting in the Ladies' gallery beside the stiff-backed Leah, and grinning, almost laughing Abby, perched high in a remote corner and whispering, 'What are you doing here? You have no right to be here! You are quite, quite ridiculous! Get up and go away, away and back to Paddington Green where you belong!'

But she turned her head and looked at Gideon, standing there among his fellows, his book in his hands, his shoulders shawled and his head covered, and she saw him not as the boy she had known for so long that he was part of her life, not as the staunch friend upon whom she leaned, but as a man. A man among others, a man of value and importance and strength.

A man she loved.

She sat there and looked at him, and let the feeling move in her as it wanted to. She could no longer deny it, and no longer wished to deny it. The man there below her, so like all the others and yet so totally unique, was for her the only man there was. For ten long years she had loved a shadow, had subsisted on the recollections of the brief months of life they had shared, had maintained her deeply passionate nature on the fragile memories of the physical love they had known so few, so pitifully few, times. And now, in the deepest shadows of her mind James stood wraithlike and transparent, looking at her with a vast sadness in every line of him; and then, at last, vanished completely. All that would ever be left of him now was a little painted miniature on the table in her sitting room at Paddington Green, the glint of red in Frederick's hair as he turned in the sunshine, a name above the door of the factory he had founded. His place, his special place in Abby's soul, had been superseded at last and she let the pain of the final parting wash over her and fill her chest with unshed tears, and then let it drain gloriously, joyously away as Gideon's figure, in all its strength and firmness, all its elegance and deep animal excitement, took James's place.

And as though he knew her thoughts were on him he looked up, his lips still moving in the words of his praying, and gazed at her, and she looked at him and leaned forwards, staring back, trying to fill her eyes with the message she so wanted to convey. The message that said she loved him, and needed him, and ached for him, and always would.

And in some way he seemed to understand, for a faint tide of colour rose in his cheeks and then subsided and he no longer spoke the words of his prayers, but stared at her as she stared at him across the broad space that separated them. And the secret separate Abby did not mock or laugh or comment, but watched in silence and knew of the irrevocable decision that had been made.


And afterwards, in the comfortable dining room of the house in Lombard Street with Leah on her left and old Nahum on her right, and facing Gideon across a table spread lavishly with white linen and gleaming silver and the most sparkling of crystal, the sense of wonderment filled her more richly than ever.

There was the way the old man sat with a great goblet of crystal filled with crimson wine before him and read those lisping singing phrases from an old leather-bound book and nodded his capped head as he sent his voice rising and falling through the antique story. From time to time he would look up to give her a simplified account in English of what he was reading, telling her how the Lord God of the Jews had delivered his people from the machinations of an evil Pharaoh, of plagues and sufferings, death of children and survival of hope, and she nodded and listened and nodded again.

There were the times they drank wine with him, a sweet and cloying wine that tasted of raisins and Gideon bade her drink it to the dregs, laughing at her flushed face when she did, and telling her of the tradition that demanded four such cupfuls should be taken on this special night.

And there was the time when Leah, the tall and stately Leah with all her aristocratic bearing held about her like a rich robe stood up and took a silver bowl and ewer and a soft white towel, and with careful humble ceremony poured water over the hands of her husband and son so that they could wash; and she caught Abby's eye on her and said with an oddly triumphant air, 'It is the privilege of a woman of our people to make such services to our men. In the synagogue the man is supreme, but in the home, oh—here, I am a queen. And as a queen, it is my pleasure and my right to humble myself in this way—do you understand that?'

'I think I do,' Abby said, and caught Gideon's eye on her, and smiled at him, but as Leah went soft-footedly to return the basin and ewer to a side table she said softly, 'I think you do not. You cannot, if you have not grown in this manner, and been taught in this manner.'

And Abby opened her mouth to speak, but had to close it again, for she could not find words to deny the truth of Leah's speech.

It was all so strange and so mysterious, the whole of it, and sometimes it was also faintly absurd, as when Gideon opened the door and they all watched a wine-brimming red Venetian glass goblet in the centre of the table for, Gideon said, 'The prophet Elijah comes to each of our houses for his refreshment at this moment on this night'—and she had to smile at that; but Leah and Nahum looked at her solemnly and did not smile.

At last they ate, a meal that was lavish and impeccably presented and served, but she could not manage to eat more than a mouthful of the excellent mutton set before her. ('It is a traditional meat for this festival,' Gideon said, and she murmured back at him, 'Dear Gideon! Is there anything you do that is not steeped in centuries of tradition?' and he had smiled and looked at her with grave eyes and said simply, 'No. Nothing.')

And then, more reading, more wine, even a little singing, with Gideon's strong young voice lifting above his father's rather cracked notes and Leah producing a startling contralto, and at last, some four hours after she had arrived in Lombard Street, but feeling as though it had been a lifetime, Abby rose from the table and followed her hostess back to the drawing room, while Gideon pushed his father's wicker chair before them both.

They sat engaging in the normal desultory small talk that could be heard in any drawing room in London after dinner and that made what had gone before seem even stranger in Abby's mind. Involuntarily she yawned, and then blushed. She had not realized how tired she was. At once, Leah looked up at Gideon and said, 'I think, my dear, that you must take Mrs Caspar back to Paddington Green. It is late and she has had much to tolerate with us this evening.'

'I will send Walter in a hackney, if that will not discommode you too much, Mrs Caspar,' Nahum said then, stirring in his chair, for he had seemed to be half asleep. 'We do not customarily——'

'I know,' Abby said swiftly. 'It is not a tradition with you to ride on these festival evenings. And I would not wish Gideon to come so far with me, so late. A footman's protection will be ample.'

'It will not!' Gideon said strongly. 'I would not dream of permitting——'

She turned her head and looked at him. 'Please, Gideon,' she said softly. 'I would truly prefer it. I have much to think about. We can talk another time.' And he looked at her for a long moment, his face unsmiling, and then lifted his eyes to stare first at his father and then at his mother, and nodded.

'If *you* wish it, Abby.'

'I do. We shall meet tomorrow at the factory after all. It is Wednesday, is it not?'

'Yes,' he said, 'Wednesday.' And he made the mundane word sound like a small prayer. 'Wednesday. Very well, I shall obtain a hack for you, and tell Walter. Excuse me——' and he bent over her hand, and brushed it with his lips and with one more swift glance at both his parents went quietly out of the room.

There was a silence for a little while and then Nahum spoke, and his voice had lost the weariness that had filled it at the end of the meal, after he had been reading and singing from his Hebrew book for so long.

'You are interested in tradition, Mrs Caspar?'

'Interested? I had not thought much about it before, I must confess. I am a practical person, Mr Henriques. One who seeks always to make the future of benefit to me and mine. I have not been much given to looking backwards.' And she knew in her heart that she was less than truthful, for hadn't she been looking backward to James for the past ten years? But that was finished now. It was the future now. The future with Gideon.

'But you have found our traditions, as displayed to you tonight, of interest?'

'Indeed. Most interesting.'

'Then I shall tell you of another that I think will—impress you, Mrs Caspar.' He stopped and coughed and Leah got up and moved softly to his side to stand beside him, resting her hand on his shoulder, and he looked up at her and lifted his own hand to set it over hers, and then returned his gaze to Abby and went on with a greater strength in his voice.

'We have a long tradition of family loyalty, Mrs Caspar. In a sense, of course, that is why I was happy to be of aid to your husband when he sought it of me. Your husband's father had been my friend and colleague. So it was apt that I should be his son's friend and colleague.'

'I have always appreciated that.'

'I do not seek appreciation, but understanding, my dear Mrs Caspar. Let me go on and explain to you that the attachment between parents and children among us is of indissoluble strength. *Almost* indissoluble. It is only death that ends contact between us.'

He turned his head to stare sombrely into the dying embers of the fire. 'We take the fifth commandment very seriously, Mrs Caspar,' he said and turned and smiled bleakly at her.

She nodded, and then said in a low voice. 'I believe we understand each other better than you realize, Mr Henriques. You are telling me that—that Gideon and you—that you have a strong influence upon him.'

'Yes, there is that. But it is not a personal influence, alone, you understand. It is built into our faith. Duty to parents, love of parents for children, care of each other—it is the cornerstone of our religion, in many ways.'

She raised her head and looked at him very directly. 'Are you trying to tell me that you dislike my friendship with your son, Mr Henriques?'

He looked back at her with his deepset eyes filled with warmth and a sort of tenderness. 'My dear girl, not your friendship. Not that. But your love. If that is what you feel.'

There was a silence then, and she could hear the embers hissing in the grate, and the faint rumble of traffic from the street below, and she looked at them both consideringly, standing there before their hearth, with their hands linked and both looking expressionlessly at her, and then she sighed and closed her eyes and spoke softly.

'Yes. Yes, I cannot say otherwise. I have not said it to him, but I cannot deny it to you. That would be a—sin, I think. Yes. I love him.' And she looked at Leah now, and saw that there had come into her high-cheekboned face and her deep eyes an enormous sympathy, even pity, and she was puzzled and let her puzzlement be seen on her face.

'Oh, I am sorry,' Leah said and her voice was deep with feeling. 'I am so sorry. It should not have happened. We should have foreseen it, and not let it happen.'

'You cannot prevent love,' Abby said. 'Can you? I tried to. I never meant to love anyone ever but James. Dear James. But he is quite dead now, quite, quite dead. And I love Gideon.'

Leah shook her head, and said nothing, but for the first time Abby felt a warmth from her; was no longer made to feel as though her attempts at communication had been repelled, and she was confused. It seemed somehow more threatening than the coldness had been, earlier that evening.

'The love of parents and children is as much a part of Gideon as his very body,' Nahum said and she almost jumped, for his voice was very strong now. 'You must know that. His faith is part of him too. He may not know how close a hold it has on him, how deeply he cares for the traditions and the beliefs, the laws and the obligations he has been taught since earliest infancy, but he is my son, and I know. He cares deeply.'

'I am sure he does,' Abby said. 'I would not have him otherwise.'

'Would you not? When you know that it is not customary for the sons of our community ever to marry any but a daughter of the yasidim—members of this congregation? That when a son or daughter of our houses chooses to marry away from the faith, they are as dead to us? That we hold services of mourning as for the dead, never speak of them again, tear our clothes and weep and sit on low chairs to grieve for the taking of our child from us? And never speak of that child, or see that child ever again? Would you not have him otherwise, knowing that?'

She stared at him for a long moment, and tried to understand what it was he was saying, and could not, and said so.

'I did not think you would understand,' he said bleakly. 'But you must try.' He leaned forwards in his chair, and immediately Leah set both hands on it to support him, and from her place behind him watched Abby with that look of sadness upon her pale face.

'If you allow this affection you have both developed to grow further and seek to consummate it with a marriage, it will mean that Gideon will be torn from his very roots. No longer will he be able to come to us as parents, to walk among his own people as their brother. He will be quite, quite cut off. Dead, you see. It will hurt us deeply, but it is not for our sakes alone that I tell you this. It is for Gideon's. You saw him tonight. You saw him there among his own people, praying to his own God. Can you take that from him? And what could you give him that would heal the gaping wound such a loss would leave behind?'

She sat very still, her hands folded upon her cream taffeta lap and tried to think. She saw Gideon again, in her mind's eye, there among the candles and the music and the splendour of his synagogue, and remembered the way knowledge of his manhood, his strength and his power had moved into her at that moment. And knew that much of the strength and power that invested him came from the surroundings in which she had first recognized it. To tear him from that would indeed be like destroying half of him, and she closed her eyes against the recognition of the huge dilemma that had so suddenly and so sickeningly opened its gaping jaws before her.

The man she loved, and the life that belonged to him; to give him her love and to take his would be to extinguish so much that made him and their love what it was.

And she opened her eyes and stared at Leah and could see, at last, just why she was looking at her with that vast pity in her dark eyes, and why Nahum was looking at her so bleakly. And shook her head and tried to speak and could not.

Behind her she heard the door click, and then Gideon's voice, in all its everyday sureness and comforting ordinariness. 'I have a hack at the door for you, Abby. And Walter is ready as soon as you are. We must see you get safe home, for you must be very tired.'

## 21

Celia had fought the blackness in her mind for three days. She had
worked about the supper rooms in a perfect frenzy of activity, rolling
up her sleeves to set to in the kitchen so that preserves and pickles were
put up, headcheeses and brawns and sausages made, and the larders left
bulging. She had made new curtains for the stage, sewn costumes until
her fingertips bled from her needle and throughout had kept her grim
silence except for orders to the servants.

Jonah had tried, at first anxiously and then despairingly, to discover
why she had fled from the park that Sunday afternoon, why she had
met his return with the children with so grim a face, but she had said
nothing. Nothing at all. All she could do was try to contain her fear
and her rage and the constant whispering of the voice in her ear; for
now it was not just that she thought her thoughts, but that she heard
them put into words.

It was a strange little voice; flat and yet filled with expression, and
sometimes she would stop her work and stand with her head set to one
side trying to listen to the actual words, but that was difficult for the
syllables would change when she paid so much attention to them,
becoming strings of rhymes and chatter almost like those of a child
when crooning itself to sleep. 'Naughty, haughty, laughing, chaffing
lady,' it would whine in its reedy little notes. 'Bad, sad, tumbling,
rumbling, humbling lady woman. Sister, father, mother, brother,
trouble, double, rubble, bubble——'

But when she was not trying to listen, then it made sense. Then it
talked to her earnestly and so reasonably, telling her to remember. So
remember she did, over and over again.

Lilith and Jonah long ago in that little room high in the attic of her mother's house, Jonah's bare legs under his nightshirt, and Lilith laughing and dimpling, her own bedgown not quite covering the curve of her breasts, her hair tumbled so prettily on her bare shoulders. It was repeated in every detail time after time after time until Celia felt almost dizzy with it, as though it were she who were going round and round in the past and condemned for ever to watch the same scene being repeated instead of it being, as she knew, *they* who made it happen. Jonah and Lilith who were to blame for it all, Jonah and Lilith who were sending their secret messages to that little voice in her ear.

Her thinking changed then, when she realized that properly. Instead of fighting down the black tide of knowledge she let it rise and engulf her, let it tell her how wronged she had been and how cruelly she was used. And when it told her she must go and tell Lilith that it must be stopped, that the messages must cease for she was getting tired of it all, she did not hesitate. Black as the tide was it had not completely cut her away from the reality about her. She could see in every aspect of his face, the way he looked at her and grieved when she just looked flatly back at him and then turned her head away, that it was not Jonah who was to blame. Oh, he was sending the cruel messages, no doubt of that —but only because of *her*. It was *she* who controlled him, and made it possible for them both to treat her so cruelly. Celia knew that as surely as she knew she breathed.

It was at five o'clock in the afternoon that she decided to go. The kitchens were ready and the servants knew what was on the bill of fare for the night, and could manage to be ready without her presence. She gave Betsy Brewer meticulous instructions about what was to be done and added sharply, 'And you are to say nothing to Mr Jonah about my departure, you understand? He will return with the children from their walk shortly, and you know nothing about where I am, should he ask. It is no concern of anyone's where I am going, and I shall return as soon as I may. Before the nine o'clock performance, I have no doubt. But you are not to say. You understand?'

'Can't say nuthin' abaht what I don't know nuthin', can I?' the woman said laconically. 'None o' my business you want to go cavortin' orf on yer own. But you'll 'ave to pay extra for the extra work as I'll 'ave to do. No gettin' rahnd that, is there?' And Celia swore at her, but gave her half a crown nevertheless and walked out of her supper rooms into the noise of Covent Garden, just beginning to fill with early evening roisterers as the afternoon light began to thicken into a grey and early dusk.

Wrapped in her sober green plaid cape and with a small neat bonnet framing her pale face, she made her swift way across the muddy gutters and the spilled fruits and vegetables from the market, still unswept from the day's trade, towards the Strand, hurrying down Southampton Street as quickly as she could. She would find a hack in the Strand more quickly than anywhere else and she felt herself impelled to make haste.

'Where is she?' she asked herself, and the little voice murmured tinnily in her ear, 'At the Haymarket, swaymarket, greymarket, poormarket, whoremarket, that's where she is, braymarket, daymarket——'

'Haymarket Theatre,' she told the cabman collectedly, gathering up her skirts above her muddy boots to climb into the dusty straw-smelling interior and he clicked his tongue and his tired animal wearily twitched one ear and went clopping away to weave through the late vans and drays and private carriages that churned the mud into an even stickier morass.

Past new Hungerford Market, where the stallholders were beginning to pack up for the day, filling their carts with their strings of cheap beads and tin trays and papiermâche boxes and ribbons and cotton lace and cheap wooden toys, and closing up the fronts of the stalls where fish and meat and fruit were sold to both careful respectable housekeepers and extravagant women of the town, where starving gutter-bred children stole and begged and capered for their suppers.

Past the hubbub and mess where the raucous Irish workmen were just ending their day's labour on the new Square, past the pile of tumbled stones and rubble that they said was going to be a great column to honour Nelson—when it was finished, which most cynical Londoners said would be never, for hadn't they been working on the Square for almost eleven years?—along Cockspur Street, into Pall Mall and then they were there.

The driver clicked his tongue again and pulled on the reins and the horse bent its head and curved right into the Haymarket, and there, looming up on her right, it stood, its six great stone pillars outlined against the smoky light of the gaslamps under the portico, the usual knot of hangers-on clustered about the doors.

'Please take me to the stage door,' she called up at the driver. 'Off Orange Street,' and obediently the hack turned right again, clattering along the narrow way past the glaring windows of cookshops and ginhouses, to stop beside the dirty little door that gave into the side of the vast building that was the theatre.

She stood there in the street staring up at it in the rapidly failing light, and let memory come crowding back into her. She had been so very small, so very young and she had been brought here by Mamma, lovely sweet-smelling Mamma, to see the new theatre being built on the site of the old burned out one. She could even remember what she had been wearing—a dress of white muslin trimmed with such charming cherry red ribbons, her hair caught in a fillet, her slippers of soft black kid, and Mamma had lifted her up and cried, 'Look at it, Celia, my precious one! You know what that is? That is the palace that is mine! I am the queen of it, and you shall be its princess and we shall do all we wish there and all the subjects will come and worship me here, and we shall be the happiest people in all the world and nothing shall ever change that!' And she had whirled about and Celia, small white-muslined Celia with the cherry red ribbons, had thrown back her head and laughed and clutched Mamma about her neck and smelled the delicious smell of her and been the happiest princess in all the world.

But Celia had grown up and Lilith had changed and now she was sending these cruel, cruel messages to steal her Jonah from her, and it must be ended. It must be ended, as soon as might be, and Celia was the one to end it. And she nodded her head and set her bonnet neatly to rights and quietly walked into the familiar little passageway that led from the stage door to the greenroom and the stage, smelling the old familiar scent of hot wax and gaslight, fish glue and lime and the dust of twenty years.

She moved quietly past the stacked scenery, through the narrow walkways where hampers and boxes were piled in higgledy-piggledy profusion, to come out at last opposite the greenroom door.

It was half open, and she could see the bright gaslight pouring out from within and stopped for a moment, not to catch her breath, for she was quite composed, not to remember, although every step she took was rich with recollections of her childhood, the agonies of growing up and the sweet and painful months when she had first known Jonah, but just to feel. A small part of her was suddenly very curious. Did she feel anger? Or sadness? Or what? And she was a little amused to discover that now she was here she felt nothing at all. The black tide that had been so much a part of her for so long was lying low, heaving sluggishly deep on the floor of her mind. She felt no fear, no anxiety, nothing but peace because she had come at last to deal with the woman who had caused her so much agony for so long.

A shadow fell across the door, and it opened wider and light again poured out, and she could see Hawks standing there, a drift of yellow frills over one arm and a tin box tucked under the other.

'It'll take me best part of half an 'our to get this lot goffered, what with the stage 'ands gettin' in the way an' all, so don't go shrieking for some rubbish yer fancies, on account of you'll 'ave to wait. I've only one pair of 'ands, and you've got the full use of 'em as it is.'

Celia could hear the response, though not the words, and it was strange; for although she had not heard that voice for ten years its cadences were so familiar, its pitch so much a part of her that it did not even have the shock of familiarity. It was just there again, as though it had never gone out of her life.

Hawks came stumping out of the room and slammed the door behind her, and went mumbling to herself down the passageway towards the distant glow of light from the wings, and Celia watched her go and then moved softly across the dusty floor to the door. She did not knock, nor even think of doing so; she simply turned the handle and walked in quietly, closing the door behind her.

Lilith was sitting at her dressing table wrapped in a blue peignoir and with her hair tied up in a white cloth. She was hunched over, deeply engrossed in whatever she was doing, and did not look up at the sound of the door.

'You'll never get the job done if you don't get on with it,' she snapped. 'For Jesus Christ's sake, you stupid drab, get out of here and get on with it, or you'll find yourself on the street tonight!'

Celia came moving quietly and calmly to stand beside her and looked down at her and she said nothing, and still Lilith went on with what she was doing. She had a little saucer full of spirit before her, with a small wick burning bluely in it, and over it she was holding a small tin pannikin by a twisted wire holder, and stirring white powder into the heavy fat that was melting in it. The faint odour of pig's lard rose smokily and she stirred carefully, the little silver spoon twinkling in the gaslight, and then rested the spoon in the gluey mixture to reach out for a pinch of carmine powder from one of the boxes that lay spread open in front of her, their dusty blues and greens and yellows glowing richly in the gaslight.

It was at this point that she looked up, her mouth open to heap more abuse upon Hawks, and saw Celia, and for a long moment the two women were quite still, Lilith holding her little pannikin over the dancing flame, and Celia standing with her hands quietly folded in front of her.

The contents of the pannikin bubbled and spat and Lilith blinked and looked down at it and then very calmly took the spoon between her fingers—a little gingerly, for it was hot—and began to stir again.

'I was of the understanding that you were never going to see me again,' she said and her voice was light and quite without any tremor. 'I was always a quick study and I quite clearly recall the words you said. "I shall not see you again," those were your words. "And nor shall he." Those too. I recall quite clearly.'

'You look very old,' Celia said, and her voice too was very ordinary. She had been staring at her mother's face, at the fine lines that ran into a network from the corner of her eyes, the way her lips, slightly pursed as she concentrated, also showed a pattern of lines running towards her nose, and despite its careful dressing and arrangement, her hair had not quite the same gloss and life that Celia remembered. 'I had not thought about it before, but you must be—why, at least fifty! Dear me. Fifty. You'll need more paint than ever now, will you not?'

Lilith set the little pannikin down on the table before her, and now her hands shook very slightly and Celia saw that and felt a small surge of triumph rise in her and suddenly smiled widely.

'Poor Mamma!' she said mockingly. 'Have I touched you on the raw? Poor old Mamma—to think that——'

Lilith looked up at her, and leaned back, folding her arms across her breasts.

'Is that why you've turned up here after ten years? To tell me that which I know, that which any woman must know about herself? You cannot jeer at me for no larger a matter than the passage of time! Look at you, after ten years! You were plain enough at sixteen, God knows, a poor dab of a creature and not one that any man would turn his head to look at, and now—la, but you are a dowd, are you not? Such clothes! Where do you find those? In some basket sent to the poor by your betters? And your face—why, if I had aged somewhat in the last few years at least I have not gone off as much as you! You have a skin like mud—what man could find anything in *you* to care for? Has he gone and left you, then? Is that why you've come whining here? Your precious Lackland gone and abandoned you? There would be none that would blame him if he did, though he was ever a fool! But perhaps he has learned after ten years with you how to——'

'You know what has happened to Jonah,' Celia said. 'You do not have to play the actress with me.' The sound of his name on her lips had started it again. That black, black tide was rising, creeping up in her mind like a living thing, and she felt her nostrils pinched and her face rigid as she tried to control the anger that the tide was pushing before it. 'And you are going to stop it. You hear me? It is going to stop. That is what I came to tell you. You have done all that you could to ruin my life, all these years you have taunted and laughed, and now it will stop, for I have said it must. And so it must——'

Lilith was suddenly looking very pleased with herself. She leaned even further back in her chair and linked her hands behind her head and, setting one slender leg over the other, began to swing her foot, so that perforce Celia had to step back a little.

'So, that's the way of it, is it?' she said softly, and laughed, a deep rich bubbling little laugh low in her throat. 'So that is how it is! I was right. I am always right, amn't I? I told you he could never forget me, and so he has not! Well, there's a thing! There is a thing indeed! He thinks of me still, and looks at you and thinks of me—oh, that is so rich!' and again she laughed and her eyes twinkled most engagingly.

'You will not stop it, then?' Celia said softly, never taking her eyes from her face, and still standing with her hands quietly folded before her. 'You will not stop telling him, and making it tell me? You will not be warned?'

Lilith looked at her a little sharply, and then shrugged. 'I do as I wish. I always have, and I always shall! Whatever I have been doing this past ten years—why, I shall continue to do so! You speak in riddles to some extent, but what do I care for that! Have I been a thorn between you all this time? I am very happy to know it! I shall go on being happy to know it! So what do you say to that?' Again that bubbling little laugh. 'What *can* you say to that? Nothing at all!'

And she bent to her table again, and picked up her little pannikin to peer at its contents and again stir the thick white mass with her little spoon.

The tide was almost at eye level now. It had come in on each side, and all Celia could see was that face, that beloved hateful face and its lines and its colours, all very large and brilliant, as though it had been set inside a telescope. That face, bending over a pannikin held over a dancing blue flame in a saucer full of spirit. There was hardly time to do anything, she knew, before the blackness would be complete, but it had to be done, and she looked consideringly at the little flame in its saucer, at that hateful brilliant face and sighed softly. And moving with an almost casual ease, she reached forwards to pick up the little saucer and held it in one gloved hand; and Lilith raised her head, startled, and stared up at her daughter, her green eyes wide and questioning.

And still casually, still with a curious slowness in her movements, Celia pulled back her hand and flung its contents directly at that face.

The last thing she saw before the black tide completely engulfed her mind were the blue flames creeping and dancing across the cheeks, the way the hair on the forehead sprang into burning light, the way the mouth opened blankly and shrieked hugely and the hands clawed at the burning robe across those once white but now reddening shoulders.

## 22

Abby was so glad to see Henry Sydenham that when he came into the manufactory she almost seized on him, to his obvious surprise and to the amusement of the workers. She had spent all morning busying herself among the work benches, had planned with Caleb a new mixture for the use of sufferers from the gripes, had found a more comfortable way for the smaller of the boys working on the grinding of powders to reach his pestle and mortar, and had given Miss Miller the most detailed of instructions so that she could get on with her efforts over the books. She had in fact exhausted all activities that could keep her mind from her own personal affairs, so the sight of Henry at the door, shaking the raindrops off his hat and stamping his wet feet had seemed like a gift from the heavens.

Which was why she had greeted him with such exaggerated pleasure and then blushed to realize how disordered her behaviour had become. She would undoubtedly have to find some way to school herself, to come to terms with the matter, but now, at least, she had other things to think about.

'We cannot talk in the office, Henry,' she said, 'for Miss Miller is there. Come to the fireside, for you are chilled to the bone, and we can discuss matters there. You look most put about, I must say! Has something happened to discommode you?'

Chattering busily she led him to the blazing hearth and pulled a bench towards it, and she hung his coat to dry against the wall, before settling him on the bench beside her.

'I am sorry about the noise here,' she said. 'I know it is quieter in the office and easier to talk there, but——'

'It is of no matter,' Henry said, and she realized for the first time that he was acutely uneasy. 'It is—important that—I mean, I would prefer that—it is better that we are not overheard, I think.'

'What *is* the matter, Henry? You look most disturbed.'

'I do not like having to come to you with the news I have,' he said, and stretched his hands to warm them before the blaze, clearly avoiding her eye. 'It is indeed, a matter of some embarrassment to me that it is all my fault that it is necessary. If I had not gone seeking Queen Eleanor's trade, then it would not—well, I did not know, after all. But I am indeed most uncomfortable about it all, ma'am, and I would not have you think I seek in any way to interfere in matters that do not concern me——'

His state of confusion acted like a balm on her. It seemed as though it was all she had needed to settle her own mixed thoughts, to make her fix her mind on business, instead of letting visions of Gideon come pushing in, and she leaned forwards now and patted Henry's shoulder and said collectedly, 'Well, Henry, there is no use going on in this disjointed fashion! If you have aught to tell me, then tell me shortly, and directly. I have more sense, I hope, than to set about you for any reason if you have not earned it! I believe you know me well enough now to know that!'

'Of course I do,' he said, and leaned back and looked miserably at her. 'It is because of the—the very real esteem in which I hold you, Mrs Caspar, that I am so put about now.'

She smiled. 'Well, get on with it. Whatever it is, the sooner it's said the sooner it's mended.'

'Well, ma'am.' He took a deep breath. 'Well, as you instructed, I took my samples and tariff to Mr Conran, and very complimentary he was, after a cursory glance. Said he liked the way we packed up our goods—he was most taken with the quality of our stone pots for our salves—and was most hopeful about the tariff. He wanted to know if we could undercut at all, and I was very cautious. Said it all depended on the size of the order, for I thought, ma'am, as if I got a really swingeing large one, that you might see your way clear to adding some extra machinery and cutting the costs that way. We'd have a smaller profit, I know, but there'd be more of it, wouldn't there? And I'd as lief make ten sets of tuppences, as five sets of threepences. It's better business, if harder work, and in the long run—well, you know how I mean.'

He stopped and looked at her, his face pink and rather shiny, and pushed his hair out of his eyes.

'Well, so far, so good, you might say. I just sat tight, and thought, well, I'll go and see him—Conran, you know—go and see him after a week or two, just to follow up. Wouldn't act too eager, and put him off, but show a nice readiness. Well, that's the way it was, till last night, when you could have knocked me down with a feather, and that's a fact. I was just settling down to me supper—about seven o'clock it was, since I'd promised my young brother as we'd go down to the Dove for a little skittles to which the boy is partial and he's a bit young to go alone, when there's this knock at the door, and my mother, who is a careful soul, as you well know, Mrs Caspar, was most anxious, seeing we don't get many calls, not at that hour of the day. Well, respectable people don't, do they?'

He was beginning to show some relish in his account, and Abby said crisply, 'Well, Henry, let's get to the point!' and he flushed and said, 'Well, yes, ma'am. But it's not easy——' He stopped, swallowed and manfully tried again, 'Oh, Mrs Caspar, ma'am, it was your brother!'

'My—who?' She stared at him. 'Jonah? What on earth——'

Henry shook his head. 'He said he was Mr *William* Lackland, ma'am, and recalling what you'd said to me about your family, well, I reckoned it must be your brother. He don't look more than six or seven and twenty, if he's that, so he could hardly be your uncle, or such like relation, could he? I didn't like to ask him whether he was connected to you when he said his name. Well, I was that flabbergasted seeing such a well-turned out gent on my own doorstep down at Hammersmith, so far from the town and all, that there wasn't much I could say! And by the time he'd got himself delivered of what he'd come to say——' his face darkened suddenly, 'Well, I decided to keep my tongue betwixt my teeth and tell only you. And sorry I am to have to do so.'

Abby was staring at the fire, her gaze unfocused. 'William,' she said softly. 'A difficult boy, William. I had not thought about it much, but of course you are right. He is five and twenty——' She looked up at Henry almost shyly. 'Not having seen him for ten years it is hard to imagine him as aught but a schoolboy. And even before—I—I left home, I had not seen him much, not for ten years. He was away at school as boys are, and really, I hardly saw him at all. William. Did he look well?'

'Well fed, ma'am,' Henry said with a small sniff. 'Not to say a bit too well fed, if you ask me. Got a decidedly stout look about him, for one so young. Does himself well, I shouldn't wonder. And dressed—well, fit to kill! My mother was sure he was some sort of lord, first go off. Soon disabused her of that notion, though, I did. He's no lord, and I hope you don't remember him with too much affection, Mrs Caspar, and that's a fact.'

'I told you, I hardly remember him at all, poor boy,' Abby said. 'Why do you say so?'

'Well, I'm glad to hear it, because I tell you flatly, Mrs Caspar, ma'am, he's a rogue. That's what he is. A flat rogue. And I've been most upset to think that I should have to be the one to have to tell you. And I'm sorry, I really am.'

And he sat with a hand on each of his knees, looking miserably at her under the lock of hair that had again flopped on to his forehead, and perspiring gently.

She smiled at him, and put out a hand to pat his shoulder. 'Well, Henry, whatever it was he said that so upset you, I absolve you of any guilt in telling me of it. I do not find it difficult to think William might have upset you. I may not remember a great deal of his company, but I know he was a boy that caused many troubles at school. He was always applying to me for more money. Rupert did, too, of course, but William was the one that really seemed to let it flow most easily through his fingers.'

'He's all set to treat your father shocking bad, Mrs Caspar.' Henry leaned forwards earnestly and dropped his voice, even though with the thump and rattle of machinery all about them it was patently clear that they were not at any risk of being overheard. 'For he as good as told me so. It's like this. He has the running of this place at Wapping, you see. It's his affair, and has been for some time, and he don't want it to happen that Nellie's—the hospital, you know—should buy its drugs and medicines anywhere else but from him. And that was why, he said, he'd got my name and address out of Mr Conran—and I bet he put that old devil through it to get it out of him!—and came all this way to Hammersmith to see me.'

He took a deep breath. 'What he said was this. He'd got a plan organized to turn the hospital into a place of fashion. Said he was sick to death o' the sort of scum people as come to it now, and wanted to get the better class o' patient. And make 'em pay. He'd got some sort of crooked system going—begging your pardon for saying it of him, Mrs Caspar—some sort of crooked scheme to show the hospital Trustees as his running of the Wapping place was vital to the hospital, that there was big profits to be made if his father could only be got rid of as surgeon, and himself set in his place. And he put it to me, ma'am— and it was this that made me really feel bad—he put it to me as there could be big money for me if I'd so arrange matters in my dealings with Conran so that the prices I was offering wasn't so likely to catch his fancy after all, and promised me as any trade I lost from Conran, he'd replace, and pay me handsome on the side. He said as if I wanted to, being a bright sort of young fellow with a future before me, if I fancied the idea, why, there was work available to me under his employment at Wapping. All he wanted was that I should wipe my present employer's eyes so as to help him wipe his father's.'

He stopped, and the indignation that had spurred his telling seemed to falter as he sat more upright, and again wiped his face. 'You see why I was upset, ma'am? And why I made up my mind to it that I wouldn't say nothing about who my employer was? I realized he didn't know— well, he couldn't've, could he, or he wouldn't have come to me, surely? And anyway——' his voice took on an even more practical note, '—anyway, he kept saying *him* and *his* whenever speaking of whomever I worked for, so he clearly don't know as it's his own sister he's trying to do down.'

He shook his head. 'His father and his sister. Oh, but he's a ripe one, ain't he, Mrs Caspar? Maybe he didn't know as it was you, but that don't make no nevermind, for what sort of man behaves so to his own father? I really—well——' and he shook his head again, marvelling at the wickedness of men.

She sat there in silence for a while, trying to sort out her ideas and to comprehend the wave of feeling that had risen in her. That William should have become the sort of man to behave in a dishonest way did not completely surprise her now she came to think about it. As she had said, they had been almost strangers to each other, but she knew he had always been a sly child; she could remember episodes when Mary and Martha, the twins, had suffered much deprivation at his hands, and been blamed for their own losses and how often she had had to comfort the girls in their helpless tears and secretly recompense them. No, it was no surprise that William was busy trying to line his pockets at his father's expense.

But that he should be trying to get Abel removed from the hospital; that was something quite other. She knew, better than most, how dearly Abel loved his hospital. She who had watched from her earliest childhood how he had nursed the first little dispensary, how he had added to its services, so painfully and yet so steadily, how it had filled him with a passion that was greater than anything else in his life. She had not seen him for ten years, perhaps, not since the night before her wedding, but she could not imagine much had changed in him in those years. If he had loved his hospital then, would he not love it even more fiercely now? After all, she told herself, he had lost so much else. Jonah, and me. And Mamma.

She closed her eyes at the thought of her mother. In all these long years she had steadfastly denied herself any thought of Dorothea. Dorothea might lie breathing and swallowing pap there in Gower Street—for Abby knew there had been no announcement of her death —but she was dead in spirit. She had died that long ago snowy afternoon outside Lilith's house in North Audley Street, her life driven from her by plunging horses' hooves. It was her knowledge that that was so that had made it possible for Abby to face the fact that she had never returned to Gower Street to visit her.

And now William was trying to take his hospital from Abel. From her father. And it was that word above all that lifted itself out of her mêlée of thoughts and remained steadfastly before her. Her *father*.

She opened her eyes and looked at Henry, still sitting staring anxiously at her, and managed a small smile.

'Thank you, Henry, for this information. You need not have been so anxious, but I recognize the source of your anxiety as a very nice sensibility and thank you for it. You are a most—most caring man, and I am fortunate indeed to have you here at Caspar's to watch my interest.' She put out a hand and he, blushing, set his own into it, so that they could exchange a handshake. 'You will not lose by your loyalty, I promise you.'

He shook his head. 'It was not in search of my own benefit as I behaved as I did, ma'am. I may always have my eye to the main chance, and why not, for no one looks after number one if number one don't, but I couldn't do it by spitting in your eye, ma'am, if you'll allow the expression, and that's a fact.' And now he blew his nose in his embarrassment, and Abby smiled at him and stood up.

'Well, Henry, what I ask you to do is nothing. I imagine you did not commit yourself in any way——'

Henry was on his feet too, reaching for his steaming ulster, and shaking it in front of the flames to try to drive out the last of the wetness. 'Indeed no, Mrs Caspar, I did not. No, it was left as I'd think about it.' He grinned over his shoulder at her. 'I didn't slam no doors, you see, in case you wanted to make some use of the situation. He went away content enough, to wait till I should call on him, at the hospital he said. He said if I sent a message as to when I wanted to see him he'd make a point of being there.'

'Thank you, Henry. You did well,' she said gravely, and helped him shrug on his coat, and led the way to the door.

'It's my pleasure, ma'am,' he said earnestly, setting his billycock hat more firmly on his head as she opened the door. 'And do remember, ma'am, as I'm available any time you may require me, if I'm not here. In working hours of course, I'm around selling to the customers. But a message to Hammersmith will always find me——' And he went plunging out into the pouring rain, leaving her staring after him through the slanting lines, her lower lip caught between her teeth.

She had to think, and after a moment she went to her office to shed her alpaca apron and put on her mantle, and tell Miss Miller crisply that she had outside business to attend to, and if anyone came, to say she was not available.

And she closed her mind to the fact that she was using this visit of Henry's to deal with the matter that was really exercising her mind. Gideon. It was Wednesday, and even if last night's visit to Lombard Street had not occurred, he would be certain to be here shortly, as he always was. But since last night it was even more certain, and it was this fact that she had been trying to hide from all morning in her frenetic busyness about the factory. She did not want to face Gideon, not yet. There were things that must be dealt with between them, things he must be told, but she could not bear to do the telling. Not yet. She had to come herself to some sort of terms with the way she had found what she most needed so short a time before she had discovered that she must throw it away. To be given and to be deprived in one evening—that had been painful enough. To give the matter words so soon after was asking too much of her altogether.

So she fled her factory, going out into the rain of the March morning with her bonnet firmly tied about her ears, her skirts held firmly in her gloved hand, in search of an answer to this new dilemma involving her father. Thinking about that would be almost a comfort, if it stopped her thinking about herself.

## 23

She stood outside the hospital staring up at its grey front in the dwindling light, and shivered a little. The rain had stopped long ago, but her clothes were still damp, and the cold had struck through to her bones. She had eaten nothing since her breakfast, and it was now past five o'clock, but she was not hungry in the least. She had spent part of the day strolling about the warehouses, ostensibly looking at silks and lace and the new French muslins like any other lady of leisure and fashion of the town, so she was tired and her legs ached a little, and she moved her shoulders wearily under her wet mantle.

It had been almost silly, she had chided herself at one point during the long day. She should have gone home to Paddington Green, to change into warm dry clothes and sit beside her own fireside and talk to Frederick on his return from school, but she had known she could not do that. Gideon was not one to be so easily put off, as well she knew. When he did not find her as he expected at Irongate Wharf Road, then undoubtedly he would make his way to Paddington Green, and there stay as long as he could. She knew as certainly as if he had told her so that he was not going to give in so easily. If she wanted to avoid him— and now she did, most desperately—then she must stay away from home until after dark. She knew he would not alarm his parents by not returning at his usual time to their home; so that would be when she could return to hers.

In the meantime, she must decide what to do about the matter of Abel and the hospital; so she had told herself as she had gone her weary way with other shoppers through the colonnades of Regent Street and in and out of linen draper's shops, shoe emporia and ribbon sellers' establishments.

And her decision had been made. Abel must be told of William's plan to depose him, however much anguish that might cause to William. She had thought carefully about the matter, wondering whether she should approach William himself with her knowledge, and thus prevent him from going any further with his schemes, but she had dismissed that. First of all she doubted she would be able so to persuade William. She had remembered more and more about him as the afternoon wore on, had recalled his stubbornness, his intransigence, and what she had regretfully told herself could only be regarded as positive mendacity. No, going to William would be of little use.

And anyway, she had whispered to herself, it is not William who concerns me. All day the picture of him had been there before her eyes, the father she had loved so dearly, the father she had understood and cared for, and in some sort protected from his own difficult nature. She had managed most steadfastly to avoid any yearning for him or for those long ago days when they had been such good friends and had found so much comfort in each other. Why, she had wondered, should she now feel so great a need to see him again, to talk to him and care for him and just be with him?

Because of Gideon. She had been standing staring sightlessly at a piece of amber-coloured Chantilly lace when the knowledge came into her mind. Gideon and his father. The way old Nahum had sat and looked at her and spelled out so painfully the strength of the bond that held him and his son so inextricably entwined. The knowledge that because Gideon had a father who loved him so dearly she could not love him equally dearly herself. The realization that never, not ever, could she let herself love a man again.

All that had filled her and made her eyes sharpen with the pain of unsheddable tears, and she had ached with an almost physical longing for her own father, someone to whom she could be bound in the same way, someone who would hold her life together, however unhappy that life might become, in the same way that she could now see that Gideon's life was held together by his father.

And she had turned and gone out into the bustle of Regent Street and hailed a hack and told the driver huskily to take her to Queen Eleanor's; and he had needed no further direction but tipped his hat and brought her here to Tavistock Street. And now she stood and stared up at the building and breathed deep, seeking within her tired body the strength to go in and find Abel and tell him what was afoot.

She would not ask his love, nor his pardon for the long ago breach between them—for she knew, still, that there was nothing that needed pardoning; she had loved and that had been all about it—nor even his interest. She would tell him her news, and turn to go, she promised herself. And if he called her back, if he made any sign of tenderness towards her, why then, and only then, might she let herself respond as she was aching to do.

She crossed the street, holding her skirts high above the mud, and then smiled wryly, for they were already shockingly bespattered with her day's walking. At the foot of the hospital's steps she paused, and frowned slightly. There was an odd silence about the place, and it puzzled her. Had she been asked she would have said she would expect any hospital to be something of a beehive, with people going busily in and out of the doors at all times; but here the door was firmly closed and she could see no sign of activity, although lights burned in the windows.

She stood back and peered upwards at those windows and saw a shadow pass and repass across one of the panes, and nodded to herself, reassured. Clearly there was some lull at the door here, but the hospital was about its usual business above stairs; and she picked up her skirts again to climb the steps and pull on the great bell beside the door.

' 'Ere, you don' want to go there, ducky.' A hoarse voice from behind her made her jump, and she turned and peered at the figure that had stopped at the foot of the steps. A bent shawled figure it was, with sharp eyes staring at her from a face so engrimed with dirt that she could not even see if it belonged to a man or a woman; and then she saw the skirts, very ragged and filthy, but skirts all the same, peeping out under the torn and voluminous man's ulster that the figure was wearing and said, 'I beg your pardon, ma'am. What did you say?'

She cackled at that. 'Cor! Ma'am, is it? One of the ladies, is yer? I said as yer don't want to go in there, if yer knows what's good for yer.'

Abby looked up at the building again. 'It is Queen Eleanor's hospital, isn't it?'

'Queen Eleanor's pest'ouse, more like,' the old woman said, and the voice had become heavy again. 'Keep aht of it, an' live to eat yer vittles another day,' and she began to shuffle off towards the corner of the street.

'Why?' Abby cried after her, but the figure shrugged, and went on moving. 'Pest'ouse, that's what it is. I wouldn't even come dahn the street if I could 'elp it——'

She stood there frowning for a moment, and then shrugged in her turn and again started to climb the steps. The fear that every hospital engendered, that was all it was, she told herself. They are places where death is more commonplace than life. That is the cause of the old woman's muttering. But all the same it was strange that there should be such an eerie quietness about the place.

There was a piece of paper nailed to the door, and she peered at it in the dimness, more puzzled than ever. There was just one word scrawled on it. 'No.' And she shook her head, bemused. To put up a written notice in a place where none but a very few could read was strange too, and to put up one so laconic in its content was stranger still. Although perhaps it was there because it was a word that even illiterates could recognize? She shook her head at her own surmising and, practical as always, reached out and pulled on the heavy iron loop beside the door, and heard the ringing peal within cry out and then die away.

She stood there a long time, shivering as the wind came whipping icily through her damp clothes, and feeling the sense of foreboding within her building up. She was not nervous about seeing her father, she told herself, staunchly. It would be strange perhaps, after all this time, but they were reasonable people after all and she had legitimate business with him. She felt so only because of the quietness and the closed door and the sign and she pulled again on the bell, this time with a sharpness born of irritation.

The door opened grudgingly, and she pushed against it to try to enter but whoever had opened it resisted, and a voice said wearily, 'No. No admission. Place closed,' and again tried to push the door shut.

But Abby, for all her fatigue, was the stronger of the two so she pushed harder and the door gave before her and she slid round it to stand on the other side, staring at the woman who had opened it.

She was of medium height, was carrying a pair of candles in a branched stick in one hand and swaying a little as she stood there staring back at Abby with lacklustre eyes. Her face had a marked pallor under the roughness of its weathering and it was lined in a way that made it look as though usually she smiled a great deal. But now her face was expressionless.

'There's no admission,' she said again. 'Closed. Best to go away. We'll be open when we can.'

'How can you be closed?' Abby said, her voice sounding young and vigorous even in her own ears, compared with the flattened tones of the woman before her. 'This is Abel Lackland's hospital, isn't it? He was never one to close his doors to those who needed him. What has changed matters so?'

The woman seemed to become more awake, and held her candle closer to Abby's face so that she could look at her more easily.

'You know Mr Abel?'

'Yes,' Abby said. 'I know him.'

'You aren't looking for care for some ill person or other?'

'No. I wish to—to speak to Mr Lackland.'

'Well, I'm glad o' that, because you couldn't get it, not if you was the Queen herself. An' if you've any sense you'll go away from 'ere and wait until such time as Mr Abel is fit to return to Gower Street, and see 'im there. This isn't the place for the likes of you, ma'am, and so I tell you. Go on—you go away and I'll tell him as you called, if you leave your name, and you can go and see him when we're over this.'

'Over what?' Abby said, and looked about her at a couple of guttering lamps with uncleaned sooty chimneys, at dusty stairs and muddied floors. The place looked sorely neglected and she looked back at the woman with the candlestick. 'Over what?' she repeated.

From above stairs there was a sound of shuffling feet, and a curious thump, and someone said hoarsely, 'You'll have to manage on your own. There's no one else I can send—I'll bring the other myself when you return.'

Abby moved closer to the foot of the stairs to gaze upwards and the woman said with a sudden note of urgency in her voice, 'For God's sake, woman, go away, will you! Ain't we got enough to worrit about without you comin' pryin' 'ere? I'm tellin' you fer your own good to get out—now be about your business, will you!'

A figure came down the stairs, bent over and moving slowly with a burden of some sort thrown across its shoulders, and as it came into the light of the pair of candles Abby could see both the bearer and his burden more easily. His stoop could not disguise his height, and he was very thin, and lifted to Abby's gaze a pale unshaven face below thinning rumpled hair. The burden he carried over his shoulder was also long and thin, and though it was shrouded in a grey sheet, its nature was quite obvious. He was carrying a corpse.

He looked at Abby blankly and then seemed to dismiss her, and went slowly along the passageway towards the rear of the building. 'Open the door, Nancy,' he grunted, and the woman with the candles hurried past him to open a door in the shadows.

' 'Ere y'are, Mr Snow,' she said. 'Mind the way now—I'll lead you down—watch it——' and then both light and sound went dwindling away as they both disappeared, leaving Abby in the faint lamplight and seized with considerable trepidation. But she was not a qualmish person so after a moment's hesitation she picked up her skirts and went purposefully up the stairs. Whatever was happening here, she had come to see her father and see him she would.

At the top of the stairs there was more light, with candles stuck on shelves against the wall. A pair of big doors on one side of the hallway stood ajar, and she moved across the dusty wooden boards to push one open and go into the room beyond.

It was big, running from the front to the back of the house, with unshaded windows at each end which shone blackly, for the room was well lit. It was crammed full with people, she realized suddenly, more than she would have thought possible, for beds stood so close side by side along the walls that there was barely room for a human body to get between them, while two rows of flat pallets were arranged down the centre of the floor, head to tail. And each and every one was occupied.

Three people were moving about between the beds, and Abby blinked as she looked at them, trying to see who they were and then a faint cry came from a far corner, and she turned her head to look and then realized what had been most strange of all about the scene before her eyes.

Despite the crowdedness of the room it had been abnormally quiet.

This was the first human sound she had heard since she came into the room, and the silence of the other people here made it seem infinitely poignant, infinitely sad.

One of the three figures moving along the beds looked up too at the cry and detached itself from the pallet beside which it had been kneeling to go as swiftly as space permitted towards the far corner, and Abby could clearly see now that it was a woman, small and neat and very sure in her movements, and almost without thinking she said aloud, 'Miss Ingoldsby!'

The little woman stopped and turned and stared at Abby and then as naturally as though they had been sharing daily communion for the past ten years instead of not having seen each other during the the whole of that time she said, 'Good evening, Abby! Your father is——' she turned her head. 'Ah, yes, there he is. In the corner.' And she nodded affably and went on to seek the source of that mewing cry which was now being repeated.

The sound of her voice seemed to have a galvanizing effect on the room, for now more people sent up little cries, as a wave of movement passed among the crowded beds. She could see the effortful heaving of bodies trying to turn themselves over, saw heads lift from the flat mattresses and across the room there was a sudden painful sound of retching which made her own throat constrict in sympathy.

The other two people who had been standing together beside a bed in the far corner looked up, and Abby saw one of them, a young woman, bend over and pull a sheet up to cover the occupant before turning away, but she gave her no more than the most cursory of glances. It was the man who drew her eyes and she stared at him intently.

Abel was in shirt sleeves, his collar unfastened and a crumpled white towel wrapped around his neck. His sleeves were pushed up to his elbows so that his arms were bare, and his hands looked unusually long and tapering. His hair was rumpled and he was unshaven, and he looked so extraordinarily weary, with his red-rimmed eyes and hollow cheeks, that involuntarily Abby stepped forwards so that she was almost in the centre of the big room to stand staring at him. He came towards her with his head down, watching his feet as he made his way past the people on the floor, and just before he reached her one of them stretched out with an emaciated arm and tugged at his trouser leg; at once he stopped and crouched beside him and took a bowl that was lying at the man's head, and shoved it hard under his chin, supporting the head with his other hand.

The man retched hugely, gasped and retched again, and Abby closed her eyes against the unpleasantness and then, ashamed, opened them again. To be offended by the sight of this man's obvious agony was in some way to insult him, she felt obscurely. If her father could kneel there and help him while he suffered, she could at least be strong enough to bear viewing it.

The man closed his eyes and subsided against Abel's hand, and gently Abel let his head down on the mattress and pulled the sheet up to wipe the cracked lax mouth, and then stood up, the bowl in his hand. And saw her standing there.

They stood and looked at each other for a long moment, and then she said quietly, 'Good afternoon, Papa.'

He blinked slowly and then without seeming to be at all surprised said, 'Abby,' and rubbed the back of his hand against his forehead.

'Give me that.' Abby turned her head to find Miss Ingoldsby behind her, her hand outstretched. She nodded briskly at Abby and gestured again at Abel, who surrendered the bowl to her hand, and she turned and went away with it to the door, passing the tall thin man and the woman with the candles as she went out.

'I told her not to come up, Mr Abel,' the woman said fretfully. 'Tried to, at any rate, but Mr Snow came down an' I couldn' stand arguin'. We'll take the other one together—no need for you.' And she moved towards a corner of the room.

'There's another,' Abel said, jerking his head over his shoulder to indicate the bed he had left. 'And the one next to him won't be long either.' His voice was very husky and Abby looked at him again, feeling the fatigue in him as strongly as if it had been her own. He was staring at her, and as she caught his eye she essayed a little smile.

'I am sorry if I have come at an inopportune time,' she said softly.

'Inopportune?' He laughed suddenly, as he moved aside to let Nancy and the thin man pass. 'Snow, she says it is an inopportune time.' The thin man looked over his shoulder at her and grinned, a humourless stretching of tired skin. 'Aye,' he said. 'She could be right,' and went doggedly on to pick up the sheet wrapped figure on the bed. Abel watched him, and then again stood back to let him pass, and suddenly yawned.

'If it is inopportune to come to a place full of cholera, then you have been so,' he said, and his voice was sharper now. 'Nineteen have died in two days, and still going like flies. The other wards are as bad as this, and worse, some of 'em. It could go on like this for—who knows how long.' He looked at her and smiled suddenly, a narrow rictus of a smile that made him look even more weary.

'Cholera,' she said, and bit her lip and looked down at the people lying on each side of her, the thin drawn faces, the yellowish skin, the lips drawn back in grimaces of pain, and without thinking pulled her mantle closer about her, and Abel laughed again and said, 'Aye. Cholera.'

'Have you no more help than this?' she asked, staring round the room. Abel shook his head.

'All the nurses, God rot 'em, ran. Every last one of them. There's Snow and me and Nancy left. Martha and Miss Ingoldsby came to help. I told them not to, but they came—and Rupert is about somewhere, too.'

'Martha?' and Abby looked across the room to the slight figure in the corner trying to see in the tired face bending over a bed the little sister she remembered. And could not.

She turned back to Abel and opened her mouth to speak, but again a cry went up from one of the beds, and he was gone, stretching his long legs over the intervening bodies and she turned away; to find Miss Ingoldsby standing behind her.

'Well, Abby,' she said, and looked up at her erstwhile charge, her face smiling gently. 'I would wish we could have met again in happier circumstances.'

'They look so *weary*,' Abby said, looking over her shoulder at the other two, and Miss Ingoldsby said, 'Yes. Even Mr Lackland is not accustomed to this degree of labour. He has not slept for two nights, to my certain knowledge. He cannot go on so much longer.' She shook her head and stared at Abel's bent back with her smooth forehead faintly creased. 'He will not be *told*! It is clear to me that if he becomes a victim of his own exhaustion he will be of no use to his patients, but I cannot convince him. He was always stubborn.' She looked up at Abby again. 'It would be of help perhaps if you would speak to him. He always listened to you, did he not?'

'That was a long time ago,' Abby said. 'Before—you remember how it was.'

'Indeed I do,' she smiled reminiscently. 'You asked me such artless questions about Gretna Green, but I knew. I am sorry you were to be so soon deprived of your husband, Abby. It was a great sadness to you, I have no doubt.'

'Yes,' Abby said, and with a sudden air of decision pushed back her bonnet, and pulled her mantle from her shoulders. 'Perhaps I can help a little. I cannot stay for too long—I must return to my son—but a little——'

'Don't be a fool, Abby,' Miss Ingoldsby said sharply, and pushed her towards the door, rearranging the mantle on her shoulders as they went. 'You would be worse than useless, for you would no doubt catch the contagion yourself and add to our burdens. I am glad you came because perhaps you can persuade him to rest a little. I will send him to you downstairs. And when you have spoken for a little while, for God's sake *go*. You will be a hindrance and no help if you do not.'

And Abby went, with one last look back over her shoulder at Martha who was still quite unaware of her, and let Miss Ingoldsby install her in a cold and ill-lit little office downstairs.

'He will come,' she said firmly, 'whether he wishes it or no. Try to remember that he is very tired.'

Abby stood there in the middle of the ugly little room and tried to collect her thoughts. To tell a man as patently stretched to the end of his endurance the tale she had come to tell him was unthinkable. She could not do it. And yet what else could she say to him, after all these years? That she had been unaccountably seized with a desire to pay a social call upon him? That would be lame in the extreme. That she had need of him in her own dilemma? That could not be considered.

She felt the tiredness that had been hanging over her all day tighten round her and let her shoulders sag a little and closed her eyes.

'Well, Abby?' His voice came harshly from the door and she snapped her eyes open and said, 'Papa! You are—come and sit down, at once! You are nigh dead on your feet——' She moved swiftly across

235

the room, taking his elbow to lead him to the curved-backed chair that stood before the desk, and he let her have her way, and when he reached the chair did not so much sit down as fall into it.

He leaned back and set his elbows on the arms of the chair and looked up at her with eyes wide and almost opaque, so enlarged were the pupils. 'It was my fault, Abby,' he said huskily. 'It was my fault.'

She slipped to her knees beside him and set her hands on both of his and looked closely at him, and it was as though she were a very little girl again, and knew herself to be Papa's favourite who could soothe him from his megrims and make him smile and even laugh when no one else could.

'Dear Papa,' she murmured. 'Tell me about it. You will feel better if you speak of it.'

He was still staring at her, and after a moment he pulled one hand from beneath hers, and reached for her face and touched her cheek, and his fingers felt cold and rough against her skin. 'Yes—it is better to speak of it. If I could only always speak of the matters that distress me.' He dropped his hand and shook his head and said almost piteously, 'It was my fault. For all my care, I brought it in here. Picked it from the streets and brought it in here. So many dying, the children, the men—' he closed his eyes, and peering at him she was almost horrified to see tears escaping from beneath those closed lids; her strong and wonderful *knowing* Papa, to weep? It was almost more than she could bear, and she put both her hands to his face, cupping it between them, and began to croon softly in her throat, a wordless sound, the one she had used so long ago for James when he had lain dying, for her baby Frederick when he had been so ill with the whooping cough. And they stayed so for it seemed to her a very long time, kneeling there with her bonnet hanging on her back, held by its barely knotted ribbons, her mantle spread around her.

And he slept. She felt his head loll and she let it rest on his chest, gently extricated her hands and stood up, and he slept on, sitting there with his legs outstretched and his hands on the arms of the chair in all the helplessness of total exhaustion.

She went softly to the door and stood there for a moment looking back at him, and could not help but smile. She had done precisely what she had wanted most to do when she had come here; although they had spoken not one word of what had happened between them in the past, although she had said nothing to him that she had wanted to say, the breach between them was healed. The time would come, soon, when she could go to her father's house in Gower Street as a daughter should, to talk to him as a daughter should, to enjoy his care and affection as a father should give it.

She went out and closed the door softly behind her, and stood in the hall outside tying on her bonnet and rearranging her mantle.

And then stopped and pondered, for there was still the matter of William's perfidy to be settled. She could not let that situation go on unchecked any longer. But how could she deal with it, with Abel in so sorry a state?

There was a clatter of footsteps on the stairs, and she looked up and saw a tall thin shape and peered more closely. And then smiled widely and held out her arms. 'Rupert!' she cried. 'Rupert, my dear boy! I am so happy to see you!'

And her happiness was not entirely due to the pleasure of meeting again a brother she had not seen for so many years; it was because she realized she had found the answer to her problem. She would discuss the matter of William with Rupert. He surely, would be able to advise her.

## 24

She reached home at almost nine o'clock, too tired even to be worried about the way Frederick might be feeling in her long absence. He was always happy enough in Ellie's company, but she knew he fretted quietly when she was away for long. The compunction she felt about him, however, was quite lost by the time her hack took her along the New Road towards Paddington Green, and anyway she was thinking about what Rupert had said.

'I shall deal with it all,' he had told her soothingly. 'There is no need for you to concern yourself at all, my dear. It was more than good of you to come to tell m'father, but I am glad you did not.' His face had darkened suddenly. 'William is a fool. He always was. I have had my problems with him myself, I may tell you. This is the last time I shall ever—well, let be. I shall deal with it.'

He had looked down at her then from his much greater height, and smiled at her. 'You are still concerned about your father's wellbeing, Abby? After all this time when he has treated you so ill?'

'He did not treat me ill,' she said staunchly. 'I chose to leave him in the manner I did. I cannot blame him if he—if he felt he could no longer regard me as a friend.'

'Well, you have a most forgiving nature, Abby,' Rupert had said and leaned across the table to pour more wine for her, for he had insisted on taking her to eat some supper ('For you are quite clearly fit to drop in your shoes, and I take no responsibility for you, as a surgeon, if you do not follow my advice!') and had swept her off to Rules eating house in Maiden Lane and, demanding a mutton chop and boiled potatoes be set before her he refused to speak of any but the most ordinary matters until she had emptied her plate. 'That is better,' he had said approvingly when she pushed it away, at last replete. 'Your colour has returned.'

She had smiled. 'Thank you, Rupert. It is strange, I must say, to have you looking after me, when I remember so clearly how I used to take care of you! But you will not recall so far back, I dare say.'

'Come, you are not so much older than I!' Rupert had laughed then, his sardonic face lifting into warmth. 'You speak as though you are Methuselah's mother!'

'Well, I am a widow lady with a son of my own, now! It is difficult for me to look upon a young bachelor and not regard him as very much my junior.'

He had become serious suddenly, looking down at his plate. 'I am sorry you went away as you did, Abby,' he had said then. 'We had need of you in Gower Street. I can see how—harsh—we have all become. M'father—he is not an easy man to live with. Or work with——'

There had been a little silence and then he had said, 'Indeed I had made plans to—to well, shall we say leave him behind, to go on with my life in some other sphere. But this past three days——' He shook his head. 'I have seen him in a new way, I think. A way I might have seen long ago, had you been there to point the direction. You always had a great partiality for him, did you not?'

'Yes,' she had said quietly. 'Oh, yes, I know how harsh and even cruel he can seem, Rupert, but he is not a bad man, you know. Indeed, he is so *very* good that in some sense it is more difficult for people to understand him. He has so much love in him, Rupert. So very much——'

'Aye,' Rupert's voice had hardened again. 'Perhaps for others. But not for his own. You cannot deny, Abby, that he has in some measure earned the scorn that William has heaped upon him. I too, in my time——' he had paused, looking sharply at her as though about to say more. And then shook his head.

'Oh, I know! It takes so much *work* to reach him. And it has hurt me bitterly these many years to be without you all, because of him. But I understand him, I believe. There is so much to understand, Rupert. He did not have a good life when he was a child, you know. That must surely colour your approach to him.'

'It cannot alter the way he has been so—very hard with all of us.

239

When Mary died, he said nothing. He never speaks of Mamma and her affliction, he shows only feeling for the people at the hospital—and he behaves there with such—such *arrogance*——'

She had leaned forwards and taken his hand in hers. 'Please, Rupert,' she said earnestly. 'Please not to be angry any more. I can understand, Indeed I can. But you cannot bid the sun rise in the west, can you? And in trying to change my father that is what you attempt. Try to——'

'I told you, Abby, I have seen him in a new light these past days. No man could have done more than he has for these people.' He had given a little sharp sigh then. 'I thought at one time it would be best to banish them all, those gutter people, to use the hospital in a different way, you know? Now, after these last days—I really do not know.'

He had smiled then and clasped her hand warmly. 'Well, that is no matter with which to burden you, after so long an absence. Let us leave matters thusly; I shall deal with William. You have no need to perturb my father with him. It will be much better for him—for everybody—if you remain silent. And now we shall speak of other matters—yourself and your son and your life. Tell me—I wish to know all.'

So they had talked companionably for another half an hour, and then she had realized the time and in a great flurry of concern for the fretting Frederick at home collected herself and almost dragged him out of Rules' comfortable sawdust-floored and steamy rooms to seek a hack in the Strand to carry her the long journey home.

And now, as the driver sent his horse clopping cheerfully westwards she smiled to herself at the thought of Rupert and how very agreeable it had been to see him again, and to talk to him on such equal terms. She had not fully realized until now how much she had lost in all these years without family contact; it was good to know that those years were now behind her. She would see much of her sister and brothers as well as her father now, she promised herself, much.

And that will help you to learn to live without Gideon, a corner of her mind whispered, and in the darkness of the musty cab she closed her eyes and tried to banish all thoughts of Gideon and his effect on her.

When her hack at last drew up outside her little house by the Green she had no difficulty at all in removing her thoughts from him, for almost before she had paid the man Frederick was running down the path, a blanket clutched around him and his bare legs peering out from beneath his nightshirt, crying, 'Oh, Mamma, Mamma! I am so glad you are home! We have been so worried about you. And it is a matter of such urgency——'

'What has happened?' In a sudden access of alarm, she took Frederick by the shoulders and pulled him close to look at him in the light thrown from the open door of the house, brushing the red hair away from his forehead, but he pulled away impatiently and dragged her up the path.

'It is not me, Mamma! I am in perfect fettle! It is Phoebe—and her father and brother! They are here—Phoebe's Papa says it is a matter of such urgency—do come, Mamma!'

She dropped her bonnet and mantle into the waiting Ellie's arms and Frederick led her to the door of her little sitting room, he with his finger to his lips in an exaggerated warning to be quiet, and she followed him in, hardly able to understand what was happening so bewildered was she to have such a welcome added to the fatigue that so filled her and indeed threatened to overcome her.

Phoebe was lying outstretched on the little sofa, her head pillowed on one outflung arm, and her feet protruding from beneath the white shawl that had been thrown over her. Curled up on the rug before the dying fire lay Oliver, his head buried in his arms so that only his tousled head could be seen.

'Oh, Mamma, she is so tired!' Frederick said in a piercing whisper and crept carefully across the room to stand beside Phoebe and look down at her, his whole face alight with adoration. 'Do but look, Mamma, how soundly she sleeps!'

'Thank God you are here!' Jonah came swiftly across the room from the window embrasure, where he had been standing staring out into the darkness, and she looked at him and narrowed her eyes trying to see him clearly, but she was so tired that her vision was blurred and she had to rub her eyes before she could see him properly. And when she did, her heart sank, for he looked so distraught that he seemed to have shed pounds of flesh from his handsome face since she had last seen him, only a few days before. His face was gaunt and tight, the lines running from his nose to the corners of his lips as deepcut as though they had been there for ever.

'I did not know what to do, Abby! I could not leave them there with those stupid servants, could I? And anyway, they must deal with customers—and I must look for her, I must, for anything could have happened, she is in so strange a mood these days, and I am frantic with concern for her—and I could not leave the children, so I brought them here to you, and then you were not here, and though your servant said she would watch over them, I could not leave them till you came—you have been so long!'

'Jonah, you must quiet yourself! Whatever has happened, it will not be aided by your getting into such a state of nerves! Now sit you down, and take a glass of wine and tell me quietly what's amiss.'

He shook his head impatiently. 'It is Celia——'

He looked over his shoulder at his sleeping children and then dropped his voice. 'It is Celia. She went out at some time this afternoon, and did not return! I can get no sense from the servants and Betsy says she knows nothing, when clearly she does, and I am afraid that there is some harm befallen her——'

Abby shook her head, bemused. 'But what time did you reach here, Jonah? It is only nine o'clock now! She cannot have gone so far! She will be at home, I am sure, and wondering with equal anxiety where you have taken the children on so raw a night!'

He shook his head and seized her hands and said urgently, 'I know I am right to be so worried, Abby! You do not know her! She has never been absent from the supper rooms in the evening, not in all the years we have been there! She believes that none but she can supervise matters. She trusts no one! For her to be away at this time—it is most unusual! I am so *very* worried!'

She looked at him for a moment, and then nodded decisively. 'Very well, Jonah,' she said calmly. 'If you believe you have cause to be concerned then I share your concern. Now, what do you wish me to do?'

'The children,' he said at once. 'Will you keep them here? The servants at the supper rooms are all dealing with the customers, and the performance—I could not safely leave them there. Please to keep them here with you until such time as I find Celia——' his voice faltered, and then went on in a little rush. 'Until I find her and take her home. You have your governess here to help, and I hoped you would not find it too great an imposition.'

'Miss Miller is away from home this evening. She has gone to a theatre. But Ellie and I can manage. We will put them to bed, and then you can go and seek your Celia. And start your search at home, dear Jonah. I have no doubt she will be there by now and most put about to find you have taken the children out so late! Come, take a glass of brandy and we will seek a hack for you to send you back to town and the children shall sleep.'

'No, no brandy. But I will help you put the children to bed——' he said, turning back uncertainly but she shook her head and firmly pushed him away towards the hall and sent Ellie to fetch his coat and hat and urged him to the door.

'You will find a rank of hacks waiting there beside the terminus where Shillibeer's omnibuses turn round,' she said. 'Send word to me tomorrow about what has happened. And do not worry about the children! I shall have good care of them.'

He stopped for a moment, and then took his hat off and bent and kissed her cheek most fervently.

'You are the best and kindest of sisters, Abby. My life would be quite insupportable without you, I think.' And then he was gone into the darkness, leaving her to close the door behind him and set about putting the sleeping children to bed.

And when she and Ellie had managed to undress the sleepily complaining Phoebe and settle her in the little room that abutted Miss Miller's, and with Frederick's eager help had managed to undress Oliver (who did not wake throughout their ministrations) and dragged him to share Frederick's own bed, she went to her own room almost in a state of collapse.

She undressed, and bathed in the big japanned tin tub Ellie had set ready for her in front of the blazing coals, letting the hot water float away the fatigue and confusion of the day. It was not until she was out of her bath and wrapped in the big white bath sheet that Ellie brought it to her.

She had come in straining under the weight of a big scuttle full of coals, and set it down and began to collect the bath things ready to take them away, when she tutted, and said awkwardly, 'Oh, madam! I'm so sorry, I'm sure, but in all the excitement this evening, it was fair thrown out o' my mind! There was Mr Gideon here most of the day, fit to bust with questions about where you was an' everything an' wouldn't take any bite nor refreshment apart from a single dish o' tea, though I offered it often enough, I promise you, and then he 'ad to go and fair put about 'e was. But 'e left this for you, madam, and said as I was to give it to you the instant you came in, and there's me gone and forgot! I'm that sorry, madam, but it 'asn't been what you might call an ordinary sort of an evenin', 'as it? I'm that sorry——' And she pulled from the pocket of her voluminous apron a large squarely-folded piece of thick paper.

Abby waited until the girl had at last gone, taking the bath and its paraphernalia with her, sitting there wrapped in her bath sheet before the fire and letting the warmth dry her. And then when at last she was alone she released her arms from the enveloping folds and, moving slowly and very deliberately, broke the small seal, unfolded the letter and began to read.

'My dearest Abby. I am nearly frantic about you! Where are you? They said at the manufactory that Henry Sydenham had come and you had gone out, and they knew no more. I have sent a message to Henry to see if he knows where you are, but have had no reply as yet.

'Dear, dearest, Abby, I do love you so very much! You know that, and I need not tell you, but what has need to do with it? I want to tell you, I must tell you and I wait only for you to tell me of your feelings. For you cannot dissemble longer. I know as any man who loves must know that you love me as I love you. I saw you there in the gallery with the light of the candles about your head like a nimbus and I knew the light came from within you. It was as though you spoke to me in loud words, shouting to me from the gallery that you knew what was in my heart. And I know what is in yours. I am certain of it. I am sure this letter is disjointed, indeed stupid, but I am so beset with anxiety, and with need for you. Please, as soon as you return send a message for me! I must see you. You cannot know how much I need to be with you. Dear Abby, I love you so very much——'

He had signed it simply with a capital letter G, a brief and sharp scrawl of a line as though he could write no more, as though his feelings had suddenly overcome him. And she folded the letter slowly, immaculately returning it to its original folds, and stood up and went to fetch her nightgown, lying ready on her bed, dropping the bath sheet on the floor beside her chair.

As she passed the cheval glass that was set between the heavily curtained windows she stopped and turned and looked at herself, almost shyly at first and then with a curiously abstracted sort of gaze, as though she were looking at someone quite different, not herself at all.

She saw a sturdy body with long hips and a slightly soft rounded belly, a little stretched from Frederick's birth, but not unduly so; her breasts were full and a little dependent, but again not unduly so. With her heavy brown hair unbound and lying in heavy sheets on her shoulders she looked young and yet mature, with a sort of sumptuousness about her, and she knew herself to be desirable and desirous.

But it had been ten years since she had shared her body with anyone, ten years since it had been anything more than a shell in which she moved and lived and worked. As a source of happiness, of contentment, of any sort of pleasure, it had been as nothing. And remembering how she had been with James, so long ago, she mourned a little for the waste of it, for the knowledge that no man would ever share that soft voluptuousness with her; for there was only one man she could share with. And he she could not have.

## 25

He had felt he must take his sister's advice, even though deep in his mind he knew she would not be there. So he had ordered the hack to carry him back to King Street and gone in to stand at the back of the crowded supper room looking about him for signs of her presence; but without any real hope.

The place was as smoky and reeking and noisy as ever when he came in but no one paid him any attention for Norah Norton was up on stage, resplendent in crimson tights and silver spangles with five inches of heavy silk fringe hanging from her low-cut bodice, and leading them all in a raucous chorus of ' 'E's got the biggest, busiest, 'eaviest one in all of Seven Dials!' a lubricious song about a man who owned a donkey, and hearing it made Jonah's gorge suddenly rise.

To think that he had spent so many of his years here, listening to songs like this; to think, heaven help him, that he had rehearsed Norah Norton in this very ditty, had shown her how to place the emphasis so that the audience were encouraged to remain good-humoured enough to join in. He who had called himself a poet, who had written the dramas and polemics he once had, to be so brought down!

And she, Celia; hadn't it been this place that had changed her, too? Looking about at the red-faced beer-swilling men and their women, bedecked in colours as garish and as ill-matched and bespangled as any ever seen on the stage, he was quite sure it had. Working so relentlessly all these years had made him weak and useless and had dimmed the passion he had once had to make his pen the weapon he knew it could be. Could it not have made her so secret and remote and frighteningly strange?

She was not here, and he knew it, but he looked dutifully for her, moving among the tables and the food and drinks being carried head high by the servants; going into the kitchen and the store-rooms to see what was happening there, but they all shook their heads at him when he asked if any had seen their mistress and made expressive faces at each other behind his back as he passed.

He escaped into the chill of King Street almost gratefully, although he was still heavy with fear for her. Quite where he intended to look he did not know, but look he must and he set out at a brisk pace, walking towards Bedfordbury and then veering along New Row towards St Martin's Lane. His long legs covered the ground swiftly and as he walked with his head up and his shoulders held very straight the capes of his coat swung about him, and many of the women of the town who passed him ogled and whispered, for he was a well set-up man in every way. But he did not notice them at all, letting his eyes move as they would over the milling crowds, past glaring cookshop windows and pavement sellers' smoky flares and the heedless plunging traffic.

Quite when the notion came into his head he was not quite sure; but there it suddenly was, and when he found himself crossing Leicester Fields, keeping close to the centre of the road for fear of the thieves and pickpockets who were known to congregate in the subfusc shadows there under the stunted trees, he moved purposefully onwards towards the top of the Haymarket and turned sharply left into its garish hubbub.

He hesitated for a moment outside the theatre, staring at the big entrance door, and then shook his head almost imperceptibly and turned back to go plunging into the dark recesses of Orange Street. If she had come here she would not behave like any gawping outsider. She who had always been part of this theatre would use the stage door as of a right, as she had all through her childhood. And he too felt that he had the same right, and went so quickly in through the little badly lit stage door that the old man who was responsible for it hardly noticed him go by.

The smell hit him almost like a physical blow. He had forgotten that mixture of heavy odours, of unwashed bodies, paint and dust and spilled beer and mutton pies and paint. He had forgotten the way cold air could suddenly come hissing round corners and go creeping along at floor level to chill his legs with a sudden cruel swirl. And he had forgotten the sense of expectancy that filled that cold air, as actors and wardrobe women and carpenters and all the other hangers-on went hurrying along the walkways between the scenery towards the noise of the distant stage.

He followed one such hurrying figure, moving through the darkness with an ease that he took for granted; it was surprising how much he had learned in those few months he had spent here in this theatre, all those years ago. He was thinking of that, feeling the weight of the intervening ten years on his back, and became so abstracted that when he did reach the wings it came almost as a surprise.

He stood there blinking in the blazing light, feeling the heat of the great gas flares above him coming down on his head, the waves of sluggishly moving air that came out into the wings from that vividly lit plain that spread before him, and he unbuttoned his coat for he felt almost stifled now though his legs still felt the chill draughts that were whistling in from the distant scene dock doors.

There was a sudden roar of laughter, as huge and as solid as a wall, and he almost flinched at the sound and blinked again and behind him someone muttered, 'Get out of the way, you fool——' and he was pushed aside against the painted canvas flat as a bewigged man in a costume dripping with lace, his legs obviously padded under his scarlet hose, went skipping past him on to the stage to be greeted by another roar from the unseen audience.

'What are you doing here?' a voice croaked at him. He turned his head to see a face that was vaguely familiar and he racked his memory for a moment to place it; and then said gratefully, 'Castleton! It is Mr Castleton, isn't it?'

The almost bald man with the scowling face who was standing there staring at him frowned even more heavily and said, 'What if it is?'

'Don't you remember me? Lackland? I'm Jonah Lackland. I—you knew me. Ten years ago, near enough——'

The man sniffed and stared at him for a moment and then shook his head. 'Can't say as I do. Can't say as I want to either. And whether you were here or not ten years ago, you've no damned right to be here now. So sling your hook. Go on, out of it. We don't want any snoopers of your sort here——'

'I'm not spying,' Jonah said at once. 'I've nothing to do with the theatre any more. Not the legitimate theatre, that is. I'm not trying to make any capital here, I promise you.' He knew enough about the rivalries of the London theatres to understand the man's obvious suspicion, and as he moved closer, clearly intending to set hands on him and hustle him out he added almost despairingly, 'You must remember me! I was a friend of Lilith Lucas! It is Lilith's daughter I am here to seek!'

Another roar came from the audience as the man in red tights shouted some comic line and capered briefly, Castleton stopped and peered even closer at Jonah and then very slowly nodded his head so that the hairless skull shone greasily in the light, and suddenly he opened his mouth to laugh, revealing blackened stumps of teeth.

'Yes—yes, I remember! Lackland, that's it. One of Madam L's bits of fun. And then went and ran off with her daughter! Oh, yes, I remember.' He laughed again. 'There was plenty of talk about it too. To think you'd want that little dab of a piece instead of her Ma! It set the lot of 'em into whoops!'

'I am looking for my wife,' Jonah said stiffly. 'I—we—arrangements made for us to meet went awry, and it—it occurred to me she might be here.'

'Gone to Grosvenor Square, then,' Castleton said confidently. 'That's where she'll be. Grosvenor Square. Number 25. Under the circumstances it's natural enough, hell's bitch though she is——'

There was a sudden roar of applause from the stage behind them and a heavy rumbling as the curtain came thudding on to the boards, muffling the audience's noise for a moment, and the actors came hustling off to primp in the big mirror set just within the wings before going sweeping on again to take a bow as the curtain once more swooped and rose to the noise of cheers and clapping hands. Jonah, pushed out of the way by the hubbub as sweating scene-shifters made way for the actors again coming off as the curtain fell, called above the noise, 'Castleton—where did you say? Gone where? And why?'

Castleton was moving away now, deep in conversation with one of the actors but he looked back over his shoulder at the sound of Jonah's voice and said shortly, 'To Madam L's. You didn't think she'd still be here, after all that, did you? It was bad—really bad. She'll not be here for a long time——'

'If ever!' said a perky voice beside him, and he turned to see a heavily-painted little face peeping up at him from under a lace-trimmed bonnet, and the girl giggled as she caught his eye and said, 'You talking about poor Madam L? Shocking, wasn't it?' But she spoke with a curious relish and went skipping cheerfully away, throwing one roguish glance back at Jonah before she disappeared into the shadows.

Castleton laughed. 'Understudy,' he said briefly. 'Well, naturally she's pleased! Gives everyone more of a chance, so everyone's pleased. But don't tell her I said so.'

And then too he was gone, leaving Jonah among the swearing, sweating scene-shifters, puzzled and more deeply alarmed than ever. He did not know why he felt that undertow of fear, but it was stronger now, and pressing up into his throat so that he had to swallow.

Grosvenor Square. Was that where she lived now? Had she reached that sort of splendour? He stood there hesitating for a moment, and then took a deep breath and went plunging back through the darkness to the stage door and the comparative peace of the traffic in the Haymarket. He had to find Celia and if that was where she had gone then that was where he would have to go to find her. He could not have said for the life of him why he was so sure Celia had gone to Lilith. He knew of the implacable hatred that had so long lain between her and her mother and yet, somehow, he believed that Lilith would lead him to Celia. She had never before, in all their difficult married life, behaved as she had today, disappearing without a word like this. Where else could she have gone but to the past she had lived before their married days? And what did that mean but her mother?

So he stood hesitating at the corner of the Haymarket for a moment, but then pulled his collar up about his ears and thrusting his hands deep into his pockets went striding through the strolling entertainment-seeking crowds of Londoners towards the elegancies of Grosvenor Square.

Again. It was as though there had been no gap of ten years. The footman who answered the big front door to him merely opened it wider when he asked, in some embarrassment, for Madam Lucas's daughter, and he went in and gave the man his coat and hat and stood there in the big black and white squared hall looking about him and rubbing his hands a little nervously together. Although this was not the house he had lived in for those few months ten years ago, it was so very like North Audley Street that the weight of familiarity again filled him. The same gilt furniture, the same rich paintings and hangings, the same overwhelming aura of wealth and possessions; this house had it multiplied thrice, but still it was so very much what he had known of Lilith Lucas so long ago.

The footman took his coat and went padding away to the stairs and he followed him; clearly Lilith was receiving in her drawing room tonight, and he put up his hand to straighten his cravat and to smooth his hair. As long as Celia was willing to come with him and did not make any difficulties they could, he told himself optimistically, be out of the house and on their way home within minutes. He would not have to spend too much time with Lilith's mocking eyes upon him, which thought comforted him; for he did not relish the thought of meeting her at all.

He was so sure that Celia would be waiting for him there in the drawing room that when the footman led him instead to a small sitting room at the back of the house he stood blinking in the doorway a little stupidly and let the man go away and up the stairs to the next floor without asking him why he had been brought here.

And when he did turn to go out of the room and seek some understanding of what was happening it was to see the black-gowned figure of Hawks coming towards him along the wide carpeting of the hallway. He opened his mouth to speak to her and then closed it as she came near enough to be clearly seen, for her face was so ravaged and so altered that he wondered if he had been mistaken, and this was not Hawks at all.

But she lifted her eyes to his and he knew it was her, and she said harshly, 'Well? What do you want? Come to crow, 'ave yer? Come to gloat over what she done?'

'Where is she?' he said stupidly. 'I've been so worried, Hawks! I could not think where she might be, and then it seemed to me that she might have come here—a—I do not wish to see your mistress, Hawks, to be straight with you. If Celia is here, please to tell her I have come seeking her and——'

Hawks was staring at him with her eyes so widely open that a rim of white showed all round the iris, giving her a look of real horror and involuntarily he stepped back and said uncertainly, 'Hawks? *Is* she here?'

She shook her 'head at him, and opened her mouth in a wide grimace and then swallowed and to Jonah's appalled surprise tears suddenly appeared in her almost lashless eyes to go spilling down her face into the harsh lines drawn there. He looked away, embarrassed, and then felt his gaze pulled back to her in a sort of horrified fascination.

' 'Ere? That 'ellcat, 'ere? After what she done to my poor darlin', do you think if she was 'ere she'd be in any fit state to be told anythin'? Oh, I tell you, you stinkin' piece of gutter meat, I tell you that if that bitch was 'ere I'd have killed 'er, I'd have set about 'er with my teeth and my nails and anythin' I could lay my 'ands on! I knew 'er all 'er life, I knew what she was, none better, for didn't I 'ave the rearin' of 'er from the month? If I'd a known what she would do, 'ow she'd a turned out, I'd a strangled 'er in 'er cradle and it's my shame and punishment that I never did and——'

And now she was weeping with a vast fury that was so great that she could only stand there and let the tears run down her face, carving it into ever deeper and craggier lines. He stared at her, feeling as though he had been physically kicked and wanting to set his hands to her shoulders and shake her, but unable to move.

The moment passed, and she regained control, scrubbing viciously at her wet face with one black-sleeved arm and she said dully, 'So she ain't 'ere. Nor likely to be, neither.'

'I don't understand you,' he said then. 'Hawks, you must tell me what all this is. I don't understand——'

'Don' understand, don't yer? Don't—ain't you seen 'er since she done it?'

'What has she done? You speak in mad riddles, Hawks! I told you, I came seeking Celia. She is—I am worried about her, for she has some maggot in her brain that makes her—she is not herself. She left home this afternoon and I did not know where she had gone, so I came seeking her, and thought perhaps, even after all this time, she might have gone to her mother, for after all there is that bond, even though they parted so long ago. And even in mutual hate people have a need sometimes——'

She was staring at him with her eyes glittering still with tears and her face set and hard, and now she nodded heavily, and again turned away.

'She come to 'er. She come to 'er at the theatre. God 'elp me, I was dahn in the wardrobe gofferin' 'er frills, and that bitch of yours come to 'er. An' if you want to know what 'appened, you can come an' look for yerself——'

And he had to follow her, the confusion on his own behalf and fear on Celia's churning within him to make him feel ever more physically ill.

She led him up the next flight of stairs, past the ornately framed paintings and the niches with the creamy alabaster figures posed in eternal maidenly surprise as they gazed out from their rigid worlds through blank and sightless eyes, along the crimson carpets and polished wooden floors until they were standing before the pair of big double doors that led to a room at the front of the house. And Hawks, with a gesture that was curiously theatrical, pushed both doors open at once and led the way in and he had perforce to follow.

A big room with deep pale carpets and walls covered with the most costly of Chinese silk hangings, a huge bed bearing cream silk curtains with golden tassels and cords, standing on a raised dais. The room was full of light from crystal lamps and from the fire that burned brightly in the great marble fireplace, and he shook his head a little against the scented heat of the atmosphere as Hawks led him soft-footedly across the expanse of carpet, until he was standing there beside the bed looking down.

It was heaped with silk lace-encrusted cushions and sheets, and a soft merino blanket was thrown casually across it, and in the middle lay Lilith, both arms flung above her head on the pillows, her head tipped so that her chin pointed at the ceiling.

He knew it was Lilith, knew the colour of those wide open green eyes as surely as he knew the colour of his own; knew the curls of that hair, the curve of those shoulders; but it was not Lilith, not the Lilith he had known, the Lilith he had watched moving weightlessly about the stage of the Haymarket, had watched beguiling all the people around her with one glance from those glittering green eyes, one lift of that dimpled mouth.

For the face was marred with an angry raw weal that spread from the nose across the right cheek and down on to the throat, a weal so reddened and angry, so blackened about the edges, so excoriated, that it made his chest heave. The hair, those curls that had been used to bounce so enchantingly on the white shoulders, was almost gone on that side, a mere thatch of blackened singed ends through which the scalp shone redly, and the shoulders, those curving white shoulders, bore the same great weal that so disfigured the face, but spread hideously wide, halfway down the arm.

He shook his head in horror, and turned his head away to look at Hawks, who was standing beside him staring down at Lilith with a look of such misery on her face that involuntarily he put out one hand to her.

She turned her head and stared at him, and when she spoke her voice was so hoarse and cracked that he could hardly hear it.

'She did that. That bitch of yours—she did that. I come in and saw 'er standing there, 'oldin' the dish in 'er 'and and laughin'. You 'ear me? Laughin' she was, fit to bust, an' my darlin' standin' there screamin' and burnin'—oh, God, the wickedness of it!' She bent over Lilith and touched her unburned cheek with one rough forefinger; but Lilith did not move, and just lay there staring at the ceiling with those wide eyes, and he could not tell if she were awake or asleep, had the benefit of her senses or was in a deep coma, so still and controlled was she.

Hawks straightened up again and still staring down at Lilith said in that same harsh tone, 'I told 'er—I told 'er as what she'd done'd get 'er 'anged, that I'd not rest till she was 'anged for what she done, but she just stood there and said nothin'. She watched me put the fire out and wrap my darlin' up and never said no word, nor moved to 'elp, she just stood there and stared, the dish in 'er 'and——'

'Where did she go?' Jonah's voice cut across the room sharply, and he coughed, and looked round almost embarrassed, but there was no one else there, and Lilith had not moved; but he spoke again more softly. 'Where is she?'

'I don' know! I daresay there's some as are lookin' for 'er. I told the Peelers, and the Inspector said as they'd get 'er, for this is grievous bodily 'arm, and it's a toppin' offence——' She raised her eyes to stare at him. 'An' when they do get 'er, I'll be there to see 'er turned off, one way or another, for she's as evil a creature as ever——'

He shook his head, furiously, and set his hands over his ears and she stopped talking and grinned suddenly, so that her face looked even more ravaged and hideous, and nodded her head, and then turned back to Lilith, to stand there with one hand gently stroking the unmarked white cheek. And he turned and went, walking out of the room with his head up and without knowing quite how he moved at all.

All he knew was that he had somehow to find her. His fear for her was now so great that he could not feel anything at all. Just the knowledge that somehow she must be found.

## 26

'You should not have done it,' Gideon said, and though his voice was soft and controlled it was full of feeling, and his father moved uneasily in his chair and twitched at the rug over his knees. But Gideon did not come at once to help him as he usually did at any sign of discomfort on his father's part. He just stood there between the windows of the drawing room, his back very straight and holding the letter in his hand. 'You should not have done it,' he repeated, and bent his head to look again at the letter.

'Already she has changed you,' Leah's voice came quietly from the shadowed corner of the room where she sat beside her little desk. 'You, who have never shown your father anything but the respect and the duty that you owe him, to upbraid him for his care of you—for you to behave so must show you how right your father was and still is. She has changed you, and will change you more. For the worse.'

He lifted his head and looked across the room at her. 'Mamma, you do not understand the matter of which you speak. You have seen my love and concern for my father—both of you—all these years and you have interpreted it only as some sort of blind faith? If you have seen it so you misjudge me, and diminish yourselves. I have loved you all my life as I love you now not for some reason of unthinking obedience, but because, simply, I love you! You are people who are easy to love. But you hurt me bitterly in your response to my need for a life of my own in addition to my care for you. I am not so limited that I can care only for my parents. I am a grown man, and it is time I sought a wife. I have found the wife I want, and you reject her, not for the woman she is, not for any cause that is based on reason——'

'The reason is deep and real, and you are not the man I took you for if you turn your back on it.' Nahum said, his voice hard. 'To marry out of the faith! You know the effects of such a happening on the congregation! I will never again be able to hold up my head, to look my fellows in the eye and——'

'Do you care more for your pride than my happiness, father?' Gideon said softly, 'I had thought better of you.'

'No!' The old man almost roared it, leaning forwards in his chair with both hands set on his knees in a tight clasp. 'It is concern for your happiness that fills me, as it always has! I know as surely as I know I shall never again stand on my own two feet that marriage out of the faith will destroy you. That your need of your roots, your religion, is something that is so much a part of you that you do not even know it is there! I know how you will suffer if you cut yourself off and I spoke of the effect on me as a way of showing you what *you* will suffer! You are as much a man of our people as I am, Gideon! If it would be agony to me to see my friends, the men of the congregation who have always been my brothers in God, turn away from me and reject me as an outcast, it will do the same to you! You are my son. I feel for you as I feel my own hands. It has always been so—we are a part of each other!'

Gideon came across the room to crouch beside his father's chair and look up into his face, and very gently he shook his head.

'You are wrong, Papa. You have misunderstood so sorely! You recognize my concern, my awareness of you and how you feel and how you think, and it has made you deny the fact that I am a separate person. It is my fault as well, I know, for I have not tried, ever, to show you any part of my separate life, but the greatest error is with you. You and Mamma may be one flesh, as the Torah tells us man and wife should be, but father and son—no, Papa. I feel for myself, know for myself, love for myself. Cannot you see how much better it is that I *should* be separate? If we were as you try to believe we are, but two parts of one person, any love I might bear you, or you me, would become a tawdry thing, a mere self-love, and what satisfaction is there in that? Try to understand, Papa. You are a man of great intellect—you can comprehend.'

The old man sat there and stared down at him, his eyes deep and dark and quite expressionless.

'You are telling me that the matters about which both of us have always concerned ourselves, the laws of God, the way of life that our people have followed through almost two thousand years of dispersion, do not matter to you? You are telling me that the loss of your faith will be of no matter to you?'

Gideon shook his head. 'I am not saying that. I do not believe that marrying Abby would mean the loss of my faith. I was born a Jew, and a Jew I will always be. Nothing can alter that.'

'A Jew cannot exist alone. The years of persecution prove that. If you are expelled from the congregation, then you are alone. And you will not be able any more to regard yourself as one of us.'

Again Gideon shook his head. 'I have the same respect for tradition that you have, Papa. I know the history of our family and of our people. I know of the sufferings of the Inquisition, and what it has done to us. I do not reject any of that. But I cannot believe that God will exclude me from the life of a Jew simply because I have chosen to love a Gentile. No, not chosen—in some way this love is God-given. If we live our lives by God—as you have always said we do—then I must see Abby as part of his plan for me, and for you and——'

'You speak blasphemy,' the old man said and leaned back in his chair, pulling away from Gideon's hand, and there was a silence for a moment and then Gideon stood up and moved back to the window embrasure.

'I think, Papa, that there is no use in speaking of religion, of laws and customs. We do not agree and that is our misfortune. Instead, we will speak of our personal situation.'

He lifted his head, and stared into the shadows towards Leah. 'Mamma, I speak to both of you. And I speak from love of you as well as—as respect for my own life and needs. And I will tell you that unless I marry Abigail Caspar, I do not marry at all. For many years I have tried not to love her, as aware as you are of the difficulties, the problems, the possible pain. But this is the way it is to be, and I am not going to fight it any longer. She is mine, and I will have her, whatever you say. I would wish us to remain as loving and close a family as we have always been—it would be a great tragedy to me to lose you. But I tell you, if you make me choose between you, the choice is already made. I will have her, if she will have me.'

'If she will have you!' Leah echoed, and laughed suddenly. 'As if she could fail to accept you! You are personable, and rich and well connected, and she loves you quite besottedly. There can be no question——'

'You are quite wrong, Mamma, and have as little understanding of Abby as you have of me. I——' he swallowed and held up the letter. 'She has written to me in terms you will applaud no doubt, but which fill me with such anger against you both that——' He shook his head. 'I do not know what you said to her while I was not with you, but I can guess. Why else should she write so?'

Leah stood up and came rustling from her corner to stand in front of him, her head up and her hands loosely clasped on her brown silk skirt.

'If you are angry with us, we have a right to know the cause,' she said and her voice was very clear, her tone very level. 'Will you read to us any relevant portions?'

He looked at her and then bent his head and unfolded the letter and she moved away to stand behind Nahum's chair in her favourite place and there was silence for a moment, and then Gideon began to read in a low voice.

'Dear Mr Henriques. You will, I am sure, understand the formality of my address when you have digested the contents of this letter. Permit me first to regret that I was absent from my counting house when you made your visit; I am glad to understand from Miss Miller that she was able to satisfy you by presenting the necessary ledgers, and that your visit was not, therefore, wasted. My absence was on a matter to do with my family, and quite unavoidable.

'I have given much thought to various matters we have discussed, and also to the conversation I had with your parents when I visited their home. It is as the result of this cogitation, and most particularly upon the content of your parents' discussion with me, that I must tell you that although I hold you in the highest of esteem, I think it better that we do not meet again for some time. I suggest that on matters of business you deal entirely with Miss Miller during the ensuing months, communication with me, and I with you, when necessary, being entirely by letter. I will of course be saddened to miss the conversations we have long enjoyed. Your friendship has always been of great value to me. But it is because I value that friendship so highly that I write to you in these terms. It is my hope that in time to come, perhaps after a year or so, you will forget the passages of intimate conversation that passed between us, will find the emotion that excited them quite subsided and we will be able to return to the easy and agreeable intercourse we have hitherto enjoyed.

'I will be grateful if you will convey to your parents my good wishes and esteem and renewed thanks for a pleasant and most informative evening spent in their company. I also will appreciate if you express to your father my lively awareness of the great debt I owe him for the friendship he displayed to my late husband and to me, in the matter of our business. I remain, your friend, Abigail Caspar.'

There was another silence when he had stopped and stood there refolding his letter and then Leah spoke, and she could not keep the faint note of satisfaction from her voice.

'So the matter is settled. There was no need for this discussion between us.'

'No need? There was every need!' Gideon said vigorously. 'You do not think I accept this as my *congé*, do you?'

'It is meant thus,' Leah said.

'Meant or not, I am certainly not going to accept it! She does not at any point in this letter deny her feeling for me. She could not, for it is there, I know it to be as powerful as mine for her, and she could not say otherwise. It is because of what *you* said to her that she writes like this— and I tell you now that although my love for you remains undamaged —it cannot be altered any more than can my love for Abby—the anger I feel will be a long time in abating! I tell you also that I will not rest until I have undone the damage you have done, and made Abby my wife. If you refuse to accept her, that will be sad, and it will hurt me deeply, for I would not separate us for the world. But any such rejection on your part will have the effect of causing such a separation, and you must know that now. It would be sad for us to lose you—but a tragedy to you, I think. To cut yourself off from any grandchildren, to be so cold to a daughter-in-law——' he shook his head. 'I hope you will not be so foolish, Papa, Mamma. But I give you fair warning now, that this is how it must be. You must think about it. Because however long it takes, she will marry me. You can be as sure of that as that tomorrow's sun will rise.'

'Are you threatening me, Gideon?' The old man said. Gideon shook his head sharply.

'Of course I am not! Not if by threat you mean some sort of—that I offer to do you harm if you will not do as I wish. Far from it, indeed, and it is an index of your disturbed thinking, I believe, that you should put any such interpretation on it.'

'He is not threatening, Nahum,' Leah said softly. 'He is right to be offended at such a suggestion. He is, I think, telling us of the inevitable nature of his situation. He will do what he must do, and the effects must happen, whatever they are. Is that not so, Gideon?'

He nodded, his face quite unsmiling. 'That is so, Mamma. I am happy that you at least see it so clearly.'

She turned her head then to look down on her husband and put out one hand to touch him, but he was sitting staring at the rug on his lap, his face a mask of stubbornness, and did not respond to her.

'Nahum,' she said softly. 'Nahum, you were ever a practical man. When your brother Reuben chose to return to Madrid to live, you looked at his proposition to you on practical grounds, and rejected it, even though it meant you would be unlikely to see him again in this world. You weighed your brother's need against your own, and made your selection on the basis of good sense. I ask you to do so now, in your dealings with your son.' She looked up at Gideon again, and then said very deliberately, 'I will never be happy to see you wed to a Gentile. I have always wanted for you the sort of marriage your father and I have enjoyed—blessed by man and God and rich in consequence. But I am not a fool—I will not reject the whole because parts are not as perfect as I would wish. I must tell you, Gideon, that if Abby will have you, then I will accept her. I must. It is now my hope your father will do the same.'

Gideon looked at her for a long moment, and then, still unsmiling, bent his head in acknowledgement, 'I do not thank you, Mamma, for that would make it seem I had begged you for a favour and been granted it. But it is not like that. I cannot beg as a favour that to which I have a right—to love the woman of my choice and to marry her. But I appreciate your wisdom, and am deeply grateful to you for being the woman you are—you have the tolerance that belongs with your great pride.'

261

Leah in her turn bent her head and they regarded each other gravely for a moment. And then Gideon said softly, 'Papa?'

But the old man wrenched his shoulders, those wasted shoulders under their fine woollen shawl, so that he turned his chair so savagely that it almost toppled. But it righted itself and he sat there straight and silent, his back turned to his son, and Gideon sighed softly and nodded, and crossed the room to kiss his mother and after a moment, bent and kissed his father's unresponsive cheek.

'I am sorry, Papa,' he said with infinite pity in his voice. 'I am so sorry. And I do not say it to apologize but to offer you instead sympathy in your loss. For that, it seems, is how you have chosen it shall be.' And he turned and went quietly out of the room, leaving them both beside the dying embers of the fire.

## 27

'Where is Gussy?' Abel said, looking at Miss Ingoldsby almost as though he did not recognize her.

She moved across the room towards him, and set one hand on his elbow and with a gentle but irresistible pressure led him towards the sofa beside the fire. He went, sitting there very upright and staring at her.

'He is gone away,' she said, and bent to unbutton his coat and help him to shrug it off. 'You cannot blame him. He saw what was happening, and chose to protect himself. I am glad he has gone. It saves us someone else about whom to worry, and he will be safe.'

'Where did he go?' Abel stood up and she pulled his coat from his shoulders and moved away to ring the bell for someone to take it from her. 'He has gone to Barty,' she said equably. 'I gave him some money and saw to it that he wore all new clothes, and disposed of those that might carry the contagion by burning them.'

He was standing very still, staring almost abstractedly out of the window at the greyness of Gower Street below, and when he spoke his voice was almost conversational. 'I brought it here. I took it to the hospital, and then brought it back here. I am fully culpable in this.'

'Now, that sort of talk, Mr Lackland, must be stopped immediately! The cholera is an Act of God and you take too much upon yourself to regard the entry of the infection to the hospital as in any sort your action. And the same applies to the appearance here. You have no right to speak so.'

The acerbity of her voice startled him out of his self-absorption and he turned and looked at her and frowned. 'What did you say?'

'Really, you are being as irritating as Gussy!' she said, and carried the coat she was still holding to the chair beside the door. 'To question and argue and be so tiresome! It is not reasonable in you to regard this disease as in some sort your personal affair. You must do all you can to contain it, of course, but that is all you can do——'

'Snow thinks, you know, that it is the water that does it,' he said abruptly, and stared at her almost abstractedly, as though he were listening to his own words for the first time. 'He says the patients throw the infection out of their bodies when they purge, and when we use the cesspit for their sewage, the disease seeps through the ground to enter the spring that feeds our well. And when we draw water and use it for patients, we pour the disease back into 'em. We draw it from the guts of the dying to taint the living——'

'Well, no doubt such talk is of use among physicians,' she said, her nose curling a little as the import of his words reached her; for all her practicality, Miss Ingoldsby was as susceptible as the next woman to dislike of disagreeable matters. 'But I cannot see that it is of use to you now to distress yourself about it. And anyway——' she stopped. 'And anyway, that suggestion should comfort you. If this is the way the disease moves from person to person—well, then, you did not bring it here to Gower Street.'

He shook his head, slowly and with a curious awkwardness for one of his usually controlled manner. 'But it is not only in the water, is it? Even if Snow is right, and we cannot be sure of that. It is on me, on my hands, in my clothes—I have come straight from those patients here. And carried the sickness with me.'

'Well, be that as it may, and I for one am not convinced, I cannot see that you do yourself or anyone any good in brooding upon the whys and wherefores. That provides no medicines for any ills.'

But for all the cool edge in her voice she was alarmed, and shot a careful glance at him from beneath her lowered lids. He was so very worn, despite the sleep he had had—and when she had found him there in the hard wooden chair in the hospital office, sleeping with the heaviness of an exhausted child she had wanted to weep at the sight of him—and, she feared, quite at the end of his rope. It would take so little to tip him over into one of his great rages, and that would exhaust him even more. There was pain enough to come, she thought sombrely, and again spoke with that strong and practical note in her voice while secretly praying it would have the effect it had always had on tired fractious children.

'It will be more to the point if, now you have been persuaded to return home, you take some rest. I have instructed a bath be prepared for you, and fresh clothes set out. When you have done that, and slept, then you can——'

He shook his head. 'I cannot be so long absent from her,' he said harshly. 'It is bad enough I brought it here—and whatever you may say, Miss Ingoldsby, that is the way of it—I must take care of her—of both of them. Now.'

She bit her lip, and then nodded, accepting the inevitability of it, and moved again to the bell to pull it.

'I cannot think what has happened to—oh,' she stopped then, consideringly, and he looked up and said harshly, 'Aye, you are probably right in your thinking. It always happens so.' She looked back at him with a wry smile on her face and said, 'Well, we managed at the hospital without any servants. We can manage well enough here, I have no doubt.'

'Rupert will be back this evening,' Abel said. 'Nancy had found some of her nurses and brought them back, and they came, albeit unwillingly, for it is clear we have contained it there now. At last.' He rubbed his face wearily. 'Seventy-five deaths, all told, Miss Ingoldsby, seventy-five——'

'Yes,' she said, and again that practical note came into her voice. 'And God have mercy on their souls, and give us the aid to take care of those that remain. You have done all you could, and I have no doubt there would have been many more dead had you not been there.'

'And you,' he said suddenly, standing beside the door with his hand on the knob, preparatory to leaving the room. He was looking over his shoulder at her, and she lifted her chin and looked at him and suddenly he smiled, a painful and thin smile, but very real in its feeling. 'I have not thanked you for your great efforts, Miss Ingoldsby. I took it as natural when I saw you arrived at Endell Street and made great use of your labour. It was not until now that I thought about it—it was most good of you to come.'

'As soon as I heard of the early cases I knew it was necessary,' she said calmly. 'There is no need for you to thank me for doing no more

265

than is my proper duty. And which it pleases me to do. Will you eat, Mr Lackland, if I prepare some food for you? I have heard often enough of your special surgeon's health, but I cannot believe you will long be free of infection if you go on abusing your constitution in this manner.'

'Aye, if you insist. A little cold beef will do——' and he was gone, leaving her to take herself down to the deserted kitchens and set about preparing not only beef for Abel, but some calves' foot broth as well as some milk pap for the two invalids above stairs. And in her usual sensible way, she cut some beef and bread for herself and made a quick meal; it was of some importance that she keep her own strength up, for without her, what would happen to all of them in the house? It did not bear thinking of; and she wrapped herself in a big calico apron, and set serenely about her self-appointed tasks.

And when she bore the tray of food up to Abel, with Dorothea's broth in a covered cup, she stood for a moment at the door looking at him, and bit her lip and then walked in very quietly to set down her tray on the table beside the bed.

For the first time that she could remember Dorothea's room looked less than perfect in its order. The early daffodils Abel had last week set in a bowl on the low table near the dead fire were drooping and curling brownly at the edges, and the fireplace with its dull cold ashes was dispiriting to look at. There was a faint sheen of dust about too, and Dorothea herself looked somewhat crumpled, as though she had been tossed about among her sheets and pillows, for her wisps of faded fair hair were disturbed and her nightgown bore the stains of her sickness.

Miss Ingoldsby turned and looked at Abel again, her eyes pricking with a sudden aching sympathy for him, for he was sitting in an upright chair beside the bed, just as he had sat in the hospital office, and was fast asleep in the self same way, his head drooped on his chest, his mouth half open so that his breath came a little noisily. He looked infinitely young and helpless and infinitely old and tired at the same time, and she moved softly to set a blanket across his knees before setting to work very quietly around him.

She washed Dorothea, lifting the flopping senseless head from the pillow to do so. With no sign of any distaste she removed her soiled gown and dealt with the exceedingly disagreeable state of the bed, for although at present Dorothea's attack of cholera was mild, still it caused some flux, and care was needed in dealing with the skin of her back and the wasted pitiful sticks that were her legs.

And when she had rubbed the freshly-washed skin with a little oil, to soften and protect it, and had set clean sheets upon the bed and removed the noisome ones to the housemaid's cupboard along the passage, and had managed to spoon some of the broth into Dorothea's lax mouth, she set to work to clean the room, kneeling before the grate to clear the dead embers, setting fresh sticks and coals, and when she had the fire crackling cheerfully dusted and swept, and finally stood by the door to look back at Abel, still sleeping helplessly beside his unknowing wife, as lost to the world as was she.

And she went away and left him peacefully there, but still doggedly working she dealt with the sheets she had removed from Dorothea and carried her brooms and dusters down to the kitchen, and then returned to William's room; and stood outside for a moment listening before very gently opening the door and going in.

He was lying much as she had left him an hour and a half ago, just before Abel had come in response to her summons; foursquare in bed, his hands on the coverlet and his eyes closed. But he was breathing heavily, and his lips looked dry and cracked. He was shivering with his fever and as she moved closer to the bed to look down on him, she felt the fear clutch in her chest. She had not spent the past week working with those patients at Queen Eleanor's without knowing the signs and she bent over the still figure and said softly, 'William!'

For a while the only response was a deeper breathing and then slowly he opened his eyes to look at her in puzzlement and tried to move his head and worked his mouth, but no sound came from him and she reached for the feeding cup beside the bed and set one hand under his head to lift it so that she could set the spout to his lips.

He spluttered a little and the liquid dribbled down his chin and she said softly, 'Aye, 'tis salt to the taste, but you need it, and must have it— come along now, for your Ingie——' and as obediently as though he were still a small child and in her care in the schoolroom he sipped and tried to swallow. But this time he choked and she set the cup down quickly and held his head as firmly as she could until the paroxysm was over and he collapsed heavily on his pillows again.

She soothed his forehead with a cold damp cloth and he turned a little fretfully on his pillow and muttered hoarsely, 'Ingie—make it better, Ingie. I feel so ill, so ill——'

And she crooned at him and wetted his lips with the water again, and he tried to smile and grimaced as his cracked lips protested, and spoke again in that faint voice, 'I am going to get better, Ingie? Don't let it not get better——'

She watched over him for a while to be sure he was asleep, and then turned and went, but she did not close the door behind her; instead she tied a towel to the knob on each side, so that it remained ajar and could not make any noise if the wind caught it, and went back to Dorothea's room along the passageway. She would sit there for a little while, watching Dorothea, she promised herself. Just a little while to rest herself and then she would return to William's room to see he was all right. Somehow, she told herself determinedly, somehow she would manage until Rupert returned this evening, until Abel woke up and could help her with the nursing.

But the disease had worked in Dorothea again, and once more she set about the labour of changing sheets and washing her and oiling the reddened skin, just as she had for so many people in the hospital these past days, and as she worked she almost wept, although she did not know whether it was with pity for Dorothea, fear for William, or concern for the exhausted Abel.

And then told herself practically that it was her own fatigue that was to blame for her weakness and that she must seek a remedy for that if she was to avoid becoming yet another burden on Abel by becoming ill herself.

She thought carefully and quickly in her characteristic way, and reached her decision swiftly, and went downstairs to her little desk to write a short letter, sealing it carefully with wax before going into the street to seek a hack who would carry it to its destination.


'Oh, why did you come?' she said, and almost stamped her foot. 'I told you in my letter—why make it so much worse for both of us by coming in this way? It is insupportable—you should not do it to me, or to yourself—no! Stay where you are. If you come closer I cannot think properly——'

She was walking up and down her little sitting room in a state of agitation, so angered with herself that she could hardly think. She had been sitting at her desk in the corner when the door had opened and, thinking it was just Ellie come to mend the fire and light the lamps continued with her head bent over her work; so that when suddenly she felt his arms about her and his warm breath on the back of her neck she had leapt from her chair, sending it flying across the room, so startled was she.

'I had to speak to you,' he said. 'It is not possible to deal with such matters in ink and paper.'

'It has to be possible. You must accept it as possible. I have made up my mind——'

'And I have made up mine,' he said softly, and went to sit on the window seat. 'Now, calm yourself. I am sorry if I startled you, but it was not possible not to want to touch you, sitting there. I had to. But I apologize and ask only that you should calm yourself and hear my reply to your letter.'

'You should have written it,' she said, and looked at him and then away; looking at him made her tongue thicken, made her agitation increase, so that she was no longer herself, the cool calm Abby she had been all her life (almost all her life, her thoughts amended, remembering James) but a fluttering stupid schoolroom miss. It was an intolerable situation; and she felt a flicker of anger within her and encouraged it. It would be easier to deal with him, she felt, if her prevailing mood was one of fury; certainly fury could be used to overcome the ridiculous flutterings that were filling her because he was so near.

She moved to her chair beside the fire, and bent to set more coals upon the embers and stir it to new life; having something positive to do helped her considerably and when the fire was burning to her satisfaction she was able to sit down in a flurry of skirts to fold her hands upon her lap and look at him with her lips set in a firm line and her eyes clear.

'I will repeat what I told you in my letter,' she said quietly, and her voice was as cold as she could make it. 'Any further passages of the sort that have passed between us are out of the question. It cannot be. I will not now or at any time accept your proposal of marriage. It is not possible.'

'Because of my family?' he said softly.

'For many reasons.'

'Because of my family?'

'I have said, for many reasons. I will not be quizzed on this matter! I have the right to make a decision without having to give chapter and verse for it!'

'Because of my family!' And now his voice was very strong, and she stared at him and breathed deeply through pinched nostrils and said sharply, 'Very well! Very well, if you so insist—in part because of your family!'

'Not in part, Abby,' he said softly, never taking his eyes from her face. 'Do me the honour of being completely truthful with me. There is too much of importance between us for it to be soiled by prevarications, by half truths——'

She closed her eyes and took a deep breath. 'All right! I would have wished to—but if you insist. Because of your family.'

He leaned back then and folded his arms and she looked up at him, almost puzzled, for his face was bright and clear, a smile displaying his even white teeth as he gazed at her.

'You make me so happy, Abby!' he said, and she shook her head, bewildered, and now he laughed aloud.

'Because you love me,' he said gently, as though explaining something very obvious to a backward child. 'Because you love me enough to go against your own wishes and desires in an effort to make me happy. Because you love me as much as I love you. How could I fail to be happy, knowing that?'

She shook her head and tried to speak, but could not. He looked so infinitely dear, sitting there with his legs outstretched in that characteristic fashion of his, that she felt herself filled with the need to touch him and suddenly the small patch of skin on the back of her neck where his lips had touched her flamed into sensation, and sent tendrils of feeling swooping down into her chest, and she drew an uneven breath and turned her head to stare at the fire.

'What is the sense of this?' she said in a low voice. 'You torment me and yourself. I know what is right, what must be done for all our eventual happinesses. You are cruel to come so to—to display my hurt to me in this manner.'

He stood up and made as though to come across the room to her, but she shrank back and cried out with an almost despairing note in her voice, 'No! You must not seek to work on me in this way! You must know that I am a responsive person. There are times when I cannot—when rational thinking is not possible because of emotion. You do us both a disservice if you use that tendency in me!'

He stood where he was, and after a moment said softly, 'You do not deny your feeling for me, Abby?'

She looked at him and opened her mouth to speak, and he said at once, 'Think carefully, Abby! You are not the sort of woman, I know, to lie on matters of importance—but you might, if you believed it practical, try to pretend that black was white. Do not treat me so—so casually as to be less than fully honest with me. Tell me of your feelings. Let me hear you say it and then we can—then will it be possible to talk of practical matters. But tell me the truth first.'

She looked up at him, standing tall and elegant in the fading afternoon light, his shape outlined against the lowering winter sky outside the window, at those deep dark eyes with their absurdly long lashes, the narrow mouth and the strong line of his jaw and her own mouth ached with a need to respond, to smile at him and tell him what he wanted to hear. But stubbornly she shook her head.

'It is not possible to separate the practical from feelings. You, of all people, should know that. You and your parents—you are very close——'

'I feel much more close to you,' he said quietly.

'Perhaps. But having affection for one person does not exclude affections that have been held hitherto.' She turned on him, letting her anger spark. 'For God's sake, Gideon, use your head! It is because you have always been on such amiable terms with your parents that you can be so casual about it! You do not know what it is to suffer the loss of parental love and approval. But I do! For ten years, Gideon, I have been separated from my family, and all because I made a marriage that did not meet their approval. I do not say it was right of my father to feel as he did about James, but right and wrong do not come into the matter. It is just the way it *is*. And it is because I have now, after all this time, made some small contact with my father again, because I believe that I may be able to—to re-establish myself with him, that I

271

know so certainly that I can never marry you, for it will mean that you will suffer as I have these last ten years.'

She stopped to draw breath and then said painfully, 'Perhaps it will show you how—how real is the feeling I have for you when I make it so clear to you that I am determined to protect you from unnecessary pain. In spite of yourself.'

'Why will you not say it?' he said. 'You love me, you do, and yet you will not let me have at least the comfort of hearing the words on your lips. That is not protection—that is cruelty!'

'I cannot say it. It would not help you, but hurt you more! You would talk even more certainly of marriage, and that cannot be. It is impossible.'

'No,' he said and the obstinacy in him was so strong it was almost as though it were palpable and he were wrapped in it. 'It is possible, it must be——'

'It cannot!' she said despairingly. 'Oh, God, if it only could! But it never can and you must know that as well as I do. I sat there in that gallery and I saw you——'

'My father had no right to speak to you as he did, no right at all. My anger with him is very great. My mother admits it was their fault to——'

'You have talked about the possibility with them? And they have told you the same thing? That marriage is out of the question?'

He was silent for a moment, and then said, 'My mother is a woman of wisdom, Abby. She knows when to bow before the inevitable. . . . And a marriage between us is inevitable.'

'When it will cut you away from your faith?' she said. 'When it will cause you to be mourned over and spoken of as dead? Forbidden to share the sacraments of your congregation?'

'We do not have sacraments. A Jew can worship God whether he enters the synagogue or not. He can worship at all or any time. I can be cast from the congregation but not from my faith.'

She looked up at him and said with infinite pity, 'But it is the sharing with your fellows that *is* your faith, Gideon. I knew that when I watched you. Your parents' words only underlined what I already knew, I think. I was an alien in your world, and that is painful. I cannot inflict the same pain on you by taking your world from you. I cannot enter it—that is very plain—any more than you will feel satisfied in mine. You may feel love now, but marry me and it will become loneliness and misery to you.'

'We can marry,' he said stubbornly. 'We will. It is impossible that we should——'

'It is impossible and that is an end of it,' she said sharply, and stood up. 'Gideon, I wish you to go away. I do not want to see you again, unless and until you have freed yourself of this impossible wish. Do you understand me? *I do not wish to see you again.*'

Before he could answer her the door opened, and Ellie stood there, an oil lamp in one hand and a piece of folded paper in the other.

'Please, ma'am, this was just brought by a man in a hack 'oo says as it was give to 'im in Gower Street and told it was a matter of great urgency, and 'e was to wait until such time as you was ready to send an answer by 'im. But 'e says the party wot give it to 'im said not to be surprised if you was to go back with 'im to Gower Street, ma'am,' and she bobbed and came across the room to give the missive to Abby, and to watch her with brightly inquisitive eyes as she opened it.

## 28

She stood in the hallway of the house staring about her, and said softly to Miss Ingoldsby, 'Nothing has changed.'

Miss Ingoldsby smiled at that, and shook her head. 'Very little ever does. Not in houses. People may change profoundly but a pair of stairs is always a pair of stairs, a mahogany door remains made of the wood from which it was cut. It is a thought in which I find great comfort.'

Abby looked at her and managed a ghost of a smile. 'It is good to see you, Miss Ingoldsby. I had hardly any chance to speak to you at the hospital. But even there I think I realized that you are in some sort a pair of stairs and a mahogany door yourself. You do not change, either. Still the sensible little person who taught me my letters and how to cipher.'

Miss Ingoldsby raised her eyebrows and turned to make her way to the stairs. 'Well, I cannot deny that I have not grown very much taller in the intervening years! But my smallness has not incommoded me too much. You will come to your mother now, Abby?'

Still Abby stood there in the hallway, looking up and Miss Ingoldsby stopped halfway up the staircase and looked back at her.

'I—is she very—how ill is she, Miss Ingoldsby?'

'Very,' she said soberly. 'Very ill, I fear. She is so frail in any case, you see, Abby. She has survived these long years only on the edge of her life. It is inconceivable to me that she should not succumb to this. That is why I sent for you. Not only to help me nurse them——'

Abby nodded, then with a decisive air took off her mantle and set it on the chair beside the door and followed Miss Ingoldsby up the stairs. To see her mother again. To see Dorothea in her physical shell after so long a time; it was a thought from which she shrank, but it had to be done. But it felt macabre to her; her mother had been dead in so many ways for so long. All that survived in the bedroom they were going to was a fragment of bone and muscle, a sluggish barely-breathing form that had no more relevance to the mother she had known than the banister rail upon which she set her hand as she climbed. And she shivered a little and let go of the banister and lifted her chin as she followed Miss Ingoldsby along the passageway.

'Your father is with her,' Miss Ingoldsby said in a low voice as she opened the door. 'He was sleeping when I left him, for he is still very weary—we will not disturb him, I think——'

But Abel was not sleeping when she pushed the door open and led the way into the room. He was standing beside the bed looking down on Dorothea, his face quite expressionless, and he lifted his head at the sound of the door opening and stared at them.

'Here is Abby come to see her mother, Mr Lackland,' Miss Ingoldsby said collectedly after the briefest of hesitations, and Abby looked at her sharply. Cool and calm as the little governess seemed, she detected in her a note of anxiety and she looked at her consideringly for a moment, at the way she was looking at Abel. And stored away in her mind the expression of concern she had detected on that small round face, and then returned her attention to her father. And Miss Ingoldsby touched her hand and went out, closing the door softly behind her.

He was looking at her very straitly, and she stared back at him, and it was as though ten years had rolled away. They were again standing confronting each other in this very room, the night before her wedding to James, and almost as though he had spoken she could hear the bitterness in his voice and the cruel words he had spilled over her. 'Will you go the way of others of your ilk, the gutter creatures—have I reared a Covent Garden whore?——'

And she knew, looking at him and at the stillness of his face that he was remembering too, and she essayed a little smile and said simply, 'I am glad to be here.'

He nodded and looked down at Dorothea and said quietly, 'She cannot go on much longer. Fifty-four years she has lived, and now it is almost finished. It is a strange thought.'

Abby moved softly across the room to stand on the other side of the bed, and she too looked down on the pale face lying on the pillow. It was remarkable how little Mamma had changed in the intervening years. Her face was still unlined, almost serene in its expressionless calm. The thin pale hair still lay in eternal neatness on her forehead, and Abby tried to imagine that face with the eyes open, with some animation moving across it, but could not. It was as though this Dorothea had never really lived, as though her memories of her mother were of someone quite different, and that the object lying here was something that had just drifted on to the bed in the most casual manner possible.

'Papa,' she said softly, 'Papa, it will be a release for her if she dies. Will it not? She has lain here too long in this state. It is time she was given her freedom.'

He lifted his head and looked at her and his eyes were opaque. 'Is it?' he said. 'Are you sure of that? You think her life here in this bed for so long has been useless? That she should have died in the street that afternoon?'

She looked down at the sunken temples and the dry lips and papery cheeks and then raised her eyes to him again.

'You do not think so.'

He was silent for a long moment, and then said, 'No. I do not think so.' He paused again. 'You find that difficult to understand?'

She did not answer, standing there and looking at him very quietly and he turned away from the bed and moved across the room with a tightly controlled energy to throw more coals on the fire and sweep the hearth. 'I will tell you,' he said savagely over his shoulder. 'I will tell you that it has been her presence there that has made my life tolerable these last years. If she had died that afternoon I could not have lived with myself ever again. The pain she suffered, the viciousness of her injury, were my fault. I, a surgeon! My fault. But I have in some small measure expiated my guilt, for she has lain there and I have cared for her, and watched over her, and been filled with concern for her in a way that——' He shook his head and stood up, and came back to the bedside.

'Her living here like this has been a balm,' he said. 'For she has freed me. All her life with me she wanted to do it, but then it was not possible. But in these last years she has done it, and I am filled with——'

he shook his head again and looked at Abby. 'I am so grateful to her,' he said simply.

'I do not understand,' Abby said. 'I am sorry, Papa. You speak in riddles.'

'Do I? Perhaps. But it is not so difficult to understand. Not when you know all that happened——'

'But I do not know,' she said softly. 'Will you tell me, Papa? I think you want to tell me.'

He looked at her, his eyes moving across her face as though he had never really seen her before. 'You have grown to be a handsome woman, Abby,' he said suddenly, and she blinked at him in surprise. 'She would have been happy to see you thus, I think,' and once more he looked down at Dorothea's silent face.

'Tell me, Papa,' Abby said again, so softly that it was almost a whisper, and he did not lift his head, but started to talk, in a flat expressionless tone of voice at first, but then with increasing strength, and she stood there and listened as the afternoon wore on and the light dwindled outside in the street, and Dorothea lay between them and lived out the remnants of her blank pale life.

He told her of his childhood, of the hunger and the squalor of the gutters in which he was born, and she could have wept for the tragedy of the lonely frightened child who had crept from his dead mother's side to seek his own survival amid the filth of Seven Dials. He told her of his swiftness as a pickpocket, of the dog-eat-dog battle for life in those same filthy gutters, and she exalted in the agility of that long ago boy who had swaggered and laughed and stolen his way through the years. He told her of Jesse Constam and Charlotte who had taken him in and she was grateful to those long dead grandparents who had loved him in their way. And he told her of Mr Witney and Lucy and Charles Bell, those friends who had loved him and helped him on his way to adulthood and the work he most wanted to do and she felt the deep pride in his ability that they must have had.

And then his voice changed and he told her of Lilith, and as she listened she felt the weight of misery he had known, the way he had suffered at her beautiful hands and how Dorothea and she had woven their complex dance through the fabric of his life, and at last she began to understand. She saw why her growing years had been marred by her mother's fears and diffidence, why Dorothea had been used to stare at her husband with those pale pleading eyes, why Abel had been so harsh and even cruel to her.

And above all she understood what her father meant about the freedom Dorothea had given him. She saw how in lying here and needing to be loved and protected she had whittled away the obsessive love Abel had once had for that sparkling, shallow and infinitely desirable creature that had been Lilith, until it was all gone. Her helplessness had been a powerful cathartic drug, had pulled from Abel the poison of his boyhood infatuation. And she looked down at her mother and knew that she would die as she had yearned to live; the dearly beloved wife of Abel Lackland, Surgeon.

Behind them the door opened and Miss Ingoldsby came in to set a lamp on the table by the bed and say in crisp tones, 'There is food ready for you in the kitchen. I am sorry to feed you there, but without servants it is difficult. I trust they will see the error of their ways and return to us in due course. Rupert is below, as well. He says that matters at the hospital are somewhat improved.'

She was like a breath of fresh air blowing the stuffiness from the room and Abby looked at her and smiled and Miss Ingoldsby smiled back pleasantly, and held open the door invitingly. 'Please to go down, Abby, Mr Lackland,' she said firmly. 'It is necessary for you to eat.'

'I will,' he said. 'After I have looked to William. How is he?'

'Far from well,' Miss Ingoldsby said. 'No, Abby, you shall go to him later. There will be work in plenty for you to do. First you must eat. And Rupert is glad you are here. He wishes to speak to you, he says.'

Abby went downstairs obediently, leaving her father to go along the passageway to William's room, to find Rupert in the kitchen, eating the pie that Miss Ingoldsby had prepared for them, and at the sight of her he got to his feet, pushing his chair back noisily.

'Abby! I am glad to see you. M'father is still above stairs? Good—I must speak to you——'

He moved swiftly across the kitchen to lead her to the big scrubbed wooden table in the centre and then carefully closed the door on to the stone flagged passage outside before coming to sit opposite her and lean forwards confidentially.

'Abby, I have given much thought to the matter you broached when we met last. William, you know? I had intended to speak to him, but as you know the contagion has come to him——' he stopped then and laughed a short ugly little laugh. 'It is positively amusing. He, of all of us, refused to give any help at the hospital, apothecary though he is. When we realized we had the cholera there Martha and Miss Ingoldsby both offered to come at once, and did so. But William, he couldn't get away fast enough. And he is the one who has succumbed to it——'

'I do not find it funny in the least,' Abby said sharply, and looked more closely at him. He seemed to have changed somehow from the way he had been the other night at Rules, seemed harder and almost sly as he looked at her with a very direct gaze, yet with eyes that conveyed no warmth at all.

'I did not mean amusing in the sense of causing laughter,' he said. 'But in the sense that it is ironic. However, let us not waste time on that. Look, Abby, it is most imperative that you say nothing to m'father about the matter. Can I depend upon you for that? I have dealt with it, I promise you, and there will be no more question of anyone trying to interfere between him and Queen Eleanor's. William did not know how far to go, nor how to deal with complex matters such as this, but I do. And I can assure you that no more will be heard of his plan. So there is no need to alarm my father with news of it. I am sure you will agree on this point.'

She looked at him doubtfully and then nodded, a little unwillingly. 'Very well, Rupert. If you can assure me there will be no further repercussions——'

'I can so assure you,' he said grimly.

'Then I will say nothing about it. I have no wish at all to cause distress to anyone. I hope the whole affair can be forgotten.'

'It will be. I can promise you that.' He laughed that hard little laugh of his again. 'It took only this little burst of cholera to send those damned Trustees scuttling! As long as m'father is there and always willing to step in in such situations, so protecting their hides from any fear of being tainted with disease, they'll lick around his shoes, whatever they may say in more piping times. They are a sorry lot—I despise 'em! Ah well, it is all old news now. I must think of other

279

matters,' he said and got to his feet. 'I am going to bed. I am fatigued beyond measure. Tell Miss Ingoldsby I am not to be disturbed at all until I ring. Oh, and tell her also that Martha will not be returning tonight. She has a notion to stay and assist Nancy and John Snow. I told her she has done enough, but she can be very stubborn. And it is no skin from my nose if she chooses to remain there——'

'I will tell her,' Abby said quietly, and watched him go and sat and pondered for a little while, wondering at the hard edge that there had been in him; and then she shrugged and ate a little bread and butter and went upstairs to see Miss Ingoldsby and her father and set to work. She had been sent for to help with the nursing and help she would. Whatever Rupert had purported by his talk of Trustees meant nothing to her, and she dismissed it all from her mind. She had more important things with which to concern herself.


The second day she sent a message to Miss Miller, explaining in a swift scrawl that she was needed at her father's house, and could not be looked for at her own until matters were better arranged. She sent her dearest love to Freddy and hoped that her niece and nephew were content, if they were still there in Paddington Green, and to tell Jonah that his presence at Gower Street would be welcomed by herself, and possibly by his father. She had no fears but that all was now well with him and that Celia had returned home, so it should be possible for Jonah to visit, and she hoped Miss Miller would show this letter to her brother as soon as might be. She feared her mother's life was coming to a close, and was sure Jonah would wish to be apprised of the situation. She gave a list of detailed instructions regarding the manufactory and remained hers truly, Abigail Caspar. And then returned her attention to the work that had to be done.

It had built up so gradually. Dorothea clung tenaciously to her flicker of life, seeming to melt away before their eyes, but every time they thought she had drawn her last breath she would seem to find some store of strength within that shell of a body and went on and on, as the third day moved into the fourth. And at the same time, William became more and more ill, throwing himself about his bed in his delirium and screaming with the pain of the gripes that seized him. He too lost flesh, becoming drawn and seeming to add five years to his age with every day that passed, and Abby would take turns with Miss Ingoldsby to sit with him and force fluids between his clenched teeth, to pack crushed ice into his mouth and wrap his limbs in cloths wrung out in cold water to bring down his raging fever, to wash and oil his grey skin in the unending struggle to clean and cool him as his body heaved and he tried to spew out the disease that filled him.

Rupert returned to the hospital on the third day, and there were just the three of them, her father, Miss Ingoldsby and herself. And then Miss Ingoldsby became ill and that was almost the most frightening time of all.

Abby had not realized just how much they had all come to rely upon her until the moment when coming down the stairs with a pile of soiled linen in her arms, Miss Ingoldsby had stopped and stood very still on the last step and then quite silently and in an oddly tidy fashion had crumpled and fallen in a dead faint.

They had borne her to her bed, and Abel had looked at her with an expression on his face that was hard to read, and told Abby harshly to undress her and wrap her in the hot sheets which he would prepare. And Abby did and discovered, as she pulled a nightdress over the head of the now conscious but shivering Miss Ingoldsby—for she was burning with fever—that she was much younger than she realized. She had been a part of Abby's childhood, after all, and she had always seen her as quite elderly in consequence, but clearly she was little more than six or seven years Abby's senior. Her body was as smooth and as curved as a young girl's.

Together she and her father had wrapped her in the sheets and fed her salted liquids and held her head when she vomited and cleaned her when she purged; and then they turned their attention to William, screaming his fear and agony along the corridor, and finally went to Dorothea; and so it went on as the hours pleated into days and the days into a week; and Abby slept when she could, upright in a chair, and felt guilty for doing so, knowing there were sheets to be laundered (for no laundrywoman would come near a house where there was disease such as this) and food to be prepared for her father and herself, though somehow she never managed to eat much of it.

It was on the last day of the week that Dorothea died. Miss Ingoldsby, who had passed the peak of her illness swiftly, for it had been a mild attack she had suffered, had wrapped herself in her sensible woollen peignoir and gone along the corridor slowly, holding on to the wall, to see if she could help Abby in any way, for Abel was fully concerned with William, who was patently moribund. She had found Abby dozing helplessly in the chair beside Dorothea's bed, but she awoke at once at the sound of the door opening, and when she saw Miss Ingoldsby standing there, swaying a little, said sharply, 'For heaven's sake go back to bed at once! You will suffer a relapse if you behave so foolishly, and then where will we be?' And she had tried to hustle her away.

But Miss Ingoldsby had stood there staring at the bed and said very softly, 'Abby.' And without turning round Abby knew, and stood there for a moment unmoving, and then very quietly turned back to stand beside the bed and look down at her dead mother.

She lay there very still, as still as she had been for all these years, but with an added quietness about her, a more remote stillness, and after another long moment Abby bent and gently set her hands upon her brow and then pulled the sheet up to cover that pale dead face. And felt a deep relief fill her as she did so. It was time, more than time.

'I shall tell him, Abby,' Miss Ingoldsby said and her voice came very clearly in the quiet room. 'I should wish to. If you will permit me.'

Abby looked at her, and unbidden the memory of the way she had stood and looked at her father that afternoon a week ago (was it only a week?) came back to her; and she gazed very directly at the little figure standing there with her thick brown hair in a plait over the shoulder of her woollen robe, her round face still haggard from her illness and she smiled very quietly and slowly and nodded. And went away to William's room to tell her father she would look after William now and that he should go to Dorothea.

He had looked at her questioningly, and she had looked away, not wanting to catch his eye, and he said nothing but turned and went, closing the door behind him and leaving her to sit there with the tossing whimpering William, to soothe his still burning forehead with cold damp cloths and ease his cracked lips with oil of roses.

And that night William died. She had held on to him while he thrashed about in one of his paroxysms of pain, grimly holding on to his heaving chest, and then felt it quite suddenly; the inner collapse, the draining away of life so that the muscles no longer resisted her, and he fell back on the bed and his head lolled ridiculously to one side, and he lay there staring at her blankly with an expression of angry surprise in his wide open eyes, his mouth hanging stupidly open and his cheeks lax.

That was when she wept. She had seen her mother's passing with no more than a mild regret; any grief she had felt for her she had worked through long ago. But William, the noisy demanding little brother she could just remember as a fat and redheaded child with a sulky face and a tendency to scream if he did not get his own way; the schoolboy who had wheedled and cheated for extra pocket money; to see him lying dead in his tumbled bed was a most exquisite pain, for he was so young, so unstretched, so wasted.

And she sat there with her head resting on the edge of the bed beside his staring empty corpse and let tears rack her weary body, her head feeling filled with wool, her throat raw and tight with the pain of her sadness. She was weeping for so much; for James and his wasted youngness as well as for William and his, for her need for Gideon and the way she must never express it, for the tragedy of her father's past as well as her own, for all the misery that living was. And she made no attempt to control her grief but let it wash over her like a vast tide. There was nothing in her world but misery.

## 29

She let events happen around her and to her, not really trying to understand or even caring very much. That evening had been a nightmare; they had obviously needed to send for help and because there were no servants, it had to be she who went. Miss Ingoldsby was in no condition, and she could not bring herself to ask Abel, sitting there beside his dead wife's bed and staring at the sheeted mound that was all that was left of her.

'I will stay beside him,' Miss Ingoldsby whispered to Abby, who was standing hesitating in the doorway looking at him. 'If you will go to the hospital, and tell Martha and Rupert—they will come home, and Rupert will know what to do——'

She had nodded and wrapped herself in her mantle and gone out into the street, and stood there for a brief moment breathing in deep draughts of the damp night air, realizing with a deep sense of surprise that this was the first time she had set foot out of doors for fully seven days; and then sought a hack. But it was late and there were none plying for hire in Gower Street and she had to go hurrying along towards Bedford Square, the wet wind blowing in her face and chilling her, and was almost beyond putting one foot before another by the time she found a lonely cab clopping tiredly along an almost deserted Oxford Street.

Martha had been asleep in Nancy's little room at the hospital, and Rupert, Nancy said, was not there at all; and she sniffed disapprovingly as she said it; but she bade the exhausted Abby not to fret herself, and shaking her head sadly over the news she brought made her sit down and drink a glass of madeira, while she went bustling away to 'make some sensible sort of arrangements for this place, on account I reckon I'll be busy round Gower Street the next little while——'

And Abby had smiled at her gratefully, seeing her rounded face as little more than a blur and deeply glad to leave matters to this capable woman, whoever she might be.

Nancy had clearly accepted that responsibility for it was she who rode back to Gower Street with the still dazed Abby and a silent Martha, she who left instructions to her nurses about sending servants to help next day at Gower Street, she who saw to it that the two bodies were laid out, and coffins sent for to be brought to the house next day, she who dealt with it all.

And the next morning, it had been Nancy who had come to Abby and wrapped her in her mantle and told her firmly that it was time she went home.

'For depend upon it, there's naught more you can do 'ere. I can manage well enough, an' things is all right at the 'ospital, for I got my best nurses back, and there won't be no rush of patients for a while. They know all round as we've 'ad the fever there, and they'll keep their distance awhile. Till they've forgot and they've got some pain or other.'

She had sniffed loudly then and put her arm round the unresisting Abby and said, 'I'm that glad to know you, Miss Abby. Knew abaht yer, o' course, these many years. But never set eyes on yer. An' you're a credit to yer family, that you are——'

It was a compliment Abby found curiously warming and she had smiled at this burly and comforting woman, and went obediently to bid her father and Miss Ingoldsby a temporary farewell.

'I shall return for the funerals,' she said softly to Miss Ingoldsby, who had insisted that she was sufficiently recovered from her illness to rise and dress as usual, and who was looking as calm and capable as ever, if undoubtedly thinner. 'You will send me word?'

'Yes, of course,' Miss Ingoldsby said. 'And I am glad indeed that you were able to come, Abby. We had need of you here, but it was more than that. It warms me so to see you and your father on terms of amity again. It is sad it had to be on such an occasion, but—well, better now than never. You are friends again, and I am very glad of it.'

'I too,' Abby said. 'You will take care of my father, Miss Ingoldsby? He is more shaken by his losses, I think, than he knows——'

'I will indeed. You may rely upon me,' Miss Ingoldsby said. At the note of fervour in her voice Abby looked at her sharply and to her amazement Miss Ingoldsby, the ever quiet and unruffled Miss Ingoldsby, flushed a brick-red and dropped her gaze in confusion.

There was a little silence and then Abby said carefully, 'Will my mother's death make you feel it is necessary that there should be changes in the household, Miss Ingoldsby?'

'I am not sure I understand you, Abby?'

'Oh, I think you do!' Abby said gently. 'You are very attached to my father, are you not?'

Miss Ingoldsby looked at her for a long moment, seeming to consider carefully and then nodded her head with a brisk little motion.

'You are clearly perfectly aware that I bear him a great deal of affection, so there would be no point in dissembling. I have for some years known that I would reciprocate immediately if he made any—any sign of bearing an interest in me.' She smiled a little wryly. 'But of course he has not. I am after all, a poor little dab of a thing. Your brothers said so to me often enough when they were younger.'

'Boys!' Abby said, dismissing them. 'That means nothing. You are—you are most personable, Miss Ingoldsby!'

'Perhaps,' she said calmly. 'I think I could be, given the chance to wear the right clothes and to hold any worthwhile position in society. Looks are very much a matter of one's station in life, after all. One never hears a lady of quality being described as anything but beautiful, while the most that will be allowed of a servant is that she may be pretty, even though any person with half an eye can see she completely outshines her betters in matters of looks. But whether or not I am personable has nothing to do with it. Your father is not one to be swayed by such attributes, I think.'

'No,' Abby said, and then smiled. 'You will not feel it necessary to leave the house, then? Your position will be no more equivocal than it has ever been, after all. My mother's helpless invalidism made her no sort of chaperone. And Martha is too young, I imagine, to be regarded in that light——'

Miss Ingoldsby smiled at that. 'Martha is a person who may surprise you, Abby. She says little, but she thinks a great deal. And she is not so young! Four and twenty, after all! It may be she who will leave now. She has said to me before this that it was only her mother's presence in this house that kept her here. I do not think I can take her into account in any future plans.'

'Where will she go?' Abby said, a little startled. 'Is she planning to be wed?' But Miss Ingoldsby shook her head. 'You must speak to her of matters to do with her. I would not for the world intrude myself. That would be like gossiping. And I never gossip.'

'No, I don't suppose you do,' Abby said. 'Not even about your own affairs. For you are clearly going to tell me nothing, are you?'

And now Miss Ingoldsby smiled widely, showing very even white little teeth and, most surprisingly, a soft dimple at the corner of her mouth. 'You are quite right, Abby. I am not. It is such a comfort to talk to someone with so keen an understanding!'

So Abby dismissed the matter from her mind, for there was no point now in thinking about it. After the funerals would be soon enough to worry about the future of the Gower Street establishment, now she could only ride back to Paddington Green in a hired carriage through the thin sunshine of the March day. She could think only about the way her very bones seemed to ache, about the headache behind her eyes that sent a sharp twinge through her whenever the carriage lurched over the cobbles, about the sense of emptiness within her.

She found Ellie awaiting her, alerted to her return by the efficient Nancy who had sent a messenger, and Miss Miller hovering anxiously in the sitting room door. All three of the children had come running out as her carriage drew up outside the house, Frederick to leap into her arms in an access of delight which almost bowled her over, Phoebe to pull eagerly at her skirts, and Oliver to stand a little to one side, shy and rather abashed by his sister's noisy demands for Aunt Abby's attentions.

'Oh, Mamma!' Frederick cried. 'I have so missed you! Are you all right? Ellie and Miss Miller would only say there is an illness in your family, but I could not understand who she meant for there is only me and Oliver and Phoebe, and Uncle Jonah of course, and we knew you were not with him——'

She was in the house now, taking off her mantle, and she looked up sharply at that.

'Jonah? He has not sent a message?' she said over the children's heads to Miss Miller, and she shook her head and said in her soft breathy little voice, 'No, Mrs Caspar. That is to say, there is no message I can deliver now.' She looked flustered as she spoke, and threw a glance at the children. 'Go out to play now, children, do, and leave poor Mrs Caspar in some peace. We cannot talk properly at all with all of you here making such a din——'

Freddy looked over his shoulder at the governess, and then back at his mother, and his young face was troubled, and then he turned and seized Phoebe by the hand and said with a sort of forced gaiety, 'Come along Phoebe! We shall have a treasure hunt in the garden, for real treasures. We shall hide a sugarplum and you shall eat it if you find it and Oliver shall have just the stone! Come on Oliver, for you never know—you may find it before she does——' and he hustled his cousins away, throwing one last look over his shoulder at his mother, who tried to smile reassuringly at him; but she was so tired her face was stiff, and she could produce only a faint grimace.

'What is it, Miss Miller?' she said quietly as soon as the children were gone, and then turned in surprise as Ellie behind her threw up her apron to cover her face and burst into noisy sobs.

'Whatever it is, Ellie,' Abby said, and fear sharpened her voice, 'do for heaven's sake, stop that noise at once! What has happened? Please will somebody tell me what is amiss before you drive me completely out of my wits?'

'Oh, those blessed little children!' Ellie gulped and wiped her nose vigorously on her apron and then sniffed again and said with a deep gloom in her voice, 'Those poor blessed motherless lambs!' and there was a relish in her tone as she looked mournfully at her employer and shook her head. 'Poor orphaned——'

'Ellie, I am sure Mrs Caspar needs some refreshment after her journey. And she is very fatigued, after so painful a time as she has had. Please to get some tea,' Miss Miller said breathlessly and the maid threw her a withering look, for there was no love lost between her and the governess, who she regarded as a jumped up little madam; but she went away obediently enough after a glance at Abby, and Abby turned to Miss Miller with her eyebrows raised.

'I am sorry, Mrs Caspar, to be the bearer of such news,' she said after a moment and reddened in embarrassment. 'Your brother—he came here two days ago. He was—he did not look well.'

'You had best tell me as shortly as possible what has happened,' Abby said, and sat down in her own favourite chair, but she did not relax, holding herself rigid, for she was so very tired that she feared that she would fall asleep if she once let go her carefully maintained control.

Miss Miller stood there, and looked at her, rubbing her hands against her skirts uneasily, and then blurted, 'His wife is dead, Mrs Caspar. Killed herself.'

Abby stared at her, and then shook her head, unbelievingly. 'Killed herself? It cannot be——'

Miss Miller nodded almost eagerly. 'It is so, Mrs Caspar. There was even a notice about it in the *Daily News*. It was the police who found her in the Long Water. In the park——'

Abby sat and looked at her but she did not see her. It was as though she were looking at a picture through the reverse end of a telescope; a small figure dressed in green, standing on the bridge over the Serpentine, one hand up to shade the eyes, and gazing in her direction. She heard Jonah's voice saying eagerly, 'How capital to meet you here like this! We were coming to visit you before we take Phoebe home, for I so much wanted my wife to meet you,' and he had turned to beckon the distant figure, and Abby too had looked and seen her running headlong over the bridge and away into the greenness of Hyde Park, and then glanced at Jonah and seen the expression of pain on his face. And she had chattered busily of nonsense, and done all she could to be cheerful and matter of fact as if nothing out of the ordinary had happened.

And now she was dead. Drowned in the Long Water in the park. Dead.

'They say they come in threes,' she said stupidly, and looked up at Miss Miller who was staring at her with an expression of mystification on her plain little face, and somehow Abby found that exquisitely funny, and she giggled. 'They come in *threes*,' she said again as though it was the most natural observation in the world, and still Miss Miller stared at her, but now with traces of alarm upon her face; it was too much for Abby and she giggled again, feeling laughter welling up in her, rising and bubbling until it burst over her head in a great salt wave and she was laughing and weeping and laughing again, completely and terrifyingly out of control of it all.

The hard reek of ammonia made her eyes smart and she hiccupped and coughed and took a deep shuddering breath and blinked up to see Ellie kneeling beside her with a bottle of smelling salts held under her nose and an expression of satisfaction on her eager face. And again Abby laughed, but this time shakily and with real amusement, not the helpless painful abandon that had so overwhelmed her. Clearly such a reaction was what Ellie expected from a lady of quality and sensitivity and her approval of her mistress was made very plain in the absurdly maternal way she helped her to her feet, and urged her to come to her bedchamber and bath and go to bed and take a little calves' foot broth to restore her before she slept.

Abby let her lead her away, but stopped at the bottom of the stairs, holding on to the banisters for her legs felt suddenly very shaky, and looked back at Miss Miller.

'Where is he now, Miss Miller? Do you know?'

The girl shook her head. 'I do not, Mrs Caspar. He came, looking most distraught, and asked if the children could remain until such time as he had made some arrangements, and in your absence I took it upon myself to say yes, for I was sure that——'

'You were quite right, Miss Miller,' Abby said, and suddenly yawned. 'Of course they must remain here as long as is necessary. Ellie——'

The little maid nodded cheerfully and again urged her to climb the stairs. 'Don't you fret none, ma'am. There's nothing to fret about, on account I can manage the three o' them, no trouble at all! Young Master Oliver ain't no worry to look after, and Master Freddy, 'e can get that impertinent little one to do all she should just with a word. We can manage well enough, ma'am, an' you come to yer bed, for you've had such a shock as could be enough to send yer to yer grave——'

And at last Abby went to bed; weary, confused and almost numbed by the happenings of the past week, she sank into the depths of her own dear and familiar sheets and closed her eyes gratefully against the late afternoon light, and the sounds of the children's voices from the garden below dwindled into the deepness of her sleep. It was so good to be at home again.

## 30

She woke suddenly to lie staring up at the ceiling of her room. It was not completely dark for the moon was full and she could see the cold light making a lattice pattern on the white plaster above her head. She closed her eyes again and tried to remember what it was that had woken her. She felt uneasy and somehow strange and she turned her head on her pillow, and tried to turn her body. And then it seized her again, and she knew at once that it was this that had roused her; a deep sickening pain low in her belly that made it seem as though some large and very cold hand had been able to slide itself into her vitals to take her in its cruel grasp, and squeeze and twist.

She lay rigid for a moment, holding her breath, thinking obscurely, 'It will stop in a moment,' and it was almost as though she were in childbed again and there was a baby within her demanding to be freed, pushing its painful way against her overstretched flesh. But it gripped tighter and it wasn't like a childbirth at all, for that had been a glorious pain, and bearable because of what it was. This was ugly and useless and so cruel and she could not help a little whimper escaping her.

It subsided then, not entirely but enough to make it possible to move a little gingerly, and then the other sensation came; nausea filling her stomach so that it seemed to press up against her teeth, filling her chest and then her arms and legs, every part of her with the absolute certainty that at any moment she would cast up her accounts, and that it would be altogether horrible and foul and somehow she must get out of bed and to the washstand in the corner; and then the gripe again, and an even more urgent need to get up and deal with these animal functions, and she rolled her head on the pillow and whimpered again.

She managed to get out of bed, half crawling and half falling across her room to reach the washstand and hold on to it, retching so pain-fully that it seemed she would be turned inside out; and the need to purge increased and added its own burden of misery and she struggled to cope as best she could, feeling more ill than she could ever remember being in all her life.

It seemed to go on for hours, as the light of the moon thinned and the room blackened, and at one point she woke to find herself lying crumpled and curled up on the floor beside her washstand and realized she must have swooned, and then gone into a deep sleep, for she was stiff and so cold that she shivered uncontrollably. And then realized that she was not cold at all but very hot and it was this that made her tremble so; and she dragged herself back to bed clutching a bowl from her washstand and collapsing helplessly on to its tumbled covers.

She lay there as the light changed again, thinning into dawn, tossing and retching and bent double over the agonizing pains that shook her, and the bed that had seemed so blissful a place so short a time ago now seemed in some sort a prison, and she wanted to get away from it, and run free outside on the grey dawnlit grass of the Green, leaving her painracked body behind. And knew, with some cool corner of her mind that she was half delirious, half wandering in her wits, and was suddenly very frightened.

But that was not all her fear. Beneath the sensations from stomach and belly that battered consciousness, beneath the distaste that filled her because of the hateful way her body kept throwing out of itself the illness that filled it, lay a greater deeper fear. She could see her mother's dead face on its white lace trimmed pillow, could see William's blank-eyed lax-mouthed stare in the midst of its tumbled sheets, each face seeming to be very small and then coming closer so that it overwhelmed her, and then receding and returning again, each in turn, over and over again. And the word rattled through her mind like an urgent drum beat. 'Cholera, cholera, cholera.'

She tried to push the fear away, but it filled her even more, adding to the burden of her sickness so much that she cried aloud, 'Don't let me die! Don't let me die!' but it came as a hoarse croak, and she whimpered again, rolling her head on her pillow and feeling the tears running down her face like hot rain.

And then Ellie was there, peering down at her with her face huge and wide-eyed and her voice chattering over her in a cascade of sound but she could not understand the words; and then there was the cool touch of air on her face, and she turned her head and saw it was daylight and the window had been opened and she shivered and someone said, 'There—don't fret—don't fret.' She looked up and blinked and the face was that of a strange man and that puzzled her and she tried to remember who he was, for there was something familiar about his face. And then she could feel a hard rim of china against her lips and liquid filling her parched mouth and obediently she swallowed and grimaced for it tasted sweet and salt together, and she felt the retching start again, and her head was being held and she felt for one brief moment a little better, not so frightened; and she opened her eyes and tried to see and could not and the fear returned.

Blackness again, sleep and dry-mouthed wakings, and more sleep and then she opened her eyes and saw lamplight and Frederick's face and was so filled with agitation that she tried to sit up and tell him to go away, right away, for it was dangerous to be with her, but she could only croak that same hoarse sound and his round face creased with anxiety and receded and she relaxed again, glad he was gone.

She began to dream. She was walking in cool woods, among shadows and sunlight, and water trickled somewhere, sweet and singing over pebbles, and she skipped and sang with it. And then it rained and it was cool rain, scented like eau de cologne and lay across her hot forehead and cheeks like a benison. She smiled in the woods, turning her face up to the rain and saw with no sense of surprise at all that Gideon was there, his hand holding hers, and stroking her forehead and bringing more of that cool scented water to her hot face. His voice was gentle but it told her what to do in a bantering sort of way and that made her laugh aloud, or so she thought, but she could not hear her own laughter. Only Gideon's voice murmuring her name, telling her to lie still and sleep, telling her to drink, and out of the rainy sunlit sky of the woods in which she was still walking came a cup and she drank from it, and it tasted cool and sweet and did not make her retch at all, and she was grateful and happy and comfortable, and breathed deeply and slept.

*

She woke in a most gentle and comfortable way, seeming to climb easily and pleasurably up shallow stairs that brought her from the depths of unconsciousness to full awareness. She lay there in lazy peace gazing at the square of her window, seeing the green leaves of the seven elms in the distance and admiring the way the morning sunlight lay in yellow bars across the sill. She felt relaxed and very happy, without a care in the world, and yawned agreeably, and wriggled her shoulders a little against the soft comfort of her pillow.

'You feel better,' he said softly and she turned her head and smiled at him sleepily, not at all surprised to see him there; Gideon sitting leaning back in a chair beside her bed, smiling at her with his face so very warm and kind.

'Yes,' she said. 'Oh yes,' and closed her eyes for a moment, so that she could think more easily about how much better she felt, and when she opened them again she was surprised for the sun had moved and it was late afternoon; she knew that because of the way the lines of shadows fell on her bedroom carpet.

She frowned, trying to understand what it was that was puzzling her, for she had woken with the sure knowledge that something was. And then turned her head and knew.

'What are you doing here?' she said huskily and tried to sit up, but he leaned forwards and with a gentle but very firm pressure on her shoulders he made her lie down again; then took a cup from the bedside table and, slipping one hand beneath her head, held it to her lips, and she had to swallow, for he was insistent, and would not take it away though she tried to splutter a refusal at him, staring up with anger in her eyes. But he just smiled pleasantly and stood there, quite implacable, so she sipped and swallowed, and was glad she had, for she was indeed thirsty, and she drank a lot before he at last let her head go again and took the cup away.

'What are you doing here?' she said. Her voice was peevish, and she knew it and was somehow annoyed with herself. 'I told you, didn't I? I thought I told you——' She stopped, confused. Had she told him? Indeed, what had she told him? It seemed to her suddenly that she was dreaming again, and she said abruptly, 'Am I awake?'

He laughed softly. 'Oh, indeed you are. All this is real, I promise you. You have suffered many bad dreams these past days, I have no doubt, but this is real. You are awake and you are better——'

His hand came down over hers suddenly, and held it with a grip so tight that she looked at him almost wonderingly; his eyes were very bright, and had he been a woman she would have said he was on the point of weeping.

'I do not understand,' she said and closed her eyes, and then opened them at once. She did not want to sleep now. She wanted to know. 'Why are you here in my bedchamber?'

He laughed again. 'So much impropriety!' he mocked softly. 'What *would* the good people who are your neighbours say if they know! Well, they would say little, I think, if they knew how ill you have been. Too ill for any dalliance, my love. So very ill——' and again his hand held hers tightly.

'Ill. Yes,' she said consideringly. 'I remember. I came home from Gower Street and went to bed, and it was bad that night—last night?' She shook her head. 'No, not last night. I cannot recall——'

'Certainly not last night. It has been nine days since you were at Gower Street——'

She tried to lift her head from her pillow, but again he made her lie still, and she stared at him in amazement. 'Nine *days*? It cannot be so long!'

'Oh, it can,' he said, and leaned over and took both her hands in his, so that his face was very close to hers. 'Nine very dreadful days, my darling. I was so afraid. So very much afraid. You so nearly died, so nearly——' he stopped and again regarded her with that bright-eyed look and blinked and bent his head and his lips brushed her cheek and she felt his breath hot on her face.

'I cannot imagine it was so long,' she said then, and suddenly frowned. 'Gideon! Nine days—the funerals—my mother and brother——'

He nodded soberly. 'Yes. That is past. It happened on a day when you were so very ill that I felt I could not leave you, but I knew, when the card came, that you would feel it sorely if you were not in some way represented. So Miss Miller stayed here beside you and I went——'

'You went? Why, Gideon! That was most——'

'You could not go,' he said simply, 'and that would have distressed you. So I did. They shared one service of great simplicity and piety.

It was all most proper. You need have no fears that they were not treated with every respect.'

She found herself crying suddenly and tried to speak but could not, for her throat was tight, and he reached over and with his own handkerchief gently dried her eyes. 'You would have done as much for me, would you not?' he said, and she managed to nod and even smiled a little, trying to show her gratitude. 'So do not fret yourself,' he finished softly.

They sat in silence for a long time, listening to the distant sounds of the house, the rattle of china and the sound of voices raised for a moment and then subsiding to a dull rumble, and someone—Miss Miller?—was in her sitting room playing on the pianoforte, and the notes came gently to their ears, melancholy and merry by turns, the cadences rising and falling and stopping and then starting again and she liked the sound, and turned her head at last, feeling his eyes upon her, and smiled.

'I am glad you are here,' she said. 'You should not be, but I am so glad.'

And he smiled back and said nothing. And she frowned a little and then said almost petulantly, 'But I do not know why, or how——'

'Frederick,' Gideon said succinctly.

'Frederick?'

'He is a boy of parts, that son of yours. Any man would be proud to be his father. I wish I was.'

She closed her eyes at that, and frowned again and he said quickly, 'Forgive me. This is no time—I will tell you what happened. The day after your return from Gower Street, Ellie and Miss Miller found you very ill, and sent for the local apothecary, of course. He told them what to do and they took great care of you, both of them, and are much to be praised for their loyalty, for I know how often people will flee from a house where there is disease. Ellie was most wise, she kept the children away from you, in the most sensible manner possible—she told Mr Corrigan—Frederick's schoolmaster, I believe—about the distress the house was in, and he took the children to school and said he would keep them there until you were well. But Frederick——' Gideon smiled. 'That would not do for your Frederick. He slipped from his bed one night—the third night of your illness—and came home to see you. Ellie was most upset for it was she who was watching by you and did not see him come or go. But the poor wretch was fairly exhausted by then and had fallen asleep. At any rate Frederick was so alarmed by what he saw that he came to me.'

'He came to you? But how—it is not possible——'

Gideon smiled. 'I tell you, he is a lad of parts. He played truant from school next day, rode Shillibeer's omnibus to the Bank and enquired for me from every business house he passed, until he found one that knew our name. A most remarkable performance for one so young! I wish you could have seen him, Abby! He stood there in the door of my counting house, his hat in his hands like the most sober of city gentlemen, and announced that he was come to fetch me at once for Mamma was most distressed and in great need of me—so very much the man of the world, you cannot imagine!'

Her eyes pricked with the ready tears of fatigue and she said huskily, 'He is a most beloved boy. Dear Frederick—but he should not have——'

'Indeed he should!' Gideon said firmly. 'He knows, if you don't, who is the person most to be relied upon when it comes to your wellbeing. I feel I have a very special ally in Frederick, Abby. Together, I have no doubt that he and I can wear away your so foolish scruples——'

'Please——' she said. 'It is not fair, now——'

'I know,' he said. 'But who is fair in love?' He smiled a crooked and very loving smile at her and again the tears came to her eyes and she was angry with herself and raised her hand to rub her face in annoyance.

'You are tired,' he said softly. 'Sleep now. We shall talk again.' He picked up a towel from the table beside him and laid it gently on her forehead and across her eyes so that she had to close them, and the scent of eau de cologne and the soothing sound of his voice as he murmured, 'Sleep now. Just sleep,' took her back to her dream and again she was walking in the woods and felt so very safe and comfortable; for Gideon was there and she was so glad of it.


During the next weeks her recovery was rapid. At first it had been all she could do to lift her head from her pillow, but she drank and ate in greater quantities every day and moved more and more, and by the end of the first week was well enough to sit wrapped in a soft blanket before the window looking eagerly out into the Green, now bright with late April sunshine, and could at last be allowed to be visited by the children.

They let Frederick come alone, the first time, and the two of them sat there holding each other's hands, very happy to be together. Frederick looked closely at her when she came in, peering into her face, and then he nodded in satisfaction and hugged her close and sat beside her.

'They said you had become thin,' he said. 'And you do look hagged, but you are going to get well soon, so that is all right!'

She laughed at that. 'Dear boy! No gentleman tells a lady she looks hagged, even if it is true!'

'Well, when I am a gentleman, I won't,' he said unabashed. 'I am a boy now, so I need not worry about such matters as paying compliments, need I? And anyway, you are my Mamma, and mammas do not have compliments.'

'Sometimes they do,' she said and hugged him again. 'Oh, dear Frederick, I am so happy to see you! And I am sorry if I gave you a fright by getting ill. I would not have alarmed you so for all the world.'

'You did alarm me,' he said and looked very serious for a moment. 'A great deal. When I came in here that night, why, you looked——' he shook his head. 'Well I cannot tell you with a compliment so I will not say.'

'Why did you go to Gideon, Frederick?' She said after a moment. 'You were most clever, I know, but why?'

'Who else should I seek, Mamma?' He lifted his clear green eyes to her face, and pushed the hair from his forehead. 'I knew that Uncle Jonah—well, that he was troubled, and besides—well, I never feel that he is a person upon whom one can rely, you know? He seems to come to you much as I would have done when I was smaller. You understand, do you not, Mamma?'

She smiled and leaned forwards to cup his face in her hands. 'I do, Frederick. For so young a person you are very knowing, are you not? I am very lucky to have such a son,' and she kissed him and he hugged her again and they were very happy together, and that night she slept better than she had all week and woke feeling stronger and more refreshed than she would have thought possible.

By the middle of the second week she was fit to be up and dressed for the greater part of the day and was visibly regaining her lost weight, her face at last being divested of the greyish pallor that had been part of it, and Gideon was hard put to it to prevent her going to the manufactory.

'You shall not, and that is all about it,' he said firmly. 'Caleb and Henry are managing perfectly well, and Miss Miller too is handling the book-keeping well enough. You will be an embarrassment if you go, for you are not as well yet as you think you are. If you have a relapse and demand even more nursing, we shall all be in trouble!'

She had looked at him at that, her head on one side. 'Why is it that you are so careful a nurse, Gideon? I have took it much for granted that you should have taken such care of me, but in all truth, it is an unlikely accomplishment for a man of affairs.'

'My father,' he said. 'He was ill for a long time, you will recall, and I was required to share his care. I learned a lot then about the needs of invalids.'

'Your father,' she said and nodded, and suddenly the bloom went out of the day. They had been so happy in each other's company during the days of her recovery. He had arrived each morning at eleven o'clock, having dealt with the urgent matters of his business in advance (and she realized he must indeed be rising early and working late into the night to be able to spend so much time with her) and sat with her through the long quiet daytime hours, talking desultorily, just being glad to be together. She had closed her mind to all that had happened to them before, to her decision, to his hopes, content to live just in the present. But now reality had intruded upon that idyllic peace, with mention of his father, and they both felt the chill that descended upon them.

They managed to start to talk again on unimportant matters, both avoiding the question that lay between them, until he was about to leave that evening. He stopped at the door of her sitting room and looked back at her and said abruptly, 'I have talked further with my parents about my plans for our shared future, Abby.'

She stared at him, her eyes big in her still thin face, and said nothing.

'I have told my father, as I tell you now, that nothing has altered my resolve. Indeed, it is strengthened. These past days——' he shook his head. 'I have come to feel so close to you Abby. You are like part of me.'

She knew what he meant. She too had found the days had wrapped them insidiously together as delicately as a spider spinning a web, had tied bonds of shared need and giving and taking between them that would not easily be released, and she bent her head and stared at the flames of the fire and could say nothing.

'Nothing will ever alter my determination. I love you too dearly for that. Please Abby, think again. What stops you see in our way, they are as nothing to the misery we will both suffer if we cannot be together. You must know that as well as I do. Tomorrow when I come you must tell me your answer, for good and all. For I love you too much to go on in this—this limbo for much longer. Tomorrow, Abby?'

She turned her head and looked back at him very gravely, looking at every feature of his face as though she were taking an inventory. He looked very dear, so very dear, standing there and she breathed deeply and said quietly, 'Very well, Gideon. Tomorrow.'

## 31

She lay awake for a very long time that night, lying quite still and staring out of her dark window at the empty sky and the tossing upper branches of the elm trees, listening to their soughing in the night wind. The thoughts ran around her head like mice, chattering and scrambling and seeming confused yet ever returning to the same point. She would make a decision and then reconsider it, and make another precisely opposite one and reconsider that, until her head ached with it all and she wished that she had never set eyes on Gideon Henriques and that she was but a piece of wood incapable of feeling. And then thought of Gideon as he had looked standing there in her doorway last evening, and felt the love she bore him rising high in her again, and was glad of it.

Quite when it was the thought came to her she did not know. She had dozed a little and awoken, and dozed again and then when she awoke she knew what the solution was. And pondered it, twisting and turning it in her mind and trying to imagine how Gideon would be when she put it to him; but could not.

She could imagine many conversations with him, on many matters, but on this it was impossible. She knew him, and loved him dearly. Every plane of his face was as familiar to her as her own, every cadence of his voice was a part of her, but there was still enough of the enigma in him for her not to be able to foretell how he would feel on this. Was he the man of tradition and form and convention his father believed him to be? Or could he free himself of such bonds with the ways and beliefs of other people and do as he wished to do, for himself and by himself? She did not know, and at last as the sky blackened into the darkest part of the night, and the clock on St Mary's Church struck half past four, her usual good sense came at last to her rescue.

'Either he will say yes or no,' she whispered into the darkness. 'And I cannot know what it will be. So I must wait, and might just as well sleep now and stop worrying.' And somehow, sleep she did.

It was almost ten before she rose, and was a little annoyed with herself for she felt she was sufficiently recovered by now to keep more businesslike hours, and was a little sharp with Ellie for letting her sleep so long. But Ellie merely smiled, setting a coddled egg and thin buttered toast before her and telling her firmly that, 'Sleep's the best medicine, an' you ain't as strong as you would like to think. You 'ad a bad time, 'eard the angels singin', an' no error. Prayed for you over and over I did,' before going back to her kitchen in high good humour; having an invalid to exclaim over was a very satisfying situation for Ellie to be in.

She fidgeted about a good deal for the next hour, and at last, unable to control her restlessness any longer, sent Ellie for her shawl (which she brought but not without considerable tutting and Awful Warnings of the fate that would overcome anyone so recently ill who was foolhardy enough to go into the dangers of the open air) and went out into her garden.

It was alight with gillyflowers, flaunting their scarlet and orange and yellow and soft golden brown, growing higgledy-piggledy against the old brick wall that surrounded it, and forsythia was blooming stridently yellow against the wall of the house. The cherry trees at the far end were thick with blossom, and she stood under the laden branches looking at the way the flowers blushed pinkly against the blue of the April sky, and sniffed their scent and was very glad to be alive. For the first time she fully realized how very close to death she had been, and she shivered a little, warm as the sun was on her woollen-clad shoulders, and she looked again about her at the lush green of the little patch of grass and the flowers and the warm red brick of her little house and was grateful they were there, and she able to see them.

She was sitting on a low stool beneath the apple tree with some of the gillyflowers she had picked upon her lap, arranging them into a tight little posy, when he came to her.

She lifted her head to see him walking easily across the grass, and felt a lurch of—what? Fear? Not of Gideon. Shyness? Not that, either.

302

How could she be shy with a man who had held her head when she was sick, and fed her and washed her face and hands, and taken such care of her? She swallowed and smiled at him, knowing what it was, both exulting in it and hating herself for it; it was indeed a burden to bear, this passionate need for physical contact that she had.

'What a setting for a lover to see his lady in!' he said and laughed down at her. 'You look like some set piece upon the stage, my word you do!'

'It was not deliberate!' she said, and reddened. 'Come, I am not a woman to be arch and to put on performances, Gideon! You should know that if you know nothing else.'

He sat down beside her on the grass, setting his curly-brimmed top hat at her feet. 'Well, then, it is most fortuitous. If I had not already offered you my heart and hand, then you can be sure I would have done so, seeing you so beautifully set off in such a place! Your gown is most becoming—did you choose those lilac ribbons because they look so springlike? Or because they turn your eyes to so deep a grey?'

His tone was light, and his eyes seemed dancing enough but she felt the strain in him beneath his banter and smiled and shook her head. He picked up the remaining gillyflowers to give them back to her one by one as she added them to her posy, stopping between each addition to regard her handiwork with a judicial eye, and then carefully placing each bloom so that it set off its neighbour most agreeably.

'Have you given consideration to what I said to you last night, Abby?' he said abruptly and she went on working industriously at her flowers, her head bent, and he put one hand out to take her chin and lift it so that she had to look at him.

'Yes,' she said. 'I have thought,' and for a long moment they gazed at each other in silence, and he took his hand away and said quietly, 'You are not going to say what I most need to hear.'

She shook her head. 'If I were to capitulate so easily, Gideon, it would mean that I had hitherto been—been wantonly capricious with you. It would mean that my reasons for refusing you first had not been carefully thought out, had been used as some sort of—oh, some sort of missish plot! There are women, I know, who regard it as proper to torment a man and refuse his proposals half a dozen times before apparently yielding to his importunities, as though they were trying to impress upon him what great treasures they are! Well, I am not like that. I could never be so. I try to be honest.'

'I never doubted it.'

'Then how can you doubt that I will remain so?' she cried passionately, and pushed the flowers away from her lap and twisted on her stool so that she was turned away from him. 'How could you believe me to be so inconstant as to give you reasons one day for saying no, and then discarding them as unimportant on another? You do me an injustice to regard me so, Gideon!'

'You are trying to fan yourself into anger, Abby, to convince me that you mean what you say,' he said quietly. 'You do not have to do that, you know. You do *me* an injustice if you think so.'

There was a pause and then impulsively she turned back to him and held out both hands.

'Forgive me. You are quite right, of course. I was behaving as though I were more angered than I in fact am. I had not realized it——'

He smiled a little crookedly. 'You see how well suited we are? I understand you even when you do not understand yourself.'

'Yes.' She breathed deeply then. 'Yes, I know. I never said we were not right for each other. I know it perfectly well. It is as though we have been cut out of one piece of cloth.'

His hands tightened on hers. 'Abby, you have never told me of your feelings—not in so many words, that is. I know what they are, I have always known. It would not be possible for me to love you as I do if you did not reciprocate. But it would please me to hear you say it. Will you tell me? Do you love me, Abby?'

She looked down at him, and smiled, her lips trembling a little, 'Oh you fool,' she said softly. 'You dear, dear fool. Of course I love you. I am half demented with it——'

His arms were round her then, pulling her down so that she tumbled off her stool in a froth of lilac skirts, but she didn't care, nor even know it had happened, for he was kissing her, his mouth warm on hers, and the sensations that she had kept battened down within her for so long came bursting up in a great flood so that she clung to him with all the fervour of which she was capable, feeling her whole body concentrated in her mouth and tongue, feeling him a part of her.

They separated as suddenly as they had come together, and she sat for a moment staring at him, and then shakily put up both hands to smooth her hair, as women always do in such situations. He laughed at that with infinite tenderness and reach for her again, but she shook her head and scrambled to her feet.

'No,' she said breathlessly. 'No, Gideon, it is not fair.'

'You are not going to refuse me, Abby,' he said very coolly and stood up too, brushing away the flower petals that had clung to his sober broadcloth coat. 'You cannot and we both know it.'

'I can refuse marriage,' she said in a low voice. 'And will.'

He frowned sharply, and there was a sudden note of impatience in his voice. 'Abby, my dear girl, you really cannot——'

She spoke very clearly then, her chin up and looking at him very directly. 'I can refuse marriage, but that does not mean I refuse to love you. That I know I cannot do. I am not so fickle, and I am committed now to caring for you. But I love you too dearly to hurt you, and I maintain that marrying you will hurt you so very badly. So——' she took a deep breath. 'So, Gideon, I have decided what I will tell you. You may come to me here at any time you wish, you may share every aspect of my life, my being——' she swallowed, '*every* aspect. We need not part ever, although we cannot be married.'

He stood very still, staring at her, and then said uncertainly, 'Do I understand you right, Abby? I cannot think that—I must be mistaken.'

She shook her head. 'You are not mistaken,' she said in a low voice. 'I will have you as a lover in every way. But not as a husband. Will you take me as your mistress, Gideon? For I see no other way.'

As soon as the word was out of her mouth she knew she had hurt him. His lips seemed to become pinched and tight, and his face, although it did not change colour, seemed to shrink and age before her gaze, and she looked at him with her eyes wide and apprehensive.

'I did not think you capable of—of so great an insult to me, Abby,' he said at length and his voice was tight with control. 'I came to you with all of myself that I can offer you. I have for you not only love but esteem and respect and——' he stopped, and then drew a long harsh breath. 'I can understand the motives that you have in thus—thus offering yourself. You believe it to be a loving and—and honourable approach to me. But I tell you I am insulted. Had I wanted some *mistress*——' and the scorn in his voice made her physically shrink back from him, '—some *mistress* I would not have come to you, for the love I have for you is too great for that. If that is your last word, then there can be no more discussion between us. I ask you to be my wife. I could not take you as any other and never could.'

They stood quietly in the sunshine beneath her cherry tree, the wind ruffling their hair a little and Abby said after a moment, 'To become your wife would be to hurt you even more than you believe yourself hurt by my offer. I will not.'

He closed his eyes for a moment and then very quietly nodded, and bent and picked up his hat, and bowed to her a little stiffly and turned and walked away across the green and golden garden, and she watched him go and felt him take the sun out of the day with him. She who had for so long sought a way to make him stop asking her to marry him had succeeded. She who had made him, at last, see what was best for him, had sent him away and was left bereft by her own actions. And she did not know how she was to live with that success.

## 32

The year rolled slowly away, a dry August succeeding an even drier July, and the newspapers were filled with lugubrious warnings of failed crops, interspersed with accounts of the possibilities of war with China. London building increased apace, much to the newspapers' disapproval of various ambitious projects, and business generally was brisk. Which was a great comfort to Abby, for she could throw herself into the affairs of the factory with huge energy and thus keep her mind from the grinding loneliness that now beset her.

She did not see Gideon again after that April afternoon. He wrote a stiff letter suggesting that any future dealings could be made by Mr Sydenham coming to Lombard Street, for, deeply as he regretted it, he felt it would no longer be possible for him to attend at Irongate Wharf Road each Wednesday. So, Henry, resplendent in the new top hat and elegant coat that befitted a young man so firmly set upon the rungs of a business career (and how carefully his mother had instructed the tailor in the making of the coat! How carefully had his father helped him choose the hat!) made his way in a hired carriage each Wednesday afternoon to wait upon Mr Henriques.

Miss Miller had now to work very hard dealing with the children at Paddington Green and could no longer come to the factory, and that too was a comfort to Abby. She worked late into the night many times and came home to fall wearily into a dreamless sleep. So she could persuade herself she was quite over the affair of Gideon Henriques and almost believe it.

And there was, too, the fact that she suddenly had so many more people with whom to concern herself. There had been a sad and painful time with Jonah when he had come to her and poured out the bitterness of his loss.

'I did love her, Abby. She was my wife and very dear to me. But she—she was so difficult——' He looked at her with appeal in his eyes and almost instinctively she knew what it was he feared and laid her hand upon his knee and said earnestly, 'She was not, I am quite certain, in any way deranged, Jonah. You fear the stain of such illness, but you need not. She lived so strange a life in her childhood, her mother is so—so *unusual* a woman that she could not fail but be marked by her experiences. You need not fear for the children.'

And she had shut her mind to the way Phoebe, little sparkling Phoebe, could swing from the heights of joy at one moment to the deepest of gloom at the next, telling herself this was but youthful spirits and not in any way an indication of a flawed reason, though she would watch and wonder and bite her lip as she did.

And she had many chances to watch, for Jonah had decided that he would leave the children with her.

'I had hopes of being a—a real man of the theatre, Abby,' he told her unhappily. 'But it is clear to me now that my talents are minuscule, that they have never been anything else. I have a gift for the sort of cheap entertainment that she—that has always been provided at the supper rooms, much as I dislike it myself, so all I can do is go on running it as it is. And she liked it. I will change nothing that she created. And anyway, I must provide for my children somehow——'

He had stopped then and after a moment said, 'I will of course pay for their keep and——'

She had rejected that idea most vigorously. 'You will not! It would be a poor thing if I took money from you for the pleasure of the company of my niece and nephew! You save your money for them if you wish, and say no more about such an idea, unless you wish to see me very angry! They are a joy to me, and to Frederick—especially Phoebe, of course, for he loves her dearly!—and it is my privilege to share my home with them!'

He had hugged her close and left it at that, arranging to spend each Sunday in Paddington Green with the children, but she knew how much of a wrench it was for him to part with them for so long a time, loving them as he did; knew that he spent six days of each week working as doggedly as she did herself, living only for Sundays. And said nothing about it.

Nor did they ever speak of what Celia had done. She had heard of Lilith's shocking injury and all that had happened, for it was too much to hope the newspapers would not obtain the story, but she made sure the children heard no hint of it. At least Lilith had survived and she was deeply glad of that, but had to admit honestly that it was not for Lilith's sake; had she died and thus made Celia a murderer as well as a suicide she feared the children would inevitably have discovered the truth for there would have been much more talk. But the story was soon forgotten, a mere nine days' wonder, and Abby thought shrewdly that this was probably Lilith's own doing. It would not please her to be the object of too much public discussion on such a score, after all. And she had much influence, and could silence the public prints if any one could.

One matter she did try to discuss with Jonah but found he blocked was the matter of his relations with Abel. She waited until some two months had passed since Celia's death and then told him gently that she had herself restored her friendship with him.

'For you know, Jonah, he is much changed. I visit him now each week, and they are most pleasant visits, for Miss Ingoldsby is still there, and Martha—quiet as she is—and we talk and prose and deal very comfortably together. Mamma's death and William's has softened him much, I think. And then Rupert deciding to go away as he did to work in the Westminster Hospital with Mr Snow—he took that very hard. He is alone at Queen Eleanor's now and I believe it meant much to him to have two sons working there with him. But there was some trouble there with the Trustees and Rupert and William—I am not quite sure what. He talks little of it, though I know it hurt him deeply. You would be surprised how—gentle he has become in some ways——'

'Gentle?' Jonah had almost spat the word out and she looked at him in surprise. 'He will never be anything but a tyrant—you hear me? A tyrant! I will not see him, not ever, and you must not ask it of me, Abby.'

'If you feel so strongly, Jonah, then of course I will not. But he asked me suddenly the other day if I knew aught of you and yours and——'

Jonah got to his feet and stood staring down at her, his hands deep in his trouser pockets, his face very tight. They were sitting in the garden, for the day was very warm and the children were picking daisies from the grass to make a chain for Phoebe and were out of earshot.

'On no account is he ever to have contact with my children, Abby. I will not have it! They have suffered enough! I could not bear it if he became involved with them, for he is harsh and——'

'Very well, Jonah,' she had said soothingly, a little alarmed by his vehemence. 'Very well, I give you my word, and we shall not discuss the matter again.' And he had subsided, and they had never mentioned Abel again, spending their shared Sundays with the children in tranquillity while the young ones grew taller and even Oliver lost some of his lugubriousness; and Jonah seemed to relax a little and learn to live with all that had happened to him.

Only Abby did not recover as fast as she thought she would. She sometimes found a memory of Gideon coming into her mind with such poignant sharpness that tears came into her eyes and she had to scrub them angrily away. She would carry herself with a bright face and a straight back, pretending that he was no more than a pleasant memory and hoping he was happy and content; and then would find Jonah looking at her anxiously and would smile and shake her head at his questioning about her wellbeing and turn the subject as adroitly as she could.

Then September came, and with it a card of invitation that made her stare and then laugh softly over the breakfast table. Miss Miller looked up, politely curious, and Abby smiled at her and said, 'Well, Miss Miller! I am to have a stepmamma! My old governess is to marry my father, it appears, on the tenth of this month, at Mr Spenser's church near Bedford Square! Is that not delightful!'

And she looked again at the card and pushed from her mind the memory of her own wedding day in that same church a long time ago. Such matters were nothing to do with her any more, she told herself.

'Oh!' said Miss Miller. 'A stepmamma? Your governess? Well, that is quite like a Mudie's novel, Mrs Caspar! I am so pleased to hear of it, and wish them joy!'

She sighed then and looked down at her plate. 'I thought it was only in novels that governesses ever came to such good fortune. I am glad it

310

is to happen in reality to someone. Governesses do not usually fare so well.'

Abby smiled at her gently. 'Come, Miss Miller! You do not fare so ill, I believe! You meet several eligible young men, do you not? The curate from St Mary's seems to me to call more often than was his wont, and Henry, at the factory, regards you with a very interested eye, I notice!'

Miss Miller reddened even more and her hair lost several pins as she shook her head with some vigour. 'Indeed, Mrs Caspar, nothing was further from my mind, I do assure you——' but she looked pleased enough.

Abby spent a great deal of thought on the matter of the wedding, and after some colloquy with Martha chose to give Miss Ingoldsby some clothes for her wedding gift and bore her off one afternoon to the warehouses to select French silks and velvets and best Valenciennes and Chantilly lace and choose ribbons and braids; and found that the quiet Miss Ingoldsby blossomed under such circumstances, showing a pretty and most elegant taste in clothes that, Abby told her candidly, made her most hopeful for the future.

'You see, my father has had a sad life in many ways, Miss Ingoldsby,' she said, 'and I would wish him to be happy in the years that remain to him.' She blushed then and said hastily, 'I am sorry! I did not mean to—to imply that he was old, for he is but one and fifty, I believe. But that his life——'

Miss Ingoldsby smiled. 'There is almost a twenty-year difference between us,' she said equably. 'I realize quite well that many will smile at such a union. But I am happy and will do all I can to make him happy. You need not fear for him, Abby. I intend to do all I can to make his declining years as you would wish to see them, comfortable ones!'

'You are mocking me!' Abby said. 'I meant only that he is out of the world in so many ways, and as I recall lived only for work and study. If you can encourage him to seek the company of friends, and to go out to dine sometimes, perhaps to a theatre——'

'That he will never do,' Miss Ingoldsby said flatly.

There was a silence and then Abby said softly, 'You know about that? About her?'

'I know. He has told me.' Her nose became pinched suddenly and small as she was she became very dignified, her anger giving her stature.

'She was a very wicked woman. She tried to damage your father—and your brother—and now——' she shook her head. 'I am glad she has suffered so. Is that very wicked? Well, in this matter I am wicked. I am *glad*.'

Abby leaned over the pile of silks and satins between them and impulsively kissed Miss Ingoldsby's cheek. 'Oh, I am so glad you are to be my stepmamma!' she said. 'You are all any daughter could wish for a bereaved father,' and they smiled at each other in great good humour.

So Abby looked forwards to the wedding with pleasure, and told herself firmly that she would enter fully into the joys of the day, a quiet one though it was planned to be, and would give no thought at all to the painful memories of her own long ago wedding, or of her present situation. And set out on the day in a hired carriage wearing a new dress of lemon tarlatan with the most handsome embroidered mantle to surmount it, and a bonnet trimmed with osprey and brown silk ribbons, knowing herself to look very well.

But the wedding service worked its insidious magic on her, as she should have known it would. She sat in the cool shadows at the back of the church beside Martha, quiet in brown merino and a severely untrimmed bonnet but looking most elegant, and looked at her father's straight back as he stood before the altar waiting for his bride. He might be past fifty, she thought with a stab of pride, but he is a most handsome man still, with his thick pepper and salt hair and his straight posture and broad shoulders. She had never regretted the loss of his company during the past ten years more keenly than at that moment, and bit her lip then took a deep breath and adjured herself firmly to look forwards and not back; and gazed about the church at the few other people there.

John Snow was standing as best man beside her father; Nancy was sitting resplendent in a crimson gown trimmed with pink ribbons that clashed most dreadfully with her high complexion, with beside her three or four nurses from the hospital; and that was all.

Abby was angered at Rupert's absence, though not because of Bart's

312

or Gussy's; Miss Ingoldsby had told her that they had not been expected to come so far from Leicestershire for such a reason 'and anyway, Mr Lackland did not attend Bart's wedding, you know, and he sees no reason why he should come to ours! I cannot blame him. I hope, in time, to arrange some reconciliation there.' She had looked at Abby with a wry little smile, 'He has been a difficult father, I know, Abby. But he could not help it——'

She was pulled from her reverie by the sound of the music as the organ broke into a solemn air and the few people rose to their feet in a rustle of silk and a shuffling of feet on the stone floor. Someone gulped and sniffed and Abby could see Nancy with her handkerchief to her eyes and smiled at Martha who looked irritated and scornful; but that was Martha—she has no atom of sentiment about her, Abby thought indulgently, and turned to look at the door of the church.

Miss Ingoldsby, in a very simple cream gown and holding only a prayer book, was standing there and looked at her from behind her small plain veil, and Abby saw the glint of a smile in her eyes and smiled encouragingly back; then, to the sound of the music now reverberating through the echoing church, she walked, holding the arm of a distant cousin she had found to perform the giving-away ceremony, towards the man who had been her employer for the past twelve years, whose children she had reared, whose wife she had cared for so devotedly, and who she had loved so helplessly for the whole of that time.

It was curious how tall and slender she looked as she moved so serenely down the carpeted aisle, her eyes on Abel. He turned expectantly towards her, and Abby looked at him, and saw the expression of peace on it and closed her eyes in a moment of gratitude. Whatever her own situation was or might be, her father, the man she too had loved so much and for so long, was to be happy. And that was much to be glad for.

And later, when she had drunk the couple's health in a little champagne at Gower Street, and hugged her new stepmother and wished her happy, she found a chance to speak for a moment to her father. He was standing in the embrasure of the window in the drawing room, watching his wife talking to John Snow and Martha with some animation, and there was a faint smile on his face.

'I am very happy for you, Papa,' she said softly, and he turned and looked down at her and smiled, and it was strange how much younger he looked, and she smiled back at him and said impulsively, 'Oh, she is so *good* for you!'

He nodded and looked at his bride again. 'Yes,' he said. 'She gives me such peace. I did not know it could be possible. I am more fortunate than I deserve to be, I think.'

He looked at her again, and his voice tightened a little. 'Abby, I feel I must—I need to say to you what I never said to her. Your Mamma——'

'Oh, please, Papa! Not now—the past is past and——'

He shook his head. 'No, I must say it. I could not be free until I did. I was not kind to her, Abby. She loved me dearly, cared only for me, and I treated her with a cruelty that fills me now with much pain when I think of it.'

'She was happy with you, Papa. She understood. I did not know then what it was that had happened, but I know now, and can see her more clearly than I ever did while she lived. She loved you in her way, and was happy to do it.'

'I wish I could be so certain,' he said sombrely. 'Be certain that she was happy——' He shook his head.

'She told me, Papa. She told me before I married James that every woman should marry where her heart lay. That I should do as she had done, and follow my own love, for that was the only way a woman *could* be happy.'

He looked at her with an almost shy eagerness upon his face. 'She said that, Abby? In those words? That she had been happy with me?'

'Yes, Papa. It was but a week or two before—before her accident. She told me.'

He took a deep breath then, and closed his eyes and nodded softly and then opened them and looked across the room at his new wife and said softly, 'I do not deserve such good fortune. To be loved by two such women——'

'I hope you can love Miss Ingoldsby as much as she deserves, Papa,' Abby said and then laughed. 'It is difficult to think of her as anything but Miss Ingoldsby!'

He laughed too, and set his glass down upon the window sill. 'Well, you must learn to address her as Maria, must you not?' he said and put his hands upon her shoulders and looked closely at her. 'Abby, I was cruel to you as well. I should not have been so angered by your marriage. I ask your forgiveness.'

She looked up at him and smiled tremulously. 'I had him, Papa, a little while. And that was worth the pain of losing you—but I am happy not to have lost you for good and all. Be happy.' She lifted her head and kissed him and he hugged her briefly and went away across the room to stand beside his Maria, and Abby saw her look up at him with an expression of such trust and adoration on her face that she was almost embarrassed and turned to go.

She was in the hall below, putting on her mantle, when Maria came rustling down the stairs. 'I saw you were going,' she said a little breathlessly. 'I could not set out upon my wedding journey without thanking you, Abby.'

'Thanking me?' Abby stared at her. 'Whatever for? I have done nothing!'

Maria shook her head. 'You do not know how much you have done. It is your warmth and understanding, all the goodness of your nature that gave me the courage that made me find myself where I am this afternoon. I loved him, you see, but I was so afraid of him.' She smiled shyly. 'I may dissemble well, but I am very ordinary below the surface, Abby. And I would not have dared to tell him of my love for him had it not been that I knew of your sweetness. It seemed to me that if you could be his daughter, could love him enough to come here as you did after so many years of bitter separation, why then, he must also be different under the surface, have warmth and springs I could not see. Was lonely perhaps and in as much need of love as I was. So I thought of you and spoke to him and——' she stood on tiptoe and kissed her cheek. 'Thank you, Abby. I wish for you only the same happiness I now enjoy. A husband who can love you and be loved in the same way. I can think of no greater felicity.'

Abby could not help it. She smiled wryly and said, 'I doubt that will ever come to me.'

Maria set her head on one side and looked at her shrewdly. 'Why not?'

Abby shrugged and began to fasten the neck of her mantle. 'Because

315

the man I—the only man who could be my husband cannot be. I love him and he me, but——' she shook her head again and closed her lips firmly and turned to go.

'Is he already married? Or committed in some other way? Why cannot you marry him?'

'You, who never gossip, asking such questions? Why, Stepmamma! I am surprised at you,' Abby said in a rallying tone, and Maria smiled and patted her arm.

'Well, I will not spoil matters by becoming some sort of ogre of a stepmother! You must keep your own counsel. But I tell you this, Abby. You are not the woman I believe you to be if you let anything stand between you and the man you want. Anything at all. I looked at your father and there were the shadows of dead women to keep us apart and anxieties about his children, about the hospital, about so many things, but it seemed to me that if I did not have the courage to face them and surmount them or the courage to help *him* face any pain those troubles might bring to him, why, then I did not deserve to be happy! So I found the courage and here I am today, quite the happiest woman alive! I can only wish you the same. Goodbye, my dear Abby. We will see you again soon, I am sure——'

She stood upon the step outside looking along Gower Street at the flat-fronted buildings with their iron balconies, the houses amongst which she had grown up, the cobbles and pavements she knew so well, and thought of her father there behind her, in his own peaceful haven at last; of her dead mother and husband, of the whole of her past life as well as theirs, and felt tears rising in her. She should be as happy as her father was, she thought, she should have as hopeful a future. And then chided herself for being so petulant. To have that she must be as strong as her father, as brave as Maria, and go to get what she wanted, whatever it might lead to, whatever pain it might cause.

She turned her head to look the other way along Gower Street, in an easterly direction, towards the spires of the City and the roofs of Cheapside and Bishopsgate, Poultry and—Lombard Street. And suddenly seemed to hear her mother's voice thin and distant, '—when it is time for you to wed, follow your heart as I did—at whatever cost to yourself and others—however your lines fall thereafter it is all a woman can ask of life. To get love is good, but to give it is so much greater!'—and it was almost as though Dorothea was standing there beside her and speaking in her ear.

Abby turned and looked up at the bedroom window on the second floor behind which her mother had lain so silent for so long and which would now be the room shared by her father and his Maria. And took a deep and shaking breath.

Had she the courage to do as her mother had done and 'follow her heart', no matter whom it hurt? Had she the courage Maria had shown? She did not know. But suddenly she lifted her chin and picked up her skirts and went down the steps to climb into her carriage. She did not know. But she could try.

# THE PERFORMERS
## Book I
## GOWER STREET
*Claire Rayner*

The streets of London in the 1880s are no place for a respectable gentleman to take his evening stroll – especially around the notorious Seven Dials.

But Jesse Constam is no ordinary man. Born a child of the gutter, he was one of the lucky ones who has escaped the squalor of the slums, and now he lives in fashionable Gower Street. So when a young lad tries to pick his pockets one evening, he makes no attempt to hand the culprit over to the law – for how could he prosecute a phantom from his own past?

And so the future of this child – called Abel Lackland – is subject to the whim of Jesse Constam. But his plans for Abel are to be thwarted by the 'adoption' of another gutter child, the rebellious Lilith, by the eccentric spice merchant of Gower Street . . .

0 7474 0740 1
GENERAL FICTION

# THE PERFORMERS
## Book II
## THE HAYMARKET
### *Claire Rayner*

Abel Lackland has risen from squalid beginnings in the slums of London to become one of the wealthiest and most popular surgeons in town. He wants his eldest son, Jonah, to follow in his footsteps, but Jonah abhors the very sight of a surgeon's knife and decides that his future lies in the field of the arts.

In defiance, Jonah steals away one night to visit the forbidden Haymarket theatre where Lilith Lucas plays to a packed house of adoring fans. After the show, Jonah manages to meet the famous Lilith and immediately falls under her spell – a fatal spell that, unknown to him, has haunted his father for many years . . .

But Lilith is all too aware of Jonah's identity – and she sees the boy's naive devotion as a chance to repay Abel Lackland for the indignity and heartbreak of the past . . .

0 7474 0741 X
GENERAL FICTION

All Sphere Books are available at your bookshop or newsagent, or can be ordered from the following address:

Sphere Books,
Cash Sales Department,
P.O. Box 11,
Falmouth,
Cornwall TR10 9EN.

Alternatively you may fax your order to the above address. Fax No. 0326 76423.

Payments can be made as follows: Cheque, postal order (payable to Macdonald & Co (Publishers) Ltd) or by credit cards, Visa/Access. Do not send cash or currency. UK customers: please send a cheque or postal order (no currency) and allow 80p for postage and packing for the first book plus 20p for each additional book up to a maximum charge of £2.00.

B.F.P.O. customers please allow 80p for the first book plus 20p for each additional book.

Overseas customers including Ireland, please allow £1.50 for postage and packing for the first book, £1.00 for the second book, and 30p for each additional book.

NAME (Block Letters) ......................................................

ADDRESS ........................................................................

.........................................................................................

☐ I enclose my remittance for _____

☐ I wish to pay by Access/Visa Card

Number ☐☐☐☐☐☐☐☐☐☐☐☐☐☐☐

Card Expiry Date ☐☐☐☐